For
Darcy

A bright and shining star!
Rock on...

Love!

WHEN ALL ELSE FAILS

The SEEDER Series

HOWARD LIBES

HAPPY MISTAKE PUBLISHING

Eugene, Oregon

Printed in the United States of America

Cover Design: Claire Flint Last and Tony Figoli

Happy Mistake Publishing
PO Box 42197
Eugene, OR 97404
www.happymistakepublishing.com

LCCN: 2017912611
ISBN: 978-0-692-92435-8

In memory of Marcia Libes Simon
You reminded me to follow my bliss.

YOR

As the door slid open to the high-security section of the Royal Library, Professor Yor Vanderlord recalled the words that led him to this moment. Yor had been eight years old, sitting on his ailing great-grandfather's deathbed when he promised to discover the truth about the old man's past. His great-grandfather bent over slowly and whispered in his ear, "Always remember, lies can be just as powerful as the truth."

From that day forward, Yor was driven to unravel the mystery. He excelled in his education, climbing the academic ladder at the Royal University from undergraduate to professor faster than anyone in Koda's planetary history. He wrote *Power Over the Future*, the best-selling history book about the SEEDER program which launched deep-space missions to discover a habitable world as the global environmental crisis threatened the existence of Koda's humanoid population.

When no livable planet was found, the SEEDER program was scrapped. At the same time, a bloodless coup ended the Global Monarchy's reign. When the Global Assembly took charge, the DOME project was initiated. The planetary economy became focused on placing domes over the most prominent cities to insure a portion of the population's survival. But before construction on the domes ever broke ground, Yor's great-grandfather Yorlik Vanderlord, who was believed to be lost in space, returned from his century-long SEEDER mission. His arrival on Koda was hailed as a triumph, but his expedition was declared a failure and its details were never told.

Now at 24 years old, Yor was convinced that one of the answers to his great-grandfather's story was his SEEDER journal, housed here in the Royal Library. Yor's entrance with a casual swipe of his identity card against a magnetic strip made him laugh. Such an unassuming gesture marked years of hard work coming to fruition. Yet access to the journal just signaled a new beginning.

When the door slid closed behind him, Yor was left alone in the silence of the cavernous library. Four floors of books lined the walls below a vaulted glass ceiling revealing the dome above. This place was a remnant of the Monarchy. In an effort to restore the planet's denuded forests, the Global Assembly mandated the creation of a fully-digital society and the production of physical books had been outlawed. Yor was captivated by his surroundings and imagined that he'd stepped back into the past where bound texts, hand-cranked presses, wood-block letters and printer's ink were the norm.

Then the Auto-Librarian whirred to life like an alien creature in this setting. This machine was solid tech: micro-circuitry and micro-processing chips with static conductors that fed off the electricity in the air to power its components. No hands needed, no muscle, just a body within the range of its proximity scanner to activate it.

The solemnity was completely shattered by the librarian's simulated female voice saying, "Good day. How can I serve you, Yor Vanderlord?"

Yor cringed when the device said his name in soft-measured syllables. His identity, along with most everything about him except for his thoughts and feelings, became known to the librarian with the swipe of Yor's card. He stepped back outside of the scanner's range and when the device turned itself off, he breathed a sigh of relief. To Yor, these contraptions with their programmed personalities were a reminder of the tech required to replace the individuals wiped out in the crisis. He grew up with them all around him and hated their presence, but in this case, he needed the librarian's information. He took a deep breath and stepped back within its range.

"Good day. How can I serve you, Yor Vanderlord?"

"Location number for the SEEDER journal of Yorlik Vanderlord."

Without a sound, not even a wheeze or a click, the librarian searched for the answer.

Yor closed his eyes while he waited. All of his life's aspirations had been directed at separating the lies from the truth. What had happened to his great-grandfather on his voyage? Why wasn't his mission—the longest in recorded history—discussed like all the other SEEDER expeditions? After so many years and so much education, Yor still had so many questions and nobody wanted to provide the answers. Silence from the government. Silence from his parents. Even his great-grandfather stayed silent without offering an explanation, except for his cryptic deathbed admonition.

"SEEDER Journal of Yorlik Vanderlord. Third level. TL 3 9 0 0 0 E. Access history available."

Access history? Maybe the journal isn't as secret as I thought. "Recall access history," Yor said.

"Only access to date was made at the 145th day of the present year."

"By whom?"

"That information is confidential and not within your current security parameters."

Although he knew better than attributing human characteristics to this device, Yor sensed a condescending tone in the simulated voice. "My clearance is level 2-A," Yor said, "By whom?"

"That information is confidential and not within your current security parameters."

Yor didn't have time to press this line of questioning any further. Even though he earned permission to review the journal due to his place at the University and the upcoming Breeze Celebration, the Global Security Service had given him a strict time limit in the library which began when the door opened.

Yor looked around for a lift to the upper levels and spotted a spiral staircase, a remnant of the library's stylized ancient architecture. Then he heard Mado's voice in his audio implant, "Yor? What are you doing in the Royal Library? I thought we discussed putting this off? I can see you on the surveillance feed. Don't look so surprised.

Chatter has already begun regarding your presence there. I'll set up the alternate feed. We can discuss this later. Now, get a move on."

Yor dashed up the staircase. By the time he reached the third level, he was winded and paused for a moment to recover his bearings, then as he proceeded down the rows of books, motion-sensitive lights lit the way in front of him and turned off behind him to conserve energy. When he found the journal and reached out for it, light intensified in that area, too. The journal's spine was blank, except for the library code and security tag at its base, and as Yor pulled the journal from the shelf, the first thing he noticed was the bright-blue Ashtecki-hide cover. The Ashtecki had been extinct for over 100 years. They were one of the first livestock animals to disappear as the climate changed and their grass for grazing stopped growing. This animal from the warmer southern clime was not only known for its succulent meat, but also its durable blue micro-fiber hide which became soft and smooth to the touch in preparation for its use in clothing and books. Yor couldn't help but run the side of his hand down the spine. His great-grandfather had chosen this volume himself to use as his personal journal.

Yor cradled the journal in his hands. Under the lights, he could see the corners of the cover, front and back, had been dinged and worn down by use. The binding had been stretched from opening and closing for over a century, probably broken and repaired a few times, and he could see where his great-grandfather added pages. Yor flipped through the thick volume which was full of writing from cover to cover, and he panicked that he wouldn't get all the pages fotoed in the remaining time.

"Get a move on," Mado said.

With the journal in hand, Yor hurried to the nearest bookstand, the overhead light following him. He peered up at the vidcam in the ceiling, then he read the first three pages to set a baseline for Mado's alternate feed. He waited a moment for Mado to get his job done, then removed the high-speed foto-scanning device from his satchel and set about his task.

When Yor was more than halfway through the fotoing process, the light flickered twelve times, then shut down. In the distance, he could hear all the bolts closing on the library doors. He had surpassed his time limit so he took a portable light from his satchel, secured it on his head with an elastic band and continued fotoing. When he was finished and put the journal back on the shelf, he switched out the foto-device's memory wafer with another one containing family and research fotos and inserted the journal's wafer into a hidden compartment in the sole of his shoe. Then he deposited the device and the light back in his satchel and braced himself.

Yor had never experienced a sonic alarm. He was told what to expect, but he wasn't ready for what happened. He heard a barely perceivable high-toned note, then his jaw tightened, his eyes watered, and the blood left his brain, his legs lost their strength and became rubbery. His first instinct was to fight the effects, but there was no way to combat it. Yor steadied himself on the shelves to keep himself upright, but his vision was blurring and he was losing consciousness. He sat down on the floor, and slumped over, feeling the coolness of the tile on his face until his cheeks went numb. In the distance, he heard the doors unlocking and the thud of boots below him, then he passed out.

RAJER

Rajer Jeps stared at the blank communication screen in his bedroom, wondering what he was going to tell his commitment-partner Mar. *How can I tell her that Yor is being held at the GSS Detention Facility and Mado expects me to rescue the boy?* Rajer thought, *Maybe I shouldn't tell her anything at all. That would save her the worry that's sure to follow.* He let out a sigh.

"Something wrong dear?" Mar called from the living room, "Did someone just screen us?"

"Yes, work-related."

"You have to go back in?"

"Just for a short period," Rajer said, relieved how easily this small white lie had played itself out. He grabbed his transpo card and hand-held comm and walked into the living room where Mar sat on the couch, reading a digi-book.

The room was designed like every other government-issued bungalow in the newer sections of the Capitol City dome and contained government-issued furniture. The only distinguishing features were the automated bluish-green wall color chosen a year ago, the couch, the paintings on the walls and the cabinet from Mar's old house displaying framed digi-fotos: Yor, Mar and Rajer at Yor's final university graduation; Yor's father; Yor holding up a copy of *Power Over the Future* at one of his readings; a young Mar looking stunning in a two-piece bathing outfit at Calem Falls before the environmental dilemma became critical. The Calem Falls foto was many years ago, before Rajer met her. Her long auburn hair was now streaked with grey, but she still possessed that slender athletic swimmer's body.

"You okay?" Mar said. She was scrutinizing him, holding the book in one hand, tapping it on her knee in a slow rhythm. She had an impeccable instinct to read people. This was a family trait: All of her childhood friends said they never could get anything by Mar's mother.

Rajer realized that he should have composed himself before entering the living room, but it was too late. Mar had already seen through him.

"You sure that you're okay?" Mar said.

"Fine," Rajer said, "Fine. Never been better." He bent down and kissed her on the lips.

"How long will you be gone?" Mar said, "Probably hard to say, huh?"

"Well, you know how it is."

"I do," Mar said, turning back to her book and slumping into the couch.

Rajer hurried for the front door, then as he pushed it open, Mar said, "When you get back here with Yor, we'll talk. Buzz me on your comm when you're headed home." Rajer halted outside on the bungalow doorstep as the door clicked to a close behind him. He smiled and shook his head in awe at his partner.

Rajer proceeded through the streets of the bungalow community where each structure looked exactly the same except for a personal touch hung from the front door like a religious symbol, a piece of art or a foto of a loved one who died in the crisis. At the rail-car-station entrance, Rajer stopped at the automated ticket-terminal and inserted his transpo card. He told the terminal his destination, then his transpo card was given back to him, and he ran down the stairs to the tracks where he jumped into the doorway of the first string of rail cars headed in his direction. He sat down at the closest seat in the near empty car. Two other people occupied the car: the government rail-car supervisor who was on every car and a power-plant maintenance worker wearing his red coverall, probably on the way to a late shift.

Rajer leaned back, feeling in-tune with the motion of the car, grasping his transpo card in hand, wondering how he would deal with the situation awaiting him. He breathed in the rail-car air that was loaded with Trianin which made a person's anxiety level decrease. He thought about the first time that he met Yor. Rajer was a stranger taking Mar on a date and Yor was a 14-year-old boy. There was a look of disgust on Yor's face, and he could only imagine the loathing Yor was feeling. Rajer didn't take it personally. He was sure other men had been in this position, and he respected Yor for being protective of his mother.

Rajer took another deep breath as the rail car slowed for a stop. The doors slid open. The maintenance worker departed. Nobody stepped onboard. The supervisor smiled at Rajer who was aware that the supervisor's optical-vid device on one of his eyes and the vidcam in the rail-car ceiling were recording him and relaying the images back to the GSS (Global Security Service).

Here I am traveling halfway across the city to get Yor out of trouble. If this was before the dome, Yor would have moved out by now, but government regulations made it illegal for a child to move from a parent's home unless they were starting their own family so Rajer and Yor were stuck together as roommates. They didn't always have similar views, but one thing that he and Yor agreed upon was making sure that Mar was happy. That was their line of demarcation. In the past, they'd have heated political arguments. Rajer worked for the government in Budgetary Standards as a financial examiner and Yor disagreed with government policies. Rajer couldn't blame Yor. His father was one of the Global Assembly's most vocal foes. In Yor's mind, his mother had partnered with the enemy.

Mar put an end to any political conversations in their home on the day that 15-year-old Yor found out the true cause of his father's death and burst into the bungalow to confront his mother. Yor entered the bungalow, slamming the front door behind him and yelled, "Aren't there enough lies everywhere, but now I discover that my mother is lying to me, too?"

Rajer emerged from the bedroom. Mar came out of the kitchen, where she had been preparing dinner, drying her hands on a cloth. Rajer had just returned from work and was still wearing his government-security badge. Yor rushed up to him and tore the badge off his shirt, creating a ragged hole where the badge had been. Then he threw the badge at his mother, hitting her in the chest.

"What is this about young man?" she said, picking up the badge at her feet and handing it to Rajer, "I won't be addressed in that tone."

"I just found out the truth about my father's death," Yor said, screaming at Mar, "And I can't believe that you are with *him* after what I just found out."

"Why don't you sit down and explain what you've discovered, in a decent tone?"

"Two reliable sources told me that father's death may have appeared natural, but he was slowly tortured and killed by the government each time that he was taken away for his 'arbitration negotiations.'"

That was how Mar described to her young son why the government officials took her husband for interrogations. "You were just a child," Mar said, "I saw no reason to tell you the horrible truth."

"One of those sources is Professor Wint, isn't it?" Rajer said.

"Why?" Yor said, poking Rajer in the chest where the badge once resided. "Are you going to report him to your superiors?"

"That's not fair," Mar said, walking over to Rajer and probing the hole in his shirt with her hand, then patting him on the chest.

"Well, you married into the government, didn't you?

The government that I just found out murdered my father. For all I know, Rajer was somehow involved."

Mar took a few strides toward Yor stopping directly in front of him. "Enough!" she said. Rajer had never heard her raise her voice.

"You did it so you could sleep with my mother," Yor said to Rajer.

"I said, enough." Mar stared at Yor for a few seconds until he began to speak again, then she struck him with a resounding slap across his face, "That's enough!"

Yor fought his emotions, his face visibly contorting, then giving way to tears. Mar looked horrified at what she had done and embraced him. Yor hugged her back, holding her tight.

"You are the most important person in my life," Mar said, "Silence was the only thing that protected you. I needed to keep you safe."

Rajer recalled that event vividly. That was the day when he began to re-examine his loyalties outside his new family and explore what was best for the future, but he kept his own counsel. He thought that was wise.

The rail car passed more stations. Protocol was not to stop unless somebody was getting on or off. They entered a rail tunnel with multi-colored lights streaming by his window, and moments later the rail car emerged from the tunnel into Capitol City's Old Quarter.

The rail car snaked through empty streets. Back before the dome, the streets would have been full of automobiles idling at the crossings and parked on the side of the roads, but they were no longer a part of the social dynamic. There were fields outside the dome filled with these abandoned vehicles. The only automobiles were government-issued for government needs and were streamlined for maximum durability, speed, and energy efficiency. Combustion engines were illegal. At this time of night, the government fleet was parked in underground garages until tomorrow when the work day began.

As they slowed into the Plaza rail center, Rajer's transpo card buzzed between his fingers. He emerged from the rail car, walking out of the station's gates and into the courtyard which was lit by ancient-Kodan replica street lamps with swirling metallic bases twice as tall as a person and yellow-glass globes like it might have been 200 years ago, except these were ion-powered. A few people wearing government-security badges ran past Rajer to catch the next rail car home before curfew. As the global seat of power, Capitol City curfew was strictly enforced.

Rajer passed through here earlier, heading home with other government workers crowding the streets. He rarely was down here this time of night. Now, on the vacant and quiet Old Quarter stone-block paved streets, he observed the merchant shops built of stone shuttered for the night like a sightseer back in the pre-dome days when people vacationed here to see the ancient marvels of the Capitol.

The Old Quarter led into the Royal Quarter where the buildings of the Global Monarchy remained. The Royal Cathedral stood with circular stone architecture and magnificent spire. The Cathedral was not a place of worship anymore and had been closed for decades. Down the street was the Royal Palace surrounded by an insurmountable fence of metal spears. The sprawling four-story stone building featured ornate cornices and stone carvings of ancient creatures peering down from the rooftops. Nobody resided there anymore, but its doors opened each day as a museum. Tours were provided for local schoolchildren and citizens who were guided through a display of the royalty's garish lifestyle and the extensive gardens containing near-extinct flowers and trees. Now, with the seventy-story monolithic Global Plaza structures looming overhead, the Palace looked less awe-inspiring than it probably did at the height of the Monarchy. Before the first dome was built here to preserve the planet's ancient structures and the global seat of power, the Global Assembly unveiled the plans for building the Global Plaza. The President compared the past and future architecture by calling them "wasteful versus efficient." Rajer thought that the "wasteful" argument could have been made for the Plaza as well.

In the Global Plaza, where Rajer worked, the government buildings were smooth metallic slabs towering on either side of an extra-wide street. The architect conceived the Plaza as mirroring the magnificence of the planet's canyons for full inspirational effect during the Breeze Celebration parade: The street would be packed with citizens and their families for the parade, and the breeze from the open dome pane making its way down the simulated canyon would affirm the government's promise to keep the population safe and thriving and some day return them to the world outside the domes. At the opposite side of the Plaza was the Arena, where the Breeze Celebration parade ended, and hundreds of thousands would gather to commemorate the continued survival of their civilization.

On a work day in the Plaza, each building was filled with workers who tabulated the taxes, set a budget for government expenditures in maintaining life under the domes, supervised the education of the masses, and policed the population to insure citizens were safe from crime and terror in the domes. Nothing distinguished the bureaucratic buildings except a sign or marker out front denoting their use. The Global Assembly building was erected on the same spot as the razed Royal Parliament building and featured the Parliament's Great Bell at the entrance. Representatives from each dome met here each year to discuss global issues and their cut of the government taxes.

The GSS building stood at the farthest end of the Plaza near the Arena and was different than the others. It was designed to appear like the blade of a knife with the two flights of stairs leading to its single front door, depicting a handle. There were no signs divulging its purpose. The only thing noticeable, other than the sentry box and the energy field, was the symbol of the Global Assembly, the planetary globe wreathed in Nafa, the mythical plant of power, on two massive stone slabs standing on either side of the building's front door.

This was the building where Yor was being held. Rajer

approached the transparent blast-proof sentry box. Inside, two helmeted Global Guards with visors and body armor stood at attention. They were armed and ready for any assault on the building. An energy field, which tapped into the dome power source, emanated around the perimeter of the four-sided building with this box as the only point of entry. In the history of the Global Assembly, no violence had ever been perpetrated on this building, but the government constantly broadcast images of individuals who they insisted were plotting to destroy the structure.

As both sentries stood side-by-side facing straight forward, Rajer held out his government-security badge. One of them peered over at the badge, then faced forward again. Someone unaware of government procedure would have thought that the sentry was ignoring him, but the sentry's visor had scanned and processed the badge's information. Then the sentry returned to searching the street in front of him for the heat-signatures of approaching combatants like his colleague. In order for Rajer to be considered for entry, the sentries required an all-clear signal from the vidcam operators inside the GSS building who were scoping out the Plaza with the surveillance cams mounted on poles lining every street.

"What can the Global Assembly do for you citizen?" the sentry said, still facing forward, examining the empty streets.

"I'm here to vouch for Yor Vanderlord," Rajer said, thinking this sentry seemed like a machine due to the lack of personal interaction and movement.

"Is there a problem, Rajer Jeps?" the sentry said, "Your heart rate is elevated indicating hostile intentions."

"No sir, I have no such intentions."

"Your voice print indicates that you are being truthful within the range of safety," the sentry said, not breaking his monotone drone, "Yor Vanderlord is being held on the 52nd floor, detention room A. You are permitted to pass. Stay within two meters of the box when passing or you will be terminated by the energy field. You have thirty seconds to pass. Enter the building and go directly to the open lift with blinking light above it. Any diversion and you will be terminated. Do you have any questions, Rajer Jeps?"

"No, I'm clear on the instructions."

The sentry reached down to a console built into the sleeve of his armored suit and pressed in a code, "Proceed, citizen."

MADO

Mado Prevor wasn't pleased. Yor agreed that now was not the time to enter the library, but he did it anyway. The chatter on the Global Security Service comm feeds confirmed that Yor had been arrested and carted off to the Detention Facility. According to the vidcam feeds Mado hacked, Rajer had also reached the GSS building. Rajer knew nothing about what was happening except Yor was arrested at the Royal Library and needed his help.

Mado thought about getting back to work on the ship, but he wouldn't be able to focus properly until Yor was freed. He attempted to quiet his mind racing with apprehension. *I should know better.* When dealing with humanoids' unreliable dispositions and fragile nature, probability was put into play. You couldn't be too sure when someone might act impulsively. Somebody might become ill or lose interest and stop being involved. A new person might enter the landscape out of nowhere and a wild card might be thrown in. One could never be certain what might happen. You had to prepare for every contingency.

When it came to their plan, Mado had performed his calculations, laying out the probabilities, especially involving the different aspects of Yor's personality. But Mado was disappointed that Yor hadn't listened to him.

He expected more from Yor. Acting rashly was a recipe for disaster and could alter their plan in detrimental ways. Mado would need to recalculate where Yor's behavior put them, and although Mado was aware that their plan would eventually change his life forever, right now he was too comfortable and content to be pleased with unplanned upheaval.

Mado had accumulated a fortune making timely moves. He was known throughout Koda for inventing the power source that kept the civilization alive. That innovation would not have been possible without his other invention, the Holographic Gaming Device. The HGD became popular as people spent more time indoors due to deteriorating environmental conditions and wanted to experience adventures in locales that no longer were available to them. For instance, a Kodan could no longer ride the rapids through the planet's most beautiful forests. Mado's device hooked into the player's brain and reproduced everything: from the player's chosen seat on the raft to the smell of the forest to the spray of water on their face as the raft maneuvered the rapids to the roar of the river, and the screams of joy from the other passengers as if it was reality. From the individual's standpoint, there was no difference than being there and they could share the adventure simultaneously with others from the privacy of their own homes. Nobody on the planet had ever come close to replicating an affordable hi-tech device like this one, that could be utilized by anyone right in their living room. As the HGD flew off the shelves, Mado's corporation, Prevor Industries, prospered. His company's stock became a high roller on the Global Market, and he invested his riches into developing the Atmospheric Ionic Device (AID).

Mado brought AID on the market when the Global Net, which provided energy to individual homes in cities and towns around Koda, started to permanently shut down sector-by-sector as the natural resources powering them were depleted forever. AID was a portable box that kept entire households humming along with power. The device was affordable for everyone, easy to set-up, and cost nothing to power-up. Mado was praised as a global hero and AID was declared a miracle. The Global Assembly and the DOME project had been searching over half a century for a clean, efficient power source for the domes. AID was the solution. Mado was contracted to use AID's tech to supply energy for every dome. That was lucrative for Prevor Industries as well.

A few days after the ceremony awarding Mado the DOME contract, he received a communication from Yor's father, Tetrick, who Mado had known for many years. Tetrick said that his son was focusing his studies on the SEEDER program and it was time that he met Mado and learned more about his great-grandfather.

Mado picked Myla Park on the edge of Capitol City for their meeting, thinking it was a significant place for the two of them to meet, where the past and present met, and where they'd possibly see eye to eye on their future together. This park used to be one of the most beautiful vistas on Koda, a jewel of Capitol City, which the Monarchy had filled with trees, flowers, and creatures from across the globe. Now, the landscape reaching into the horizon was leafless, dead, brown and devoid of life, and nearby the foundation for the Capitol-City dome was being excavated.

On his way into the park, Mado disabled the vidcams. The park was low priority so the GSS wouldn't send out a vidcam repair team until he and Yor were long gone. He also probed a specific radius around the park for GSS listening devices with tech of his own invention to insure that nothing would pick up their conversation. Although the dome excavation being in earshot made it so nobody within three meters could hear them.

Mado waited for Yor on a bench and he was mesmerized by the cacophony of the three four-story digging machines crashing their buckets into the hard dry ground and their engines groaning as they dug up dirt and dumped it into waiting trucks, one after the other. He was so transfixed that Yor's tap on his shoulder startled him. Yor stepped back at Mado's reaction, then approached tentative and nervous. Mado had seen this behavior in regard to his fame before and he found it silly. He hoped this wouldn't be a problem for Yor. They were in two different places in their lives. Mado was a successful scientist and businessman, and Yor was an intelligent teenager, starting his collegiate career. If they were going to end up in the same place at the end of their conversation, Mado was mindful that he'd have to steer it.

Mado motioned for Yor to sit next to him on the bench.

Yor said something, but Mado couldn't hear over the excavation's mechanized racket and pointed to his ear. Yor leaned toward Mado practically yelling, "Maybe we should go somewhere else so we can talk and actually hear one another."

"No, this is fine," Mado said, raising his voice, "Please sit."

Yor sat at the other end of the bench. Mado waved for him to move closer, but Yor stayed put so Mado slid over to him and said, "Glad to make your acquaintance. We met once when you were a small child. You probably don't recall." He spoke in a loud volume, close to Yor's ear.

"I don't, but my mother told me the story," Yor said, leaning his face closer to Mado's ear. "It's an honor to meet you."

Mado shrugged. "I think it's the other way around, but let's see how you feel after we know one another better."

Yor smiled. "My father told me that you had an interesting sense of humor. I've been wanting to meet you."

"Yes, he told me," Mado said, "He told me that you have a deep interest in your great-grandfather's history and the SEEDER program, and the debacle of the DOME project. Is that correct?"

Yor appeared surprised and looked over both his shoulders. He didn't know what to make of Mado's treasonous words about the DOME project, and he was sensitive to the government's surveillance. Mado liked that Yor was cautious.

"You don't need to be afraid of me, my boy. I may have a contract with the Global Assembly, but my actions are more acquitted to a future plan than any affinity with the government's policing structure or their misguided policies. They are driven more by greed and ignorance than wisdom and scientific fact."

Yor was silent, examining Mado's body language and face for the truth. The boy had inherited his mother's ability. Mado simply waited.

Then a smile spread across Yor's face. He nodded and laughed, gazing around at his surroundings again, then said, "Now I get it. You *are* a friend of my father's."

Mado smiled as well as he could and nodded. Yor reminded Mado of an old dear friend. "Your father said that you're quite the prodigy. He also said you're planning on entering the university at 14 years old," Mado said, "In two years, when you enter the Royal University, you come work with me while you're studying. I have a project right in line with your interests. Let's keep in touch. You can tell people that we've met, but you have to keep this conversation between us."

Tetrick died shortly after the meeting and Yor began working in Mado's lab sooner than planned. Mado thought the diversion would be good for the boy, and he was impressed by Yor's intellect and his facility at comprehending complex ideas. As their relationship developed and they grew closer, Mado felt like Yor was the son he never had.

That was twelve years ago and Mado was confident they'd made the right steps together to remain undetected by the government, but recently Yor had grown impatient and they'd argued about speeding up the plan.

The last time, after a full day working on the ship, Yor had left for home, but returned hours later, demanding that they speak. He was clearly upset.

"What's wrong? Is everything okay at home?" Mado said.

"Yes, I never got that far. I paced around the rail car station and walked the streets for awhile, then came back here," Yor said, "We need to talk about moving forward with the library part of the plan."

"The library is too dangerous and risks uncovering all of our work. We agreed that we'd wait until the ship is ready and we're closer to a Breeze Celebration. I know that you want to see the journal, but now is not the time."

"I don't want to wait any longer. We don't have time on our side. Turn on your viewing channel. I heard about it on my way to the station. Today, thousands were killed when part of the Mauan dome collapsed. That's over a dozen dome accidents in the past five years with tens of thousands killed. How long can we wait and watch more murdered?" Yor said, "I've waited my entire life while I've watched this world disintegrate around me."

"I appreciate your empathy, but I think you just want to see the journal and have your questions answered about your great-grandfather, and now is not the right time."

"I think that you're stalling on finishing the ship."

"Stalling. That's how you see it? If working all day to keep this corporation running, spending my evenings working on the ship with you, and getting no sleep is stalling, then you're correct. I'm stalling."

"The corporation is fine. You just need to make the ship more of a priority."

"The corporation pays for the ship," Mado said, "If you stop and think instead of acting with your emotions, you'll recall there is so much more to making the plan work than the ship."

"I've got everything under control."

"Under control? How about losing that asset in Shamba?"

"I've tasked Insol to deal with it."

"I'm not talking about putting someone else on the job. Since the Global Assembly captured the asset, we have no idea what they know and until we find out, we need to proceed with caution," Mado said, "Now take a deep breath and think about your mother and Rajer and Insol and all the other people that you care about. Your actions have consequences."

"Once we act, they'll all be fine and Kodans will realize how they've been duped."

"That's what your father thought."

"That's not fair."

"I respected your father, but you know it's true," Mado said, "So why don't we talk about this again when the ship is closer to being finished and we'll reconsider where we are in assembling the plan? You need to make sure that our network is solidly in place and you could use more practice with the scanner. If you're concerned about thousands being killed in the past five years, then consider how many we'll jeopardize when we don't get our end right."

Yor agreed that they'd postpone the library until the right time presented itself, but now he had broken his word and possibly ruined everything by being impetuous. Entering the library and scanning Yorlik's journal was the start of the dangerous portion of their plan. The Royal Library's high-security section was reading only. Copying in any fashion was illegal. There was no way to steal the journal without being caught so they required a way to secretly scan it.

Mado invented a high-speed foto-scanning device for the task, which appeared like an ordinary scanner, but was ten times faster than a normal one, and he would alter the surveillance feeds. Yor practiced scanning a fake book which was the exact length of the journal with a timer and was steady under pressure although he had the tendency to become distracted by historical curiosities, and he'd never seen the library or the journal.

Mado was confident and the odds were high that Yor would copy the entire journal, but the only way to finish the job was surpassing the time limit, being knocked unconscious by the sonic alarm, and getting arrested. There was always the probability that the sonic alarm could knock Yor unconscious before he could swap the memory wafers. If Yor was convicted, then he would disappear for the rest of his days, nullifying all their years of work together. If there was no crime charged, then Yor would be released, but after the arrest, he would come under constant scrutiny by the GSS as a suspect of interest. This meant that their plan would be persistently under threat of being exposed. For both of those reasons, Mado argued that entering the library should happen right before they were ready for their presentation.

Mado watched on his viewing screen as Rajer sat in the reception area outside the detention room where Yor was being held, and Mado pondered his own youth. He understood what it was like being idealistic. He felt for the loss of life on Koda, but caution was imperative. Mado perceived the surveillance state all around him and he was mindful of the danger. Over the years, he had built an influential corporate empire to harbor his activities, the Vanderlords had become his family, and he labored toward a better future for all Kodans, but he feared losing it all before he completed the plan. *Maybe I've grown too comfortable, but there is a way to proceed where everyone comes out safely.*

Then Mado picked up a conversation on a comm channel far outside of the ordinary GSS comms where Yor was mentioned with familiarity. In a quick search through the government database, Mado could not find the government-security ID number of the person speaking.

Mado clearly heard the man say, "Don't release him

until I get there. I want to interview him myself. If he is released, I'll have your head. Do you understand? Am I making myself perfectly clear?"

The person on the other end of the comm tripped over his tongue as he spoke, "Yes, yes, I will, I understand, sir." Then there was a click. "Will there be anything else, sir? Sir?" The unknown person had disconnected.

The wild card had arrived.

YOR

Yor awoke on a cot in an all-white room. The walls were white. The ceiling was white. The floor was white. The door was white. The table and chairs in the middle of the room were white. The cot was white and the pillow and sheets were white. His brown satchel and the foto-scanning device laid in the middle of the table, out of place in this monochromatic environment.

Yor sat up. The room was filled with a constant *whoosh* sound like water running through pipes in a wall, which Yor had experienced in Mado's simulations for this part of the plan. Yor couldn't locate the source of the sound. It seemed to be coming from every corner of the room. He didn't spot a vidcam either, but he assumed he was being watched. The room was so bright that Yor's eyes hurt, but he thought that might be an after-effect of the sonic restraint, too. He laid down on his back and closed his eyes.

Yor wasn't worried. A government interrogator would enter the room and ask him questions about why he exceeded his time in the library and why he had the device on him. Yor would tell him that he never used the device in the library and would offer to show the contents of the memory wafer. The interrogator would run down a list of possible violations if Yor were caught again in similar circumstances, then release him with no charges. He and Mado had gone over the scenario from every angle.

Yor opened his eyes to the sound of the door sliding open and sat up on the edge of the cot. A man entered and stood in the doorway, observing him. Yor was instantly aware that this wasn't the typical overworked government civil servant.

This man in his fifties had a tanned bronzed complexion, perfectly coiffed jet-black hair and was clean shaven. He wore a white button-down shirt with one loose button at the collar and no government-security badge on his lapel. With the security in the GSS building, he probably stopped and took the badge off before he arrived at the room, choosing to conceal his identity. His black pants were recently pressed and his black shoes were polished to a shine. He stood frozen in place as he gripped the door frame, scrutinizing Yor, then examining the objects on the table. When he took a step forward and closed the door behind him to the click of the lock, the *whoosh* now sounded louder to Yor.

"Yor Vanderlord," the man said, holding onto the last syllable *lord* like he intended to sing it out for the both of them. "Would you mind sitting at the table, please?" The word *please* sounded less like a polite request than a demand.

The man never averted his gaze from Yor as he crossed the room and pulled out a chair, deliberately scraping the legs on the floor, sitting down with his hands clasped in front of him. Yor never rose from the cot.

"Well?" the man said. He unclasped his hands, striking the table twice with both palms, producing a sharp metallic rattle, and the objects on the table jumped in front of him.

Yor immediately rose from the cot and seated himself across from the man. "Yor Vanderlord," Yor said, holding out his hand to the man, "And you are?"

The man stared at Yor's hand, then back at Yor. "I know who you are. Do you understand the gravity of your situation, Yor Vanderlord?" He pronounced *lord* the exact same way as before.

Mado told Yor that he should refrain from showing outrage at the arrest especially if the interrogator was a tough one. They both knew that this arrest would occur with the activation of the alarm. Mado strongly suggested being surprised that the arrest had happened in the first place especially with Yor's clearance from the Global Assembly to visit the Royal Library, "I'm not sure why I'm here," Yor said, "I was in the library one minute and woke up here the next."

"That's a convenient answer. Are you making light of the situation? This is a serious crime that we're investigating," the man said, clasping his hands in front of him again, but this time, Yor noticed the back of his hands were deeply scarred. This didn't look like an accident, but a deliberate attempt at pain.

Yor searched for an answer, but couldn't find anything appropriate to say. That wasn't like him.

"I won't ask again," the man said in the same controlled tone as when he walked in. "I can simply throw you in a holding cell and let you rot. Would you like that?"

In his head, Yor could hear Mado chastising him for entering the library before they were ready, then words came to him, "No. Sorry. Feeling a bit woozy. Sorry."

"That's the affect of the sonic restraint. Some people are affected longer than others. Although I'm surprised, your father was sturdier stock."

Yor paused for a second to take in what the man had said. "I was reading the journal when the lights went dim, then I was knocked out."

"Did you not notice the lights flashing beforehand?"

"Did they? I was focused on reading the journal. I had a time limit."

The man breathed in and exhaled forcefully through his nose and shook his head. "And what is this here?" The man unclasped his hands and put one on the foto-scanner. "You with your brilliant intellect and position of authority should know better than to bring such a device into the high-security section of the Royal Library. You should know that use of such a device is not sanctioned there."

Yor explained how he used the device at the University Library, researching a new book specifically about his great-grandfather and forgot he had it in his possession when he entered the Royal Library. "It was an honest mistake. I had it on my person, but never used it."

"We've already checked the memory wafer and we've seen that it wasn't implemented in the Royal Library. This interview is standard in cases when an alarm is triggered.

I'm sure that you're aware of that," the man said, "You broke no laws, however..." The man placed his hands palms down on the edge of the table and pushed himself to a standing position, then he leaned toward Yor, raising his voice. "...in your case I have my suspicions. You're too smart for a lapse in reasoning like this one. You entered the university at 14 years old, the youngest student in history. By 20 years old, you graduated with the highest degree that you could achieve in the field of Global History. At 22, you're a full professor at the university, heading your own department on the SEEDER program, and published your best-seller. Then you and Mado Prevor, convince the Global Assembly to let you restore your great-grandfather's spaceship for the new Global Museum due to your book's wave of popularity, your standing in the academic community and Prevor's influence within the government, and here we are...in an interrogation room at the Global Security Service Detention Facility because you forgot, made an honest mistake. You expect me to believe that?" The man yelled the last sentence in Yor's face, and Yor got a strong whiff of the man's putrid breath.

"I'm not asking you to believe it. That's the truth."

"Your great-grandfather was an impressive man just like you. The journal wasn't a bad read. What was your favorite part?" Now, Yor knew who read the journal before him.

Mado speculated that the interrogator would ask "If you didn't scan it, then tell me about what you read."

Luckily, Yor possessed a fotographic memory so he recalled two passages that he read as Mado setup his alternate feed.

"My favorite went, 'I've watched my planet disappear from view over the past week. The blue globe with distinct patches of brown reminding me why I'm out here, heading into the darkness speckled with points of light, one of which might be our new home. Right now this pressurized life raft is a measure of hope. Maybe the last hope for the people of Koda. I have faith in myself, but the mission is daunting. My greatest fear is loneliness, which I've trained myself to overcome. As I pass further from Koda, messages from home will become like precious stones on a beach, washing up on shore at random intervals over great lengths of time.'

"The other part that stood out to me, 'As I've watched Koda become just another point of light among the others, the humbling nature of life like ours on Koda becomes magnificent in its improbability. Thus I must discover the improbable.'

"Those are my favorite two," Yor said, "Although I didn't have a chance to read the entire journal in the time allowed. I'm hoping to apply for another viewing."

As Yor spoke his great-grandfather's words, the man sat down, leaned back and observed Yor with his hands clasped in front of him. When Yor finished speaking, the man continued appraising him, seemingly taking Yor's pulse from a distance. The *whoosh* filled the room again. At first, Yor thought the silence was a victory, and his recitation had dumbfounded his interrogator, then as the silence went on and on, Yor came to the conclusion that this was a ploy to coax him into saying something incriminating to fill the void.

In that time, Yor got a better look at the man. He concluded that this man had done terrible deeds in his lifetime. The deep scars on the back of his hands were an indication of painful acts perpetrated on him which had drained him of empathy. If necessary, this man had no problem inflicting excruciating pain to wrench the truth out of people.

"That was very, very good. I had read that your memory was first-rate. I didn't expect anything less. And although I'm not a fan of your namesake, I have to say those were eloquent passages." The man unclasped his hands and pushed the satchel and device toward Yor until they lay at the edge of the table in front of him. Then he pushed back his chair, scraping the legs on the floor, and left the room with the door locking behind him.

Yor felt exposed. He wasn't surprised that the GSS had a file on him containing his personal history, considering his family and the restoration project, but he wondered how much more they knew. If he was being monitored, then he had no idea for how long and what intimate details they'd obtained about his life or if they had any knowledge of his plan with Mado. Yor felt vulnerable, and he was concerned for his well-being and the people who he cared about. He felt angry at himself for thinking that he was smarter than everyone else and felt his resolve coming apart at the seams.

The *whoosh* seemed louder now, and Yor didn't know how much time passed as he questioned his choices. His mother always said doubt was normal, but she had no clue what he was actually doing with his life. Sometimes he wondered whether his course of action was wise and the best use of his skills. *How did I get here?* If he was honest with himself, he had to admit that his life decisions hinged on the words of a 199-year-old man when he was young and impressionable.

Yor was eight years old when his father took him out of school for fifteen days to spend quality time with his terminally-ill great-grandfather. Yor hadn't seen him in awhile since his father was busy lecturing and his mother was focusing on her med practice, but he frequently visited the 10-bedroom Vanderlord estate as a small child. He loved running around the rooms and up and down the stairs of the large building and playing on the grounds.

The estate resided far outside Capitol City on rural lands. Yor's great-grandfather had amassed his own wealth on top of his family fortune and retained the estate which was built by his father. The structure was constructed from materials which had been depleted for over two hundreds years by the time of Yor's childhood. The foundation and walls were made of stone from exhausted quarries. The vaulted ceilings and wood paneling in the living room and library were cut from the ancient forest that once surrounded the house. The craftsmanship utilized to put together this kind of building had disappeared and most of the structures like this one had been torn down and their components sold and re-purposed long ago. Yorlik Vanderlord's home was a remnant of his planet's past, just like him.

On this visit, Yor's great-grandfather was only awake for short periods a day which left time for Yor to wander the estate. He began to comprehend that the estate offered more than a place to play. The library walls were lined with shelves of books on two floors. There were books covering plant life, animal life, the stars and planets, physical science of the universe, history, and biographies. There were story books and tech manuals. Thick volumes. Thin volumes. Books filled with fotos and illustrations. When Yor wasn't eating or passing the time with his father and great-grandfather, he stretched out on the cushions of the library couch and poured through the volumes. He absorbed all that he could, falling asleep there most nights and carried off to bed by his father. Over breakfast, he would ask his father questions from a list he had typed into his digi-tablet from his previous day ensconced in the library. His father answered most of them, then they'd present the unanswered questions to his bedridden great-grandfather.

More times than not, the elderly man arrived at the answer without so much as a pause, showing that his body might be failing him, but his mind was sharp. Before the question-and-answer session ended, Yor would always ask about space travel. His great-grandfather would launch into stories of his days as a test pilot pushing aircraft past the known limits for speed or breaking free of Koda's gravitational pull into outer space where he would race for the nearest moon, slingshot around it and rocket back home. In the moments when he described these experiences, with high spirit in his voice and vivid detail, Yor was transported back to the past with him. With the images of those stories reeling in Yor's mind, he would turn to his father who was just as fascinated and Yor knew why his father had brought him here. Yor waited for those moments each day. That was probably when the seed was planted in him to become a historian.

His great-grandfather's illustrious past was on clear display in the estate's living room. The framed Royal Medal for Valor presented to his great-grandfather by the Monarchy, which gave him the title Yorlik the Great, hung on the wall there. The fireplace's stone mantle was lined with framed physical fotos. The frames were constructed of a metallic substance which glowed and lit the foto in the darkest room and glimmered blue when light reflected off them. The material called Murotum was mined from a planet's moon in the years when the SEEDER program built outposts as they traveled further and further into the universe, hoping that they were headed toward a momentous discovery.

The fotos showcased life on and off Koda in the centuries before the environmental collapse and the domes. There was a foto of his great-grandfather as a young man with a thick dark brown head of hair wearing a white lab coat standing next to a skinny, balding bearded man in a laboratory. Both were smiling and held beakers up toward the cam. In another, his great-grandfather appeared older, his hair was cropped short and he was resting on an experimental aircraft with trademark Vanderlord broad shoulders and big chest filling out the flight suit. There was a foto of his great-grandfather standing in a space-suit on a moon, waving at the cam. He was helmeted but Vanderlord was printed on the suit. Then there were the family fotos: his great-grandfather, early 20s, in an expensive suit and a flower in his lapel with his arm around the waist of Yor's great-grandmother wearing a white dress in front of a four-tier cake on the day of their partnering; his great-grandparents with his grandfather and his great Aunt Yara as small children taken in this room with large logs burning in the fireplace. They were dressed up in the wealthiest finery of the time as if they were on their way to a festive event. Some of these fotos were taken more than 160 years ago and Yor was struck at the lavish lifestyle that his forebears lived. Another foto taken on the estate's dock captured the family—the children as teenagers—standing next to a sailboat in leisurely summer attire. His grandfather stood, tall and lanky having not filled out his body yet, with his right hand on the stern of the boat named When All Else Fails, with great-grandfather and the rest of the family fanned out beside him. Behind them, the dock built back to a green lawn with the estate in the distance.

Yor was most intrigued by the foto of his great-grand-father standing in the control room of what Yor assumed was his SEEDER ship, When All Else Fails, also known as the WAEF, with a view of space in the window behind him. His great-grandfather wore a broad smile on his face. He was older than the other fotos with a head of flowing grey hair, but appeared strong and vital and he looked joyous as he was turned partway pointing to the window. Peering at this photo, Yor was seeing tech that few of his generation had ever seen. He could almost make out the readings on the screens, the settings on the dials. Yor picked up the foto from the mantle and sunk into the cushions of the living-room armchair and stared at the foto for he didn't know how long as the light in the room faded and day turned into night and the glow of the frame lit the foto. He got lost thinking about his great-grandfather's voyage and compiled new questions for him.

Yor was roused by a hand on his shoulder. His father stood beside him.

"I've been searching the house for you. I even looked in this room before and you were here all along," his father said, switching on the nearest lamp. As Yor's eyes adjusted to the light, he observed that his father resembled his great-grandfather in the foto, the way that he stood there smiling down at him.

"Have you seen this?" Yor said, holding the foto out to his father.

"Ah, yes," his father said, "The foto of all fotos. I figured that you'd find it sooner or later, the way that you've been scouring this house like a squiggle meezer."

"A squiggle meezer?"

"Yes, a squiggle meezer," his father said, tickling Yor

with both hands.

Yor curled up in a ball on the armchair, laughing hysterically, and squealing.

"That's exactly what a squiggle meezer sounds like," his father said.

When the tickle barrage stopped, Yor jumped to his feet with the foto in hand. "Is great-grandfather still awake? I really want to ask him about this."

"No. He's asleep. You can talk to him tomorrow, if he's got the strength."

Yor brought the foto to bed with him, and he couldn't fall asleep, speculating about the story that his great-grandfather might tell him. Over the course of Yor's childhood, his father told him bedtime stories about his great-grandfather who was a scientist, pilot, and space explorer, who left the confines of his planet and voyaged into space for 122 years on his own. Yor found it hard to equate the larger-than-life man of adventure with this old person around the estate. His father entered the room, took the foto out of Yor's hands and placed it on the night table, then tucked him in, and kissed him on the forehead. Yor fell asleep and dreamt of standing in the control room of the WAEF sailing amongst the stars with the spry version of his great-grandfather in the foto.

The next day, Yor arrived in his great-grandfather's bedroom with the foto clutched in his hands, and his great-grandfather carefully eased himself to a sitting position on the bed when he heard Yor scampering toward him. There was no doubt that his father had told his great-grandfather about the excitement his son had displayed at seeing the foto. When Yor reached the bedside, his father lifted him to sit next to his great-grandfather. Yor had not been this near his ailing great-grandfather since they arrived days before. The elderly man hugged him with a strength that surprised him, then he tussled Yor's hair while taking the foto from him. The foto brought delight to his great-grandfather and Yor could see the younger man from the foto under the aged face.

"So you found the foto?" his great-grandfather said as if Yor was meant to discover it.

"Yes, great-grandfather," Yor said, "Please tell me about it."

"This ship was my lifeboat, my home for many many years," his great-grandfather said, "But I can't tell you much about this foto."

"I want to know everything," Yor said, bouncing up and down on the bed, "I'm not going anywhere until you tell me everything."

"Calm down now," Yor's father said.

The old man smiled and looked over at Yor's father. "That's okay. The boy is right to be excited," his great-grandfather said, "I can't tell you much, my boy, but this foto says more than I can currently tell you about the outcome of my voyage. I want you to remember that fact after I'm gone from this world. I want you to keep it. It's yours."

Yor was speechless. He didn't know what to say. Then his great-grandfather reached out, squeezing Yor's shoulder with one hand and handing him the foto with the other. "Promise that you'll never give it to anyone, and you'll keep it as yours no matter what."

"I promise," Yor said, embracing the foto, "Now tell me."

Yor's great-grandfather regaled him about the anticipation on the days leading up to the WAEF's launch. This was the final expedition of the SEEDER (Space Exploration Endeavoring Development of Extraterrestrial Relocation) program. Five expeditions had never returned and were presumed lost while sixteen others came home from twenty-plus years traveling in the vast expanse of the universe, but without a promising discovery. Kodans were counting on his great-grandfather's expedition to succeed where the others had failed. His great-grandfather described himself sealed up inside the ship, strapped into the WAEF's pilot seat, awaiting the go-ahead for takeoff, "...and then I pressed ignition. The engine's roared and the ship began moving upwards toward space and the start of my mission," his great-grandfather said and gently took the foto from Yor, gazing into it again and breathing a long sigh.

"...and then...?" Yor said.

The old man handed the foto back to Yor. "You remember what I said about this foto," his great-grandfather said, tapping at the transparency covering the image, then glancing over at Yor's father.

"Your great-grandfather is tired," Yor's father said, picking up Yor and placing him beside the bed.

"I am tired and I can't tell you much more than I have, my dear boy. I'd love to spend hours telling you about the details of my journey, but I can't."

"Why not?"

"Ah, why not?" his great-grandfather said, "Well, it's hard to explain, but I no longer have those memories. They were taken from me. I know that you won't understand right now. Some day you will, but come back here for a moment." Yor's father placed Yor back beside his great-grandfather. "Come closer," his great-grandfather said, then he bent closer to Yor and whispered in his ear as if he only wanted Yor to hear, "Always remember, lies can be just as powerful as the truth."

Then the old man kissed him on the cheek. "I need my rest now. Just listen to your father. He'll tell you what you need to know when the time is right. You go and play." Yor's father carried Yor from the bed and closed the bedroom door behind them. Yor was disappointed at not hearing the story about his great-grandfather's foto, but Yor's father told him the day would come when he would learn everything.

Now, sitting here in the interrogation room, Yor understood with greater clarity than ever before that once the truth was buried, the liars would do anything to protect the truth from being revealed again.

Shortly after Yor's childhood visit to the estate, his great-grandfather died. The funeral was private and the Great man was buried on the grounds of the estate next to his partner. The only people in attendance were Yor,

his mother and father, Joro Camtur—a family friend—
and the family's religious prefect who presided over the
ceremony.

The day was hot. There weren't cold days anymore.
The burial plot was beneath an ancient tree with limbs
like outstretched arms that clung to life in the oppressive
weather and must have had deep roots. Yor could see his
father's eyes welling with tears and Yor attempted to hold
himself back, but once the prefect began speaking, he lost
control and wept hysterically. His mother held him tight.
He never heard a word the prefect said, and at the end of
the ceremony, he felt a great loss like part of himself was
now missing. The cylinder containing the Great man's
remains was lowered into the ground and the hole filled
by an automatic burial device. Yor's father, mother, Joro,
and himself took turns putting a rock that signified their
personal mourning on the finished mound. His father's
was a volcanic rock. Joro's was a rock from the sea that
he collected as a child. His mother found rocks on the
estate's lakeshore for herself and Yor. His father shook the
hand of the prefect who walked back to the house and
the mourners formed a semi-circle around the grave, then
his father stepped forward.

"My great-grandfather Yorlik Vanderlord was a complicated man who placed himself at the center of this
planet's crisis, doing what he thought best to make life
better for everybody on Koda. By taking that responsibility, he missed watching his children grow up and never
getting to know them, but his sights were set towards

the well-being of future generations. He truly believed in what he was attempting, and invested his life force into it. When he left Koda, he never grasped how different it would be upon his return and that cost him the truth of what he had accomplished. The people in this circle are the keepers of that truth." After an extended silence with their heads bowed, Yor's father walked over to Yor and put his hands on his shoulders. "Time for you to start understanding the truth, my boy." Then Yor's father took his hand and led him to a motorized cart that had carried the coffin to the site and motioned for him to sit in the passenger seat. Yor looked over at this mother and she said, "It's okay. Go ahead. I'll be okay. I need to talk to the prefect."

His father sat in the driver's seat and started the cart. Joro sat on the back. They drove down a paved path through a grove of short, thin trees clinging to life with mostly barren branches, then came over a hill where an immense manufactured block building stood with a door that stretched its width and a smaller personnel door at its center. The building was out of place, an industrial warehouse in a country setting.

The cart pulled up to the building, stopping by the smaller door. His father turned off the engine and jumped out of the cart. Yor followed him to the personnel door. While his father pulled out a set of keys and searched for one in particular, Yor noticed that they stood on a driveway, the width of the large door, that led into the distance where he assumed was the main road. His father inserted a key in the personnel door's lock, turning it to the clicks of an old tumbler system and he pushed the door open with a creak, then he waved for Yor to follow. When they were inside, Joro closed the door, cutting off the outdoor light, plunging them into darkness. The interior was much cooler than outside and musty, although Yor noticed the low hum of an air-circulation system.

His father took his hand, then there was the distinct sound of a switch being thrown and light flooded the room. When Yor's eyes adjusted, in front of him was a three-story high object, filling the length and width of the warehouse, covered with some sort of tarp. Yor gawked at the object and quickly knew what it was. His father let go of his hand and disappeared for a few moments, then appeared next to him with Joro who held a remote-control pad. Joro pressed a series of buttons and the room was filled with the sound of motors humming to life, then he pressed another and ropes that were connected to the tarp grew taut and the tarp slowly rose from the object, revealing his great-grandfather's spaceship, When All Else Fails. Chills ran up his spine and he began to cry like he had at the funeral, but the tears at the funeral were for the loss of a man who he loved, who would never be able to tell him the truth of his journey. The tears on seeing the SEEDER ship were tears of joy as if the old man had been resurrected. His father pulled him to his side and held him close.

When the tarp concluded its rise upwards, the motors shut down. Joro pressed a few more of the remote buttons and lights posted around the ship, turned on. The hull of the ship was dark around the edges, but otherwise the silver hull gleamed in the lights like in the historical vids on the day it was launched. His father took Yor by the hand again and they walked by the four wheels of the landing gear which towered over them, and under the fuselage until they stopped under the tail with the six hyperdrive engines, three on top of three. Yor's father yelled over to Joro that they were all clear. Yor noticed they stood in front of a long piece of tape which had been adhered to the floor. The loading bay doors opened above them and a ramp lowered touching ground at the edge of the tape by their feet.

Yor's father squeezed his hand. "You ready, my boy."

"To go up there," Yor said, "I was born for it."

"Truer words were never spoken."

They ascended the ramp into the empty loading bay, then took the stairs up into the ship. The interior was so large that the lights streaming through the windows only provided a dim view of the inner chambers. They climbed above the engine room with its six towering power conduits, and reached the third floor walking through the med bay, the science lab, the sleep chamber, and the living chamber. They finally entered the control room which was illuminated the best, because of the large window in front of the pilot chair and the lights set up in the rafters at the front of the ship. Yor recalled the foto of his great-grandfather with the room full of consoles, computing devices and viewing screens. The room was much larger than he imagined, but it was now pitted where viewing screens once resided and there were open consoles with heaps of wiring hanging from them down to the floor as if the ship had been ransacked and left for dead.

To Yor's joy, on the main control console sat the foto. He picked it up and gazed at his smiling great-grandfather pointing out into space.

"I thought that this would be lost in the estate sale or the government would confiscate it for a museum," Yor said.

"No, I saved a bunch of books, family fotos and mementos from the estate. Your great-grandfather gave this to you. He wanted you to have it so I kept it for you."

"Thanks, father," Yor said, placing the foto back on the console, then slowly walked around the ransacked room taking a closer look at it. "What happened here?"

"Your great-grandfather wanted the ship so the Global Assembly took a large percentage of his fortune, the integral tech of the ship and erased the data connected to the voyage as payment. Last but not least, they removed your great-grandfather's memory of his journey as final installment."

"His memory?"

"Yes, his memory. You're great-grandfather thought that this ship was worth it."

"I don't understand. Why agree to those terms for this ship?" Yor said, "There's nobody alive who has the earnings and technical know-how to bring it back to life, and the story of his journey is gone forever."

"Because your great-grandfather was smarter than them," Yor's father said, grabbing a handful of wiring hanging from a console, letting it go and leaving the room.

Remembering the day of his great-grandfather's funeral, Yor's rationale for infiltrating the Royal Library sooner than later seemed correct on one count: He had told himself that this was his family legacy and his duty to uncover the truth of his great-grandfather's accomplishments. He also convinced himself that the government wasn't watching him more than any other Kodan. In that regard, he may have deluded himself, and he didn't relish the future conversation with Mado regarding his actions.

The interrogation room door slid open and the man entered holding a memory wafer with the Global Assembly symbol on it. "This is a summons for a hearing in 42 days to review your case in front of a panel of judges. You're free to go until then," the man said and handed him the wafer.

Yor gathered the scanner, placed it in the satchel and headed toward the door.

The man stood in his way. "I knew your father well, Yor Vanderlord. He was a stubborn man. I hope for your sake that you're less hard headed than him."

ORN

Orn Shiv watched as Yor Vanderlord walked out of the interrogation room, disappearing down the bend in the all-white hallway leading to the reception area. He caught the distinct whiff of fear from the young man as he passed by. Maybe Orn had done his job and put him on notice. *He is a Vanderlord so you never can tell.*

Surveillance and spies were important to Orn's work, but he learned early in his career that instinct was his best ally. In this case, not only did he mistrust any Vanderlord, but his instinct told him that this supposed mishap in the Royal Library was part of a larger scheme. He wanted to lock up the boy in the Detention Facility, but when it came to anyone affiliated with Mado Prevor, further action would require a conversation with the Leader.

Orn dealt with the Vanderlord family more than a few times in his career, starting with Yor's grandfather, then his father and his great-grandfather. To say that Orn disliked the Vanderlord family would be an understatement of gigantic proportions. Orn took miscreants into custody every day. Citizens who were too vocal in their disagreement with Global Assembly policy. Most of those times, he could extinguish their activity with no more than a threat. Sometimes it took a harsh interrogation or a few nights locked up to set them straight, but usually they'd return to society as loyal citizens. Vanderlords never seemed to learn their lesson.

Seventeen days ago, Orn read in his daily planetary intelligence briefing about a Shamban who was caught hacking into the security mainframe of the government's central military facility there. The traitor had been tortured for days by GSS operatives and they'd obtained nothing useful. Orn's instinct told him that this could be important. The majority of Shambans rejected living in the domes and resided in the cave networks of the regions' mountain range. They were reported to have a vast separatist militia, but they were rarely caught and hacking was far from their usual subversive activities so Orn decided to take charge of the investigation. This was Orn's prerogative by direct order of the Leader on any case that he deemed suspicious. He commed ahead with his demands for the necessary interrogation environment to be fulfilled before his arrival.

Then Orn flew in a military cruiser from the Capitol City dome to the central Shamba military base. The region experienced heat in excess of a hundred-degrees daily so measures were taken to protect sensitive military equipment. The cruiser landed on a pad equipped with a hose which connected to the cruiser and projected cool air inside the chassis of the aircraft so the circuitry of the vessel wouldn't be fried in the heat. An air-cooled vehicle attached to the cruiser with an airlock, and Orn stepped from the cruiser directly into the vehicle which sped off to the hangar where the traitor was being held. The driver handed him a remote with one switch on it.

When Orn stepped into the hangar and the door closed, he waited a moment and listened, then headed toward the sound of labored breathing. Orn had ordered for the hangar's interior to be pitch black with no outside light seeping in, and the air-cooling was turned down to the lowest setting so the heat inside the hangar was unbearable. The traitor seared in the heat of the day and received little relief at night when a flood light was turned on above him in close proximity at random intervals for an indeterminate length of time.

In accordance with Orn's demands, the traitor was kept in the hangar for days without food or water. He was regularly checked on by a military medic, and he was kept alive with an intravenous saline drip when it looked like the depravations would take his life. Orn wanted to insure that the traitor was still alive when he showed up here.

Orn took great pleasure in his job. He approached the labored breathing and flipped the switch on the remote. The flood light turned on, revealing the traitor who was naked and strapped down—arms, legs, torso, head—on a metal bed. He was black and blue all over his skinny body where the previous interrogators had beaten him and his nipples were charred from electrocution. His head had been shaved. His eyes were closed. He was barely alive. Beside the bed was a metal table with a tray containing two hypodermic needles with fluid in their chambers.

Orn flipped open the switch on the tube connecting the solution on the I.V. stand to the traitor's arm, starting the flow of saline. "Hello," Orn said a few times, slapping the man's face until his eyelids opened and his eyes turned toward Orn.

"Who are you?" the traitor said in a sing-song Shamban accent.

"I'm here for you to tell me what you know."

"Drop dead. I know that you're an asshole."

"You Shambans. Surly to the last breath."

"Kill me now. I'm not going to tell you anything."

"Don't be so sure. Pain is a wondrous lubricant to loosen the mind," Orn said, flipping off the I.V. drip. The traitor's eyes widened as he attempted to inspect Orn from his limited point of view with his head strapped down. Orn moved closer to give him a better look and placed the remote on the tray, then picked up one of the hypodermics. "Here is some lubricant," Orn said, placing the hypo in front of the man's face, "But I will give you a chance to avoid it. Just tell me who hired you to hack the mainframe and what you were attempting to do."

"I'm not going to tell you anything. You can beat us, you can torture us, but in time you will be defeated."

"Oh that old tune. I have to admire your spirit, but from my vantage point, you aren't defeating anybody," Orn said, tapping the bubbles out of the hypo solution, "This is a concoction of my own making. It's used in interrogations throughout Koda."

"You must be so proud."

"I am proud," Orn said, tapping the traitor's strapped down arm with his fingers, searching for a vein. It was difficult to find one with the dehydration. "This solution will begin to burn out your veins, arteries, nerve endings and vital organs within moments after injection. For the last time, I'll ask you. Tell me what the Global Assembly wants to know."

"I will not…"

"Yes, you're not going to tell me anything," Orn said, "I know. You say that now, but let's see what my little concoction can do." Orn moved the needle towards the traitor's arm.

The traitor thrashed in his restraints as if there was some hope of breaking free. Orn let him expend his strength for a few moments, then stroked the man's cheek with the back of his hand which made the man thrash harder. Orn was delighted at the look of disgust on the man's face.

The traitor pursed his cracked lips and attempted to spit at Orn, but the result was dribble down his chin and neck. Orn ran his fingers across the traitor's chin, mopping up the spittle and the man thrashed in his restraints again. Orn licked his fingers like a child who was allowed to taste the frosting. "Hmmm…I don't think you have much life left in you." Orn tapped at the hypodermic once again, found a vein and injected the traitor. "You should feel the…"

The traitor screamed as if somebody had plunged a knife into him. He gulped at the air and screamed at every exhale.

"That was quicker than usual. You're pretty weak,"

Orn said, placing the empty hypo on the tray, picking up the other one and tapping at it. Orn shouted over the screaming, "This hypodermic contains a solution that will counter the effects of the first one. Just tell me what I want to know. Who hired you to hack those mainframes? Give me a name and the intent of the hack and this can all be over."

The traitor continued screaming and his limbs began to violently spasm, creating a cacophony of crashing against the metal table.

"I don't think you have much time left. I've been told that it's like burning from the inside out. The longer you wait, the worse the permanent damage. Anything from loss of taste to brain damage. You're not a pretty picture right now," Orn said, "It's superb."

The arteries and veins in the traitor's body appeared to be level with his skin now, turning black. His corneas were turning bloodshot to solid red. The traitor continued screaming, but less energetically.

"You better tell me something quick or there's no turning back."

"All I know," the traitor said, sputtering the words, "All I know is…when…all…else…fails…"

Orn took a moment and surmised the traitor's condition. "You know. I believe you," Orn said. He put the hypo down on the tray and began walking toward the hangar's door.

"You said…" the traitor yelled through the pain, "You said…"

"Oh yes," Orn said, continuing his walk to the exit, "But I don't think so."

The man screamed louder than ever, then silence filled the room.

Now, standing in the hallway of the GSS building, Orn thought about what the traitor said and his interrogation of Yor Vanderlord, then took his comm out of his pocket. First, he called a cruiser to the GSS rooftop landing pad, then pressed the button for his line to the Leader.

MAR

Mar sat on the couch as the door closed behind Rajer. She and Rajer had been together for 10 years now and she was fascinated that he still tested her ability to tell whether he was being truthful or not. This developed into a game between them as their relationship matured: He would lie about something and see how long before Mar called him on it or determined the lie he was covering up. It was all in the name of play. Nothing devious. Rajer had even become better at covering up his tells over time.

However, Mar knew right away that Rajer was lying about going back to work, which meant whatever happened was serious because he didn't have time to fashion a ruse. She figured that it probably had something to do with Yor. She was aware that Yor was up to something for quite some time that would earn her disapproval. Sneaking around. Hanging up on comms and lying about who was on the other end of the call. She was hoping that he'd eventually tell her. She was concerned, but she trusted him. Now she would make sure he'd come clean, because whatever he was doing obviously had gone too far. Rajer was too worried about Yor and upsetting her to work out a better lie. She should be angry, but Rajer's behavior made her love him even more.

Rajer was fond of Yor, although Yor never made it

easy. The boy was too smart for his own good and at the beginning of her relationship with Rajer, Yor's defense of his own father was a shield that he carried in battle against Rajer daily. There was no doubt that Rajer would never be like Yor's father, Tetrick. They were different people, but they were similar in being awful at lying and loyal to their family.

Loyalty ran deep in the Vanderlord's. This was never more apparent when it came to Tetrick's father, Naivim, a renowned marine biologist. When Yorlik the Great was presumed lost and the SEEDER program was shut down for good, Naivim made the decision to produce a less expensive faster privately-funded hyperdrive spaceship using the family fortune and units from investors who believed in the program. When the project appeared to be moving toward success, Naivim died in an explosion during an engine test.

At that time, Mar and Tetrick were a serious couple. Tetrick was teaching at the Royal University and Mar was finishing Med School. As one would expect, Tetrick didn't take the news of his father's death well, and with the help of other sources, he developed a conspiracy theory that the explosion was executed by the government. In Tetrick's mind, it only made sense. Naivim's death guaranteed the spaceship would never reach its potential and restart the SEEDER program. This meant the DOME project would move forward without any competing views on how to tackle the worsening environmental crisis.

"Why? Why would the government do such a thing?"

Mar asked Tetrick, "Do you have any evidence this is true?"

"I know its true," Tetrick said, "But I can't tell you how."

"Do you know how that sounds?" Mar said. "I understand that you're overwrought by your father's death, but when you don't give me or anybody else evidence for this theory, you know how it sounds? Delusional."

Mar surmised that Tetrick's obsession with his father's death would pass with time. They were partnered. Mar began her med practice at a Capitol City clinic and she became pregnant. Then came the news that deep-space viewing spotted an object heading toward Koda. A few scientists theorized that it was Yorlik the Great's ship. Skeptics said this was not the WAEF, but a comet, asteroid or meteor. All doubt was erased when the object made an obvious course correction and the shape of the ship was clearly seen on Kodan telescopes. Global excitement for the WAEF's return mounted. A countdown for the ship entering Koda's atmosphere was set at 156 days. All viewing channels maintained a countdown clock in the corner of their broadcast screens.

Knowing that Mar was pregnant with a boy, they decided to name him Yorlik, and as the day for the Great man's arrival grew closer, Yorlik the Great's only living ancestor Tetrick was inundated with requests for interviews. Mar pleaded with Tetrick not to mention his conspiracy theory when the interviewers inevitably asked about Tetrick's father and his relationship with Yorlik the Great. Tetrick couldn't help himself, igniting a storm of discontent over government policies. Citizens wanted to know if and why the Global Assembly would act this way. The DOME project was decades behind schedule and quadrillions had been spent on research and development with no construction date in sight. The Kodan population called for government hearings to investigate this accusation.

That was the first time that Tetrick was asked by the GSS to come in for questioning under the guise of "learning what he knows about this tragedy." He was gone for an entire day. Afterward he gave an interview where he expressed his theory again and talked about his questioning by the government and how he informed the interrogators that he wouldn't stop speaking out. The GSS detained him again for four days. When Tetrick returned, he appeared exhausted as if he hadn't slept the entire time he was gone, and there was a distinct adjustment in his attitude towards the theory that he adamantly pledged true a handful of days before. He said things like "It's possible that it didn't happen." A government statement was released that Tetrick had a nervous breakdown when his father tragically died and his theory was born of his grief without any foundation of fact. Tetrick did not confirm or deny this statement. The bruises on his body told Mar why her husband had altered his story, but they never spoke of it for a long time.

At 104 days on the countdown clock, life on the spaceship was confirmed. Yorlik the Great's cheery voice was heard as he communicated with a makeshift ground control that had been thrown together since there hadn't been space travel in over a 100 years. Celebration broke out around the planet. There was speculation about what Yorlik had discovered and how he survived longer than the effectiveness of his renowned invention, Rejuv Serum.

Yorlik Vanderlord and his lab and business partner created the Rejuv Serum as contracted scientists for the SEEDER program. They were attempting to lengthen the life span of explorers for their extended voyages into deep space. The Rejuv Serum restored the cells of a person back to their younger stronger structures and extended life spans beyond their natural lengths with Kodans reaching an average of 135 years old.

The viewing channels debated how Yorlik the Great had survived in space for over a century when the effects of the Serum would have worn off a half century ago. Since an equipment malfunction on the WAEF made face-to-face communication impossible, the viewing channels prognosticated on how Yorlik would appear, broadcasting speculative fotos of his appearance as an ancient and decrepit man.

As the day drew nearer for the landing, deep-space viewing broadcast clearer images of the spaceship, which appeared unscathed and unaltered like the day the ship left the planet 122 years ago. The viewing channels reviewed the ship's location on its final communication with Koda before its disappearance, wondering if there were any planets in the charted vicinity which might be their new home. If there was a habitable planet that far away, people wondered whether resources could be made available to build enough ships to save the entire population as the livability of their planet neared an end and the DOME project wasn't ready to begin. Scientists, philosophers, spiritual figures, and politicians including the President of the Global Assembly were marched out to hypothesize about the future depending on the news from the Great man. Again, the viewing channels wanted to speak with Tetrick, but this time he refused.

When the countdown clock ticked to zero, everyone on the planet would look upwards for the Great man's arrival. That would be a day of planetary celebration. Revelers around the globe would crowd the city centers and watch enormous viewing screens on the side of buildings to rejoice together. Long-range cams were pointed at the exact location where the ship would enter the outer atmosphere to capture the first glimpse of the ship before it circled the planet a few times on its descent. Planetary dignitaries would be present at the landing. The government had already told Yorlik of his son's death and his daughter Yara's natural passing years ago so there would be no surprises upon landing. Tetrick and a pregnant Mar would be the family contingent to greet him. They were flown by military cruiser to the military base where Yorlik would land, then setup in travel lodging nearby.

Mar and Tetrick had never stayed in such a luxurious establishment. The cost would have been far out of their means. A three-room air-cooled suite. Candy on the pillows. Complimentary butler and wait staff. King-size bed. They were placed on the twentieth floor, the top floor, and had a clear view of the brown drought-ravaged valley below with rusting irrigation systems in the barren fields. This was once Koda's most fertile land, but no more. In the distance, Mar could make out the sprawling military base bordered by fences with guard stations at the entrances and twelve circular landing sites dotting the compound with a handful of military cruisers parked there.

The government chose this site for Yorlik's landing as a precaution. All the security questions had been asked and answered correctly by the person who the government assumed was Yorlik Vanderlord and the analysis of his voice further confirmed his identity, but there wasn't a scientist on Koda who was absolutely sure what bacteria or virus he might carry with him aboard the ship. For that reason, the government wanted the site far away from any population centers.

On the morning of the landing, Mar woke earlier than Tetrick. The dawn was spectacular with the sun peaking out over the horizon and its rays beaming out over the lifeless landscape. Mar wondered what this new day meant for her family. Tetrick was sure to tell Yorlik about his conspiracy theory, then who knew what would happen. She heard the tales of this Great man who forged his own path to the stars and altered the course of planetary history with his mind and will. But this man had been gone for over a century, and nobody had a clue what to expect from him.

Mar was about 90 days from giving birth to her child. She had attempted to keep the anxiety associated with Yorlik's countdown and Tetrick's incarceration to a minimum. As the clock counted down to the landing, she balked at naming the boy Yorlik. She was concerned about putting any undue influence on her son's character after he was born. The name itself carried its own baggage, and she was concerned that giving him the same name as the Great man would levy a formidable standard on the boy. Tetrick was obstinate about the name and in the end, they agreed on one change. They'd name him Yor.

Staring out the window, she took a deep breath and hoped for the best from the new day's tidings. She woke Tetrick with a kiss on the lips and he pulled her down onto the bed for another kiss, then gently put his hand to her belly. "Hello my two darlings," he said, "We have one magnificent day ahead of us."

They prepared themselves for the government automobile to pick them up. Mar unpacked the box of clothes that the government purchased for them to wear. She was bought a simple green maternity sundress and comfortable cloth shoes. Tetrick was given a casual light brown suit and a pair of slip-on shoes to match the suit. The materials were practical for the weather outside. In the early morning, Mar felt the room's window and the outside heat through the glass was already burning to the touch. The box also contained a potent sunscreen lotion. The showers in the room were the type only wealthy Kodans experienced. The water was cooled and the pres-

sure of the spray was soothing to the pores. Mar didn't
want to leave the shower, but Tetrick needed his turn and
she wanted to dress and prepare herself. She was mindful
that the eyes of the planet would be judging her since
she avoided the viewing channels during the countdown.

When the comm in the room rang and the voice on
the other end of the line said the vehicle was downstairs
waiting for them, Mar felt a surge of anxiety. She looked
over at Tetrick, and they inspected each other.

Tetrick said, "You look particularly pretty in your
costume."

She laughed and they hugged, then she pulled away
from him and smoothed out her dress. "Don't want to
mess with perfection," Mar said.

Then there was an authoritative knock at the door.
"Your vehicle is waiting," a man's voice said.

Outside, on the walk from the lodging to the black
limousine, the temperature was scalding hot. The driver
wore a black suit and opened the back door for them,
seemingly unfazed by the heat, not a drop of sweat on
his brow. Mar assumed he was a local. Once they were
inside the vehicle, the door was closed with a thud, then
there was a pressurized sealing sound and the interior
temperature rapidly cooled.

The driver entered the front where he sat behind an
open partition and said, "Good morning, Vanderlords.
Big day," and the vehicle moved forward.

Even though Mar had slathered her exposed skin in
the protective cream, she felt like her shoulders were burnt

from the less than two-dozen steps in direct sunlight. She had brought the tube of lotion with her and Tetrick put more on her shoulders.

"There are a few boxes in the back for the both of you," the driver said. The limousine drove down a paved road with a thin layer of dirt covering it. The driver deftly avoided an occasional mass of weeds blowing across the road into the vehicle's path. Then they approached a line of vehicles entering the base and theirs slowed to a crawl.

In one box was a pair of sunglasses, and a pair of hi-tech binoculars.

"Best tech on the market. Expensive. We could never afford this brand-new," Tetrick said, examining the binoculars. "I'm going to hold onto mine."

Mar removed two hats, a man's and woman's, from the other box. She handed the flat-brimmed square hat to Tetrick and put the floppy cloth one on her head and pretended to model it. "High fashion. Expensive. We could never afford this brand-new," Mar said, "I'm going to hold onto mine."

They laughed. Maybe it was the cool air and the finery, but this was a rare moment of levity between them since the spotting of Yorlik's ship and Tetrick's controversy.

"Let's see what we've got here," Tetrick said, pointing at the viewing screen mounted in the ceiling in front of them. He turned on the screen and the binoculars and tinkered with both of them until they interfaced. The screen now showed the view outside their window where Tetick was pointing the binoculars, then he turned up the magnification pointing toward the military base's fence, moving the view closer to a transparent dome covering the viewing stands where individuals were lined outside in a cue going through security. A transparent tube snaked from near the landing pad to a smaller non-transparent bubble, a juncture, which was connected to another non-transparent tube which led to one of the buildings on the base. Mar assumed that building was the place that Yorlik would be quarantined, physically examined, and debriefed before being released to the public.

As their limousine neared the base's gate, Tetrick turned off the binoculars and viewing screen, handing the pair to Mar. They folded into a thin hand-size device that fit in her dress pocket. Through the open partition and front window, Mar noted that each driver of the vehicles ahead of them handed credentials to an armed guard standing outside a sentry box who examined the information, passed the creds back to the driver, then the gate went up and the guard waved the vehicle into the facility, pointing to the right where the other vehicles had gone. When their vehicle reached the guard, he took the creds and had some words with the driver that Mar couldn't hear and pointed to the left.

The gate opened and their limousine sped off, away from the viewing stand and landing pad to what seemed like a deserted part of the base.

"Where are we headed?" Tetrick asked the driver in a concerned tone. The driver didn't answer. Assuming that the driver hadn't heard him, Tetrick asked raising his voice, "Where are we headed?" The driver closed the partition between them. They approached a parked limousine identical to theirs, then stopped beside it. Tetrick knocked on the partition. "What is happening here?" he yelled with panic in his voice, "What is happening here?"

A moment later, there was the sound of the doors unsealing. A man stepped out of the other vehicle, entered theirs, bringing the searing outdoor heat into the limousine with him, then sat across from them and the doors sealed again. The man was in his late twenties, early thirties—about the same age as Mar and Tetrick—with perfectly coiffed jet-black hair and a bronzed complexion. He seemed unaffected by the heat outside and wore a white button-down shirt with one button loose at the top and black pants and plain black shoes with black socks. The shoes were polished to a shine, not a scuff on them. Mar smelled the scent of cheap soap.

The man stared at them for what seemed like a long time, nodding his head with a curious look on his face and it seemed like he was about to speak when Tetrick interjected, "What is happening here? What is this all about?"

"Funny I get that a lot," the man said, smirking, amused by himself.

"Who are you?" Mar asked.

"That's the least important detail here," the man said, clearing his throat loudly and covering his mouth with his fist. The back of his right hand was brutally scarred in thick protruding lines as if a whip had struck them many times and they'd scarred and healed over many violent sessions. "If it makes you feel more comfortable, I work for the President of the Global Assembly."

"So what is this about?" Tetrick asked, pulling on the door handle. The door was locked.

"Well, this is partly because of you, Tetrick Vanderlord." He said the last name in two separate words. Vander. Lord. Almost singing the second word. "We asked you here for obvious reasons. You're family to Yorlik Vanderlord and we need to maintain decorum, but you can't mention your speculation related to your father or express any anti-government remarks today. This is an event to be celebrated…"

"I will…" Tetrick began to say, but the man put up his hand with forefinger up, then opened his entire hand with his palm toward Tetrick like he was directing traffic to stop. As silence filled the air, he placed both his hands on his knees. Mar noticed the back of the man's left hand was brutally scarred as well.

"You will comply," the man said, smirking again. "You will comply. You will enjoy the event and be overjoyed to see your grandfather. If you do not comply Tetrick Vanderlord, I believe that you already have some idea of the consequences and I believe your wife and child will want their husband and father capable and in the home caring for them. The outcome of non-compliance will be unwelcome."

Then the man reached behind him and knocked on the driver's partition and the doors unsealed. He stepped outside, then turned and ducked back in holding the door open. The heat rushed in. Beads of sweat began flowing into Mar's eyes. The man was visibly unaffected by the heat. "The President will join you shortly at the viewing stand. Please enjoy this historic day," he said in an exaggerated jovial tone, then closed the door which sealed. The partition between the driver and Mar and Tetrick opened.

Time passed as the interior of the car cooled and the vehicle idled. Mar said nothing. Tetrick said nothing. They were both stunned. The vehicle's cooling system was the only sound in the interior. Suddenly the vehicle started forward, turning around and moving towards a queue of vehicles dropping off guests in front of the viewing-stand dome. Mar didn't know what to say. She assumed whatever she said would be relayed back to the man from the driver. She was angry. She wanted to go home. Tetrick was furious. She saw it in his eyes and the way his nostrils were flaring with each breath. "It's going to be nice meeting your grandfather," Mar said.

Tetrick inhaled, then blew out an extended breath and turned toward her. "Yes. I'm excited about seeing him, too. I'd love to catch up, but we probably won't have the time. I'm sure there will be time when he's released from quarantine." Mar got the message. Tetrick was promising to behave himself for now.

The doors unsealed when their right-side door was in line with the blue carpet emblazoned with the symbol of the Global Assembly which led to the entrance of the dome. The heat was grueling in the ten steps from the vehicle to the cooled enclosure where a man in military dress uniform greeted them at the entrance and led them to their front-row seats. Mar recognized government officials and political leaders in the crowd.

Before they sat down, the President's limousine pulled up and a musical group in the far corner of the enclosure, began performing the Global Anthem. Then the limousine's door opened, and everyone in the stands stood and the military personnel clicked their heels at attention. The President exited wearing a sharp-blue suit, white shirt with blue tie. The same fashion as Tetrick and every man in the enclosure. He walked the carpet toward the viewing stands, waving to the crowd, flanked by guards.

The viewing-channel reporters with their vid-operators by their side emerged from the crowd and intercepted the President, briefly interviewing him before he walked off toward where Mar and Tetrick were standing. The vid-operators stayed in place, but followed his movements. Guards surrounded the President with one extra-large guard both wide and tall in front parting the crowd with his forward motion and nothing else.

Finally, President Vidor Plemso stood in front of Mar. He was taller than Mar imagined from what she saw on the viewing channels. He was a bachelor. Never married. He was young for a person in his position. Thirty-eight years old. He was the son of a prominent global businessman and had an extensive and impressive military background, known for his leadership against the separatist revolts. He ran against an unpopular incumbent and won the election by a landslide. Political pundits said that his good looks, bright eyes, broad smile with white teeth and upbeat personality didn't hurt on the viewing screens and helped in his election victory. He was known as a ladies man, too. Mar saw there was something magnetic about this man who was ten years older than her.

"Is your wife okay?" the President asked Tetrick.

Mar had been staring at the President, and didn't know it. She was embarrassed.

"She's just overwhelmed by the heat and the event," Tetrick said.

"Well please sit down, both of you," the President said, "Being overwhelmed is understandable. This is quite the momentous occasion. The entire planet is overwhelmed. Nobody knows what to expect. The man has been missing for over a 100 years." The President turned toward the stands behind him. "Please sit," the President said, raising his voice so everyone could hear him, then he made a downward motion with his hands signaling the crowd to sit down. Everyone sat and began buzzing with conversation. He directed Mar and Tetrick to sit so he could seat himself between them, then the President addressed Mar, "This must be thrilling for you two. A family reunion of sorts. I've been reading up on Yorlik the Great, watching old vids. He was a remarkable man. A pioneer the likes Koda has never seen. I'm honored to meet him. It's like he's leaping out of the history books."

Mar nodded her head as he spoke. She was fascinated by him. Not just by his presence, but how his words seemed rehearsed as if he was playing the role of President. Somebody groomed him his entire life to reach this station. Mar thought *I don't trust this man. He's fake and programmed. A man like this isn't trustworthy.*

Then there was an explosion above their heads. The crowd gasped and were agitated. The President stood and turned to the crowd, holding out his hands as if to contain them. "Citizens, citizens please," he said, raising his voice, "There is no need to be alarmed. Please look over to that quadrant of the sky. Our guest of honor seems to be earlier than expected." He pointed in the direction that Mar's seat was facing.

The President seated himself and leaned toward Mar, saying with genuine excitement in his voice, "We've got front-row seats to Yorlik the Great's entrance." He pointed to the sky in front of them.

In the distance, high above the horizon, Mar could barely make out a dot coming toward them at a high velocity until it shot overhead and another explosion occurred. A sonic boom. Mar heard about them, but never experienced one, much like the majority of people in this enclosure. Tetrick nudged her from behind the President and held out the binoculars from the limo to remind her to use them. The ship shot over the base again with another boom. Again, the ship disappeared into the distance.

Mar wondered if the Great man was making a show of it. She turned on her binoculars and peered in the direction the ship had flown, increasing the magnification. The binoculars locked onto the ship and zoomed in closer, automatically tracking the ship as it banked back toward the base. Mar had seen historical fotos of When All Else Fails, and the outer hull looked precisely the same except for some blackened areas around the edges. The hair follicles on her arms stood on end in bumps as the WAEF headed back toward the base, she attempted to zoom into the control room window and glimpse the Great man flying the ship, but to no avail.

Mar looked over at the President who was leaning forward, peering through his own binoculars, which were larger and she assumed were military-grade. Tetrick was doing the same. She reached behind the President, nudging Tetrick and said, "You see it? You see him?"

"Yes," Tetrick said, "Magnificent. I can't see into the control room though. Seems like he has the radiation shielding down for some reason. We'll see him soon."

When Mar looked up again, she didn't need the binoculars to see the hull as the ship slowed directly over the base. The roar of the engines reversing, then making the ship hover was deafening. Many people held their hands over their ears. The sheer size of the WAEF was awesome. This was a lengthy three-story building gracefully pirouetting through the air to position itself over the landing area marked by a red circle. Mar turned to state her sense of awe to Tetrick again, but he couldn't hear her over the engines which held the ship motionless over the landing site. Then the ship began descending to the ground as if it was connected to an invisible string, seamlessly lowering to the pad.

She put the binoculars back up to her eyes to catch

a glimpse of the Great man behind the controls as the ship faced them. She increased the magnification over and over as she aimed at the control room window. All she saw was black. *Odd,* she thought, *Maybe he can see out, but we can't see in. Some sort of radiation shielding, but why would he need that here.*

The roar of the engines was ear-piercing now as the WAEF lowered landing gear, positioning itself perpendicular to the stands, preparing to touch down. Everyone in the stands had their hands over their ears now. The force of the engines pushed on the enclosure to the point where it seemed that the entire thing might be torn from the ground, exposing the revelers to the elements, and the heat emanating from the engines began to cook the air in the cooled enclosure. The government had not prepared for any of these factors. The viewing stands should have been placed further from the landing site, but there wasn't a citizen alive who experienced a SEEDER ship landing in person. As the ship neared the ground, a cloud of dirt and rocks shot in their direction, blocking their view for an instant. A few people screamed as the enclosure violently rattled, but held its ground.

Tetrick peered into the cloud that enveloped them. He couldn't wait to meet his grandfather. Mar was interested to see if Yorlik lived up to his legend. "Most of it was true," Tetrick's history professor colleagues told her when it came to Yorlik the Great folklore. He was brilliant and funny. Everybody who knew him loved him. He was tenacious in getting his way. History told that he petitioned the Global Monarchy incessantly to get his mission okayed, and when he hadn't returned to Koda and was presumed missing, people talked about how his stubbornness to discover a livable planet might have been his undoing in the hazards of space.

When the ship eased to the ground, the roar of the engines powered down to silence and the dust cloud settled, revealing the WAEF safely landed, towering over the viewing stand. The people in the stands bolted to their feet, whooping and applauding at what they'd witnessed, chanting "When All Else Fails, When All Else Fails, When All Else Fails..." Mar and Tetrick stood along with the President who turned to the crowd and took in the jubilation. His face showed no emotion and Mar wondered whether he was enjoying the crowd's celebration. Then the President held up his arms and motioned his hands downward for the crowd to calm and sit down. Mar and Tetrick sat, too. The President was handed an amplification device and spoke into it, "My dear citizens, we've all witnessed a magnificent day in Koda's history," he said, gazing down at Mar and winking at her. He had heard Tetrick talking to her when the WAEF was landing. "The return of Yorlik Vanderlord to our dear Koda is unexpected and unparalleled in our planet's history. His return to our planet gives us hope for the future and although we have high expectations and await the details of his journey, I would caution against any conclusions until we have all the facts at hand and can examine them from an objective, scientific and rational place in applying them to our current planetary emergency."

The crowd applauded. Mar could tell that Tetrick was annoyed at the rhetoric. The President continued, "May the Powers-That-Be bless our global union and bring the Kodan people safely out of our crisis so we may prosper in the future." The crowd gave the President's speech a standing ovation. Mar and Tetrick stood and applauded, too. The President held up his arms, signaling a triumph for his people. When the applause waned, the President turned to face the WAEF.

On cue, a ramp lowered from the rear and beneath the WAEF and touched down to the ground, and a person wearing a silver and orange spacesuit presumed to be Yorlik the Great descended to the landing pad. Yorlik was not wearing the suit for dramatic effect. This was a discussed safety precaution against spreading disease on a planet where crisis-level problems abounded already.

The landing crew drove up in their vehicle, extended the quarantine tube to the edge of the landing pad, securing it in place before jumping back into their vehicle and racing away. Yorlik bent down at the end of the ramp and touched his gloved hand to the ground. The crowd erupted in applause and cheered. Yorlik stood and turned toward the viewing stand and waved to the crowd as he walked toward the tube, the sun glistening off the suit and helmet. The crowd roared and chanted "Yorlik…Yorlik… Yorlik the Great" over and over again. Yorlik waved, then touched his hand to his heart and simulated it beating for them with his hand. Mar recognized the historical significance of this event for Kodans and her family and peered at the Great man through the binoculars. 'Vanderlord' was printed over the right breast of his spacesuit. Yorlik held up his hands in triumph, much like the President had done at the end of his speech, and the crowd cheered louder, continuing to chant his name. Mar noticed that the binoculars took digi-fotos and snapped a few off. Yorlik waved to the crowd one more time, blew a kiss to them and disappeared into the tube. Mar closed the binoculars and placed them in her dress pocket.

"Follow me," the President said. Four of the President's guards surrounded Mar, Tetrick, and the President. They walked to the rear of the viewing stand where there was a back doorway in the enclosure. The President stopped and said to Mar and Tetrick, "Remember. When we meet him, we will be viewed by the entire planet." He pointed to the gigantic viewing screen lowering in front of the viewing stand so everyone there could see their meeting with the Great man. "I will also have a trip switch in case something unexpected happens."

This was a warning for Tetrick, but nobody had any idea what to expect when Yorlik removed his helmet, too.

"We're ready," one of the President's guards said, then the President placed his palm on the door's DNA scanner. The door slid open, and one guard entered the doorway and a moment later, re-emerged signaling for the President to follow.

When the entire entourage was in the tube, the door was secured behind them and they moved forward. There were no sounds in the tube except for their footsteps and the quiet whir of the cooling system. The tube was a sterile sealed environment. At one point, the guards halted the group and one went ahead and the other went back to the enclosure's door to insure that all was secure, and as they waited, Mar felt a sense of euphoria. Happier. She looked over at the smile on Tetrick's face and realized that the tube was being pumped full of Fretopin, an airborne pharmaceutical used by the government to keep potentially volatile crowds under control at large indoor gatherings. She was positive that the guards and the President were vaccinated against it. While they waited for the guards, Mar attempted to pull herself back from the intense Fretopin high, thinking that she could control herself against its effects, but she was too far gone.

The lead guard returned and they continued forward. Mar thought it was funny that they were going down a tube. She even released an involuntary giggle, like a bubble generated by the Fretopin, then restrained the flow of others that she felt rising up. The tube ended at a transparent wall. On the other side of the wall was a chamber that was a junction with two tube connections where Mar assumed that the tube leading from the landing pad ended, and the tube ending at the military-base building began. The tube leading from the WAEF was closed off by a door. Vidcams were mounted on every corner of the chamber. On their side, centered in the tube's ceiling directly beside the transparent wall were two cams, one facing in toward them and the other pointing out through the wall into the chamber.

One of the guards held his finger to his temple. He was listening to somebody, communicating with him through an audio implant. He turned to the President and said, "Ready when you are, President Plemso, sir." Mar and Tetrick were instructed to situate themselves side by side behind the President who stood with the cam in the ceiling pointing at him. Two guards stood to the side of the tube and the one with the audio implant moved a few paces to the rear, counting out loud, "6, 5, 4, 3, 2, 1" and the door in the chamber slid open. Yorlik the Great stood there in his spacesuit, stepped into the chamber and the door slid closed behind him. Mar's heart raced. She felt the baby kick.

A voice from an unseen speaker that Mar presumed came from one of the buildings on the base said, "You can remove your helmet now, Colonel Vanderlord." The figure in the suit tapped a few buttons on the right bicep of his sleeve and there was an audible hiss. He pressed a few more buttons, then reached up and released a clasp connecting the helmet to the suit and lifted the helmet off his head.

Long strands of grey hair fell over Yorlik's bearded face. His beard was mostly grey, too. He unclasped his gloves and put them in the helmet which he placed at his feet, then he took both his hands and pushed his hair back into a small tail which he secured in place with what looked like wiring that must have loosened when he removed the helmet.

Then Yorlik picked up the helmet, placing it under the crook of his arm and stepped toward the transparent wall and the President. His motions were deliberate with no rush. Mar concluded that he'd been in space for so long by himself that interacting with other people was simply foreign to him by now. There was no ceremony to him except his own routine.

The President said, "Colonel Yorlik Vanderlord, I am President Vidor Plemso of the Global Assembly. May I welcome you back with all the gratitude of Koda's citizens for your service. We're all amazed to see you return after so many years. Everyone thought that you'd been lost. Welcome home."

Mar saw a distinct family resemblance between Yorlik and Tetrick. Yorlik was a tall broad shouldered man like Tetrick, too. Mar had seen fotos of Yorlik before he left. He had aged but not as much as she would have thought. He must have found a way of replicating a new serum. He appeared around 60 years old, maybe younger. His full head of hair counterbalanced deep wrinkles from old age in the skin of his face between his eyebrows, in his forehead and particularly around his eyes which seemed to be diligently observing the surroundings.

"The entire planet is watching," the President said, "Would you like to say something to the citizens?"

There was no way that they'd let him speak freely, Mar thought, *He must've been fed words to say by the government.*

Yorlik stood facing the President, scrutinizing him. The silence began to verge on awkward, then Yorlik distinctly shifted his gaze from the President to Tetrick and a broad smile crept across his face and stuck there. Mar knew that mischievous smile. *A Vanderlord thing.* She girded herself. She felt the baby kick again.

Yorlik peered directly at the President and spoke. "I'm thrilled to return home, President Plemso. For years and years, I've dreamed of my loved ones, of my family and friends, and this wondrous planet full of life that is seemingly unique in all the universe," Yorlik said in measured words with a tone of complete sincerity, then he took a step back and looked directly into the cam above the President's head, "But I was aghast as I approached the globe and took readings on the environment and noted the degradation that has taken place in such a short planetary period of time. I can only imagine the greedy forces at work to maintain the status quo in the face of such a disastrous tide…"

The President reached to his right and hit a red button attached to the tube. A metallic partition slid over the transparent wall between the President and Yorlik the Great. The President never lost his composure and spoke directly into the cam. "Our thanks to Yorlik Vanderlord for his service to the planet and I'm sure that we will hear more about his journey in the days to come. Until then, may the Powers-That-Be bless our dear Koda." The President put his hand over his heart and waited.

The guard with the implant said, "The transmission is out." The two guards who stood to the side of the tube carefully grabbed hold of Mar and Tetrick and moved them against the wall of the tube.

The President turned to Tetrick, pointing at him and said, "That was completely uncalled for. Don't think there won't be consequences." The mask was gone from Vidor Plemso and Mar saw him for the truly selfish spiteful pampered little boy who got everything that he ever wanted. He stormed off down the tube with one guard ahead of him and another behind. One guard remained to escort them back to their vehicle.

"What do you think?" Mar said, walking beside Tetrick.

That same mischievous smile that she'd seen on Yorlik's face spread across Tetrick's. "He is everything my father talked about and more." The baby kicked and Tetrick saw her reaction and held his hand to her belly.

Mar recalled that moment as if it happened yesterday while she sat on the couch in her bungalow, worrying about her son. She was concerned that there was too much Vanderlord in him, and naming him after his great-grandfather hadn't helped, but his great-grandfather was quite a man, a great man.

RAJER

When Rajer first entered the Detention Facility reception area, an older woman sat hunched over, sobbing until she was escorted past the reception desk by a guard and disappeared down a hallway. This was a reminder of what this building represented, reigniting Rajer's concern for Yor, but that didn't last long and he lapsed into a state of calm, closing his eyes.

Rajer felt a tap on his shoulder and opened his eyes to a tired looking Yor standing in front of him.

"How was your nap?" Yor said.

Rajer rubbed at his eyes and stretched his legs. "Did I fall asleep? You look like crap."

"Must have been the Trianin that they pump in here. And thanks, you look wonderful yourself," Yor said, "Let's get out of here."

Rajer shook off the sleepiness and stood to shaky legs. "Wow, that stuff is powerful. Do I need to sign anything?"

"No, we're good if you can call it that. Why are you here anyway?"

"Mado commed me. He thought that it might be a good idea for me to come down and vouch for you. Flash the government badge. I'm glad you're okay," Rajer said and squeezed Yor's arm.

"Appreciate the effort. Really. But let's get out of here.

This place gives me the creeps."

When they left the GSS building, curfew had already begun. The sentry gave them passes with their name and ID code, a unique number given to all dome residents. The curfew pass allocated a specific amount of time before it expired, taking into consideration the lack of rail cars this time of night and the most expedient path home. Upon expiration, the pass transmitted a positioning signal to the proper authorities. At that time, if Yor and Rajer did not arrive home or another indoor shelter, then they'd be arrested.

The streets were deserted as Rajer and Yor walked in silence through the Plaza and the old part of the city to the rail car station. Rajer intermittently looked over at Yor who was deep in thought, brow furrowed, looking off into the distance. Rajer had no idea what was happening with him. He decided that he would let Yor ponder whatever was on his mind and wait until they reached the rail station to chat with him.

A Global Guard at the station inspected their curfew passes, reminding them in a firm tone to get off the streets before the passes expired.

As they waited for the rail car, Rajer commed Mar and told her that he was headed home, but didn't mention the actual reason he left the bungalow. He didn't want to talk to her about Yor's situation until he and Yor returned home together.

"Your mother will want to talk to you about tonight," Rajer said, thinking this was the best way to break the silence, but Yor was still lost in thought. "Yor, did you hear…?"

"Yes, I heard you," Yor said, "Did you tell her where you went? I noticed that you didn't mention me."

"No. I didn't want to worry her."

"She'd be concerned."

The rail car pulled into the station. They boarded an empty one. After curfew, there was no supervisor although the vidcams never stopped working. Rajer waited for Yor to sit down and seated himself beside him.

"Yes, she'd be concerned," Rajer said, "Would you expect anything less from her?"

"You didn't tell her anything?" Yor asked.

"Like I already said, I didn't tell her anything. I didn't know anything. Mado told me that you were taken to the Detention Facility and it might be prudent for me to go down there and see if I could do anything to clear up the situation. I told your mother I was called into work."

"Nice move. Lying to my mother. I bet she had it figured out before you left the bungalow."

"Oh I have my moves," Rajer said, giving Yor a playful shove.

Yor began laughing.

"Oh you find that funny, do you?" Rajer said, "I can keep some secrets from your mother."

Yor bent over, laughing.

"You find my relationship with your mother amusing."

Yor made an effort to stop laughing, and released a

few more giggles before he stopped. "Sorry. Thanks. I needed that."

"I'm not insulted. You're correct in finding humor in what I said, and you're welcome," Rajer said, "So what happened at the Royal Library? Why did you get dragged into the Detention Facility?"

"It's all a misunderstanding," Yor said, "But I've been given a summons for a panel to review the incident in 42 days."

"A hearing. That's not good."

"I'm not worried," Yor said, "No big deal. There's nothing to review. The alarm went off before I was done. A simple error on my part."

"If they didn't think there was something more to it, then they wouldn't bother calling a review of the incident," Rajer said, "Is there something that you want to tell me?"

"Are you saying that I'm lying to you?"

"Come on, Yor," Rajer said, "I know you're smart. I know you have an agenda when it comes to your research. I know I'm supposed to think that this was all academic, but I know you better than you give me credit for. We've lived together long enough that I can tell when you're burying the truth under your smile and impeccable logic so don't even try."

Yor leaned forward and put his head in his hands, covering his eyes and held himself in that position as the rail car pulled into a station, the doors opened and closed and the car sped up again. Rajer saw a maintenance worker walking away from the rail car.

"You okay?" Rajer said.

Yor rubbed his eyes with his hands and sat up. "Tired," Yor said, "It's been an exhausting day."

"I'd prefer that you not change the subject."

Yor smiled. That Vanderlord smile. Mar said that Yor inherited it from Tetrick. That sly smile with something hidden behind it. Rajer was now truly concerned. "Now you're scaring me. What do you have planned?"

Yor whispered in Rajer's ear, "The less you know, the better for you and my mother." Then he put his fingers to his lips before Rajer could respond. "Trust me. You and my mother will be fine and you need to keep her in the dark for now, for all our well-being."

Yor looked around the vacant car and at the vidcams in the corners of the rail car's ceiling. Whatever Yor had planned, it made him paranoid enough, that he feared the government might be spying on him.

"I don't know anything. You haven't told me anything," Rajer said, "I can only tell her that I went to the GSS building to pick you up."

Yor reached around Rajer and hugged him with one arm. "Exactly. I need to meet up with Insol. I'll be home in the morning," Yor said as the rail car pulled into a station. He stood up, waved good-bye and exited the car, running up the station stairs and out of sight.

This was typical of Yor's behavior. Always running off to do his own thing. Soon after Rajer met Mar, Yor entered the Royal University. When Yor wasn't in classes or studying, he was usually off researching his great-grandfather's history. Mar was concerned about her son's obsession with uncovering Yorlik's past, and how he wasn't friends with any other students and was only social with his father's old University colleagues.

As Yor's internship with Mado intensified, he was more preoccupied and quieter than usual. To ease her mind, Mar talked to Yor. He gave her no answers. He was sullen and upset that she'd question him. Mar thought about talking to Mado, but Yor would have seen it as going behind his back so she asked Rajer to have a talk with the boy alone.

So Rajer decided to take Yor for an outing to the Royal Library's Museum which housed SEEDER-program artifacts and was only open to government employees and citizens with special permission. Rajer and Yor weren't on the best of terms, but Rajer knew that Yor would put up with him to visit this place.

Rajer was correct. Yor's enthusiasm at viewing these objects from the past was unbounded and it didn't matter that Rajer was present. Inside the museum, Yor was enthralled by a shovel and transparent container full of soil from a planet discovered by Harl Maksin on the first SEEDER mission. Maksin believed he discovered a viable planet, but when his readings were analyzed, the planet was rejected by the Board of SEEDER Scientists which included Yorlik Vanderlord.

Yor put his hands on the glass of the display case and peered inside, attempting to get a closer look at the soil until a curator told him to move away from the glass.

The curator was a thin fragile-looking man with a pale complexion.

"Sorry," Rajer said to the curator, "He's a little excited. First time here. This is Yorlik the Great's great-grandson."

"You don't say," the curator said, looking over at Yor. "I can see the family resemblance."

"Who do I ask about viewing special requests?" Rajer said.

"That would be me," the curator said.

"I'm Rajer Jeps. I'm a friend of Lek's."

"Yes. I spoke with Lek. Your request is ready. Would you like to see it now?"

Yor had returned to the SEEDER exhibit and moved onto a detailed model of a Transit Point Station. These way stations were meant to orbit moons or planets for refueling and resupplying ships on the way to the viable planet. Passengers would disembark here for a few days before journeying onto their new home. None were ever built.

"Yor," Rajer said.

Yor didn't budge, immersed in his examination of the model.

"Yor! I've got something for you to see."

"I'm checking this out."

"You can come back to that. You'll appreciate this. Follow me."

Yor groaned and mumbled something under his breath, then reluctantly followed Rajer and the curator. They passed through a security door bearing a 'No Admittance except Authorized Personnel' sign, and entered a wood-paneled room filled with overloaded bookshelves, smelling of mold.

"What's all this?" Yor said to the curator as they walked down an aisle between the shelves.

"This is where we keep books and documents that we consider worthy of restoration for the library."

"Is my great-grandfather's journal around here somewhere? I'd love to see it."

"That journal is in a secure section of the library and off limits. Sorry."

"Can you do anything about that?" Yor said to Rajer.

"No. I actually asked, but it's above my clearance. You may like this though."

They reached the other side of the room and the curator unlocked a door with a large key. This was an ancient building and keys were rarely used or made these days. Metal for keys was hard to come by. They stepped into a small room with no windows. A desk with an outmoded viewer sat in one corner and an object covered by a cloth about as tall as Yor stood in the other corner.

"This is it?" Rajer said to the curator.

"This is what Lek requested for you. How do you know him?"

"From University."

"We actually grew up a few houses from one another."

"That's what he told me," Rajer said, "He's a good man, a good friend."

"He sure is," the curator said, "I need to get back out

front. When you're done, pull the door behind you. By the way, Lek told me to tell you, 'Any time.' Nice to meet you, young Vanderlord."

"You as well." Yor said.

The curator exited, leaving Yor and Rajer alone in the room.

"You ready," Rajer said.

"Not sure, but I'm curious."

Rajer grabbed a handful of the cloth covering the object and pulled it with a flourish. Before them was a mannequin wearing Yorlik the Great's silver and orange spacesuit including helmet. Rajer kept an eye on Yor's face which went from not knowing what to expect to utter disbelief, mouth agape.

"Holy…What did you do? Oh my! This is unbelievable. How did you pull this off?" Yor said.

"I'm not without my connections."

"Can I put on the helmet?"

"Just you and me. I don't see why not. I won't tell anybody."

The helmet wasn't secured to the rest of the suit so Yor gingerly lifted it from the mannequin as if it might fall apart in his hands.

"So it's okay?"

Rajer smiled and nodded. "Go ahead."

With both hands, Yor lowered the helmet over his head and slowly let go.

"How does it feel?" Rajer said.

"Incredible. How does it look?"

"A little strange in this room, but I can see you wearing it in space."

"Looks like there are some displays in here, but I can't see them without having the suit completely on and powered up, but we probably don't have time for that."

"No. Sorry."

A short time later, after Yor basked in the helmet and thoroughly examined the suit, Rajer exited the office with him. While walking back in silence between the bookshelves, Rajer felt a poke in his back, stopped and turned around.

Yor said, "Thanks for doing that, Rajer. That meant a lot to me. I know that I've been rough on you since you got together with my mother. Maybe even gone out of my way to be a jerk sometimes. But I'm grateful for what you've done here and I know that my mother loves you so that means a whole lot...and you're growing on me."

"That's nice to hear you say," Rajer said, "I wanted to talk to you before we went home. Your mother and I have been worrying about you lately. You're more withdrawn than usual."

"My mother worries about me. That's her job, but now she has you to bring in on her worrying," Yor said, patting Rajer on the arm. "I'm fine. You guys need to relax. I'm 15 years old and I'm a University student with a full course load and I'm learning about groundbreaking tech from the most gifted man on the planet. I've got a lot on my plate, but I've got a handle on it."

Rajer laughed. "Okay that's good to hear."

Now with this arrest and the hearing to come, Rajer was concerned. Yor's intelligence made him believe that he could outwit everyone around him, but Rajer knew the system all too well. The system was rigged to catch people who played it.

When Rajer stepped out of the rail car at the station near his bungalow and it sped off, he was greeted by a man in his 50s with perfectly coiffed jet-black hair, tanned bronzed complexion wearing a white button-down shirt with one button loose at the collar. He stood directly in Rajer's path. They were alone on the platform.

"Rajer Jeps," the man said, "I believe that you have an idea of my occupation. There's no need for you to speak." He was GSS. Rajer had met a few of them on his interviews for his current position, and around the office. Most of them were ex-Global Guard officers who were recruited for their keen sense of observation and their ruthlessness. GSS personnel looked at you like they could take your life without a thought. This man fit the bill. "I have only a few words to say, then you can make your way back to Mar. We believe that Yor is treading in territory that will create disaster for your family. That includes jeopardizing your cozy Global Assembly position which can easily be filled by a long list of candidates. Global Assembly jobs are hard to come by and excuses are made every day to release citizens from their employment with no recourse. Once you're terminated from your position and the reasons are officially sealed from the public, then finding another Global Assembly job will be impossible.

You'd have to move out of your cozy high-tech bungalow and move to the old part of the city which would be more affordable on a maintenance worker's pay. So keep an eye on your boy. Oh sorry, that's right. Not your boy. You've never been able to have children. But we'll hold you responsible if he gets too far out of line."

"What did Yor do?" Rajer said, his words coming out shaky, revealing his quivering and fear.

The man clasped his hands in front of himself, then shook his head and smirked. Rajer noticed the scars on the back of the man's hands. Deep scars. Jagged scars. "You don't know?" the man said, "Maybe you should ask him." Then the man did an about-face with military precision and strolled out of the station like this was a walk in a park.

Rajer walked home in a daze. Yor had never told him why he was brought to the Detention Facility. Rajer's life and livelihood were in the balance and he didn't know why. Over and over he reviewed how his life course and his future with Mar could be irreparably altered due to Yor's actions. His daze turned to anger. He felt like his life which seemed on track was suddenly out of his control.

When he reached home, Mar was asleep on the couch. He closed the door to their bedroom and pressed the button on the comm to speak with Mado who immediately appeared on the screen. He was still in his lab.

"Is everything okay?" Mado said.

"Can we talk?" Rajer said. That was planetary language for 'Are we on a secure line that can't be tapped by the government?' True secure lines of communication were illegal without high-security clearance. Mado had one of them, but it was safer to ask.

"Always," Mado said, "You meet Yor at the Detention Facility?"

"Yes." Rajer said and told Mado the entire story from leaving the GSS building to now. "What do you make of it?"

"Not good," Mado said, "Not good. I'll talk to Yor tomorrow and assess what's happened and get back to you."

"Please do," Rajer said, "I have to admit that I'm shaken up by that man."

"For good reason. Get a good sleep and we'll talk tomorrow. You might wait until we talk again to tell Mar anything."

"I'll do what I can do. You know how she is."

"I'm aware," Mado said and the comm disconnected.

Rajer attempted to compose himself. He paced around the room for awhile, then he opened the bedroom door. Mar was standing on the other side and she did not look happy.

YOR

Yor knocked on the door of Insol Renta's apartment in the Royal University building for housing out-of-dome professors. Posted on the door was the Shamban regional flag, straight lines emanating in a circle from a central blank point. The flag represented the Shamban myth that millions of years ago the birth of all creatures on Koda flourished from an exploding star.

Yor knocked again. The door opened and his friend Mellick Zonor stood in the entrance. Mel was a man of short stature, but large presence, with flaming red curly hair and a booming voice. He was ten years older than Yor who recruited him for the SEEDER-program studies faculty. It was an easy decision to choose Mel for his staff. Mel was the planet's foremost historical expert on the origins of the SEEDER program. When Yor was a teen, entering the University, he read a published paper by Mel and they started a long-distance correspondence, based on their similar interests. Mel's research was the foundation for Yor's book.

"Hey brother, how goes it? Mel said.

"Rough night," Yor said, "What are you doing here so late? Where's Insol?"

"Come on in," Mel said, "Earlier, she wanted me to come over and discuss her upcoming communication with her network. She didn't want to discuss it over an unsecure comm and I'm only a few floors down." Insol administered discussions with a support group for survivors from the southern climes, both living in the nine domes and struggling outside them. Their discontent with the Global Assembly was deep-seated and at Insol's word, they were ready to mobilize.

Yor walked past Mel into the room of the apartment which served as a kitchen and living room. The walls were covered by multi-colored Shamban tie-dye tapestries. The saving grace of the small room was the one window looking out onto the campus green. Insol's bedroom door was closed and the shower was running in the bathroom.

"She wanted me to wait here and let you in," Mel said, pulling at his hair as if he wanted the curls to stand out straight on the strength of the tug. He did this habitually. "I should get going."

"No. Please stay. The three of us should discuss what happened tonight," Yor said, sitting down on the couch.

Mel placed himself in an armchair across from Yor, and picked up a cup from a low table between them and sipped at it. "Would you like a hot beverage?" Mel said, holding up his cup. "I just made some."

"No. My stomach's upset. Not feeling that great. Had a run-in with a sonic alarm," Yor said, "And my head is still aching."

"Poor baby," Insol said. Yor likened her accent to purring. She stood in the bedroom doorway wearing a towel, her black shoulder-length hair wet. They first met at her interview for a position in his department and she was hired for her intellect, although Yor was stunned by her beauty. After she got the job, they learned their attraction to each other was both intellectual and physical, and they'd been dating for a few years now. She gazed at him with those dark eyes of hers, and Yor was lost in the vision of her.

"You two sure you don't want me to go?" Mel said.

"No," Yor and Insol said simultaneously.

"That's a first," Mel said, laughing. "What happened must be serious?"

"Our esteemed director of SEEDER-program studies decided to go ahead and attempt a foray into the Royal Library, and he received a summons for a hearing," Insol said.

"I knew that you obtained entry," Mel said, "But I thought we decided to wait until we had more of the movement's infrastructure in place, just in case something went wrong there."

"Insol?" Yor said, noticing she was no longer in the doorway.

"I'll be right there," Insol said from the bedroom. "Slipping into something more appropriate."

"I thought the towel was fine," Yor said.

"You would," Insol said, "But we have company."

"You two sure that you don't want me to leave?"

"Normally, I'd push you out the door, but not now," Yor said, "My foray as Insol put it has caused some problems we should discuss, although I just realized I don't have a jammer on me."

"I still have the one that you left a few days back when we met with Ador here," Insol said from the bedroom.

"Right. I'm definitely not thinking straight," Yor said, "I was looking for it today in my office and remembered that I left it here."

"Should we call, Ador?" Mel said.

"He lives halfway across the city and he wouldn't be able to come here anyway because of curfew," Yor said.

"Ah the curfew," Insol said, bounding into the living room wearing a purple nightie that ran down to mid-thigh with a low-cut neckline and thin shoulder straps. The thin material clung to her body and accentuated her curves. She placed the signal jammer, which resembled a forefinger with a base, on the low table, and activated it. A light on its base blinked six times, then stopped to a steady light. Insol plopped down on the couch beside Yor and planted a kiss on his cheek. "The curfew is the Global Assembly's way of controlling dome residents for 10 of our 29 hours a day. There's no need for it. The last DOME riots happened eight years ago. Wasn't that the rationale for them?"

"Yes," Yor said, holding his head in his hands. "But we've got other problems."

"Let me massage your shoulders. That might help with the tension from the alarm. Scoot forward," Insol said. Yor moved and Insol slid behind him with both legs straddling him. She kissed his head, then began massaging his shoulders.

"That feels fantastic," Yor said, turning his head and kissing Insol on the lips. "I can fill in Ador tomorrow."

"I'm all ears," Mel said.

Yor recounted the entire experience from the Royal Library up through being released from the Detention Facility. "I have to admit that I was extra paranoid on the rail car ride and the walk over here. I noted all the vidcams recording my movements."

"Yes, those things are despicable. The longer they're up there, the greater chance we'll forget about their presence," Mel said.

"Privacy is no longer a given. That's for sure," Insol said, still rubbing Yor's shoulders.

"Yes. Back to the issue at hand," Yor said, "I don't think we can wait for the hearing to make the plan happen. Who knows what they might know and what they might uncover in the 42 days between now and the hearing? Can we risk it? Are we ready to proceed?"

"Before we get into that, I thought we were going to wait for the library until at least another year to build the movement in all the regions, and Mado needed that long to finish the ship," Mel said, "I'm not sure why you decided to make this unilateral move without discussing it with us first. You were aware of the inherent danger and the exposure to what we're attempting to put together here. What we're doing here isn't all about your fixation with your great-grandfather."

Yor said, "That's not fair..."

"I hate to say it, darling, but I believe that Mel's statement is fair," Insol said, moving out from behind Yor and sitting with her legs crossed next to him.

"I thought that it was worth the risk."

"You thought," Mel said, "You thought. Last I looked this isn't all about you."

"Yes, I thought," Yor said, "Up until now, we've seen no evidence of Global Assembly interest in our activities. I considered the risk and even if I was caught, there was a high probability that they'd let me go. All they know is I was reading my great-grandfather's journal and I took too long."

"You know that your great-grandfather, your father, your entire family is a touchy subject for the government," Mel said, "Their job is protecting their interests. You think this man isn't going to pour over the vidcam feeds and come after the people closest to you, the people who spend the most time with you to find out what the library was all about. That exposes everything we've been working toward because of your whim."

"Mado didn't think it would be a big problem," Yor said.

"I recall you telling me that Mado said the library was the biggest danger looming so we needed to put it off for now, and you agreed," Mel said.

"Of course it's not a problem for Mado. Even if they suspect him, even if they find evidence, they'll let him get away with it," Insol said, "The Global Assembly can't survive and literally can't stay in power without him."

"That's why he's such an important part of what we're

doing here. He's been our cover," Yor said, "And you're correct, Mel. He did say that. He meant that it was dangerous but manageable or that's how I interpreted it."

"You know my opinion about Mado," Insol said.

"I know. You don't trust him," Yor said, "If it helps, he didn't know that I was going to do this now either, and he's going to be angry with me, too. And I hear what you're saying, but again we've been over this before, if it wasn't for him, then we wouldn't be as far along in organizing the movement and he was a close friend of my great-grandfather."

"Again, this isn't just about your great-grandfather anymore," Mel said. He rose from his chair and took his cup to the sink, then walked back and stood behind the chair with his arms crossed.

"Mado is a good friend of mine, too," Yor said, "That's the bottom-line here. I have my suspicions, but I don't believe that he would turn on us."

"Your line of reasoning is thin," Insol said, "Getting back to your original thought, in light of this evening, I would agree that we need to forge ahead with the plan now instead of later. We were all in danger before tonight, but Mel is right. The events of tonight and this pending hearing means they'll be closely monitoring you and all of us from here on out. We can't wait around for them to round us all up. As far as Mado, he is too key to our current plans to not implicitly trust him. If you decide that you no longer suspect him, then we trust you."

"I completely agree on all counts," Mel said, sitting

back down in the armchair, leaning towards Yor. "If we can't trust Mado, then we'll need to come up with a completely different plan right away."

"Just so we're clear," Insol said, "We need to know that you're all good with Mado and he is definitely on our side otherwise moving forward with the current plan will be a complete disaster,"

"Just like this evening's blunder," Mel said, "I don't know what you were thinking. It was impulsive. It was reckless. It was egotistical. This isn't just about you. This is about the survival of the Kodan people. We've built this movement over the past couple of years together, and we needed to be consulted before you acted. In many ways, you've been the spokesperson especially with the success of your book, but this was out of line."

"I understand that you're upset," Yor said.

"Of course I'm upset. Is your family lost somewhere in a refugee camp or out there wandering the desolation?" Mel said. His position at an inland university gave him a favorable number in that region's DOME Residence Selection Process and kept him alive as he watched the ocean's rise, destroying his home city of Nor. His family didn't make it into a dome so they were displaced and Mel couldn't locate them in refugee camp listings. He never gave up thinking that they were still alive.

"Let's not go there," Insol said, "We've all had family and friends lost because of the Global Assembly's actions and that's our biggest pitch when it comes to our movement. Not many people on Koda have been spared from loss because of the government's policies and they continue to be affected by them."

"I get it. I'm sorry. I screwed up," Yor said, picking up Insol's hand and kissing it, "I'm tired. I will talk to Mado and we'll have a meeting tomorrow. If anything positive comes from today, I attained a complete scan of the journal and I'm hoping that outweighs the consequences of my actions. If anything concerns me, it's the man who interrogated me."

"We'll find out soon enough where this leads," Mel said, "I've got an early class and have to catch some sleep. See you tomorrow." He waved as he left the apartment.

"What about you?" Insol said, jumping to her feet and standing in front of Yor. "Come to bed. I'll make sure you feel better."

"I'll be there in a little while," Yor said, "I need to think and maybe take something for this headache."

"Okay you know where the pain relievers are. Don't keep me waiting too long," Insol said, kissing Yor on the lips and skipping into her bedroom.

Yor took a deep breath and laid down on the couch. Looking up at the white ceiling, his mind immediately went to the interrogation room. *How did everything go wrong so quickly?* Yor thought. *How will I deal with Mado?*

Yor remembered that he first met Mado less than a year before his father died. That was a tumultuous time in Kodan history. The environmental crisis was devastating the planet with fires, violent storms and floods. Citizens in the distressed areas were traveling to the DOME (Domes Over Metropolitan Environments) construction zones so refugee camps encircled the cities, causing food shortages and clogging up vital roads for the transportation of building materials for the domes. The Global Assembly suspended laws, sending armed forces to stop the flow of people. Despite the warnings and roadblocks, the transients didn't stop coming. Vehicles in the roads packed with families were bombed from the sky by military cruisers. Hundreds of thousands of lives were lost. All civil laws and elections were suspended until further notice. The Global President was designated the Global Leader and given sweeping powers to act. Riots broke out across the globe.

Yor's schoolmates who were five years older than him were dying in the streets. Yor wanted to fight by their side, but his father demanded that Yor stay indoors. "Listen to me," his father said, his voice weak from illness and his spirit waning. "Listen to me. Remember what your great-grandfather said. He knew things that will save this planet. Remember what I've told you. You're already doing the work to make things right. Study. Learn from Mado. Follow him."

I followed him, Yor thought, *I followed him and he only did right by me.* When Yor arrived on the first day of his internship, he was awestruck by the Prevor Industries Complex, which sat on the edge of the Capitol City dome. The Global Assembly deeded the land to Mado as part of the deal for the development of the DOME-project power source. This was the heart of Mado's business empire, consisting of eleven buildings. A handful were still under construction.

Mado's personal research building stood in the midst of the complex. The state-of-the-art, hi-tech, five-story rectangular building was designed with an empty middle where another five-story building could have been built. Yor followed Mado onto the second floor balcony, which ran around the entire perimeter of the interior, then they descended together to the middle of the empty space.

Mado held up his hands as if to present the nothingness. "What do you think?"

"Not sure," Yor said, "Seems like an inefficient use of space."

"That's funny," Mado said, laughing and slapping Yor on the back, "That's funny in more ways than you know."

"I don't get it."

"You'll understand soon enough," Mado said, "This space is where we will truly get to know one another."

Yor's internship consisted of Mado teaching him about his inventions and how they worked. Yor could wire up a portable power plant and fix a faulty gaming device with the best of them and he was handy at programming the sub-routines for Mado's projects in development.

Mado became a close friend. Yor met with Mado regularly over a meal to discuss life. Mado was a great listener. The death of Yor's father was a trying time, and Mado was there for him. When Yor and his mother were given a favorable number in the DOME Residence Selection Process to live in the Capitol City dome, Yor was surprised. His mother told him they were lucky because there was a demand for med professionals. Yor always thought Mado had something to do with it.

In the fourth year of interning, Yor received a comm from Mado, saying that he had a surprise for him, a project for them to work on together. Yor was excited. He considered Mado a friend, teacher, and mentor, but now Mado was asking him to be a colleague.

Yor found Mado in his main lab where he was speaking on the communication screen to a government official wearing a lapel pin of the Global symbol on his jacket and the photo of the Leader behind him.

"I think that's an outstanding idea," the official said, "Especially with this young man working alongside you. His University records are impeccable and his professor's call him a rising star. I believe this project could be a beacon of hope for the youth of the planet in these hard times."

"Yes," Mado said, "I believe we're thinking along the same lines. Please let me know if you need my assistance in making this happen."

Yor tried to stay out of view, but the official on the screen spotted him. "Is this the young Vanderlord?" the official said, pointing at Yor.

Mado was surprised. He didn't know Yor was in the room behind him. He held out his hand as if to present Yor to the official, waving Yor closer. "Yes, this is Yor Vanderlord, the great-grandson of his…Great namesake," Mado said, chuckling.

The official on the screen laughed along with Mado. "We are proud of you and your family's legacy young man, and we look forward to your presentation in front of our committee. I must go. Late for a meeting." The screen flipped to blank.

That was when Mado told Yor of his plan to restore the When All Else Fails. Together, he and Mado gave a pitch to a Global Assembly committee about restoring the spaceship to its former glory as a centerpiece in a new Museum and for a future appearance at a Breeze Celebration. In their pitch, they showcased the WAEF as an example of what planetary minds achieved together in the past and what could be dreamed in the future. Mado would pay for the majority of the project, which would run into tens of millions of units. When the proposal was approved, the WAEF was airlifted from the Vanderlord estate through a pane in the dome that was only opened for Breeze Celebration, then the retractable roof over the middle of Mado's building was opened and the ship was lowered inside. The WAEF perfectly filled the space. The curious design of Mado's building now made complete sense. Restoring the WAEF was Mado's intention all along.

Yor was 17 years old at the time and the WAEF restoration was timed to be finished in 8 years. On Yor's 22nd year, Mado made an endowment to the Royal University for the formation of a SEEDER-program studies department with a director and staff. No favoritism was necessary. Yor was considered the best candidate for the directorship and the University leaders found it appropriate that the Great man's great-grandson and namesake should be the first to hold the chair.

At about that time, Mado admitted to Yor that he had been tinkering with the WAEF's systems and could make the ship fly again. He didn't want the Global Assembly to know. He reiterated his frustrations with the DOME project and how it was handled. He was disgusted how his friend, Yor's father, had paid with his life for his dissent, and he thought the SEEDER program was the right idea for the planet. "I want to change the course of Kodan history and place it on the right path," Mado said.

When they first met, Mado told Yor his sentiments about the Global Assembly, but Mado had never mentioned a desire to work against them. Yor was taken aback by Mado's confession which seemed to come out of nowhere. Paranoia had become normal in Kodan society and Yor couldn't help but be suspicious of Mado's remarks. Mado was in regular contact with the upper echelons of the Global Assembly including the Leader, and he was beholden to them for his riches. Yor was conflicted, but Mado laid out an ingenious plan that would blow the lid off the Global Assembly's nefarious lies.

Sorting out the truth from the lies. Wasn't that the task great-grandfather handed me all those years ago? Yor thought. As far as Yor could tell, Mado was truthful, but there was one instance in their relationship which planted a seed of distrust in Yor.

That was the day they finished rebuilding the WAEF's

main control console with the spatial coordinate positioner, which displayed the numbers denoting Koda's place in the universe.

Yor said, "Have you ever seen my great-grandfather's foto inside the WAEF's control room? It was taken sometime during the mission. I've magnified the foto and read the coordinates of the WAEF's position when the foto was taken, and it doesn't make any sense."

"Yes, that foto. I've seen it," Mado said.

"My great-grandfather gave it to me," Yor said, "I have it at home on my night stand. I'd love to show it to you. The coordinates don't make sense."

"No, that's not necessary. I don't need to see it. Just another foto of your great-grandfather. Seen one, seen them all. Glad you have it. I thought it was lost."

Yor wasn't as good as his mother at reading people, but it was obvious that Mado was feigning indifference and he was aware Yor possessed the foto. Over time, Yor attempted to bring up the foto and the coordinates in conversation, but Mado never showed any interest and changed the subject, which was odd since Mado was one of the most inquisitive people that Yor ever met. When Yor asked him why he was changing the subject, Mado said he didn't know what Yor was talking about.

As Yor stared up at Insol's living room ceiling, he saw no reason why Mado would invest millions in the WAEF and support the movement to sabotage their efforts in the end. That didn't make sense. Mel and Insol didn't know Mado like he did, but if he was going to confirm his trust in Mado to his colleagues, especially Insol who he told about the foto, then he knew what needed to happen.

Yor walked to the bedroom, removed his clothes and slipped under the sheets to the warmth of Insol's body. She had her back to him and he thought that she was asleep, then she flipped over and kissed him.

"How are you feeling?" Insol said.

"Not great. I'll be better in the morning."

"Doing some heavy thinking in the living room?"

"Yes, attempting to work out this situation I've created."

"Why did you go to the Royal Library in the first place when it wasn't planned for another year?"

"A lot of what Mel said was correct. I have no logical excuse. It was impulsive. It was reckless. When you get right down to it, I wanted to know the truth and I couldn't wait any longer."

MAR

When the bedroom door slid open, the fear on Rajer's face said it all. Whatever happened on his trip had filled him with dread. She heard the majority of the story that Rajer told Mado through the door. She wasn't one to eavesdrop, but she had her suspicion that Rajer's quick exit from their home involved Yor, and her concern for her son outweighed any discussion of privacy in her own home.

Mar asked Rajer in the calmest tone possible to sit down with her on the living-room couch and tell her what happened. When Rajer was done, instead of crying, Mar's body went cold. This was her visceral reaction to fear and despair. She felt the warmth of Rajer's hand on her back and moved against him for body heat. She made Rajer describe the man in the rail car station in greater detail: She asked exactly how he appeared and how he spoke and asked him to describe the back of the man's hands. After Rajer gave his answers, she felt even colder and nuzzled further against Rajer, wrapping her arms around him and burying her face in his chest.

"I know this man, Rajer," Mar said, lifting up her head and peering directly into his eyes, "And you should be frightened for yourself and this family."

Mar told Rajer the events leading up to Yorlik the

Great's arrival on the planet. Rajer was aware that she was present at the landing, but she never told him this part of her personal history in detail. Once Tetrick was gone, this past history felt better left behind. She didn't see how any of it was relevant to her relationship with Rajer.

Mar reached the point in the story which included the first meeting with the man at the landing site and Rajer confirmed this was the same person, then she continued to the incident in the tube. "Let's just say the President or now the Leader of the Global Assembly wasn't happy in the least. He was furious as he walked away. Tetrick was full of pride for his grandfather who he already deified without ever knowing him. I already had my hands full reigning in Tetrick and now I had two of them to keep in check, and a baby on the way.

"The limousine drove us back to the travel lodge and they informed us that once Yorlik was cleared from quarantine we'd be permitted to visit him. Days went by and we never left the building. There were many days when I just wanted to go for a walk, but the environment outside was too harsh. We also received a memo slid under our door telling us to use the building's dining area for meals or order room service at the government's expense. The memo said in no uncertain terms that we were not to fraternize with any of the other guests who were either military or government officials or viewing-channel reporters. I assumed the government's biggest fear was Tetrick meeting with one of the reporters and speaking his mind about Yorlik's statement. This was before the major clamp down on information during the riots and the acquisition of the viewing-screen channels by wealthy Global-Assembly sympathizers. Yorlik's statement got through to the planet and the channels were abuzz, wanting more from him. They saw Tetrick as the next best thing to explain Yorlik's words and they clamored for a statement from him. Tetrick believed that if the words of the Great man were explained well enough over the channels, then Kodans would see their government's folly. I barely slept keeping Tetrick out of the reporters' clutches.

"Twenty-three agonizing days went by. Before we left home, we were told by the authorities that the trip might be lengthy so we brought our personal viewers to get work done while we were cooped up in this place. That didn't make the days go by any faster. Finally, we were informed that we could meet with Yorlik at the military base. The time for our pickup and the precise length of time for our meeting was broken down in another memo slipped under our door. We were told that the initial meeting would be recorded by the viewing channels, then we'd receive what they called private time, but we both knew that our meeting with Yorlik would be watched by the government.

"When we arrived at the visitation site, a barracks cafeteria, it was vacant except for Yorlik, a government official and the viewing-channel vidcam operators. Yorlik hugged Tetrick, who was grinning ear-to-ear at meeting his grandfather up close, kissed me on the cheek, then he bent over to say hello to his unborn great-grandson who kicked at the sound of his great-grandfather's voice. We were told that the viewing channel feed had ended, and the crews packed up and departed with the government official.

"Yorlik looked around to make sure the cams and official were gone, then embraced Tetrick tight, and tears ran down the Great man's face while he sobbed out loud. Tetrick wrapped his arms around him, too. Through his sobbing, Yorlik apologized to Tetrick for his father's death. He was told how it happened when they debriefed him on the state of his family, past history and the current planetary situation.

"Tetrick told Yorlik that he had no reason to be sorry and said, 'You're back now and that's what matters. We can make a difference now.'

"Yorlik let go of Tetrick, then simultaneously patted him on both shoulders, holding him at arm's length. He scolded Tetrick. He could hear Naivim's cavalier attitude in his voice, and he told Tetrick he needed to 'apply patience and strategy to produce change, and avoid rushing into precarious positions.'

"Tetrick attempted to talk about his anti-DOME ideas, but Yorlik tightened his grip on Tetrick's shoulders and gave him a shake, jarring Tetrick's massive body in its place a few times. Yorlik still had a great deal of strength in him even at his advanced age. He told Tetrick they'd have plenty of time to catch up and talk about politics now that he'd returned.

"I remember at that moment baby Yor kicked hard,

and I told Yorlik that it seemed our baby boy liked the sound of his voice. Yorlik was elated that we were expecting a boy and pointed out there were an overabundance of males in the Vanderlord line. He put his arm around me and I realized he was even taller than Tetrick. The legends said Yorlik the Great filled the room with his personality and charismatic demeanor. I wondered if his physical presence had anything to do with it. I felt at home in the crook of his arm and Yor kicked again. Yorlik made a point of telling Tetrick that he could see himself growing fond of me and how Tetrick needed a strong woman like me, like his grandmother, then he became distant and sad.

"I asked him if he'd like to feel the baby kick and I took his free hand and moved it to my belly and on cue, the baby kicked, and Yorlik's face lit up. Tetrick let out a booming laugh and Yorlik kissed my cheek.

"Later back at our room, I asked Tetrick to sit down. I told him that he needed to heed the words of his grandfather about rushing into 'precarious positions' and counseled patience. I was tired and fell asleep, but awoke with Tetrick out of bed and found him gleefully stomping about the suite. He was exhilarated, feeling as if the Great man's return would usher in a reasonable debate of the DOME project versus the SEEDER program, and his father's death may not have been in vain.

"I told him that we should tread carefully, especially after meeting that horrible man, plus his grandfather insulting the President had probably placed us on the Global Assembly's watch list. Tetrick told me that he was sure the Great man already had a plan in play, then he let out a joyful scream and lifted me off the floor and swung me around the room. He was big man who often confused his physical strength with being able to strong arm and willfully make happen whatever he deemed appropriate in the physical world. That was his fatal flaw, but I loved him for his optimism. When he swung me around the room, in that moment, Tetrick was ecstatic, and I wanted to believe he was right. That the return of the Great man was the spark necessary to awaken the global population against the tyranny in the Global Assembly and the single-minded greed, fueling the DOME project. That the Great man's return would mean a better future for our son. The only other time, I had seen Tetrick that happy was when I told him that I was pregnant.

"I recall telling him, 'If the Great man has an idea on how to proceed, I'm onboard, but work together with him. Lunging headlong into danger wouldn't be smart for any of us—you, me, or our son.'"

Mar stood up and walked over to a cabinet that was moved from the house which she had shared with Tetrick. The cabinet not only displayed fotos, but old paper books from the Vanderlord estate, and Tetrick's academic and published works in physical-book form. They were produced before digital became law. She moved the cabinet away from the wall at an angle so she could access the back, then squatted and knocked at a secret compartment on the lower half of the cabinet to open it. If anyone just happened to look at it, the outline of the compartment door appeared to be thin shallow cuts in the wood. Back in the days when it was used more often, Mar could just knock a few times and the door would pop open. Now she hadn't opened the compartment in years, and the cabinet's wood had warped with temperature change, jamming the door shut. Rajer moved towards her to help, but she put her hand up to stop him.

"Please sit," Mar said, "I can handle it." She took a knife from the kitchen and inserted it in one of the compartment door cuts, applying more and more pressure, the cabinet rocking on its feet, until the door flung open and paper pages flew out from the compartment onto the floor.

The scent of Tetrick's cologne rushed out from the compartment. All the paper inundated with the odor from his touch had been trapped inside the compartment for years. Mar recalled the last time this compartment was shut—the day of Tetrick's funeral. She began to cry and sat on the floor. Rajer began walking towards her again. "Please stay where you are. I'm okay," Mar said, "Give me a moment."

Rajer didn't listen and headed her way.

Mar began picking up the paper from the floor in a harried manner as if she didn't lift them quick enough they'd stain the carpet. They were an assortment of Tetrick's published articles about the government's lack of attention to the environmental problems, the defunding and cancellation of the SEEDER program, and the DOME project's shortsightedness. She placed them back on the top shelf where the remaining pile of paper was higher than she remembered.

Rajer hunched beside her now, lifting paper from the floor and inspecting them.

Mar searched for a specific memory wafer among the hodgepodge of them on the bottom shelf. Many were labeled with dates in Tetrick's handwriting. She scooped them up in her hand and picked through them. When she found the one, she placed the rest of the wafers back, and tore the paper that Rajer was studying from his hands, stuffing them back in the compartment and slammed the door shut.

Rajer jumped up, strode around the couch, and kicked it. "So that's been there the entire time," Rajer said, "I don't mean to sound angry or maybe I am angry. Yeah I'm angry. You've been hiding what I can only assume is your late husband's seditious writings in our home. Materials that could get us sent to the detention lockup for a considerable amount of time. You've been hiding them right under our noses, the house where I live, your son lives…and you never told me."

Mar sat cross-legged on the floor watching Rajer rant. In daily life, he was a logical man, but he was emotional behind that façade and he was more afraid now than she'd ever seen before. She stood and slid the cabinet back against the wall, then crossed the room to Rajer and hugged him. He didn't hug her in return.

"You're right, Rajer," she said, holding him tight, "You're right, but to be completely honest with you…"

"Yes. Let's start now," Rajer said into her ear. "Now would be a good time."

Mar released Rajer and took a few steps back. "I completely forgot about this hiding place until you reminded me of that man and I thought about Tetrick. Truly. And that cabinet was searched by the government more than a few times when they were harassing Tetrick and they never found anything so you don't have anything to concern yourself about it."

"But you brought it into our house and never told me. You never thought about telling me when we moved in together."

"I did, but I thought it was better if you didn't know."

"You know you're probably right. I would have told you to burn all of it," Rajer said and pointed to the memory wafer in Mar's hand, "What's that?"

Mar looked down at her hand, wondering how to explain why she revealed the hiding place for this wafer. "It's bigger than I can explain in words. You just have to see it, and I need to reformat it. It's 24 years old and definitely won't work in this viewer right away."

"I thought that we were done with this part of your life."

"Obviously, Yor is his father's son in ways I never imagined. I recognized long ago that he wasn't a model citizen, but he's obviously gotten into similar territory than his father. I'm afraid that Mado may be involved in this, too. I didn't believe a word of his innocent tone over the comm to you," Mar said, "And I'm sorry for listening to your conversation with Mado. I actually woke up and was walking by the door and couldn't help myself when I heard Yor's name mentioned." She wrapped her arms around Rajer again.

"I forgive you for eavesdropping, but this hidden trove of illegal materials in our home without my knowledge is going to bother me for quite some time," Rajer said, hugging her back.

"I completely understand and I'm sorry."

"I'm drained from all this drama. You coming to bed?"

"I'm wide awake. I'm going to reformat this vid, and I'll be in shortly."

When Rajer closed the bedroom door, Mar removed her viewer from her briefcase and sat down on the couch, inserting the memory wafer. Reformatting was in progress, and Mar sunk back in the couch's cushions and remembered Yorlik with fondness and frustration.

As the days passed following Yorlik's landing and he remained in quarantine, anticipation boiled to a frenzy on the viewing channels. Everyone wanted word on what was happening to the Great man. Daily discussions on the channels speculated about Yorlik's condition. The government stated that further tests were required to not only insure Yorlik's health, but to guarantee that no alien virus' or molds were unleashed on the planet. Mar and Tetrick petitioned for information about Yorlik through their Global Assembly representative, but no word was forthcoming. Only one foto of Yorlik talking to a physician was released to the viewing channels and digi-media in the 93 days of his quarantine.

Finally, a media conference was announced. The eyes of the entire planet watched on viewing channels as Yorlik the Great, clean-shaven and his flowing grey hair cut short, wearing a suit was introduced by the President. The wildman from space who disembarked his spaceship and insulted the Global Assembly appeared tamed.

The President stood smiling beside Yorlik who answered questions from the viewing-channel reporters. He was feeling fantastic with a clean bill of health. No, he had not discovered any viable planets. He had been gone longer than his mission parameters because he refused to return without the discovery that his fellow Kodans truly needed. He felt the weight of what he was tasked to do so he kept searching. He had gone out of his way to find the elements to refuel the WAEF's power cells and that extended his voyage, too. Yes, this was him and not a clone created by an alien species. He had found a way to extend his life beyond the ordinary results of the Rejuv Serum, but he ran out of the substances he procured from planets which were light years away, and there was no way to replicate them. Yes, he did regret being away for such a great length of time because he missed his family and home cooking. He did not know what he would do now except acclimate to being home and spend time with his family. He was excited his grandson's partner was about to give birth to his great-grandson. He understood the resources for space travel no longer existed and were being funneled into a more constructive way to save the planet's population. Yes, he had heard of his grandson's theory about his son's death and although he respected his opinion, he read the investigator's report and agreed with the findings which concluded the incident was caused by malfunction and not sabotage. No, he did not mean to discredit his grandson. He just respectfully disagreed. He was sure they would discuss it.

Then the President put up his hand and told the reporters that the question-and-answer session was finished, but he had an announcement of his own. The Vanderlord estate and all its grounds which had been turned into a museum and government-run park would be returned to Yorlik Vanderlord as compensation for his service to the planet and he would be endowed a generous stipend to live out the rest of his life equal to his family fortune which had been absorbed by the Global Assembly upon Yorlik's partners death and Yorlik being lost without a will.

Mar viewed the press conference with Tetrick at home, and Tetrick wasn't upset at Yorlik's answer regarding his father's death. He trusted that Yorlik was on his side. Tetrick was so enthused by his grandfather's return to Koda that he began his anti-DOME campaign in earnest, traveling from city to city, from university to meeting hall, spreading his gospel. The Department of Education and Well-Being followed him from city to city. They endeavored to use the local viewing channels to create dissent against Tetrick's views, but pockets of supporters flared up every day who believed in Tetrick's message against the DOME project which was still in its planning stage.

The majority of Tetrick's supporters were young people with no fear of the government's wrath and felt like they had nothing to lose. *Youth harbors the idea of immortality*, Mar thought. That was one of Mar's worries regarding the latest turn of events for her son.

With Yorlik settled back at the estate, at their first dinner there, he apologized to Tetrick about his comments. That was the beginning of them growing close. Mar was happy for Tetrick's friendship with his grandfather.

Tetrick never had a close relationship with his parents who never planned on a child. Tetrick's conception was a surprise. He was an unexpected Rejuv Serum baby. Before Yorlik left on his mission, he gave his partner Rejuv Serum for his children who were youngsters at the time. In case his mission went longer than planned, he was hoping that the Serum would elongate their lives and he might see them on his return. Naivim was 108 years old with Serum when Tetrick was born. He was focused on his scientific research and had no interest in being a father. Yorlik felt responsible for his son's shortcomings, and attempted to fill that void.

When Yorlik's life resumed a semblance of normalcy, he made a point of spending time with his family. He was at the hospital when Yor was born and cried when he held Yor for the first time. Every few days, he visited their home in Capitol City with a bag of groceries, cooking a meal for everybody and bearing children's books that he would read to Yor at bedtime. Or they would travel to the estate on days off from work, and Yorlik would spread out a picnic by the receding shoreline of the lake. Inside the estate, Yorlik created a nursery for his great-grandson. He painted the room himself with glowing constellations on the ceiling which he said were astronomically accurate. He built a crib and a hand-painted mobile with planets spinning and a replica of the WAEF, flying around them.

One consistent event in all of these get-togethers at the estate was Tetrick and Yorlik leaving for walks after Yor fell asleep. Sometimes the two of them would be gone until sunup and they'd apologize for losing track of time. The first couple of times this happened, Tetrick attempted to make up a story about learning more about his father, but Mar could clearly tell this was a half-truth. Tetrick was a horrible liar. He once told Mar that his father would berate him when he caught Tetrick in a lie and say, "If you're going to lie at least be good at it." *That inability to lie with conviction might have been what killed him in the end.*

One night, Tetrick returned from one of those walks with a story that he had told her before about Yorlik venting his frustration over the increased use of his Rejuv Serum and the exponential increase in population which accelerated the environmental crisis. Mar called him on it, and they argued until Tetrick came clean. He admitted that he and his great-grandfather were working on a plan to alter the Global Assembly's policies. Tetrick didn't want Mar to know any of the details, because he and Yorlik agreed it would put her and Yor in harm's way.

"I'm glad that you two are deciding my future for me," Mar said.

"I'm hoping that this will make the future better for you and Yor…and everybody else on the planet," Tetrick said, "The less you know, the safer you'll be."

"So you take all that risk and I'm supposed to be happy about it?"

"At first."

"What does that mean?"

"You'll see," Tetrick said, "I can't explain it right now."

That was a turning point in their marriage. Mar was unhappy with being cut out of plans that were affecting her future. She and Tetrick argued over it while he conspired with his University colleagues and with Yorlik. Tetrick increased his public writings and lectures in dissent against the DOME project. Again, Mar attempted to tone him down as the Global Assembly was widening their crackdown on what they defined as "terrorists against global unity," but Tetrick disregarded her.

Eventually the arrests of Tetrick started again along with the torture. The GSS men began to appear at their front door to escort Tetrick for "interviews" with great frequency, and Tetrick returned home appearing as if he'd been in a lengthy brawl and hadn't slept in days. Mar threatened to go public with what the government was doing to her husband. Tetrick told her to keep out of it. They yelled and screamed at each other. Tears were shed. She was losing him, but he wouldn't change course. *When does bravery become stupidity?* Mar had thought as Tetrick charged with reckless abandon at the Global Assembly agenda.

When Tetrick was on a lecture tour of the major universities around the globe, giving his *Doom of the Domes* speech about how the domes were financial giveaways to the wealthy and they were not sustainable environments in the long term, Mar decided to confront Yorlik about the plan. She borrowed a vehicle from a friend and traveled to the estate with Yor, who was nearly four years old, and always excited to visit his great-grandfather.

The Great man greeted them at the door of the estate. Since he landed four years ago, he was noticeably older. He walked with a cane that he carved from a rare tree on the estate known for its limb's strength. He had begun to shrink, and the amount was extraordinary, too. Yorlik was at least a head taller than Mar when they first met and now he was nearly eye level with her. This kind of change in normal aging would take 20 years and with Serum deterioration about 10 years. Mar read med research about the individual effects of the Serum's overuse, but Yorlik's change was another thing entirely. She theorized this was due to overuse of the experimental serum that kept him alive for years in space. His cells were now aging at breakneck speed, and she wondered how many years the Great man had left. That being said, his mind was sharp. There was no slowing down there. Historically, he had a reputation as always being the smartest person in the room. Maybe he was originally far above everyone's intelligence his entire life and now there was degeneration, but nobody was alive who knew him before he left the planet so there was no way to measure the loss.

Yorlik led them into his study where a large conference table was strewn with sheets of paper and digi-tablets, and at one end was Mado Prevor inspecting an array of both.

Mar had never met Mado before. Yorlik told Mar and Tetrick that he met Mado shortly after his release from quarantine and he was so taken by the man's brilliance that he introduced Mado to the right people to help Mado's business kick into high gear. One of Mado's first investors was Joro Camtur, the grandson of Yorlik's old business partner. Yorlik the Great was the perfect middleman. Everybody wanted to meet him so everyone returned his calls. Due to Yorlik's help, Mado earned fame and fortune with his Holographic Gaming Device and was already one of the richest men on the planet. Yorlik had introduced Tetrick to Mado, and they had met a few times afterward, but Mar was never invited.

Yorlik said, "Mado, come over and say hello?" Mado made a slight bow, and Mar walked the length of the table to meet him.

Yor jumped up and down with his arms up wanting his great-grandfather to pick him up. Yorlik put his cane aside and told Yor to stand on a chair, then lifted him in his arms.

Mado was average height and average looking, slightly balding and mid-40s. He seemed socially awkward for a man of industry, and there was something else strange about him, but Mar couldn't put her finger on it. He stood waiting for Mar to come near as if he was not confident about how to approach people.

"Pleasure to meet you," Mar said, shaking Mado's hand, "I've heard lots about you. Maybe you can keep an eye on my boy while I have a word with his great-grandfather." Mar looked over at Yorlik who was holding Yor. The Great man was smiling and joking with Yor who was giggling.

Mado appeared petrified to be alone with Yor. Mar saw trepidation in his body language and in his eyes. "I really don't have much experience with your children," Mado said to Mar. She thought that was an odd thing to say.

Yorlik said, "I think what Mado means is he's not experienced in dealing with children one-on-one." He seated Yor on a chair, and Yor grabbed a digi-tablet from the table and began pushing buttons, engrossed by whatever was on the screen. Mado looked horrified at Yor's actions and strode toward Yor to take the tablet away from him. Yorlik stuck out his arm to block him.

"Nothing on there of great importance," Yorlik said to Mado, "And it's all backed up. Just let him be. If he walks off just follow him around the house until we get back. It'll be good exercise. We shouldn't be gone long and we'll be right outside if there's an emergency."

"He'll be fine. Won't you?" Mar said to Yor, mussing his hair. He didn't look up from the tablet. Mar noticed that he was flipping through images of star clusters.

"He plays with one at home and already knows the ins and outs of the device. He can distract himself for awhile," Mar said to Mado.

Mado was agitated searching around the table, pushing aside the paper and tablets, then slid a comm across the table to Yorlik. "If you have this, then I'll feel better."

Yorlik laughed and hooked his arm around Mar's. "Oh these confirmed bachelors."

"We'll have to find him a woman," Mar said.

"That's not necessary," Mado said.

Yorlik laughed again and Mar along with him.

"No, really," Mado said.

Yorlik picked up his cane in his right-hand and Mar hooked her arm around his left-arm.

"We'll be nearby if you need us, dear," Mar said to Yor who still didn't look up from the screen.

Yorlik and Mar strolled outside to the back patio where Yorlik plunked himself down with a sigh of relief in a padded antique wooden chair and rested his cane beside him. "I'd say let's walk over to what's left of the lake, but I don't have it in me."

The weather was warm and dry. The brown lawn extended out to the lakeshore. Since Yorlik had reclaimed the estate, the lake had receded further from the shore and was a mere puddle of water in the distance.

"In the past, this must've been a beautiful and temperate place to sit and lounge in the early evening," Mar said, seating herself in a similar wooden chair beside Yorlik.

"Yes, among other things on Koda, the thought of

returning to this wonderful place helped me persevere while I was gone. A cool summer breeze coming off the lake would be perfect right about now," Yorlik said, his voice trailing off, staring into the distance. Since Yorlik returned, he frequently turned melancholy when reflecting on the life he'd left behind for his mission. Mar decided to change the subject.

"That Mado is an odd one," Mar said, "What are you two working on?"

"Yes, one might say that he's not from around here," Yorlik said and laughed. "I should've made some refreshments for us."

"That's not necessary," Mar said, "I saw those star clusters that Yor was looking at. Is that part of what you two are working on?"

"Mado is helping me organize a few things."

"What would those things be?"

"Nothing for you to worry about, my dear."

"That seems to be the overall sentiment these days when it comes to me."

Yorlik looked over at her and said, "I'm sorry. You've lost me."

"I doubt that's the case," Mar said.

Yorlik grabbed onto his cane and began tapping on the ground in front of him. "I'm not sure what to say, Mar."

"That's difficult to believe. You're by far the most intelligent person that I've ever met, and I'm pretty sure that you know the reason why I drove all the way out here to talk with you while Tetrick is halfway across the planet."

"I appreciate the compliment," Yorlik said, clearing his throat, "I'll start by saying that nothing is being done to insult your intelligence. I mean that sincerely. I have a great deal of respect for you personally and for your intellect."

"Doesn't seem that way to me."

"You're the constant that's counted on for everything to happen around here. You are the mother of my great-grandson and the one person who keeps Tetrick sane in what he's doing."

"And what is he doing?"

"I would think that's plain to see."

"Yes, on the surface," Mar said, "His actions are orchestrated by a plan you two have set in motion. Your long walks gave that away, and Tetrick has pretty much told me so. But he truly believes that you are the savior of our world and if you asked him to do it, he would walk off a cliff for you. My concern is that you have him on course for the exact same result."

"Your insights are valid, my dear,"

"Well, it's always nice to be validated, but I'd prefer some clarity."

Yorlik stopped tapping his cane. "You're correct there is conspiring happening between myself and your husband. He has taken the danger upon himself and I respect him for it. I made certain that he was doing it by his own volition and not out of worship for me. I know how he sees me," Yorlik said, "When I stated that you're the constant here, I meant it as a compliment. You keep an even keel, and are holding the family together, but I can't tell you what's happening."

"That's infuriating. You have to know that."

"I hear it in your voice, but you're playing an important role by not knowing anything, by not being part of Tetrick's campaign, by not approving of it, by being annoyed and angry at what's occurring around you. I know this might not be what you want to hear or what makes sense and you may hate me for it, and I will begrudgingly live with your negative feelings towards me. If it helps, this is the only way to keep you and Yor safe into the foreseeable future."

Yorlik used his cane and his other arm on the chair to lift himself to a standing position as the chair creaked under his weight.

Mar stood and looped her arm around Yorlik's arm taking on some of his weight. "I trust you," Mar said, "I know that Tetrick trusts you, but I have a bad feeling about all of this. I don't see it ending well. Tetrick is a strong man, but I can already see him fraying at the edges. I think you can stop him, but I get the impression you both are like-minded on this subject."

"That's a good way to put it," Yorlik said, "No matter the good or bad that comes of this, it will all make sense in the foreseeable future."

Is this the foreseeable future? Mar thought the past was behind her with Tetrick's death, then Rajer told her about being confronted by the man with the scars on his hands and she had the terrible feeling that the past with all of its pain and loss had been brought back into the present. As the reformatting was near completion, the image of Yorlik the wildman from space with his long grey hair and beard appeared on the viewer's screen, looking out at her. The man behind the transparent window. In a way, it seemed like he had returned again.

MADO

When Yor arrived at Mado's office in the morning, he removed a memory wafer from his satchel, then stood there turning it in his hand. "Got the journal," Yor said.

Mado rolled his seat away from his desk and said, "You're not going to read it that way."

"I actually read it this morning and was disappointed. Some incredibly descriptive passages, but it doesn't reveal anything new. I can definitely use parts of it in my speech."

"Hand it over and let's see if you missed anything."

"I doubt it." Yor handed it to Mado.

"Don't be so sure. You don't know everything," Mado said, "And what were you thinking yesterday? We agreed to put off going to the Royal Library for awhile."

"I know," Yor said, "I'm beginning to realize it wasn't the best decision. Learned a lesson, I guess."

"A ill-advised decision. You set things in motion that could've been held off, but now we'll just need to deal with it," Mado said, "You know that you'll need to address yesterday's incidents with your mother. She has been down this road before,"

"You said 'incidents.' Did I miss something?"

"A GSS man threatened Rajer after you two split up last night."

"I had no idea. My mother must be beside herself," Yor said, "What did he look like? Any distinguishing features?"

"Hideous scars…"

"On the back of his hands," Yor said, "That's the same man who interrogated me."

"That's disconcerting. Look at this feed." Mado began typing into the keyboard of his viewer and a hacked vidcam feed from the Global Safety Bureau appeared on the screen. On the vid, there was an empty rail car station. A car pulled into the station, then Rajer stepped onto the platform and the feed went to static. A few moments later, the static cleared and Rajer stood on the platform appearing stunned as if he'd seen an apparition.

Mado rewound to the rail car arriving at the station and restarted the feed. "Take note of the time," Mado said, pointing to the active vidcam time clock in the upper right-hand corner of the screen. After the static, the clock skipped time. The cam had been disabled.

Mado continued, "Whoever this man might be, the government has made a distinct effort to keep his identity unknown. That worries me the most. An enemy who is wiped from the record and can't be tracked, located or identified is nearly impossible to defeat. I know we were thinking of making the WAEF presentation at a Breeze Celebration next year, but we'll need to jump to an earlier Celebration before your hearing."

"I agree. That's something that I was thinking too," Yor said, "How do you know about the hearing?"

"Rajer told me," Mado said, "We have to assume that

you're being followed and monitored at every moment."

"I can confirm from my interrogation that the GSS has a file on me," Yor said, "And probably you too?"

"I didn't receive my Global Assembly contracts without scrutiny," Mado said.

"But there's no telling how much they know."

"They don't know what's happening here and they're not listening in on me. I know that for certain. We do have to assume they have an idea that something crooked is happening, especially after your activity at the library. What was your plan if I hadn't caught you and created the alternate surveillance feed of you reading the journal?"

"I assumed that you'd catch me."

"I appreciate your confidence in me, but your arrogance could have got you locked up at the GSS and jeopardized all our efforts," Mado said, "I'm disappointed in you. I talked to the Leader this morning and he said that he knew nothing about you being monitored, but we should assume that he's not telling the truth."

Mado saw remorse on Yor's face so he decided to move on. He walked across the lab toward the window with Yor trailing him. From the window, Mado looked out on the When All Else Fails, surrounded by repair mechbots and welding sparks flying. There were open gaps in the outer hull with wires hanging out of them. Tools, pipes, industrial spools of wiring, and outer hull panels laid on tarps surrounding the ship.

Mado said, "I know that it looks daunting, but we'll prioritize the essential systems and we'll see what we can finish quickly to make our window before the hearing. We'll just have to work a little harder and sleep a little less."

"Wouldn't be the first time."

"So let's get to work," Mado said, exiting the lab.

"Hold on," Yor said, grabbing his satchel, and following Mado into a lift.

On the ground floor, the lift doors opened to the racket of the mechbots, then they climbed the loading bay ramp into the interior of the ship. Mado climbed the stairs to the top level with Yor beside him, then they walked through the med bay, the science lab, the sleep chamber, and the living chamber.

Since they began the WAEF's restoration, the government inspectors had visited a few dozen times to check on progress and before they arrived, any sign of work to activate operating systems was cleared away. For the ship's residence at the Museum of Global History and Information, the façade was the inspectors primary concern. Other than the outer hull's metallic surface glistening for them, each chamber on the top-level had been visually restored to its pre-launch glory like the reclining seats in the living chamber were reupholstered to the original bright orange.

The Museum also wanted interactive elements. The motion sensors in each room were reproduced so when a person resided in the chamber long enough, the lights would increase to full intensity and shut down to preserve energy when the person exited. The door's between rooms slid open at a person's approach and closed as they passed through. The living chamber's food replicator was rebuilt with a simple menu for visitors.

Much of the tech in the med bay, science lab and control room was destroyed in the gutting of the ship and obsolete so the government had no idea that anybody on Koda could recreate functional versions of them. The inspectors were delighted by the tech display in the science lab and the med bay which they assumed were nonfunctional replicas but actually worked. Inside the control room, Mado installed fake control panels directly over the operational panels.

On the last control-room inspection, the director from the Museum sat in the pilot's seat practically squealing in delight at the blinking lights in the panels, and the switches producing sounds to simulate the activation of thrusters. Mado was pleased at the success of his show, striking at the heart of what the Global Assembly was expecting from the project: a museum exhibit showcasing the visual and functional elements of the ship. They never imagined that the ship would ever perform again in its true capacity.

"Everything in here is close to one-hundred percent ready," Mado said to Yor, spinning around and holding out his arms in the control room. He acted like he was dizzy from his performance to get a rise out of Yor, who always ribbed him for his clumsiness, but Yor didn't crack a smile.

"Everything will be fine." Mado walked up to Yor, reaching up with both arms and grasping Yor's shoulders.

Yor was taller than Mado which wasn't the case when Yor began interning for him. "Look at me, my boy. Do you trust me?"

Yor reached out, placing his arms on Mado's shoulders and said, "I'm not sure."

"I suspected as much, but I'm glad that you finally admitted it," Mado said, "Especially considering our current situation." He releasing his grip on Yor, and Yor did the same.

"What do you mean? You suspected? All these years?" Yor said.

"Not the entire time, just since we started concocting our plan and other people became involved. Considering my position in Kodan society and my government contracts, I knew there was a radical element in the movement who would question my loyalty over any little thing. Maybe even Insol."

"You never said anything."

"I trust you, and I figured a high probability that you'd eventually say something to me."

"That's a relief," Yor said, "Now is a good time to clear the air."

"Absolutely," Mado said. "You have questions, and with the timeline pushed up, I have something to tell you as well. Let's go sit in the living chamber."

Yor led the way ahead of Mado. They entered the living chamber, and the lights turned on, increasing to maximum intensity as they sat down in the recliners. Mado seated himself across from Yor with a game table between them. Mado pressed a button on the table and a space opened in the floor and the table folded up, descending into the space which closed behind it.

"How do we start?" Mado said.

"I stopped by my office this morning to pick this up," Yor said, pulling the foto of his great-grandfather out of his satchel. "How about this?"

"Yes. The foto."

"Every time I ask you about it, you change the subject. Do you deny it?"

"No. Not at all. In fact, if you hadn't noticed, then I would've been worried about you," Mado said, thinking that he was being funny. Yor was not amused. "So serious. You've always been that way. I understand. I used to be like you. No way you could have achieved your level of competence in so many areas of life without it. I'm glad you have Insol. You need someone in your life like her."

"Are we going to keep playing this game?"

"Sorry. I wasn't playing. You know how my mouth just runs off sometimes," Mado said, "What would you like to know about the foto? I know why your great-grandfather gave it to you."

"That wasn't my question, but let's start there. Why did he want me to have it?"

"He saw how it roused your interest in his past life and the SEEDER program. You two had a close bond and he knew that you'd never give the foto away and you'd keep it safe. It was special to him and to me."

"To you?"

"Yes. My friendship with your great-grandfather goes back much further than anybody on your planet knows. That's what I need to tell you."

"You've never mentioned that before, but let's stay on the subject of the foto."

"There's a reason for that. I'm not being evasive. I'm about to tell you something that will come to answer your questions about the foto."

"Okay, proceed," Yor said. Mado could tell Yor was exasperated by Mado hijacking the conversation.

"Well, let's start with baby steps. How old am I?"

"It's in all the media materials, and I've heard you tell people that you're 64 years old."

"Incorrect. In your planet's way of measuring time, I'm 317 years old," Mado said, noting the serious look on Yor's face, shifting to amusement now. Yor laughed.

"That can't be true. You're kidding, right? No Kodan ever lived to that age, even in the Rejuv Serum years."

Mado remained silent as Yor gazed at him for an uncomfortable period of time. He wanted Yor to come to the conclusion on his own.

Yor said, "That's impossible. Is this some sort of joke and I'm just not getting it? Is this one of your tests? Not exactly what I was seeking in this conversation."

"No joke," Mado said, "And I'm not testing you. Well sort of. I thought that it'd be best to start with a question and not come right out and tell you. I'd like you to see the truth for yourself so you can understand why I've withheld what I know about the foto all this time."

"It's kind of annoying, but go ahead."

"Did you ever wonder how I could rebuild this ship when all knowledge of this tech had been censored, wiped clean from the public's access, and nobody else on your planet has a clue about this tech?"

"Because you're the smartest man on the planet. A great inventor. Did you work with my great-grandfather as a scientist in the lab that discovered the Rejuv Serum?" Yor said.

"No, here's a bigger clue. I met him after he left Koda and before he returned."

Yor stared intently at Mado as if he might see something that he was missing. "Wait. You're not a man to misspeak. Sometimes you scramble up a thought or two, but you're the most precise person with words when it matters. You've said, 'your planet' three times and now you're saying that you knew him on his SEEDER mission. There's a deduction to be drawn here, but it's unbelievable."

Mado leaned forward in his chair, pointed at Yor, saying, "You got it."

"This has to be one of your jokes. I don't believe it."

"By the end of this conversation, I think you will."

Yor moved closer to Mado, examining him. "If I take your word on your age and you didn't work with my great-grandfather in the Rejuv lab and your uncanny knowledge of this ship isn't just a reflection of your genius and you met my great-grandfather on his SEEDER mission, then you're saying that you're from another world. If I believe all of it, then that's the only conclusion to reach." Yor continued inching towards Mado, scrutinizing him as if by moving closer he'd see the alien in him. "I never noticed you looked any different than any other Kodan and you speak our language fluently. I need some proof other than your words to believe you haven't just lost your mind."

"Just to be clear, where I was born, the tech is generations ahead and scientific knowledge has advanced far beyond what is known here," Mado said, "I do have physical proof, but I'd like to tell you my past history and how I came to meet your namesake before I unveil my true self, so to speak."

"Of course," Yor said. He leaned back in the recliner, smiled and held up his arms. "I'm your captive audience. Go right ahead. Not like I have anything better to do."

Mado spent almost 12 years working with Yor and he could tell by the look on his face that Yor didn't believe him. *Why would he?* Yor must've still thought this was some sort of test.

"Where to start," Mado said, "Where to start. I was born on a planet far from your solar system. The planet is covered with oceans and the diameter is twice yours, but the amount of land is similar. Space travel has been an occupation of ours for nearly 2,500 of your years. The closest approximation in your language to pronouncing the name of my planet is Prevor. I took the planetary name as my surname since individuals have only one name on my planet.

"Much like your namesake, I was a pilot and scientist—astronomer, physicist, chemist, engineer—which are prerequisites for a Space Traveler, an occupation that is highly valued on Prevor. We send out more than a few expeditions at a time to compile new resources for our already bountiful world. Prevorians are all of the same species, from the same source and we work together toward common goals to make life better for the Prevorian Protectorate. We have our squabbles, but we have none of Koda's political problems. We consider our source, our mother, the oceans from where we came.

"Our spacecraft are fast and travel at a speed that I won't get into here, but suffice to say the speed at which we travel is hard to fathom compared to the WAEF. Our lifespan is ten times your normal span, and we have the ability to hibernate which lengthens our lives, so we're suited in this way for extended journeys in space.

"So combine the speed of our spacecraft with our capability to live considerable spans of existence, then our journeys easily take us across large expanses of the universe. We never colonize or interfere with other civilizations. We keep clear of planets where civilizations have been established. In our earliest travels, we attempted relationships with other planets, but our presence always seemed to create fear and sometimes violence against us. We decided to focus on uninhabited worlds and mine resources out of the reach of any other interplanetary species. Our knowledge of the universe and our mapping prowess is extensive.

"I was on a mapping and resource discovery expedition. My twenty-second of the sort when my spacecraft began to experience mechanical problems. I attempted to land on an uninhabited planet with gravity and atmosphere similar to Prevor and with the necessary ores available to fashion the parts to fix my spacecraft and continue on my way. Standard procedure for a Prevorian expedition. On attempting to set down my craft, I realized the damage was far worse than I had originally perceived and the problems got greater with a rough landing. My communication array was damaged beyond repair on landing too so I set up a distress beacon and went about fixing the spacecraft the best I could with the elements available. Unfortunately, after working about a quarter of your year, I came to the conclusion that the damage was too extensive and I'd be living on the planet until I was rescued. Without my communication array, I had no clue when that would happen.

"Luckily, I landed in a lush and pleasant spot. The weather was well-suited for my species. There was plenty of moisture in pools and falling from the atmosphere. Four of your years passed and no contact from my people. I hibernated for a large percentage of that time, and in the meantime, I fixed whatever I could on my craft and catalogued the planet's resources on extended hikes and by sending out orbital drones. I kept about my work. I harbored hope that my people were coming for me. There are only a few instances in our extensive history of space travel where a craft was lost, so I made the planet my home and set up a daily routine to keep my wits about me.

"Around that time, one of my drones, picked up the

WAEF entering the planet's atmosphere and adhering to Code 5225 of our Space Travelers Code, I made no effort to make contact, but Yorlik knew that I was there. He landed nearby and approached my craft. I wasn't sure what to do. The odds of meeting another intelligent being who walked on two legs and mastered space travel was extremely rare, only five recorded circumstances. All of the Space Traveler Code relating to first contact didn't seem to fit this experience. In this case, Yorlik searched me out and there was no way for me to avoid contact, because my craft was low on power and I couldn't flee or camouflage the craft into the environment."

"I'd like to see you camouflage the spacecraft," Yor said. Mado realized he still didn't believe his story. "So you just wanted justification to break the rules?"

"You know me too well," Mado said, "All I could do was sit in my craft with the door shut while Yorlik arrived there every day, then twice a day, then pitched a tent in front of the entrance to my craft and camped out there. Not that he'd stay all day, he'd be gone most of the day. Later I found out he'd been trekking out and taking soil samples and cataloguing much like I had been doing. He knew I was inside my craft by the recent tracks around the craft and the disturbance of flora where I had placed my equipment.

"So I was trapped inside for an extended time. This was many years ago and I haven't thought about this part of my life in awhile. If I search my memory, maybe this lasted close to 35 days in your time. Each evening, I just sat in my control room watching him on the monitor, as he sat in his chair outside my craft's door, speaking to me, saying whatever he was saying. I had no idea what he was telling me but the sounds were pleasant enough. I figured out later, when I learned your language that he was telling me about his life; your great-grandmother, your grandfather and great Aunt, and how he came to be on this planet with the dire situation on yours. He showed me fotos of Koda's people, cities, and landscape and his family.

"Then one day, I awoke and he was gone. His chair, his tent and all of his scientific gear were gone. I did a sweep of sensors and the WAEF still resided where Yorlik had landed so I continued my vigil inside my craft. Days passed but no sign of your namesake and the WAEF was still there. At first, I thought this might be some sort of trick to lure me out, then after more days passed, I took more readings and noticed no power emanations from the WAEF. So I made a decision and logged in my spacecraft's circuitry that even though there was a chance of contact I was headed out of the vessel due to an emergency situation involving the craft's environmental system."

"Good one," Yor said, "Can't be inside the ship if the environmentals are broken."

"I thought so too," Mado said, "I also did a bit of fixable sabotaging on the environmental workings of my spacecraft to cover my tracks, because when I returned home, this incident would surely be investigated. I can still recall when my spacecraft's door slid open and I was outside. The moist air felt incredible on my skin. There was a drizzle in the air. Just enough. Like a curtain of moisture falling from the sky. For my species this is heavenly. I remember it well because it was the last time that I would experience such a sensation in my current life span and this led to meeting your great-grandfather.

"I searched but saw no sign of recent movement around my craft and gathered gear for a hike to a spot overlooking the WAEF and camped there for a day or two to get a closer look at this creature from a different vantage point. I mean your great-grandfather, who was really just a creature to me at that time. When darkness came on the third day, there was no sign of your namesake so I crept down to the WAEF to confirm my earlier readings. The WAEF was dead. No power. No circuitry turned on. I put a sonic scope, a device that your people don't have yet, against the hull and listened for interior movement and sounds. I concluded that Yorlik wasn't inside and if so, he was not alive. Maybe he was in trouble. Infectious disease, poisonous flora…anything can go wrong out there.

"Sanctity of life is a central canon among my species. I contemplated breaking into the WAEF. Early the next morning, I noticed drag marks where Yorlik had recently brought his heavier equipment back into the WAEF and fresh tracks left by him leading off into the thicker flora so I decided to follow the tracks for a day until dark came and returned to my craft. The next day, I packed up for a few days hike. On the end of the second day of the hike, the weather became dry and hot. I hadn't experienced this sort of heat on this planet before. Then

I found a skid mark at the top of a steep embankment that went down into dense flora below. I could see where a body had bounced until the bruises in the landscape disappeared into the flora. I was at an impasse. I assumed from the length of the drop and the dents in the dirt that the creature was injured. My species is double-jointed and flexible, but that steep a drop would have caused catastrophic injury to parts of our bodies, too. I didn't have proper rope to propel down safely and I was low on provisions. I was taught survival skills as part of my training, but I had no idea how your great-grandfather had been trained, although I assumed that a species that could space travel and land on other worlds would have at least minimal survival training."

"So obviously you found him," Yor said. He was becoming impatient, but trying to be respectful.

When Mado spoke, he was aware that he had the proclivity to tell every detail and he could go on with minutia. That was part of his training in logging the specifics of his journeys. "Took me awhile," Mado said, "I finally searched around enough and heard his cries of pain as he attempted to climb out. He had tumbled inside an old lava tube covered by fallen flora. I made a rope from the vines in the forest and used the trees by the tube as the tie off point. I quickly realized the heat was volcanic activity all around me. I rappelled down to where Yorlik was stricken. His leg was severely broken, the bone sticking through his leg at the worst part of the break, and he huddled on a ledge a good distance down the tube."

"I remember him limping when I was a child and massaging his leg all the time, but I thought that was old age. Probably was this accident," Yor said.

"Probably both," Mado said, "I would tease him when we returned here and I heard people call him Yorlik the Great. I'd say 'If only they could see you helplessly hanging to a ledge and some alien creature had to save you.' Definitely wasn't funny when it happened but in hindsight with all of our time together, it was funny to us."

"And..." Yor said, "Obviously you saved him."

"He was cut up, bleeding and bruised. He had ripped off parts of his uniform to tie off and stop the bleeding. I unraveled one crude bandage to reveal a deep cut. I knew nothing of your anatomy, but seeing Yorlik in this battered state, I clearly knew that his condition was serious. His breathing was shallower and his complexion was paler than those days when he was sitting in front of my craft. I assumed that he needed mending soon to avoid severe trauma. Eleven days had passed since I had last seen him and I figured that he'd been down there at least half that time. Knowing what I know about your anatomy now, his survival all that time alone until I got there was incredible.

"So I picked him up and threw him over my shoulder to wailing and screaming and crying and climbed up the tube with this bleating creature over my shoulder. I was concerned that my makeshift rope would snap under all the weight. I could clearly hear the climbing vine cracking with stress even though I'd doubled the vines and twisted them together for strength.

"Once I retrieved him from the tube, I had no idea how to help him. I just stared at his injuries. Our species are different, but basic med training like needing to stop bleeding seemed common between us both. I had no idea how to mend broken limbs and more extensive internal damage. Yorlik kept saying, 'My ship, my ship.' I know what he meant now, but back then I thought that he was praying to his deity for help or saying a loved ones name. That's what I would have been doing. He grabbed at me and pointed to the sky saying 'My ship, my ship.' Darkness was coming I didn't know whether this creature would make it to the next day, and I was torn between my training and beliefs. Again, Prevorian training said don't get involved and our beliefs called for sanctity of life. In final training, we are told when these two contradict one another that we should adhere to our training, even if we are compelled to do the opposite by our beliefs. I decided to break protocol. I had to live with myself and although I had passed training with high marks, I realized being a Space Traveler was less important than saving this life.

"So I remotely called for my craft. I had repaired the engines to the point where the craft could fly in the planet's atmosphere, but not break its gravitational pull. I activated the engines using the remote in my travel pack, sent the craft our coordinates and while I carried Yorlik to a clearing, I waited for the sound of the engines. When the craft hovered above us, my loading bay lowered a platform and we were lifted up to the craft. I carried Yorlik to my med bay and left him there strapped in so that I could fly the craft to a less volcanic area to land. When I returned to the med bay, Yorlik was passed out. I had no idea how close he was to the end of life. He lost a great deal of internal fluids and I wasn't sure how to fix him so I needed him awake to communicate with me. That was his only chance. I injected him with a mild stimulant from my med cache hoping that it would work on his metabolism and not kill him. It worked and I got him talking to me. Through pantomime, I understood what 'My ship' meant and flew my craft closer to the WAEF.

"I carried him into the WAEF and he voice activated the med bay and showed me how to repair him. His leg was gravely broken and fixing it was the most difficult task. Although he limped for the rest of his days, I believe that I did an adequate job considering the extent of the break. He was severely bruised and cut, too. He taught me how to use the food replicator and I cared for him while he healed and gained his strength. Took time. I was surprised. My species heals faster.

"That was an interesting time. Our ships were parked close enough to one another that it was our own village. My people wouldn't have been pleased about my fraternizing with another species, but I was beyond worrying about what they thought and began striking up a friendship with your great-grandfather. The language barrier was difficult at first, but I took the lead and learned yours since the language of my species is more complex and uses sounds that we both quickly understood your anatomy could not create with accuracy. While Yorlik recuperated, I not only taught myself your language, but took advantage of the WAEF's computer data to school myself on your global issues and overall makeup of your civilization. I was taken aback by the violence between your species in daily life, which doesn't exist on my planet, and I actually decided to be careful around Yorlik which of course over time, I discerned was unfounded.

"I'm sorry," Mado said, standing up from the recliner, walking over to the kitchen dispenser and filling a glass of water. "I've been talking for a great deal of time. You must have a few questions."

"That is one fantastic story," Yor said, "But it's just a tall tale without grounding in reality and empirical evidence."

"Understandable," Mado said, "I'd like to put this place on lockdown before I reveal what you're asking for. You okay with that?"

Yor nodded. Mado walked over to the nearest console in the living chamber and accessed the building's security system locking all doors to any security codes and shuttering the windows to the space where the WAEF was parked. Each day before starting his work day, Mado would confirm that the jamming field around the entire building was operational so no GSS bugging devices could hear or see what was happening inside.

"Okay," Mado said, turning to Yor, "I take these prosthetics off for maintenance and cleaning every 45-to-60 days and they're on pretty firmly so it's a bit painful. Bare with me."

ORN

Orn stared at his reflection in the silver doors as he rode the lift in the Global Assembly building up to the 63rd floor. He wanted to make sure that he appeared in proper uniform for the Leader. He wore his daily apparel, pressed for the occasion, but with tie and suit jacket bearing his Global-Guard pin. The doors opened and he walked down the hall lined with paintings of the past Presidents of the Global Assembly before the Leader put elections on hold. None of these men and women stood out in Orn's mind. They were feckless politicians in expensive suits who somehow endeared themselves to the citizens, serving a term or two. *The Leader is the only man to guide the Kodan people*, Orn thought, *The only one with the vision and understanding on how to properly use his authority.*

Orn entered the waiting area for the Leader's office and stopped at the receptionist's desk. "He's expecting me," Orn said.

"Yes, please take a seat," the receptionist said. She was a diminutive young woman who the Leader had chosen for the position because of her bubbly and non-threatening personality. The Leader had asked Orn to perform the background check on her and she was as non-threatening as her façade: average student, everyone liked her, never late for work, always worked after hours with no complaints, performed tasks exactly as her superiors told her and never took initiative on her own. When it came to people crossing the line and demeaning her boss, she had a no-holds-barred attitude like a mother protecting her cub.

"I'm fine here. Thank you," Orn said observing the receptionist's desk. All the desktop items—viewer, office intercom, digi-tablet for taking notes from the Leader, personal comm—were in a neat symmetry side by side across the desk of dark wood from extinct trees that once graced the office of the Global Monarchy. Orn ran the fingers of his left hand in the deep scars of his right hand to pass the time.

On the wall behind the receptionist, hung a large painting of the Leader when he was first elected Global President close to 26 years ago. The painter was the foremost loyalist artist from the Mauan region. The Leader was a strong man who appeared like he belonged here, leading his planet. On another wall was an aerial foto from the top of the dome looking down on the Arena and the Plaza. Otherwise the walls were bare and painted the color of the Global symbol. The small room had three chairs including the receptionist's. The unique facet of this room was there wasn't a doorway other than the one to enter the reception area.

"You sure you don't want to take a seat?"

"Would that make you more comfortable?" Orn said. If it was anyone else he wouldn't care, but if she was happy, then the Leader was happy.

"No, I'm more concerned about your comfort."

Orn was aware she was upset with his presence. He had that effect on people. They always felt that way about him. At an early age, he was told by his elders he could change that perception, but he preferred to remain the same and as circumstances panned out, that's why he was so good at his job and was so close to the global seat of power. It did put a damper on being social, having friends, but serving the Leader was his life so that wasn't a problem.

"I'm fine where I am," Orn said, crossing his arms in front of him. The receptionist glanced up and her eyes landed on the back of Orn's hands. He saw the horror in her face as she cleared her throat and looked back at her viewer. Her squirming gave him pleasure.

"The Leader should be ready for you in a few moments. He's running a little late today," the receptionist said and began typing into her viewer, doing her best to ignore him.

Orn thought about how he would approach the Yor Vanderlord situation with the Leader. An urgent investigation was necessary, but it would bring him within close proximity of Mado Prevor, and Orn was aware the Leader had his own notions about Prevor's loyalty and the need for the WAEF restoration. Getting through to the Leader, no matter the intelligence Orn presented, was going to be tough.

The receptionist's intercom played four identical beeps in a row and she said, "The Leader will see you now." She pressed a red button on the side of the intercom and the wall to the left of her slid open to the size of a doorway.

There were three doorways along the bare walls and none would open without the Leader allowing it and they would randomly open, one at a time for visitors.

The receptionist said, "Have a pleasant day," and Orn entered the Leader's office. The room contained two large couches, the color of the Global symbol, facing one another in the middle of the room. The white office walls were covered with paintings of Koda's magnificent ancient landscape in wooden frames. In the past, they'd hung on the walls of the Royal Palace. The only painting that stood out as different was an artist's rendition of Capitol City from outside the dome with the visible skyline of the Plaza and Royal Quarter inside. At the far end of the room was the Leader's ornate hand-carved wood desk, which once belonged to the Global Monarch, with a wall of weapon-proof windows behind it overlooking the Plaza. The Leader sat at the desk staring at his personal viewer. The desk was bare except for the viewer and a framed digi-foto of his wife and two boys.

The office door slid closed and Orn stood at attention, waiting to be addressed.

"Please sit down, Orn," the Leader said, not looking up from his viewer. "You're making me nervous."

"Sorry, sir," Orn said and sat down in a chair, another wooden relic from the Monarchy, in front of the Leader's desk.

The Leader closed his viewer and pushed it to the side of the desk. "What is eating at you, Orn? You know that I don't like you being seen here, but your comm was rather insistent, which I didn't appreciate."

"I meant no disrespect, sir. I foresee imminent danger to the status quo with this Vanderlord incident," Orn said, holding the arms of the chair. The wood felt odd in his hands.

"That's what I gleaned from your report on his arrest," the Leader said, "I just don't see how this Professor is such an immediate threat that you need to communicate with me in person. You arrested him in the Royal Library. Is he going to attack us with ancient books?"

"It's tricky, sir."

"Are you saying I'm not smart enough to understand it?"

"No, sir."

"Then explain yourself."

"You know how I feel about the Vanderlords?"

"Yes. Yes. Back when Yorlik the Great landed, you suggested that we take them all including the pregnant mother to a remote area and extinguish their lives."

"Correct, and you decided to not take my advice."

"And it worked out unbelievably well. I negotiated with the old man and it all worked out for the best. I negotiated a great deal. Once you dealt with the rabble-rouser grandson…what was his name?"

"Tetrick Vanderlord."

"Yes him. Once you dealt with him, it's been smooth sailing. Are you telling me that this young man is somehow a threat the level of Tetrick Vanderlord and the old man? He writes books and teaches at the Royal University.

He's never spoken out against us in public. How dangerous can he be?"

"Examining the vidcam surveillance over the past 22
days of his University colleagues and reviewing the people
that he was consorting with on his book tour, I believe he
is in the midst of a plan to destabilize the government."

"You're telling me, and I read this in your report too,
that this group of eggheads are a problem for the powerful
Global Assembly and you reached this conclusion after
you detained the boy for going over the time limit at the
Royal Library. Do you understand how that sounds? "

"Yes, sir. But it all adds up especially with Mado Prevor
in the mix. He's at the center of all of this."

"Maybe you're just bored with your work and I need
to station you somewhere a little more dangerous," the
Leader said, "Do I?"

"If that's your desire, sir."

"Mado Prevor is a friend of the Global Assembly and
myself. If it wasn't for that man, the people of this planet
would be in dire straits. If your theory is based on Prevor
being at the center of this plot, then your hypothetical
egghead revolt is even more off-base."

Orn tightened his grip on the arms of the chair.

The Leader rose from his desk and turned his back
on Orn, peering out the window in the direction of the
Prevor Industries Complex. "Mado Prevor is the lynch-
pin of Global Assembly plans—past, present and future.
I'm trying to understand this theory of yours, Orn," the
Leader said, turning to face him, "I really am, but what

you're saying doesn't add up. Your perspective is off. Everything is going so well and you seem to be looking for problems. Look how far you and I have come."

"Yes, sir. We have, sir, but that is why you have me around, and it seems clear from the information that I accrued through the Shamban interrogation that Prevor's restoration of the When All Else Fails may have something to do with this, too."

"Ah, yes. The Shamban traitor who muttered 'when all else fails.' That is a bit of a reach. Don't you think? It's a common term. Maybe he just didn't finish a sentence." The Leader sighed and shook his head, then walked around his desk and stood directly in front of Orn. "Restoring that ship is a stroke of political genius," the Leader said, "Presenting it at Breeze Celebration will boost our popularity with the citizenry for decades to come."

"That ship is dangerous. It's a rallying cry for all the supporters of the SEEDER program."

"That's where you're wrong. The program is gone. It will never happen again. The domes are built. The ship is nothing more than a shiny hunk of metal for a museum. The work is under constant inspection and I was out there for a viewing-channel spot just recently. Mado Prevor has done a tremendous job."

"I have intel that he's using the black market to obtain items to make the ship functional."

"Prevor is a perfectionist. He's trying to make sure the ship is historically accurate. He told me about making purchases on the black market and I approved it. He might be going overboard, but he's doing it on his own units," the Leader said, "And do you hear yourself? If that ship were to fly again how would it get out of the dome? You know that I respect your abilities, Orn, even the unsavory ones, but this theory of yours just doesn't pass muster."

"Do you mind if I breakdown what I see and you can decide from there?"

"You're already here, so I might as well hear you out, but make it brief. I'm losing my patience." The Leader sat back down behind his desk and pushed in his chair.

"I'm sorry, sir. I will do it as quick as I can," Orn said, "You have Yor Vanderlord. He has a higher than average intelligence, like his father and his mother, and he's maybe as smart as the Great man. He is brought up in the radical views of his father. He was schooled in the legends of his great-grandfather."

"As we all were."

"Yes, sir. As we all were, but this is family. Through his association with his father's University colleagues, he has an idea on how his father met his end. The boy has developed a deep interest, based his entire existence on learning about the past as it pertains to his great-grandfather. He has scavenged whatever information that's available to learn about that past. Mado Prevor takes him under his supervision and nurtures his intellect, then funds the promotion of his book."

"Prevor feels a debt to the Great man in helping him make his mark and take his place in Kodan society."

"That may be true, sir, but Prevor funds the promotion of the book which is historically in-depth, but romanticizes and glorifies the SEEDER program and it hardly mentions the program's lack of tangible accomplishments. Yor Vanderlord flies from dome to dome promoting the book, meeting with known subversives related to his father who are now miraculously in touch with Vanderlord's University staff who all have their own subversive leanings. On top of that, Prevor convinces some Global Assembly lackey to push the WAEF restoration idea to your advisors as a worthy public relations maneuver or what I consider a public relations stunt. Now, Vanderlord is snooping around the Royal Library attempting to dig up more information regarding his great-grandfather and I could tell in my interrogation with him that he was lying and hiding something."

"I don't like your tone," the Leader said, "I make the decisions. I was advised and decided. And I signed off on permission to view the journal and the WAEF restoration which you just called a stunt. Are you saying that I was wrong?"

"No, sir. I would never."

"Then what are you saying?"

"I'm simply pointing out that these series of events point toward a societal disruption happening in the near future and I believe that Vanderlord is at the center of it."

"All I see is a series of events that have no connections except your obsession with the Vanderlords. That family has always spun your head so far around you don't know your ass from a hole in the ground."

"I'm sorry you feel that way, sir. I'm only doing the job you appointed me to do," Orn said. He could feel himself sweating through his shirt. Luckily he was wearing the jacket.

The Leader looked down and tapped his fingers from right to left on the desk. Orn had been around him long enough to know this meant that he was reaching a conclusion.

"I've read in your report that you've called for a hearing to review Vanderlord's violation of the time limit," the Leader said.

"Yes, sir."

"If you can discover tangible intel that connects all these moving parts to a deeper scheme, then we can take it up at the hearing. So continue doing your job. See if you can confirm this theory of yours," the Leader said, standing up from his desk, "Will that do? Now, I have things to do that are less theoretical."

"Yes sir," Orn said, standing up from his chair. "I appreciate your time, sir. I will do my best."

"That's all I've ever asked of you," the Leader said, "You've never failed me before and that's why I'm giving you leeway here, but there are a few boundaries you can't cross. I forbid you from approaching Mado Prevor. I've already talked to him this morning. He was quite upset at your harassment of Vanderlord and his family. I told him that I knew nothing about it. I need Prevor on our side so if you insist on pursuing this theory of yours, then you'll need to avoid using your usual methods on Vanderlord and his family. Go crack a few eggheads and make Yor Vanderlord rethink his allegiances, but I don't want this coming back to me. Keep your usual profile. Do I make myself perfectly clear?"

"Yes, sir. I will comply with your order sir."

"Make sure you do," the Leader said, "Now away with you. Leave by the side door and go out the underground entrance. I don't want you being seen around here."

Orn turned on his heels and marched out of the room. He would make the Leader proud.

YOR

Yor waited as a shirtless Mado turned his back and placed both his hands behind his neck and reached down his spine toward his waist, stretching further than Yor had ever seen anyone do before. Mado's flexibility was incredible, but that wasn't evidence of anything.

Yor found it unbelievable that this man who was a friend and confidante for 12 years was supposedly a space alien from a planet called Prevor. He had respectfully listened to Mado's tale of being from another planet, meeting and befriending his great-grandfather, but Mado was an eccentric man and maybe he was going through a nervous breakdown from the stress of Yor's detention and their plan going sideways. That rationalization seemed far-fetched, but not as much as Mado's story.

Yor heard a wet snap like when a soaked towel is thrown against a hard floor, then a tearing noise. Mado's skin across his entire back was now loose, then he pulled at the skin around his chest until there was another wet snap, and tussled with the skin on both sides of his head until it was loose. He lifted the skin from his upper torso, neck and head over what Yor presumed was his real head. Water flowed down Mado's back. With this fake skin removed, Mado's upper torso, neck and back of his head appeared like the scales of a fish with bluish-silver hue.

On top of his scalp jutted what appeared to be two small fins. Yor had never seen a fish. By the time he was born, they were extinct, but in school he viewed historical vids of them.

Mado said, "I'm going to turn around now. You think you're ready?"

Yor had experienced life-altering events like the death of his great-grandfather and father, and living in a dome, but nothing as strange as this one. "You couldn't be any uglier than before," Yor said.

"Humor," Mado said, "I'll take that as a good sign."

Mado turned around slowly. His skin shimmered in the light. On the side of his neck, Yor thought that he saw gills, then Mado faced him. He had no nose but a bump there. A mouth but no lips. His eyes appeared to protrude from their sockets with an eyelid that seemed to hardly blink.

Weirdly enough, Yor thought, *Still kind of looks like him wearing a fish mask.* Maybe Mado was wearing a fish costume under the fake skin, but that was ridiculous. Then it hit him and he felt lightheaded all of a sudden. Mado was some sort of upright walking aquatic creature. "Holy crap," Yor said, "This is not some sort of trick. You're not pulling a joke on me."

He picked up the neck and head piece that Mado had just removed and looked at the face. This was the Mado that he recognized. Since Yor had known Mado, his hair had thinned to a bald space down the middle of his head so he shaved his head bald for fashion's sake. Yor now realized this was a ruse to make Mado appear like he was from Koda and aging.

"I know what you're thinking," Mado said.

"How could you know what I'm thinking?" Yor said. He was bewildered. "Has someone that you've known for 12 years revealed himself to be an alien from another planet?"

"No," Mado said, "That's not what I meant. I just wanted to say that I am the same being. I've been here all along."

"Is that really what your hands look like?" Yor said.

"Actually not," Mado said, "The skin appears like on my face and neck, and I have four fingers which includes something that looks like your thumb."

Yor had trouble connecting Mado's voice exiting this alien face, and he felt like he might pass out.

Mado walked closer and said, "You don't look well. Even though it happened last night, this is probably an after-effect of the sonic alarm. It's an offshoot of the sonic restraint and has the same results."

"That damn sonic restraint. I had no idea it would be so paralyzing and it was more painful than I thought. I'm not sure I like that you invented it."

"If you recall, I invented it to prevent more killings at the riots. Restrain the rioters instead of murdering them. Fortunately, the Global Assembly bought it. I estimate it saved tens of thousands, and I earned a hefty reward in units which I put back into the WAEF."

"You're right. I'm feeling disoriented right now. I

should drink some water," Yor said, attempting to stand up, but his legs wouldn't carry him and he fell back to the recliner.

"Stay where you are," Mado said, walking over to the dispenser and returning with a glass of water. "I know this is a lot to take in all at once, but I didn't think there was a better way to do it."

"No, you were right. Might as well just rip off the bandage or the prosthetic head in this case."

"That's a funny one," Mado said, laughing and pointing at Yor.

Yor didn't think his remark was that funny, but he always found Mado's laughter infectious and broke out laughing himself.

When the merriment died down, Yor said, "Thanks Mado. That made me feel a little better."

Mado handed Yor the glass of water and Yor sipped at it, then he asked Mado to finish his story about meeting his great-grandfather.

Mado said, "I heard nothing from my people about a rescue, and we stayed together for about half a year in your time. As I said before, I learned your language until I could speak and read it well enough for us to share more detailed information about each other's planetary cultures, technology and eco-systems. He told me about his family and I told him about my clan. We grew up on very different planets, but our true bond was science and the desire to see our families again. We explored the planet together. We became friends. Of course, Yorlik was determined to discover a planet to resettle the population of Koda and accomplish his mission. Unfortunately, the planet that we were inhabiting was tectonically active and there was not enough habitable landscape for your people.

"Eventually, Yorlik decided that he had to move on and keep exploring. Although there weren't planets nearby that fit into the parameters of his mission, I shared my knowledge of a few sectors with potential. The sector with the most viable planets was nearly a hundred years away using the WAEF's propulsion system. Your great-grandfather could be a convincing man. I'm sure you've heard the stories in your research, and they were true. He lobbied me to give him the spare parts for my propulsion system to convert the WAEF to something closer to the speed of a Prevorian vessel. I told him that my people would never allow it. The rescue team would arrive soon to fix my ship and they'd inventory my systems and spare parts and note the parts missing and they'd find out that I'd shared too much Prevorian knowledge with an alien species. Such an act was treasonous.

"He pled for the life of his people. It took everything that I could summon not to give him what he wanted. So he finally left me, but we found a way to synch up our comm systems so he would be less lonely on his voyage and we could keep tabs on one another. He launched, but we spoke almost every day.

"Then shortly after Yorlik left, I saw a spike in tectonic activity. At first, I noted it as a part of the geology that I'd mapped out, but I decided a more extensive look at the planet was necessary. I took readings of the entire sphere from as high an altitude as I could establish with a drone. I didn't want to risk my craft which could still not achieve orbit. After about 60 days of research, I concluded that the entire planet would begin a tectonic event, the likes of which myself and my craft would never survive.

"I transmitted a dire emergency signal on the beacon to my people, but the only sure way to be safe was attempting to escape the gravitational pull and reach space. I had my misgivings about this maneuver, but the alternative was nonexistence. My attempt failed, and I damaged the hull on a rough landing in a less hospitable place than before with lava flow around me. I had no way to repair the damage before my predicted time window for a planetwide tectonic event.

"I kept your great-grandfather appraised of what was happening and when the crash occurred, he told me that he was turning around and coming back to get me. I told him there might not be enough time, and he said that he'd push the WAEF's engines and gave me an estimated time of arrival, cutting close to my predicted time for the event. He checked in and communicated with me every day and in the meantime, I stripped my craft of all tech and propulsion systems that might be transferred to the WAEF, all the star chart data, all the food systems to keep me alive, and even metal from my ship for building my next craft.

"So you know what happened, here I am! Yorlik arrived in the nick of time, as your people would say. From the safe confines of orbit, we watched the land masses rip apart. Quite the scientific event. The readings were spectacular." There was an awkward silence, then Mado said, "I'm hoping this doesn't change anything between us, but I know that's a great deal to ask of you right now."

"I'm not sure what to say, Mado," Yor said, "I'm definitely in shock, but not just from last night. Look at you."

"I am a handsome specimen," Mado said and winked at Yor.

This time Yor didn't have a laugh in him.

"Seriously, I understand," Mado said, "I'm happy to answer any questions."

"I've collected an enormous amount of questions about my great-grandfather over the years," Yor said, "And you probably know the answers to many of them, but this revelation is frustrating. You've been sitting on this knowledge for as long as we've known one another, understanding what it means to me and you've waited until now to tell me. Why?"

"I'm not sure you'll like the answer," Mado said, "Your great-grandfather thought that if I told you the truth about me, about the foto, then you might be content with the knowledge and not develop the skills that you'd need to get Koda headed in the right direction. He also strongly believed the longer a secret is out there the harder it is to contain, and this was a big one. He used to say, 'There's a time and a place for everything' and this happened to be the right time. You have to admit, I may have withheld information, but I never lied to you."

"Wait a minute," Yor said. He picked up the foto from his lap and pointed at it. "I always thought the camera was on a tripod, but you took this foto, didn't you?"

"That's correct," Mado said. He walked over to Yor, patted his hands on Yor's shoulders, looking him in the eyes. Yor was going to stand up, but he sat there and examined Mado's alien face. His eyes were the same though. This was the same individual even if he had a different appearance. Logically, he still wanted to question Mado's story, but the evidence was in front of him. *Why would I stop trusting Mado now? He's literally bared himself to me.* Yor noted that Mado put his hands on Yor's shoulders fairly often especially when he was being sincere. Yor wondered whether this was simply a Prevorian custom. He had lots of questions, but a specific one entered his mind.

"Why did you come here with my great-grandfather?" Yor asked, "Why didn't he take you home?"

"We'd need more time to tell that story, but in our voyage together, he became my close friend, my family, and I came here and stayed to fulfill Yorlik's vision for Kodans to survive."

Yor stayed seated and said, "I still consider you my friend, Mado. No need to concern yourself on that front. I certainly believe this story you've told me, but this is quite a lot to swallow. And we haven't discussed last night and how that might change..."

"Yes, I was thinking..."

"Yes Mado, I know you well enough to know that you've already got another plan in mind," Yor said, "I don't have time to talk about the details, but I agree we should start working towards this coming Breeze Celebration. I have to stop at home before I teach and I have a meeting, so I need to get out of here."

"Will you come by this evening?" Mado said, gripping Yor's shoulders tighter.

"Without a doubt, we've got lots of work to do, and I've got lots of questions. I'll leave the foto here," Yor said, "But can I ask one thing of you?"

"Of course, anything."

"Can you put old Mado's face back on?" Yor said, "I think it'll take me some time to adjust to your true appearance."

MAR

Mar awoke on the couch. She had curled up and fallen asleep waiting for the vid to reformat, and since she had a late shift, she was aware that she could sleep in.

Rajer wasn't in the bedroom and the bed was made. In the kitchen, she found a digi-tablet next to a ready-to-heat cup of morning beverage. She touched the tablet and it lit to a note from Rajer, 'Dearest, I woke this morning with greater understanding. Sorry to press you on a subject that couldn't have been easy to dredge up. Talk later this evening. Love, Rajer. PS Prepared this beverage for you' She heated the beverage and sunk back down on the couch, touching the keyboard of the viewer. The dark screen lit up revealing the image of Yorlik the wildman from space, staring back at her. *Here we are again*, Mar thought and closed the viewer.

The bungalow door opened and by the way it banged to the doorstop, she concluded right away that it was Yor. She turned around to confirm it. Standing in the doorway with the light behind him, the frame of his body and the way that he stood reminded her of Tetrick and Yorlik. That wouldn't have been her thought a day ago, but considering last night, they both were on her mind.

"How are you, mother?" Yor asked, shutting the door behind him.

"Better now that I see you alive and well," Mar said, "Come over here and sit."

"I'm running late to class."

"I don't care," Mar said, "Come over here and give me a hug."

Yor complied and Mar was happy to have her boy in her arms.

"Now what're you thinking?" Mar said, holding Yor at arms length, "What have you gotten yourself into?"

"Nothing for you to worry about."

"Don't tell me not to worry. You end up at the Detention Facility and the same night, Rajer is threatened by that horrifying monster. Why has he entered our lives again?"

"You know that GSS man?"

"I had a few run-ins with him in the past and he got to know your father too well. He's not a man. He's a monster, and he terrifies me. What did you do?"

"Mado warned me, but I didn't listen."

"This has to do with your great-grandfather and the WAEF, doesn't it?"

"How do you know?"

"Rajer told me you were detained because of an incident at the Royal Library. Your great-grandfather's journal is there, and for as long as I can remember, you've been obsessed with it," Mar said, "Seems like Mado is involved, and you and him are collaborating on rebuilding the

WAEF. What else but the WAEF and your great-grand-father would attract that monster's attention?"

"Everything will be fine."

"Doesn't seem fine to me. I always thought the Breeze Celebration presentation was a little too extroverted for you and more like your father, but you're becoming more like him everyday. You're taking the lead, bringing this danger onto yourself. That worries me the most," Mar said, "I want to know what's going on here."

"I don't know if it's smart to involve you."

"Listen to me, young man. I'll be damned if I'll be shut out of whatever is happening here."

Yor kissed her on the cheek. "I'll tell you, but I can't right now. I need to pick up my class notes and head to the University or I'll be late."

"You promise?"

"Yes. I'll probably sleep over at Mado's, but I'll come over tomorrow on your day off," Yor said. He kissed Mar on the cheek again, running into his bedroom, then back into the living room and out the front door.

Now it all made sense. It was more than a coincidence the past was coming back to haunt her family as the WAEF was being overhauled. The WAEF had been in the middle of controversy before. One of the only times, Mar saw Tetrick in a disagreement with Yorlik was over recovering the WAEF from the government. That was about six years into Yorlik's return.

Up to that point, Yorlik had expended a great deal of energy, trying to convince the Global Assembly to let him possess the WAEF. He argued the ship had been his home for well over a century and the craft belonged to him more than them. He proposed, taking his argument through the court system, but Tetrick pointed out how the judges were controlled by the government and Yorlik would never win.

Yorlik never believed the government would destroy the WAEF so he waited for the opportunity to arrange its return. Due to years in space, the hull was radiated at low levels, but high enough that the metal was not valuable for recycling in government construction projects. Many argued its scientific value for study in the future, and others stated the ship was important for its historical value.

One late evening, after dinner at the estate, Yorlik asked if the family could stay the night and he told Tetrick that he wanted to show him a structure that he intended to build on the property. Mar and Tetrick both had the next day off from work so they agreed.

Mar watched as Tetrick and Yorlik climbed into a motorized cart and sped off down a path into the woods. She took Yor onto the patio and read to him. Yor had already been accepted into a school for gifted children, and his great-grandfather insisted on paying for a private tutor. After each session, the tutor raved about how Yor was far ahead of children twice his age. Yor was a Vanderlord in intelligence and since he was a baby, she recognized the stubbornness, too.

Mar put Yor to bed and she fell asleep next to him.

Tetrick woke her later. He was upset, talking fast, loud, and incoherently.

"Calm down," Mar whispered, pointing to Yor, "You're going to wake him. Let's go to our bedroom."

Tetrick bent down, wobbly on his feet and kissed Yor on the cheek. He was inebriated, partaking of Yorlik's Malrap stash.

In their bedroom, Mar ordered him to sit down on the bed. "Now, lower your voice so you don't wake your son and tell me what this is all about," Mar said.

"He can't do it." Tetrick said, "He can't do it. It's insanity. That's what it is. It's going too far for that damn ship. Who knows what could happen? I won't let it."

"Slow down," Mar said in a hushed tone like she'd speak to Yor when he was throwing a tantrum, "Take a deep breath and start from the beginning." Mar sat down next to Tetrick on the bed and he took a deep breath.

"So after dinner, grandfather shows me where he's building a hangar. Right now just the foundation is built, but it's huge. Building materials stacked up all around the site. Definitely not a hayloft. Maybe a city block in size. Yorlik tells me that the WAEF will be housed there. I got excited for him. I didn't know that he worked out a deal with the Global Assembly. Then he tells me that there's a catch to the deal, and I'm not going to like it, but he's got a way to make it all work out in the end.

"Right away, I'm concerned at the serious tone in his voice. He first tells me that this catch was his suggestion. Then he tells me that the Global Assembly will return the

WAEF to his ownership with all essential tech stripped from it, which was their idea, and they'll take possession of his spacesuit and journal for posterity, which was his idea, but the catch is they'll erase all data related to the discovery and they'll use the available tech to remove his memory of the discovery."

"What discovery?"

"I'd promised not to tell you, but you need to know if you're going to be involved in the procedure."

"What discovery? What procedure?"

"Sorry. I'm drunk."

"I can see that," Mar said, shoving him. He fell off the bed and landed with a thud on the floor. Mar laughed out loud and covered her mouth, concerned that she'd wake Yor.

"I'm sorry," Tetrick said, using the bed to elevate himself to a standing position. "Wait one moment." Tetrick left the room and went downstairs. He was gone for a considerable amount of time. Mar assumed he had fallen asleep on the couch in the library where she would usually find him in the morning after a Malrap binge.

As she nodded off, she heard him returning, taking the stairs two at a time up to their room. He carried a viewer under his arm and a memory wafer in his other hand. Mar could tell by his reek that he stopped for a few more swigs of Malrap while he was gone.

"Did you really need more Malrap?" Mar said.

"Sorry. I needed it for courage to face you," Tetrick said. He forced a smile.

"That's encouraging," Mar said.

"I'm sorry."

"And stop saying your sorry and get on with whatever you want to show me."

Tetrick sat down next to her on the bed, inserted the wafer into the viewer, then placed the viewer so they shared it in their laps. "What you're about to view was slipped to me by Yorlik on the day that we visited him after his landing?" The wafer uploaded and a start-up image appeared on the screen of Yorlik, the wildman from space. "Here we go," Tetrick said and pressed the start button.

"Hello Tetrick," Yorlik said, "So much time has passed, so much has happened to me that I wouldn't know where to start. Once I'm released, then I can tell you more. Sorry to be so clandestine. I'm being watched every instant so I'm using a jamming device to keep them from knowing about this recording. I don't have much time to convey this information before they suspect that the static on their surveillance screens is not just a malfunction in their systems so I will cut to the facts.

"It appears that my findings and what the current political establishment want Kodans to be aware of are two different things…" Yorlik pushed back his chair and observed the room, turning his head back and forth, then stayed motionless listening for sounds. After a few moments, he leaned towards the viewer's camera, lowering his voice, "I found a planet, a beautiful planet that is perfect for the habitation of the Kodan people. The planet is far from here, but in my travels, I've come across a faster means of propulsion for space travel..." He stopped and looked both ways again. "Someone coming. Must end transmission." The screen went black, then showed the start-up image of Yorlik's face again.

Mar was stunned. "You never told me about this vid? This vid. Arguably the most important news in Kodan history."

"I asked Yorlik if I could tell you and he said the fewer people who knew the better," Tetrick said, "Silence about his discovery was part of the deal to get him out of quarantine. That's the main reason he hasn't talked about it."

"I knew there was something more to his release. So now they want to finish what they started and erase all record of the mission including this world-changing discovery and Yorlik's memory?"

"That's about the size of it."

"This news could change everything for every Kodan citizen and they are holding so tightly to their greed that they won't let the news out. I knew your cause was correct, but now I see why you've taken it so far."

"Yes, I know that we've been fighting about my zealotry, but now you see what this is all about. It's so much larger."

"I'm still perturbed that you feel like it's okay to sacrifice yourself, not thinking about how your actions affect myself and Yor."

Tetrick closed the viewer and put it beside him, then placed his hand on her thigh where the viewer had been.

"That's all I think about."

"Well, think a little harder the next time those goons come and take you away. They'll eventually do permanent damage."

"I'm not sure how to stop that unfortunate effect of what I'm doing."

"Maybe find someone else to be the headliner. Take some of the heat off yourself," Mar said.

"I'm the face of the movement now...but I could try."

"Yes try. For me and your son, try," Mar said, putting her hand on Tetrick's thigh, "And what are we going to do about Yorlik's situation?"

"He is adamant he'll go through with it. He says the ship is the most important piece of his plan."

"Why is that stripped hunk of junk so important?"

"He won't tell me. I've tried to get it out of him. It's infuriating."

"Join the club," Mar said, patting Tetrick's hand on her thigh.

Tetrick stood up, wobbling for a moment before standing upright in front of her. "It's insanity. I don't care about the medical success rates. He can't let them take his memory much less erase the data. He's made the most important discovery this planet will ever know and he wants to erase it from history." Tetrick's voice was getting louder with every word. "He can't do it. He just can't do it."

"First of all, lower your voice," Mar said, "Your great-grandfather is a highly intelligent man. We can both agree on that, can't we?"

"Yes, but…"

"And one would think when he says that he has a way to make it work, then we should listen to him."

"He said that he's doing it for you, me and Yor, and for the entire planet, but he can't tell me the plan right now, we have to trust he knows what he's doing."

"I'm not happy being in the dark either, but I trust him," Mar said, "You should, too."

Tetrick fell down on both his knees with a thud in front of Mar, grabbing her calves. "I know my darling, but this procedure will happen on one of the most brilliant minds this planet has ever known. I asked him how he could be sure that they wouldn't erase his entire mind and he said he would calibrate the machinery himself and he wanted you to help him. He said he's been researching the idea for a long time and this option wasn't his first choice, but now it's the last best one."

"I've read about the memory erasure tech in the med journals. It's been around for years, but its never been perfected. It's still experimental. They've used it on deviant prisoners and at first it took more memories than the targeted ones, but they've honed it with use and success rates have gone up."

Over a year passed between that scene in the bedroom and Yorlik's successful memory erasure. Yorlik wanted to insure that the WAEF was locked in the hangar on the estate before the procedure happened.

In that time, Yorlik supervised the WAEF's move to

the hangar on the estate. Flight wasn't possible, because the power source for the WAEF's engines had been depleted for safety reasons upon landing so the 75-meter long, three-story spaceship was conveyed by ground transportation on slow crawling carrier. This was a logistical nightmare due to the distance of the journey: There was bureaucratic wrangling across each political jurisdiction and only specific roads could be used, making the path from the military base to Yorlik's estate a zigzag instead of a straight line.

The move was a publicity juggernaut worked by the Prevor Industries Public Relations office. The daily route was posted on all media. People would line the roads to watch the WAEF pass by. Yorlik appeared on viewing-channel shows, and when he was inevitably asked the details of his travels, he said just enough to produce a rumor that he was writing his memoirs. Century-old nursery rhymes about Yorlik the Great and the WAEF's travels were revived around the globe. The Kodan people adored Yorlik like never before which the government didn't mind as long as Yorlik kept his discovery quiet.

Mado helped with the construction of the hangar: He hired manpower through human resources in his corporation and used their expertise in building holographic-gaming-device factories to facilitate the work. Prevor's legal team worked out the tedious bureaucracy for each city, county, and region along the WAEF's passage, too.

So Mado became more of a fixture around the estate while the WAEF crept across the Kodan landscape toward the hangar. Since the day they first met, Mado was an oddity to Mar. She could never get a read on him, but Mado seemed to care about Yorlik's well-being so she accepted his presence nonetheless.

When the end was nearing for the Great man, Tetrick and Mar cared for him at the estate. They sat vigil by Yorlik's side for five days while he passed in and out of consciousness. On the sixth day, Mado arrived. When Yorlik became conscious and saw Mado, a smile spread across his face. Yorlik reached out and grasped Mado's hand and said, "Carry on, my friend. Carry on" then released a final gasp.

Tetrick walked over to the body and saw that he wasn't breathing. "He's gone," Tetrick said.

Mar burst out crying and Tetrick embraced her and began weeping, too.

Mado placed each of his hands simultaneously on Yorlik's shoulders, then he spoke something in a language that Mar had never heard before or since that moment. The words and sounds were spoken in a sort of melody and there was a beauty to its sing-song quality. Mar assumed that this was a prayer, and as Mado continued, Mar stopped weeping and Tetrick wiped away his tears. They were hypnotized and Tetrick placed his arm around Mar as they both listened. When the prayer ended, Mar felt uplifted, more overjoyed than sad. She thought about Yorlik's life and it dawned on her how full and wondrous his existence had been.

Mado released his hold on Yorlik's shoulders, breathed

out a long sigh, then turned to them and said, "We have lost one of the best beings I have ever known in my existence. As your people would say, I loved him dearly." Then Mado placed one hand on Mar's shoulder and another on Tetrick's, bowed his head and closed his eyes.

A sense of loss overwhelmed Mar and she began to weep and wail in grief and so did Tetrick. When Mado finally let go of their shoulders, the sadness subsided. Mar could have sworn that Mado's hand on her shoulder had somehow been the conduit for sharing his feelings.

Mado stared down at the lifeless body. "Goodbye my old friend. I will keep my word and finish what you've started."

"What was that you were singing?" Mar asked, feeling drained from her grief, "It was beautiful."

"That was a prayer of passing that my mother taught me when I reached the age of maturity," Mado said, "A transcendent prayer among my people."

"Your people? What was the language?" Mar asked.

"I think that we can save that for another day," Tetrick said.

"I was just curious. I know so little about Mado."

Tetrick said, "I don't think now is the time."

Mado sat down on the bed next to Yorlik's body and put his hand on the blanket in the middle of Yorlik's chest. "This being had an incredibly giving heart."

Mar's attitude toward Mado changed that evening. She was endeared to him for his obvious love of Yorlik. That's why she didn't argue the idea when Tetrick told her about Yor interning with Mado.

Now, besides herself, Mado was the only living connection to past events involving the WAEF and the Great man. Whatever was creating the recent turmoil in their lives, Mado was at the center and it only made sense that the restoration of the WAEF had something to do with it. She didn't have a clue what was happening, but she wasn't going to sit around and let it play out without her having her say.

YOR

As he progressed down the corridor of the Royal University building toward his office, Yor began knocking on doors on either side of the hall until he arrived at the entrance to his office. He turned to see his colleagues peering at him from their doorways.

"Meeting in my office," Yor said to them, unlocking his office door. The lock was modified to DNA-scanner tech so the door would only open to him. Yor installed the Prevor Industries tech himself on a night between academic terms when the campus was nearly vacant.

This was one of the oldest buildings on the 527-year-old campus and in his position as Chair of SEEDER-program studies, Yor's office was more prestigious and spacious than others. The walls were paneled with dark wood from extinct trees. Shelves of books, four shelves high, lined the wall on the right leading up to Yor's desk at the far end of the room. To the left was a round wood conference table where Yor met with his staff. Between the table and the bookshelves, there were three overstuffed armchairs for more intimate discussions with students and staff.

Yor opened the shutters on the windows, the light streamed in, and he sat down at his desk. When a student or colleague was seated across from Yor, they could gaze

Howard Libes

past him through the four side-by-side windows and view the artificial turf of the campus green.

Due to Mado's endowment, the department possessed the funding for a new handpicked staff. Yor chose the most qualified intellects from around the globe like Mel and Insol, but the University trustees were not pleased with his candidates. They criticized Yor for hiring historians who were known for speaking vehemently against the DOME project, touting his father's views. Yor assumed the pressure was coming from the Global Assembly and told the Trustees that his father was an inspiration for many SEEDER historians and assured them that the staff was hired for academic achievement, not political intrigue. He lied.

Yor was relieved to be off his feet and looked around at his surroundings. He once thought this scholastic life would compose his future. He laughed at the time it took him to get here and how soon he'd be leaving.

"What's so amusing?" Mel said, standing in the doorway.

"Just thinking about the future," Yor said, plucking a jamming device from his satchel. He activated it and placed it on his desk.

Mel snickered and stood by the conference table. "That's funny. Considering you're a historian."

"Funny," Yor said, "Why are you always the first one here and the last one to leave again?"

"Nor tradition, but thanks for always pointing that out."

"I just want you to remind you what a pain in the ass you are," Yor said and they both laughed. They placed themselves across from each other at the roundtable. Mel was not only a close friend, but Yor's right-hand man in the movement. He was a master at causing ripples of doubt in the digi-media regarding the government's policies. He had volunteered to test his strategies over the past few years and had been called into the Detention Facility more than a few times for an interview. He was told by the GSS that he was close to contravening the laws and long-term detainment, so Yor concluded Mel was performing his job correctly.

"Where is everybody?" Mel said.

"They'll be along soon. You going to be ready on your end?"

"Do you really have to ask?" Mel said, pulling on his hair.

"Always good to ask even if you assume you know the answer. Life is unpredictable."

"Especially after your foray last night. In our case, let's hope that we work out all the odds…"

There was a knock and Insol stood in the doorway. Today, she wore a short sun dress that showed enough of her cleavage and shoulders, and the length of her legs to distract Yor.

"Would you like me to leave?" Mel said, pulling on his hair.

Yor snapped out of his trance. He didn't know how long he'd been staring. "No, we're fine. I mean, I'm fine.

I don't want to talk for Insol. Everything is fine, I mean."

"You sure that's what you mean?" Insol said, "May I come in?"

"Please come in," Yor said, standing and pulling out the chair beside him.

"Wow, I didn't get that kind of treatment," Mel said.

"Maybe you need to sleep with him," Insol said, sitting down. She moved her chair up against Yor's and placed her hand under the table on the upper part of his thigh, then whispered with her tongue in Yor's ear, "Sorry I'm late. My class went long." Insol Renta's field of expertise was the study of women and minority Kodans in the SEEDER program.

"I can give you two a moment or five alone if that's necessary," Mel said.

Insol starting massaging Yor's thigh and he reached down to hold her hand as he could feel his face flushing. "No I'm good," Yor said.

"I'm not," Insol said, "We may need to have a private meeting after this one."

Yor wanted to be professional, but Insol's hand on his thigh wasn't helping him concentrate. He was getting stirred up so he decided to change the subject.

"By the way, I talked to Mado and I'm confident that he's on our side and we can proceed."

"What did he say?" Mel asked.

Yor knew what he couldn't say, "Mado is an alien who came here with my great-grandfather and stayed to fulfill my great-grandfather's wishes."

"Yes, what did he say?" Insol asked.

"Where are the other two?" Yor said, "I saw them in their doorways a moment ago."

"In your doorway now," Ador Wint said, strolling into Yor's office with Harmin Leeno next to him.

Ador and Harmin were the oldest of Yor's staff. They'd been professors at the University with his father, so Yor knew them as a child. They were the first staff that Yor recruited when he was given the chair.

Ador was the foremost expert on the controversy of the DOME project versus the SEEDER program and the discussion for and against both of them. He once shared this field of study with Yor's father. His connections were deep with the anti-DOME factions and their leaders. He was a closer friend of his father's than Harmin who was an expert on the impact of the SEEDER program on the planet's intellectual history. Harmin was the consummate player at promoting his career. He possessed a broad-range of contacts in the viewing-channel community. He harbored animosity towards Yor for being awarded the chair.

When Yor was awarded the chair, a rumor spread that Mado bought him the position. Mado swore more than a few times, in Yor's moments of doubt, that Yor obtained his job on his own merit. In the end, that gossip was traced back to Harmin.

"So we're all here," Yor said.

"Let's get this over with quickly," Harmin said, "These meetings seem to cover the same ground every time."

Yor wasn't surprised by Harmin's rumor besmirching him. He always trusted him the least. As a teenager, he recalled overhearing his father ranting in a nearby room about how the University community didn't support him due to their Global Assembly funding and he referred to Harmin as a "backstabber." By hacking Harmin's comm devices, Mado confirmed that Harmin was a government sympathizer, so Yor wanted Harmin at these meetings. His presence was useful.

"Why don't you just listen for a change, Harmin?" Mel said.

Yor said, "Everything has changed and we're readying to make a move in the near future. So make sure all your connections are in place and ready to mobilize."

"Why is this happening now?" Harmin said.

"You know full well why we don't have that discussion," Yor said, "Everyone in this room needs deniability if the time comes, and I want to make sure we're all on the same page here."

"I'm with you, buddy," Mel said.

"Me too…buddy," Insol said, kissing him on the cheek and squeezing his thigh.

"I stand with you, too," Ador said.

"All I questioned is why this is happening at this time or at all. This has been my argument since we started this little cabal. The domes are up. All the decisions have been made. There is nothing we can do to possibly change things."

"Can you remind us why you're here again?" Mel said.

"Please tell us. You saw on the viewing channels today that the Msituan dome had a catastrophic collapse. Thousands dead. Seems like these incidents are happening daily. If you have no empathy towards the damage that's already been perpetrated on the citizens of this planet in the name of greed, and the disaster that awaits everyone in this room and on this planet, if we won't stand up to the tyranny, then I don't understand why you're here."

"Please spare me another diatribe," Harmin said.

"I'm curious why you're here too," Insol said.

"I don't have time to get into this debate again," Yor said, "Harmin was one of my father's closest friends. I've known him since I was a child and I trust him to join us. If he wishes, he is welcome to bow out of his involvement. Is that the case?"

"As I said in our previous meeting, I'm onboard. I do have a question. When is this actually happening?"

Mel and Insol groaned.

Yor said, "As we've discussed before, when it gets closer, we'll have a meeting and I'll hand out your assignments. I'm not getting into details here."

"Sounds like your father's paranoia speaking. Maybe it runs in the family genetics."

"Maybe you should leave!" Mel said, standing up and leaning over the table towards Harmin.

"You aren't half the man," Insol said.

"Now, now, everybody calm down. Mel sit down. We're all friends and colleagues here and we want the same things. It's only constructive to question why things are happening the way they are," Yor said, "I don't know about paranoia running in the family, but I do know my father was correct about the government spying on their citizens."

"Do you have any empirical evidence?" Harmin asked.

"No, I have my father's word that he experienced government recordings of himself at home and on his comm and that's all the evidence I need. I'm positive I'm being monitored along with members of my family, but I'm pretty sure the people watching us have no idea what's about to happen."

"And neither do any of us?" Harmin said.

"Nobody here is following blindly," Mel said, sitting and pushing in his chair. "For years, we've all discussed that something needs to change. The establishment needs to be shaken up. I trust Yor, and I'm ready for whatever I'm required to do for the betterment of this planet."

"If I have to live with these parameters, then I will," Harmin said, standing up and leaving the room.

"I vote for letting Harmin out of this right now," Mel said.

"We're all in this together," Ador said, "Whatever we do, I believe we're stronger working together."

"I agree with Ador," Yor said, "Now, I have to end this meeting early. I've got lots to do today. I'll comm you all soon." Yor stood and so did everyone else. He embraced each of them before they left the room and shut the door.

Yor deactivated the jamming device, placed it in his satchel and closed the shutters, then there was a knock at the door. His heart raced. He could only assume this was how his father felt throughout the final years of his life. He never knew if the person behind the door was someone who'd take him away. He debated whether to answer it, but whoever was out there obviously was aware that he was inside and they continued knocking. Yor needed to get out eventually. He calmed himself. *Probably Insol.*

Yor opened the door. Ador stood there and said, "We need to talk." He entered the room and Yor closed the door behind him.

"Something you need to discuss?" Yor could tell from the look on Ador's face that this was serious. "Do I need to turn on the jammer?"

"I don't think so," Ador said.

"I'm going to set it up anyway," Yor said and activated the jammer.

"So I had a visit today from an old acquaintance of your father's and mine. He asked me questions about what's happening in this department and about you, in particular. He told me what happened last night."

"Yes, I was going to talk to you after I locked up here," Yor said, then told Ador about the previous evening's experience.

"Probably wasn't wise to poke at the government," Ador said, "I wish you'd come and seen me before you went to the library. I would've counseled you to wait until we were closer to making what we've been planning a reality. You're a Vanderlord and that just sets off all the alarms even if a decade has passed since they've had to deal with one."

"I get that now. I feel awful about it. I made a big mistake, but I'm hoping we can overcome it," Yor said, "You said that you know this person who visited you."

"Yes, he was a person who threatened, detained and even tortured your father and a bunch of other colleagues who spoke out against the domes. He is a cunning and frightening man who you don't want to cross."

"Scars on the back of his hands?"

"That's him. After he told me about last night, asked his questions, and threatened me, he said he presumed I was involved in whatever you were doing. He said I should tell you that he's watching and you'd see each other soon."

"Sounds like he's threatening me, too."

"I wouldn't put it past him," Ador said, "I assume you acquired the journal like you planned. Did you read it yet? You must've. You probably couldn't put it down and the speed that you read, I bet that you already finished it."

"I read the entire thing."

"So don't keep me waiting. What did you find?"

"Poetic prose about my great-grandfather's frustration over searching for a new Kodan home and finding nothing worthwhile, about missing his family and friends. The journal portrays his staunch dedication to saving the Kodan people and disgust with the crisis. Material I can use in my speech."

"Nothing about a discovery?"

"No, in that way, it was disappointing. Although Mado said I might've missed something and I have to believe he might have some insight into it." Yor realized right away that he said too much.

"What do you mean? He read it, too?"

"I'm not sure what he meant, but I'm looking forward to finding out."

MADO

In the WAEF's sleeping chamber, Mado stared at himself in the mirror. He spent so much time wearing the prosthetic device that when he took it off, he liked to remind himself of his true appearance. Yorlik and now his great-grandson said he resembled the aquatic species that once lived on Koda before they became extinct. Mado had investigated historical materials and could see how a Kodan humanoid would think such a thing, but how could they know any better. They didn't know his people. In these moments, Mado dreamt of Prevor, wondering if he'd ever return there.

After Yorlik saved Mado's life, they observed the planet's seismic activity on viewing screen via hyper-telescope from orbit, and Mado watched his spacecraft along with the long-range emergency beacon being swept away by the lava flow, disappearing beneath the magma. That was the saddest day in his young Prevorian life. He thought, *How will I get back home? What will become of me? Maybe I should have gone down with the ship.*

Then he felt Yorlik's hand on his shoulder. Yorlik was unaware, but this gesture was an act of bonding among his people. A connection being made. "Condolences, my friend," Yorlik said, "We'll figure out a way to get you home. You saved my life. I owe you everything."

"I need to be alone," Mado said, "I'm going to hibernate." For the Prevorian species, hibernation was actualized by closing an secondary eyelid housed behind the outer one. Set in motion, hibernation lasted about 15 days by the Kodan clock. If preferred a Prevorian could sustain hibernation by reclosing the inner eyelid as soon as it opened at the end of the 15-day period. Despondent at losing his spacecraft, Mado hibernated for two runs and awoke in the sleeping chamber bed where he had laid down, but there was a blanket over him.

Mado waited for the strength to return to his legs and walked to the control room where he found Yorlik on his back, halfway under the bottom of a console with tools splayed around him.

Yorlik said, "Good timing, I could use an extra pair of hands. Can you hand me the spanner with the red handle? Should be over there." Yorlik waved his right arm over a collection of tools.

"I know 'red', but not sure about this word 'spanner,'" Mado said.

"Oh sorry. I completely forgot. We never talked about tools."

"Just hand me the objects from over there," Yorlik said and moved his hand with palm down over the area on his right side. Mado handed him a few objects before he gave the correct one. "I'll be out from under here soon, I think."

Mado looked out the control room window. The WAEF was still orbiting the lava planet, reminding Mado once again of his loss. "We're still here."

"Yes," Yorlik said, "I thought it would be rude, not kind, to leave this area of space without asking you. I know you lost your ship, but your people might come looking for you."

"That's…kind of you," Mado said, "Can I take a look?"

"My ship is your ship, my friend."

Mado turned on the viewing screen which was still connected to the hyper-telescope and an image of a blackened cooled lava landscape appeared. "Is that…?"

"Yes, that is focused on where we last saw your ship. I'm sorry."

Mado said in Prevorian, "I'm lost."

"What was that?"

"I'm lost," Mado said in Kodan, "I'm lost." He couldn't take his eyes off the screen. Once the long-range emergency beacon's signal was shutdown his planet's regulations were clear. Rescue missions would be halted and returned home. Mado was aware of that fact when he watched it disappear in the lava flow. That's why he extended his hibernation, but he wasn't hibernating anymore and this was not a dream. "They won't come for me now."

"My people have a saying," Yorlik said, his voice sounding less muffled. Mado turned to see Yorlik standing now with his tools at his feet. "If you have a plan, then you're never lost, and I have a plan."

Mado needed to sit. His legs were still weak from his long hibernation. He attempted to turn the pilot's seat from facing out the control room window toward where

Yorlik stood, but it was stuck. Yorlik came over, popped a release on the side of the chair, then began gathering his tools and placing them in a box. Mado turned the chair toward Yorlik and sat down. "On the planet's surface, I told you about Prevorian Space Traveler regulations, about no mingling with other species. You can't simply drop me off on Prevor."

"Would you rather I kicked you out the docking-bay airlock and get it over with?" Yorlik said, securing a panel over the bottom of the console. He flipped a switch and the console, which covered part of a wall, lit up.

"That wouldn't be my first choice."

Yorlik carried the toolbox over to the holographic map table or holo-device, opened a door below it and put the box inside. "Well, that's one plan we both agree on. And that's a start."

Later, Yorlik said he surveyed the sector, which Mado recommended for viable planets, on his long-range hyper-telescope. He found two planets in the sector that might work for his people, but Mado was correct that they were nearly a hundred years away with the WAEF's propulsion system. Nevertheless, Yorlik had a plan. He suggested that Mado assist him in accomplishing his mission by outfitting the WAEF with his craft's propulsion. In return, Yorlik would somehow get Mado home within the parameters of the Prevorian Space Traveler's Code.

Although he saw no other choice, Mado pondered Yorlik's proposal. Before he left the lava planet, he conceived a rescue which might just maneuver him around the Space Traveler Code even if he hitched a ride with Yorlik. The plan entailed building an escape pod, which was standard training in becoming a Prevorian Space Traveler, with the parts and materials that he salvaged from his craft. He'd ask Yorlik to drop him off on a planet with the pod where he could survive for awhile, then activate a long-range emergency beacon. When his people arrived, he'd explain why his craft was missing and how he was safely on another planet. That plan fell short because the two beacons supplied for his expedition were lost: One beacon was damaged in his first landing and the other was destroyed when the lava flow blocked him from where it was posted and he was unable to retrieve it.

Now, since he had no way to build another beacon with Prevorian tech and send out a long-range distress call, Mado concluded he had no other option available, but to leave on this journey with his new friend. After Yorlik's mission was done, Mado could pilot the pod into space near Prevor, then send out a short-range emergency signal to the Prevorian Protectorate to pick him up, and he could easily explain his way around the Code.

The next day, Mado approached Yorlik in the control room, where he was performing a systems check, and told him about his idea.

"Sounds like you came up with a plan all by yourself," Yorlik said, preoccupied with his task.

"I took parts from my craft that might make the escape pod possible and make your ship faster," Mado said, "But I'll need the drawings of your engines to see if we can manage it."

Yorlik was doing something odd with his mouth where the two ends were turned up.

"Are you ill?" Mado said, "You're doing something strange with your mouth."

Yorlik put his hand to his mouth and the ends of his mouth turned up more. "You mean smiling," Yorlik said, "My people do that when they're happy."

"Odd."

"I'll teach you how to do it," Yorlik said, walking over to the holo-device and pressing buttons on the console. A three-dimensional drawing of the WAEF's engines appeared. He pressed a few more buttons and the entire interior design of the propulsion system rotated to face Mado.

"We call these blueprints," Yorlik said, "Will this suffice? I mean help in your work."

"Yes, these blueprints will suffice," Mado said, "Some of the making yours into mine..."

"Conversion?" Yorlik said, "Changing the engines from mine to yours."

"Yes, some of this conversion will need to take place outside the hull."

"You can use one of my space suits, and change the oxygen settings and pressurization to work for you. We can space walk, but I've already found an asteroid belt where we can land and do the repairs."

The conversion of the WAEF's engines took 188

days which was much longer than either Mado or Yorlik had imagined. They needed to weld and bend metal and invent parts in order for the transition to be complete and safe. Apart from the time-consuming engine construction, energy-field generator units were built from scratch, using Prevorian tech and placed around the WAEF's hull so a barrier of energy would encompass the entire ship. This insured the hull's integrity when the engine's were operating at full capacity, otherwise the ship would be torn apart. Mado's craft had no use for these units since its structural integrity was designed for his engines.

Mado was delighted to teach Yorlik his planet's tech and enjoyed Yorlik's wonderment and quick grasp of the science. They talked for hours about physics, astronomy, and engineering, and reached solutions by combining their knowledge base. Mado concluded that the Space Traveler's Code might be holding his people back from advancing scientifically. Maybe if he shared his experience with them, when he returned home, any wrath regarding his violation of the Code might be disavowed.

In-between their work on the engines, Mado noticed Yorlik losing sleep and spending long hours in the science lab over his need to produce a new batch of Rejuv Serum. Yorlik told Mado that if he had followed mission guidelines, then he would have headed back to Koda already, but he saw no logic in returning without a discovering a viable planet. He missed his family, but his success was the only way they'd live on. The converted engines would decrease the travel time to the viable planets by half, the estimated time of arrival was 15-to-20 years and another 25-to-30 returning to Koda, but if a new Serum wasn't created, then Yorlik's life would end before he returned home.

"I haven't known you for long," Yorlik said, "But our experiences together make me trust you. There's a chance that I won't be able to extend my lifespan. If you tell me that you'll travel to my planet and bring back the information that's integral for my species' survival, when I don't make it, then I trust you, otherwise I don't believe this trip is worth the effort."

"Trust," Mado said, standing up and placing each hand on each of Yorlik's shoulders and looking him in the eyes. "I will do this for you." He owed Yorlik his life so this was the least he could do.

The flight tests on the engines took around 20 days. The tests were not without danger and they came close to crushing the WAEF's hull a few times, but when the WAEF reached a sub-light velocity near the speed of Mado's ship, they celebrated. Mado broke out the Prevorian delicacies from his food stores, but Yorlik found them distasteful so he opened a beverage from Koda that elevated a person's mood called Malrap.

Yorlik pointed out that Mado tended to be too introspective for his own good. Mado's people had given him similar evaluations of his personality. After a few glasses of Malrap, Mado felt that personality quirk wash away. He strolled from the living chamber toward the control room, his balance deceiving him and saying sentences that mixed together Prevorian and Kodan. When he arrived at the new main control console he and Yorlik built to monitor the converted engines and the hull integrity, Mado whooped aloud in joy. He couldn't remember the last time he made that sound. Yorlik had followed him there, and laughed.

"I enjoy when you do that," Mado said, slurring words in two different languages

"Laughter?" Yorlik said, somehow interpreting Mado's babbling. "You said that your people don't do it, but the sound you just made is similar in sentiment. Does that mean you're happy?"

"Defining that word is difficult…" Mado said, collapsing on the deck. Yorlik lifted him and placed him in the pilot's seat. "I am ill."

"The Malrap might have something to do with how you're feeling."

"That might be the case, but I don't believe I've ever felt this way before, and it doesn't feel good."

"You may have overdone it." Yorlik bent down and hugged Mado who had never experienced this display of emotion before.

"Is this something else your people do when they're… happy?" Mado said.

"We do this also when we feel affection for another person," Yorlik said.

Mado stood as well as he could with Yorlik's help and wrapped his arms around him. "I am happy in that way, too."

On the day of launching the WAEF with the new engines, Mado re-checked Yorlik's analysis of the two planets in the sector. He ran the data through tests that Yorlik didn't know existed and he agreed that Yorlik's hunch was hopeful.

"I have good news," Mado said, entering the control room.

Yorlik had moved his pilot's chair, which had looked directly out the main window, to the left and had taken a similar chair from the rear of the room and secured it to the floor, to the right of his pilot's chair.

"I have something to show you, but you first," Yorlik said.

Mado told Yorlik about his confirmation of the planetary data and while he was explaining his analysis, he programmed the fastest route to the sector, which was clear of meteors and hostile societies, into the navigation system.

"That's excellent," Yorlik said, smiling, patting the seat of the newly installed chair.

"What did you want to show me?" Mado said.

"The chair," Yorlik said, patting the seat again.

"Yes," Mado said, "The chair. I see. You moved things around."

"This is a momentous event," Yorlik said.

"I don't know what that means."

"I'll tell you what the words mean later," Yorlik said, "This chair is yours."

"It's like the other one. It's nice"

"No, you don't understand. I'm not making myself clear. My fault. I get this way with surprises which means...I'll just be clearer," Yorlik said, "I put this chair here for you. From now on, this is not my ship, this is our ship. This is the ship that will get us to the sector, find the new planet for my people and get me home, but this ship, which is also your ship, will get you home. This is our ship now. Does that make sense?" Yorlik patted the seat and waved Mado toward him. "Sit, sit."

Mado was slightly confused, but he saw this as a sort of gift from Yorlik and he didn't want to insult his friend. He sat down, and Yorlik excitedly sat down next to him. Yorlik turned to Mado and laughed.

"What? I understand. We share When All Else Fails now," Mado said.

"No. I mean, yes," Yorlik said, shaking his head and laughing some more, "Buckle up."

Yorlik asked Mado to monitor the engines and the stress on the hull and began pressing buttons. The engines began to hum, and the ship moved forward under impulse power, maneuvering to Mado's programmed course.

"How does it look?" Yorlik said.

"All good."

Yorlik pointed to the four switches on the control console. Two each controlled the engines and the energy field units on each side of the ship. "Please do the honors," Yorlik said, "Sorry, I mean activate when ready."

Mado placed his hand over the switches, then peered over at Yorlik who was staring out the window lost in thought. Mado had been a Space Traveler for far longer than Yorlik and he understood what was going through Yorlik's mind. One could get lost pondering the vastness out there. The infinite nature of space was daunting, and the distances necessary to complete a journey made it so you'd never return the same person as the moment you left.

"Are you ready?" Mado said.

"Ready as I'll ever be," Yorlik said, "Just a long way to go, having some second thoughts, which is natural. Let's see what these engines can do."

Seventy-five later, Mado can still recall flipping the switches and the engines powering up, the ship speeding forward faster and faster, the momentum pinning him to his chair until the energy-field generator units stabilized the hull, normalizing gravity within the ship. Mado watched the stars rush towards him, then turned to Yorlik who was smiling at him.

Now, Mado stared at himself in the sleeping-chamber mirror. He had practiced smiling over the years, but could never quite get it right, although he enjoyed laughter which was like the whoop of his people. He worked out an awkward smile remembering the launch. The memories of Yorlik had begun to come back to him as the restoration of the WAEF edged closer to completion.

Mado returned to his lab where he stood on the balcony looking out at the WAEF with all the repair gear and cranes surrounding it. Soon all of this equipment would be removed to ready the ship for another launch. Mado needed to explain a revised plan to Yor. That could wait, but not for long. He had learned the concept of planning from Yorlik. On his planet, the Space Traveler was given mission guidelines: scout a planet, collect soil samples and specific data, then return home. If a Traveler saw a useful moon orbiting a planet, then he took note and reported back, but he didn't go and collect data on his own. Every detail of the mission was laid out and a Traveler would be penalized by loss of pay or grounded if they diverted or improvised from their planned path with the exception of emergencies. Planning was a skill for others.

Yorlik was the master planner. In the 51 years, Mado spent on the WAEF, he was schooled in the art of both short-term and long-term planning. Yorlik had the keen ability to assess a situation on the fly and figure out how to reach his goal with the greatest efficiency in time and effort and least expenditure of resources. Mado observed as Yorlik factored in the probable likelihood of each outcome along the path to achieve the desired conclusion. On a voyage of the magnitude they took together, in a ship barely equipped for such a journey, this skill was invaluable. On Koda, Mado's success in business and his work with Yor were based on these teachings.

Mado thought about Yorlik's journal. He walked over to his main viewer console and opened the scanned files.

ORN

Orn didn't have an office in the GSS building with fotos of the Leader or his compatriots in the Global Assembly. No space with a desk where he could be reached during office hours. When he required an area to work on his own, he simply appropriated an interrogation room, which seemed right, because this was where he got most of his job done anyway.

He now sat at a table in the middle of an interrogation room by himself. A viewer was open in front of him as he meditated on his next step in dealing with his Yor Vanderlord conundrum. He had already visited Ador Wint and was formulating a strategy for handling him and Vanderlord's other colleagues. His instinct was screaming at him that more expansive moves were required, including arresting and using tougher interrogation methods on the Vanderlord boy. Within those conditions, he was confident he would get the expected answers and enjoy it, but he was limited by the Leader's orders.

Orn was not deterred. He would just need to get more creative to obtain the necessary results. He closed his eyes and listened to the sound of the *whoosh*— installed here to create a sense of disorientation and agitation among those being interrogated. One of the more prominent med-tech corps was paid millions of units to come up with the concept. The sound had the opposite effect on Orn. He found it soothing.

Orn activated his viewer and called up as much surveillance footage as possible on Mar Jeps. He thought that maybe he could use her to get the Vanderlord boy to confess his plan. Orn watched her shopping and working at the med clinic. He watched her walking the streets and riding a rail car. There was no evidence from the vids that she was part of Yor's scheme.

One thing stood out for him. If she wasn't at work or going back and forth from the clinic, then she was with Rajer Jeps. They were affectionate towards one another more than half the time—holding hands, one arm around the other, kissing—and here Orn saw a weakness he might be able to exploit.

Orn had been watching Mar and Tetrick Vanderlord before he met them at Yorlik's landing site and after Yorlik's speech in the tube, the Leader who was President at the time, gave him the order to make Tetrick Vanderlord cease his treasonous actions by all means necessary. Orn was Tetrick's handler. He called for Tetrick's arrest and performed the interrogation and torture himself, then sent him home from the Detention Facility.

One day, he heard from his subordinates that Tetrick's partner was kicking up a fuss. She was making it difficult for them to arrest Tetrick and yelling at them when Tetrick returned home. Neighbors were taking note and complaining to their local Global Assembly reps. So Orn had Mar arrested and brought to him when Tetrick was out-of-town on one of his speaking tours.

Most Kodans when they enter an interrogation room are frightened at the prospect of a diminished future with far less freedom. If you're brought into one of these rooms, the assumption is you've been accused of breaking the law whether you've done it or not, and the system is determined to tag the crime on you.

When Mar entered the interrogation room, she reminded him she was no ordinary citizen. "You? Why have you dragged me here?" Mar said as the interrogation-room door closed behind her.

"Please sit," Orn said, standing at the far end of the room.

"I will not," Mar said, "I'm leaving. This is madness. You have no grounds for bringing me here." She attempted to open the door, but it was locked so she frantically pushed at it.

"Please stop shoving the door and sit down."

"I will not," Mar said, stomping across the room and stopping a few feet from Orn. "I have a toddler at home who needs my attention."

"That's unfortunate," Orn said, "But we're not savages. I've provided a child-care worker to watch over him and he's a smart youngster, ahead of every child in his age group. You should be proud."

If it were possible, Mar appeared angrier. Her nostrils flaring as she glared at Orn. "Haven't you done enough to disturb my family? Tetrick told me that you've been behind his arrests and torture. Why are you doing this to him? To us? If what he's saying isn't true, then how detrimental are his actions to the government?"

"You're a smart woman, Mar," Orn said, "You know why this is happening to you and your family. You know what needs to be done to stop it. You need to reason with your partner."

"Tetrick has a mind of his own."

"He is a stubborn one. Weaker men would have cracked by now."

"I've tried to reason with him, but his dedication goes far beyond reason."

"I'm well aware," Orn said, "All he needs to do is stop his anti-DOME campaign and that'll be the end of it."

"So why did you bring me here?" Mar said, raising her voice. "Did you bring me here to tell me how much you admire Tetrick's strength and your inability to torture it out of him?"

"Torture is such an offensive word. I like to think of it as physical persuasion."

"Whatever helps you sleep. Can I go now?"

"No, we need to talk," Orn said, "If you're not going to sit, then suit yourself." Orn refused to move from his position. He didn't want Mar to think he was intimidated by her so he stood his ground.

"I'm fine standing right here."

"All right," Orn said, "I've heard from my men that when they pick up or escort your husband home that you're hostile to them, alerting your neighbors to our activities."

"So? Are you afraid that the world will know what you're doing?"

"I prefer a little more discretion surrounding my work."

"Your work. You wouldn't want the population to know you're suppressing the will of the masses."

Orn took two steps toward Mar. If he took one more, then they'd be nose to nose. "Those are the kinds of words that will get you locked up. I can appreciate your mothering instinct and protecting your mate, but be careful of crossing the line. You don't want me becoming your active enemy. You won't like the consequences at all," Orn said, "I brought you here to tell you that you need to back off. Don't make a scene with my men otherwise your son might become an orphan and a smart one like him would be valuable to the Global Assembly's cause. Do I make myself perfectly clear?"

Mar nodded her head. Orn could tell that he was getting through to her. Her face was transitioning from anger to a more sober emotional state. If he pushed her any further, he could make her cry.

"One more thing," Orn said, crossing his arms over his chest. Mar looked at his hands. Rather than horror on her face, he saw clinical wonderment. As a med practitioner, she was fully aware of the violence necessary to cause his scars. "Your boy cannot know what's happening to his father."

"I would never. He's too young."

"You can't tell him ever. Do I make myself clear?" Orn said, "Decades down the road, I don't want to bring your son to this room, because he had a hatred of the Global Assembly planted at a young age which has festered into treason."

"Other people might tell him."

"Yes and I will attempt to silence those people too, but I'm talking to you now. You will stop making a scene in front of your neighbors and you will never talk to your son about your husband's visits here. If you break your word, on either of those two points, you will be back here for an extended stay, and I will send your son off to an Allegiance Camp to set his mind straight, then government-run boarding school."

Mar was stunned by Orn's threats. He could see it in her eyes. She left the interrogation room visibly shaken.

Over the years, she kept her word. Orn collected informants inside the University and he was told it was Tetrick's colleagues who filled Yor with stories of his father's treatment. Orn had dealt with some of these academics, pulling them from their positions and making certain that they were given unfavorable picks for dome residency, but the damage was done. He was later told by an informant that Yor was enraged when he discovered that his mother had been hiding the truth from him. Mar's maternal instinct was strong. She gave herself to her family and they loved her back with the same ferocity.

Orn continued to watch the compiled Mar Jeps' vids and he began focusing on the vids of her with Rajer and an idea dawned on him. He pulled out his comm and made a call. "Yes, it's me. I have an assignment for you. I'll meet you in your office at the beginning of the next work day and tell you about it."

A message popped up on his viewer, 'You have a rail car to catch.'

Orn closed his viewer satisfied he might get to the bottom of Yor Vanderlord's scheme after all.

YOR

Yor was riding the rail car to the Prevor Industries Complex stop. The car was more than half-full of Global Assembly workers, coming off their shifts at the Plaza, and here and there sat students staring into their digi-tabs, who had jumped onboard at the University stop like Yor.

The rail car lines were upgraded—tracks, cars—before the dome was finished, and they became the only way to commute across the city. That's when the vidcams appeared everywhere. Yor never felt the vidcams presence before like he did now. His experience the night before had torn away the veil of familiarity. He saw them everywhere he turned.

The car pulled into a station. The doors opened and people got on and people got off, then Yor felt a painful grab at his shoulder. He looked up to see the man from the interrogation room. The doors closed and the car sped forward.

"Move over," the man said.

"I could say no," Yor said.

The man stood unmoving and silent, glaring at him. Yor didn't want to make a scene so he slid over on the bench seat, placing his satchel in his lap.

"Smart boy," the man said, then sat next to Yor, crowding him even though there was plenty of room for the two of them to sit comfortably. Yor thought about saying something about it, but he didn't want to acknowledge this intimidation tactic. So they sat in silence as the car stopped once and approached another stop. Yor was becoming petrified by the discomfort. He thought if he stayed quiet and didn't make eye contact, the man would never know, but when the car stopped again and pulled away from the station, Yor couldn't control himself.

"There's plenty of room on the bench," Yor said, looking straightforward.

The man pressed against Yor harder, squashing him into the car wall until it was difficult to breath. None of the other passengers noticed.

"What are you doing?" Yor said.

"My job," the man said and let up pressure.

"Your job?"

"Yes, my job."

"Is that what you were doing with my step-father and colleague?"

"Doing what I need to do since you won't tell me the truth."

"The truth. That's funny coming from somebody like you."

"You're acting pretty brazen. Your fear is bringing you courage. Maybe you're smarter than I thought," the man said, poking Yor with his elbow.

Yor grunted in pain.

"Just so you know, going to the library was stupid," the

man said, "You just alerted us to your little scheme, and that journal is worthless so your plans have been turned upside down for nothing."

"I'm a historian doing research for the WAEF Breeze Celebration so that journal is invaluable to me, and this harassment of my friends and family is unjustified."

"You're hiding something," the man said, "I don't believe you."

"That's too bad," Yor said, turning to the man who was still glaring at him. When their eyes met, Yor immediately looked away, more frightened than before.

The rail car slowed into a station. "That's too bad for you and the people who know you. Looks like we're going to see lots more of one another," the man said, standing as the rail car came to a halt. The doors opened and he strode out of the car.

Yor let out a long sigh as if he'd been holding his breath and clutched at the satchel in his lap. His palms were sweating. It was clear this man wouldn't stop until he received answers that satisfied him and he would do anything necessary to acquire them. Again, he questioned his actions in acquiring the journal pages.

Yor was aware Yorlik the Great's 400-page handwritten journal was a SEEDER-mission relic which possessed more personal than scientific value. Each mission had one for posterity, an expression of the mission commander's thoughts. The detailed daily log containing the scientific information was stored in the spaceship's data banks.

With the erasure of the data from his mission, Yorlik

offered his journal to the Global Assembly with the understanding that it would reside in the Royal Library in perpetuity and the Global Assembly agreed. The library had once been staffed and open to the general public for any citizen who desired to read valued and rare books from Koda's past, but at the time of Yorlik's donation, sections of the library were converted to permission-only entry and hi-tech security. The SEEDER Journal section was only open to those with top-level clearances. These coincidental changes at the time of the donation were suspicious. Like other academics and skeptics of the government, Yor speculated his great-grandfather told the Global Assembly the journal contained sensitive information regarding his journey, like the discovery of a habitable world, so they locked it up tight.

If not, why impose such impenetrable security? The Global Assembly was reluctant to let Yor near the journal, too. Mado petitioned until he obtained Yor's entrance with a time limit attached. This piqued Yor's curiosity and contributed to him impetuously entering the library earlier than planned. After reading the journal, Yor understood they placed a time limit on him, because the later pages contained his great-grandfather's disgust over the government's handling of the crisis, and these words would have been considered seditious.

So the library sojourn was a success in one regard. Yor had procured his great-grandfather's thoughts for the WAEF Breeze Celebration speech. The Great man was still one of the most popular figures in Kodan history, and Yor was hopeful his great-grandfather's views on the bungling of the crisis might encourage the populace to fight for their survival.

Yor appreciated how his great-grandfather could inspire people. His great-grandfather had propelled him on his life's path, but there was another motivation rooted in Yor's actions. He sought to avenge his father's death by exposing the domes as a sham and inflicting a certain degree of payback for his father's treatment at the government's hands. His mother would kid that the Vanderlords were genetically predisposed towards family loyalty so they'd go to greater lengths than others to uphold their family honor. Yor's grandfather died attempting to validate his father's legacy. Yor's father worked himself to exhaustion and endured the government's wrath so his father's death wouldn't be in vain. *Mother is right,* Yor thought, *Here I am doing the same because I feel some need to uphold my family's honor.*

One of Yor's last meaningful interactions with his father, occurred on a visit to the hangar where the WAEF was stored. Since his great-grandfather's funeral, which was four years prior, Yor had not returned there. The pavement of the driveway leading from the main road to the hangar was immaculately clean, and the hangar appeared to have a new roof. His father stopped their vehicle by the hangar door and turned off the power. He kept the air-cooling device running, and stared out at the structure. Yor did not say a word. During the drive from their Capitol City home to the hangar, his father talked incessantly about his frustration with his cause. In this silence, Yor cherished being together as purely father and son.

His father was lost in thought. He was somewhere else. Maybe he was dreaming of the past with his grandfather. Every time his father spoke of the Great man, Yor heard an abundance of admiration and love. "Here was a man who stood for his convictions," his father would say, "Here was a man who stood for something greater than himself, giving up his family to save his planet." In a way, Yor saw his father in this statement. *He was much the same,* Yor thought, *Except he gave up his health.*

When Yor was a boy, his father was a tall broad-shouldered man with boundless energy and limitless strength. One time, Yor watched as his father readied to swim a man-made lake: He took off his pants with his bathing suit underneath and removed his shirt revealing his barrel chest. "I'll be back in a flash," his father said, diving like an arrow into the water, shooting across the lake with powerful strokes and kicks. He quickly became a speck in the distance and Yor lost sight of him. Then a few moments later, Yor saw him heading back, and he arrived on shore beside Yor hardly winded. Boys looked up to their fathers as heroes, but Yor swore his father was larger-than-life.

Before they left for this trip to the hangar, Yor walked into his parent's bedroom and his mother was helping his father put on his shirt, which he obviously couldn't do himself. His torso was black and blue and gaunt with his ribs prominently showing through his skin. His father turned away when he spotted Yor, and his mother told him to leave the room. On the drive here, Yor saw the remnants of the man who swam across the lake. Life had been drained from him. He was stoop-shouldered. His movements were measured, slow and careful. His face was gaunt with dark circles under his eyes as if he never slept, and he spoke in a strained tone like he was in pain all the time. His father was middle-aged, but he had become a broken old man.

"So," Yor said in order to get his father's attention, "I love spending time with you, but you never told me why we drove all the way out here."

A smile spread across his father's face and he turned toward Yor. "Sorry. I kind of got lost thinking about the old man and how his return to Koda gave my life meaning. Not that meeting your mother and your birth didn't do the same. You know what I mean. What I'm trying to say is…"

"Father," Yor said, patting his father on the knee. "No need to explain. You've told me before and I understand exactly what you mean. You named me after great-grandfather, didn't you?" Yor would have hugged him, but the vehicle was a cramped two-seater and it was difficult to turn and embrace so he gave him a playful shove.

His father laughed. Yor hadn't seen that in awhile. When his father was home these days, he fought with his mother or he was dour about the anti-DOME movement or overly concerned about Yor's education, lecturing him on the importance of applying his knowledge toward Koda's future.

His father continued laughing until it poured out uncontrollably and he attempted to say something through the laughter, but couldn't make himself clear. The joke wasn't that funny, and Yor was slightly disturbed by his father's display, but he didn't say anything. When the laughing subsided, he said, "Thanks, son. I needed that. Let's go."

When they opened the vehicle's doors, the outside heat hit Yor like he'd suddenly opened an oven. The air quality was terrible too, reeking like rotten tires and producing a cough every five or six breaths.

Although the hangar door appeared the same, the personnel door mounted in its center was different. The wooden door with key locks from the day of the Great man's funeral had been replaced by an impenetrable-looking sliding metal door. The locking system was hi-tech with DNA scan and password required for entry. Below the number pad read 'Prevor Industries.' His father typed in a series of numbers, then placed his hand on the scanner. The sound of heavy-duty tumblers activating and locks opening followed.

"That was easy," Yor said, "I thought you'd need to pull out a piece of paper with a complex password."

"No, it's simple. The password is the date of your birth," his father said, pushing open the door. "I can't forget that, can I?"

They entered the hangar and lights mounted far above

them in the rafters clicked on one by one. The WAEF towered over them. No tarp this time. Yor heard the purring of a hi-tech climate-control system. Large boxes marked 'Prevor Industries' were stacked three high around the ship.

"I'm always amazed at seeing her. She's a beauty," his father said.

"Don't let mother hear you say that."

"I don't think she has anything to worry about," his father said in a serious tone, completely missing the joke, "Follow me."

They climbed the ramp into the ship and ended up in the control room. Everything appeared the same as the day of his great-grandfather's funeral with the lights from the hangar illuminating the room.

His father said, "I have important things to tell you. Sit down." He flipped a switch on the main control console and the overhead lights came on, then he hit a release at the bottom of the pilot's chair facing toward the window and spun it around, presenting it to Yor with a flourish of his arm. "Sit, please."

"Who got the lights up and running?" Yor said, "Has someone been repairing her?"

"Mado Prevor has been tinkering around in here."

"Is that a good idea?" Yor said, sitting down, facing his father.

"If anyone can figure his way around here, Mado can."

"What are his intentions? He's in bed with the government, isn't he?"

"Mado only has the best of intentions," his father said,

"And that's part of what I want to talk to you about."

Yor began spinning around in the chair and tinkering with the dead switches on the main control console.

"Mado is a good friend of the family. You know that. You've been asking to meet with him forever and when it comes to tech, Mado is beyond anybody on Koda. Now, please stop with the damn switches and listen to me!" His father spun Yor around to face him, leaned over him and said in a stern tone, "Please. I need you to be serious. This is important. Are you listening to me?"

"Yes," Yor said, "Sorry. You have my undivided attention."

Then his father started pacing about the control room, mumbling to himself, and finally turned toward Yor. "I'm sorry I jumped down your throat. I know that's uncalled for," his father said, "I'm going to need you to grow up faster than your peers. I know that's already happening with your schooling, and your mother and I are proud of you. The bottom line is I don't have much longer to live."

"What? Why?" Yor said in shock as if he'd been punched in the nose. His body went cold.

"Please," his father said, "I know this is sudden, but this is what I've been told by my doctors and I can feel it in my bones."

Yor began sobbing, tears streaming from his eyes. He wiped the tears away with his shirt sleeve.

"I know. I know," his father said, "There is no easier way to say it." He removed a handkerchief from his back pocket and handed it to Yor. "You're a smart young man. I've seen the looks you've been giving me. You knew something was wrong."

"Can't anything be done?" Yor said.

"No, my organs are failing. Your mother and I thought it best that we wait until the specialists were positive about the results before we said anything to you, and for the record she wasn't pleased about me dragging you out here. I wanted to tell you here because there's more to say and I'm positive this place isn't bugged by the government. Mado has seen to it."

"So you're still convinced the government is listening in all the time?" Yor said, wiping away the tears.

"I know it for a fact!" his father said, snapping at Yor again. "From this day forward don't you ever forget it. This is no laughing matter."

"I'm not laughing. But how do you know?"

"You'll have to believe me. I have no evidence to present, but I've heard the recordings first hand. Do you believe me?"

"Yes. I believe you."

"Good. Now, I've set up a meeting between you and Mado Prevor about an internship. That'll happen in a few days. You haven't seen him since you were a child and you probably don't remember him. I know on the surface this appears outside of your interest in the SEEDER program, but he is the utmost expert on the tech inside this ship, and having the most famed and impactful scientist and entrepreneur on the planet as a reference won't hurt when you start applying for higher levels of study and University employment."

"That's fantastic news," Yor said, "I can finally talk to him about great-grandfather, and any student on Koda would be envious. I'm not turning it down, but how does Mado know so much about the WAEF?"

"He learned a great deal in his friendship with your great-grandfather," his father said, pacing in front of Yor as if he was working out these ideas as he went along.

"Well, learning about the tech on this ship can only be helpful when I get to writing about great-grandfather."

"The work with him will be hands on," his father said, "And I want to stress that this ship is your legacy. Your great-grandfather's achievements might be the best hope for the survival of our people. More than one person will need to know how a ship like this works."

"I'm not sure what you're getting at."

His father stopped pacing and took three long strides toward Yor, putting himself directly in front of him, then bent over and was face-to-face with him. "That's because I haven't gotten there yet," his father said, "I haven't said this out loud in such a long time even thinking about saying it seems unreal." His father threw up his hands and began pacing again. "This is information only a few people on Koda know. Well, the government knows, but your mother, myself, and Mado Prevor are the only people alive who know. Soon, it will be just the two of them…and you, and you are to tell nobody else, it's too dangerous."

His father began pacing in circles, throwing his arms around as he spoke, "The government doesn't want anybody to know and they will not allow the public to be aware, and I fear for you having this burden. You can't tell anybody, it's too dangerous, but in fact it's wondrous and marvelous and you need to keep it secret until the time is absolutely right or bad things will befall you. Do you understand?" He stepped toward Yor, stopping in front of him again, his eyes shifting back and forth in their sockets.

"I understand you're serious," Yor said, "But I still don't have a clue what you're talking about." His father stood there, frozen in position. Tears welled up in his eyes and he covered them with both his hands as the tears streamed down his cheeks. Yor never saw his father act this way. He'd seen him sad, but never crying so uncontrollably, and he'd seen him speak passionately, but never this manically. Yor was becoming scared.

Then suddenly his father turned and marched out of the control room. The sensors on all the doors throughout the ship were disabled so Yor could hear his father's footsteps going deep into the heart of the ship, fading until he could hear them no more.

Yor spun back around to the main control console, and looked out the window. He craned his neck. His father wasn't on the hangar floor and the personnel door was shut. There was no sign of his father.

Then Yor heard footsteps moving towards the control room and turned around. His father entered the room with his eyes puffy from crying.

"I apologize," his father said, "With the doctor's news, I'm not myself lately. Just feeling overwhelmed. I was losing it and needed to step away. I'm sorry."

"It's understandable, father. No need to apologize," Yor said, "What did you need to tell me?"

"I just want to make it clear. I'm telling you this now, because I'm positive the government isn't listening in. You cannot tell anybody. Your mother cannot know you're aware of this fact and you cannot tell Mado. Neither of them are aware I'm telling you, and your mother would be furious. You'll know when the time is right to reveal what you know. That may be years from now, but I'm pretty sure when the time comes it'll be clear. I'm telling you now because…" his father's face clenched, forcing himself not to cry again. "I want to share it with you myself, because I don't know when I'll get the chance in the future."

That was when Yor was told that his great-grandfather had found a habitable world. For years, he only half believed his father, but now with everything happening, he presumed anything was possible and it was time to tell Mado.

Yor exited the rail car at the station by the Prevor Industries Complex and walked down the street lined with restaurants serving food and drink from around the globe. The best minds on Koda were employed by Mado and this was the place for them to eat on their breaks. Yor recognized a few of the technicians seated outside eating and waved to them. When Yor reached the gates of the Complex, the guard recognized him, waving him through and he headed straight for Mado's building where the DNA-scanner locks on the outer and lab door opened to him.

Mado was skimming through Yorlik's journal on the viewing screen and flicked it off as Yor entered the room. Mado had placed his prosthetic back on.

"Just me," Yor said.

"Yes, I heard footsteps on the landing outside. I see that now," Mado said, "How are you?"

"I'm tired and I know we've got work to do," Yor said, sitting in Mado's hi-tech work-table chair, which literally embraced your body. Only a person of Mado's means could afford such a luxury. "Been a long day, and coming over here that man confronted me in the rail car."

"I'm glad you're all right," Mado said, "You should alert your University colleagues about him."

"He's already visited Ador, but I need to tell Insol and Mel. I've got something to tell you though."

Then Yor told Mado the story of his father driving him to the WAEF and telling him about Yorlik's discovery. "I never believed my father. His state of mind was confused and scattered at the time. I spent years seeking the truth in my research, and I assumed if my father's story was true, then I'd dig it up someday, maybe in the journal. That's another reason why I wanted to see the journal so badly. Now, I've screwed things up," Yor said, "I didn't want to disrespect my father's trust in me by telling you or my mother before it was necessary. He told me I would know the time to tell you and with the events of the past 29 hours, this seems like the right time."

"Your father never mentioned he told you, but I'm not surprised. Your great-grandfather always preached compartmentalization of the plan so nobody would know what they needed to know until the time was right."

"What do you know?" Yor said.

"I know quite a bit, because I was there, but I'd like to tell you how we got there first."

MADO

Before telling this tale, one thing you need to understand. Your great-grandfather Yorlik possessed a love-hate relationship with being named Yorlik the Great. Before he left Koda, he was respectful and fond of the commendation, because there was a connection to the Global Monarchy. Upon his return to Koda, he was surprised people still used that title since the ruling royalty were relics of the distant past. Since it was considered the planet's most prestigious honor, he understood it would seem petty to ask people to stop calling him Yorlik the Great, but he hated the moniker for the reason he received it.

As you know, the SEEDER program was developed when Koda's climatologists predicted a catastrophic environmental crisis within a hundred years. The Royal Parliament granted funds to Koda's best scientists to devise applicable concepts for deep-space travel like the design and propulsion of the ship, the navigation system, and food replication. After years of exhaustive research into extending deep-space missions up to 60 years, Yorlik and his business partner Klim Camtur at V-C Industries discovered the formula for the Rejuv Serum which halted aging and maintained an individual's virility upon injection.

When the news of the breakthrough leaked out, the popular outcry for commercial distribution caused the pharmaceutical industry to lobby the Monarchy for its immediate release to the public. With Parliament members in financial cahoots with the Serum's potential manufacturers, the government legislated the licensing of the Serum for distribution to the global population, decreeing that the people's taxes paid for the Serum so it should be available to everyone on Koda. Klim Camtur was elated at the prospective royalties earned from the licensing of the Serum and the riches that would come his way.

Yorlik was horrified. He sued the government to stop distribution. He used his personal finances and tried the case himself. He argued that allowing the entire Kodan population with their penchant for youth, access to the Serum, would quadruple the planet's population in 50 years, further disrupting the delicate balance between humanoids and the Kodan eco-system—signing the death warrant for the planet and its people. In his closing arguments, he stated the universe was larger than anyone could imagine yet the probability of complex life forms occurring was the rarest of circumstances. Somehow on Koda all the elements aligned to gather a spark and now these intelligent beings existed, making it the duty of those individuals in authority to be the stewards of what some might call a miracle, and halt the destruction.

Yorlik lost the case and attempted to direct V-C Industries' profits into SEEDER research for the design of spaceships, but Klim thought the program was folly. Other business associates convinced Klim that domes over metropolitan areas was the way to stem the human cost of the crisis. Klim saw the licensing of population-control drugs for the DOME project as a more profitable opportunity for the company. Their split over the direction of V-C Industries dissolved their partnership.

Yorlik threw himself into the idea of deep-space travel. His guilt for creating the Serum ate at him and drove him. He was a pilot already, but emerged as one of the top test pilots of high-speed aircraft. He flew the crafts he designed rather than risking any other lives. He broke airspeed records. He launched outside the planet's atmosphere traveling further and returning in faster and faster record-breaking times. He traveled with crews to build outposts on a nearby moon so research could occur in space. He designed the propulsion system for the SEEDER ships, utilizing a chemical reaction that generated at least one-hundred years of power without need for renewal, and producing never before seen rates of acceleration. He worked himself to the bone innovating at a pace that placed the program far ahead of the timeline for its first long-range launch.

In a speech hours before the first lift off, her Royal Highness awarded Yorlik the highest medal of honor on Koda and dubbed him Yorlik the Great for his service to the planet. Few had ever achieved this honor for anything outside of military service. Yorlik understood he was receiving this distinction for his progress on the SEEDER program, but he was only working so relentlessly to atone for his sin in producing the Serum. For him, this award was a badge of shame. His absolution would only come with the success of the program.

Yet the SEEDER missions departed the planet and returned in failure one after the other. Yorlik wasn't deterred. He built faster ships to travel further into space, but no matter how far the ships traveled, the few prospective planets never met the standards required for livability.

Thirty-five years after the Serum was brought onto the commercial market, Yorlik's predictions were coming true. Kodans decided that they could extend their youth with the Serum, halting their aging at 25-to-40 years old and having more than one family or breeding larger families and those offspring would do the same. Simply more people were living longer. The planet's population increased at an exponential rate, draining the planet's vital resources, dumping more toxins into the environment and accelerating the predicted timeline for the crisis.

Panic and calls for accountability fell on the Global Monarchy which was dissolved in a trumped up scandal of exorbitant runaway spending. A globally-elected Assembly with a President was created to hasten constructive change. Population control was put in place. The Rejuv Serum was made illegal and removed from the market. The SEEDER program was cancelled, and all future funds and resources would go toward the DOME project.

That's when Yorlik petitioned the planet through viewing-channel appearances for one more SEEDER launch. He used his fame as Yorlik the Great, the persona he hated, to rally Koda's population behind the launch. This time, he would go into space and nobody else. The populace supported Yorlik and the fact that the Assembly members and the President desired re-election made the launch a reality. Also, lobbyists and the wealthy were hoping for a high rate of return on their DOME project investments and removing Yorlik from the debate, the most popular voice of dissent on the domes, was preferable.

Koda's love for Yorlik the Great, this man of incredible talents whose only focus was the survival of his people, passed into legend with the SEEDER program's final launch. On telescopes across the planet, the Kodan population observed the When All Else Fails shooting into the infinite expanse with a few planets as initial goals.

I understand these historical moments are in *Power Over the Future*, but your great-grandfather told me his feelings on these events and I can't help but tell you my impressions, too. When I met him, Yorlik was 46 years into his journey. He ran out of Rejuv Serum, but he refused to return home. None of the other SEEDER missions had lasted that long, and he had traveled beyond where anyone on Koda had gone before. He could have returned home and been hailed a hero even if the mission was a failure, but his sense of responsibility for the plague he unwittingly unleashed on his planet haunted him every moment of his voyage. He vowed to himself that he'd never return until he discovered a viable planet.

I admired him. He was willing to acknowledge his part in the crisis and take it upon himself to find a solution that would help future generations move beyond their own shortcomings and flourish. So with the new propulsion system and an estimated time of 15-to-20 years to the sector with the viable planets, we settled in for the long haul.

Yorlik started every day viewing vids of Koda's scenic vistas, the vids of his family before he left and those transmitted from his wife and children. The last ones received from his family were seven years old by the time of our first meeting. His partner told him that the Global Assembly was officially designating Yorlik as lost so they could permanently shut down the program offices. His partner pleaded with Yorlik to send a transmission to help promote his mission, but by the time his message reached Koda, the SEEDER program would have been history and there would be no reviving it. By watching the vids of his children playing on the estate—swimming, running, jumping into his arms—and the ones of them growing into adulthood, he was reminded why he was traveling so far from home and how he might be the last hope for Koda. In this way, he regained his purpose for the start of a new day.

We had a daily regimen of everyday tasks like maintenance and checking the ship's systems. Yorlik spent a great deal of each day on an upgraded hyper-telescope scanning for closer candidates to replace Koda, and while he was at it, he made sure our path was clear of any dangerous obstacles—black holes, large and miniature meteors—that might damage the hull, which were not on the charts. He found nothing useful in a planetary way, but he did spot plenty of obstacles so we'd recalibrate for the most efficient flight path to our destination. In our travels, there were many times that we changed course to avoid damage, altering our arrival time in the viable planet's sector by days or a year.

Along with time, doubt weighed heavily on Yorlik. He would say, "What if we go all that way and come up short of the goal? What then?" I heard that lament more times than I cared to count in the years heading toward the sector. I felt for Yorlik's agony. I could never truly understand it, but I could clearly see his pain as time dripped away. Luckily there was more than enough daily chores on the ship to take his mind off this quandary.

When Yorlik finished his systems check and hyper-telescope scanning, he ate a meal, then headed down to hydroponics. As you know, the food replicator can manufacture self-replicating spores into meals filled with nutrients from the planetary menu. In deference to my dietary needs, Yorlik programmed the replicator to make Prevorian delicacies with my advice and sketches. In hydroponics, Yorlik grew fresh spices and vegetables from the seed bank he'd compiled before lift off. All the menu items got tiresome and the hydroponics plants helped add flavor, and even that got old after a year or five due to the finite plants and cooking combinations. We both forgot how eating could be pleasurable and ate out of necessity.

That being said, Yorlik took great pleasure and peace of mind in making sure the hydroponics bay perpetuated itself. He had gone without it for many years when the original stock of soil enrichment processor was exhausted but he found an ultra-rich soil on the lava planet that lasted years longer than expected.

When I was done with my share of the systems check, I worked on the short-distance escape pod for my eventual return to Prevor. I catalogued whatever I scavenged from my craft, then built the usable parts into what I conceived for the pod. The basic focus was building this pod with as many parts and materials from my defunct craft as possible, even producing rivets from my craft's scrap metal to hold the pod together. Upon my landing back on Prevor, an intense investigation would commence on whether I violated the Space Travelers Code. Questions would be asked. I would need to come up with believable answers. The craft would be probed for alien parts, down to the bolts. Before Yorlik rescued me, I took this into consideration and was mindful that my craft might be permanently grounded in the lava so I stripped away parts of the hull that were damaged, then transferred those materials onto the WAEF.

While I labored on the pod construction, Yorlik would finish his hydroponics chores, then exercise and set about the difficult task of formulating a replacement for the Rejuv Serum. This was an immense problem. How could he create an entirely new serum without the key ingredients from the original serum and only the elements onboard? An impossible task.

Yorlik explained to me how the original Rejuv Serum could be applied three times, then the serum lost its ability to work at all. In basic terms, the Serum rejuvenated Actopurlieus which are repetitive nucleotide sequences at the end of chromosomes that kept a cell vital. The Serum wasn't recommended for people until they reached 45 years old when cells start running out of Actopurlieus and aging begins. The average person who applied the Serum could live upwards of 135 years: 60 more years due to the serum—3 injections every 20 years—starting at 45 year old, then living possibly another 30 years of real aging.

Yorlik had discovered the Rejuv Serum at 28 years old and he was focused on the SEEDER program by 30 years of age. When Yorlik left Koda at 70 years with Serum, he had already injected himself two times and brought his last dose with him. Now he was off-planet at 116 years old with Serum, and he had been off the effects of Serum for 11 years. His body's age was 56 years old and he could not allow himself to get physically older. He was in fantastic condition. Part of his daily routine was running 32,000 meters on a treadmill and lifting weights in-between hydroponics and locking himself in the science lab to formulate a new Serum

There was one thing that baffled him. When the Serum was gone and he entered true aging, he began taking cell samples of himself, and analyzing them. In his observation of those samples, he was dumbfounded by the results. He was off the serum for 11 years and supposedly his body was 56 years old so why did he have the cells of a 49-year-old Kodan? That became the starting point for his research.

When he was alone on the WAEF, the daily routine to maintain the ship was a full day of work for one man which didn't leave much time per day to conceive and create a new Rejuv Serum so I took up many of his chores. For instance, the rebuilt engine's were based on Prevorian tech so it was easier for me to perform the daily checkup and maintenance. This freed up Yorlik's time, but his challenge was still monumental. We put our brains together on the analysis of the cells which weren't all that different from my chromosomal makeup.

One of the big differences in our physiologies was my necessity for hibernation. On the one hand, Yorlik hated it. He became accustomed to my companionship after years by himself and we enjoyed each others company. Yorlik was concerned about his state of mind without me being around and how to proceed if the engines developed a problem that he couldn't resolve. I told him to wake me if he needed me.

Of course, while I was in hibernation, Yorlik's research slowed, but he arrived at a solution to everything. That's why I considered him Yorlik the Great. The man had the knack to find an answer to the most difficult problems by coming at them from a creative angle. You might call him a singular mind. That is why, in my estimation, he attained greatness.

That brings us to two years into our journey. I awakened from hibernation with Yorlik standing over me. I gasped and caught myself from falling off the sleeping-chamber bed.

Yorlik put both hands on my shoulders. I immediately calmed.

I said, "Did you awaken me?" I laid still and gathered my breathing to a normal rate as I'd do if I had normally awakened from hibernation.

"I apologize. I happened to be here when I heard your breathing radically change," Yorlik said, "I figured you were awakening or dying on me so I should be ready for any contingency." He held up a med kit.

I worked out a smile for him which I'd been practicing.

"That's a better one," Yorlik said, "And right out of hibernation, too. When you're vertical come into the lab. I want to show you something fascinating."

After I shook off hibernation, regaining circulation in my limbs, eating and hydrating, I visited Yorlik in the lab. "Any progress?"

"I haven't solved the formula to a new Rejuv Serum yet. I reached a conclusion that may explain the reason why my cells are not aging at a normal rate," Yorlik said, "I'm currently 50 years in my cellular age. I should be 57, going on 58. After approaching the quandary from many angles, I thought it might be the highly oxygenated environment of the ship which we bumped up to accommodate your needs, but that was only recently and not significant. We also hadn't seen this twist in the cellular aging in other SEEDER missions either."

"You've been in space the longest though."

"True, but that wouldn't create these results, so I decided to run a full check on the oxygenation system," Yorlik said, "I found that all the oxygen filters required cleaning. A fine residue coated them. If I hit the side of a filter on one of the lab tables, the residue would spill on the floor. Took me eight days of maintenance work, but I cleaned all of the ship's filters. I wondered if the residue had impaired the settings or the generators. I checked the oxygen-levels throughout the ship with a mobile detector and the settings were where I had placed them. I looked over the oxygen generators for any malfunction and they were still running at top-rated efficiency. With those results, I concluded that the residue wasn't affecting the amount of oxygen released into the ship." Yorlik opened a lab cabinet and there were ten jars the size of a man's head full of a brown substance. He removed the lid from one. I ran my hand through a fine granular silt. "From my initial analysis, this is non-toxic."

"What is it?"

"That's the question," Yorlik said, "So of course I analyzed the substance and arrived at a conclusion. This is dirt. We're in deep space. Where did it come from?"

"The lava planet?"

"Correct," Yorlik said, "The dirt must've made its way into the filters from hydroponics since I'm using the soil from that planet there in conjunction with heat, moisture and fans. I've grown plants down there for 40 years and I've never seen this filter problem. Before I used the lava-planet dirt, I studied and compared it to the enriched Kodan soil and the substances composing both were close to identical which I thought almost miraculous, because it would allow me to keep growing my own plants utilizing the seeds from Koda. I thought it too good to be true, but I'm a scientist and trusted my analysis. Maybe when the lava dirt became moist and heated by the lamps, then a microscopic top layer formed and this silt made its way into the filters via the fans. I hardly ever check the filters unless the oxygen level drops and I monitor it daily but this silt is porous enough to make no change there, and it accumulated over the past two years without me noticing."

"That's intriguing," I said, "But what does that have to do with the slowing of your aging or if I might interpret where you're headed with this story, are you saying the answer is this dirt?"

"After my leg healed enough for me to hobble around and we set up our camp together, I produced my analysis of the soil, then filled a dozen barrels with it, placed the barrels in storage and planted a new crop with the soil," Yorlik said.

"I remember. My back is still aching from helping you."

"A smile and now a joke. Hibernation suits you," Yorlik said, "The next cell sample was from the day I lifted off and said goodbye to you. That sample was no different than the previous ones. But the sample from when I turned around and headed back to the lava planet to rescue you demonstrated not only a slowing of the aging process, but remarkably the aging process had reversed itself. As you know the Rejuv Serum arrests the aging process. We never figured how to reverse the aging process, but here were the results. I'm not sure how it happened, but from that day forward, there was a reversal of cell degradation so that's why I'm 50 now instead of 57 or 58."

"So you're saying that we've got a lead, but we've got our work cut out for us."

"And it appears we've got time on our side or at least my side."

"Or at least hope," I said.

So the research moved forward as we made progress toward the sector where the viable planets orbited. Yorlik approached the problem by making a thorough examination of the soil. I decided to see how my metabolism and hibernation might be applied to slowing or stopping the aging process in Yorlik's species. Other than that, the routine of our existence on the WAEF centered around research time. Yorlik began talking about how the research was hopeless as day upon day passed with no results. He was anxious and worried. He began sleeping more and I began picking up his chores. Yorlik eventually self-diagnosed himself with depression. I didn't have a solution for this malady, because my people don't experience such a thing.

When enough time passed, I required hibernation and when I emerged, Yorlik was in a better mood, and seemed to have overcome his depression, but his state of mind concerned me. He explained that he was "giddy" because he had found a way around his dark mood. I saw a kind of hysteria in his happiness, but he told me that it was normal among his people and he wanted to show me what he'd been building.

The hallway leading up to the storage compartments was lined with shelves three high to the ceiling. Yorlik had built them when I was in hibernation. They contained bins filled with the WAEF's spare parts and the engine components that we removed to install my craft's propulsion onto the ship. I assumed the larger parts were in other part's of the ship.

"Solid craftsmanship," I said, pointing at the shelves, "Is this what you brought me down here to show me? Did this chore make you happy again?"

Yorlik laughed and slapped my shoulder. "No, and once again hibernation brings the joker out of you."

My statement and question had been serious. "So what was it you wanted to show me?"

"You enter first," Yorlik said, standing outside a compartment, "I want to see your reaction."

So I entered the room and the lights turned on, and in the far right-hand corner of the square room was a work station with plans pinned up on both walls in the corner and a table strewn with parts and tools. As you know, the compartment is 5 meters tall and about 400 square meters. Up against the left wall was a machine, which occupied about half the room, with a recliner next to it like the ones in the living chamber. A cord led from the machine to a device laying in the seat of the recliner.

I walked over and examined the machine with no clue what it did, but I noted spare parts from the control room, the science lab, a spare data drive from my ship and a spare optical sensor for the hyper-telescope. The engineering was a dense design of servo-boards and wiring. The machine was about two meters tall, which was somewhat eye-level for Yorlik and would make the machine easier to repair with no climbing involved.

"This is what you've been doing while I've been hibernating? You've been busy," I said, "Not working on the Serum? What is it?"

Yorlik had been standing in the doorway observing me as I looked over the machine. "This machine," Yorlik said, striding into the room and patting it like a pet, "Is going to speed up the process of figuring out a new Rejuv Serum." He picked up the device at the end of the cord and handed it to me.

I turned it in my hand. I'd seen Yorlik wear an item that he called sunglasses on the lava planet. They were two dark lenses to cover both his eyes from harsh light which were connected via clamp that fit on his nose. The device appeared to have the sunglasses mounted into the encased brick of wiring, servo-boards and more spare parts from the hyper-telescope. As I turned it, I noticed tech that appeared recently manufactured: I'd never seen it before and the condition of the soldering was fresh.

"You've got my attention," I said, "Now that you've given me the tour, I know you're jumping out of your skin to tell me about it."

I handed Yorlik the device with the sunglasses and he sat down in the recliner facing the machine, "I had this idea years ago when the Rejuv Serum was in development. One night I sketched it out at home. I wanted to start a tech division, but the Serum took up all my time at work. So I thought of this concept as a hobby until I could free up time and hire more staff, but that never happened. The Rejuv Serum consumed our efforts, but I attempted to construct this in my shop at the estate. Free time was at a premium especially when the company fell apart and I took responsibility for the SEEDER program and my children were born. I never constructed a complete functioning unit so I downloaded the schematics and a brain-mapping program that my company had developed for a med project into the WAEF's data-core. I was positive I'd have the time on this voyage to get the project up and running. I thought once it was finished and functioning that it would help pass the time.

"But one thing or another—daily and emergency maintenance, changing course, spying the galaxy for viable planets, working on a new Rejuv Serum, meeting you, installing the new propulsion system—got in the way of making this tech possible. During your hibernation, I hit a dead-end on the research and depression and loneliness started to overcome me and I thought about waking you. I stood over your hibernating body for I don't know how long thinking about what I'd say if I disturbed you, then I wondered what it would be like to hibernate.

Would a deep sleep, putting my mind, my conscious mind off my research, so far off my research that my subconscious would be working on it lead to an answer?"

"Unthinking?"

"Yes," Yorlik said, "So I built this machine."

"You still haven't told me what it is," I said, "What it does?"

"If you try it, I doubt it will work on you. The settings are based on brain mapping for my species and your eyes and brain are different, but let's give it a shot," Yorlik said, handing me the device with the sunglasses and standing up from the seat. "Please sit down."

Yorlik pressed a button on the machine's control board and the whirr of surging power brought the distinct sound of switches being automatically thrown in the machinery. Heat emanated from the towering conglomeration of gear packed together.

"Now, what you'll experience is walking through the WAEF. You'll start in the control room, but you can simply walk through the ship as you'd normally do. This concept called *Virtual Practical Reality* has been an engineering feat that my people have been attempting to optimize for years, but getting it to reflect true reality to the point where the subject can't tell the difference between reality and the machine simulation has been the difficulty. The training applications are endless, and this would have been a boon for my company," Yorlik said, flipping switches on the control board and lights glowed in a few places. Yorlik pulled a helmet from behind the machine with more wiring and circuitry covering it and clipped the device with the sunglasses into the front of it. He demonstrated how to place it on my head, then handed it to me. "Now, put on the helmet and we'll see what happens."

I fitted it over my head and only saw darkness. "I don't see anything."

"I haven't activated it yet. Sit back and relax. Here we go."

I heard another switch thrown and the darkness dissolved into an image. At first, I couldn't make out exactly what I was perceiving, then I turned in a circle. I was shocked at first. I was in a completely different place, although I knew consciously I was sitting in the compartment with Yorlik standing over me. *Where was I?* Then it came to me. I was standing in the control room, but the ship was flying upside down and I was firmly planted on the deck. The walls were glowing. I began to feel the sensation of my fluids running to my head, pressure building in my brain as if I were upside down with the ship's gravity effecting me. Before asking Yorlik to turn off the machine, I wanted to see one thing. I peered out the control room window and there were the stars as the ship sped through space.

"I'm done now," I said and the control room dissolved to black. Yorlik removed the helmet.

"How was it? You were in the control room, correct?"

"Yes. Like I was really there, but I knew I was here. I bet you can forget that rather easily after a time. How did you render it?"

"A cam that I invented before I left Koda which captures the tactile nature of a place. All the cam's data is transferred into the machine which translates it to create the captured environment in an individual's mind. Then through the individual's perception the machine can manipulate and change the details of the environment as if you're practically there."

"Didn't work perfect for me. I was standing on an upside down ship and all the colors were vibrating and glowing."

"I'll need to map your Prevorian brain with the scanner in the med bay to make it work properly," Yorlik said, holding the helmet like a fragile child and placing it next to the machine. "How long do you think you were perceiving the environment?"

"As long as it takes to walk from the middle of the control room to the window by the pilot chairs. A few moments."

"No. You were immersed in that simulated place for the time you perceived multiplied by thirty in real time."

"I trust you, but I'd need empirical evidence to believe it. That's not what I perceived time-wise."

"I figured you'd say that. Keep seated," Yorlik said and walked over to the table in the corner of the room, returning with a tray of my favorite post-hibernation Prevorian snacks which was the last of the original supply from my craft. As he carried them over to me, I could smell them so they were freshly made. "While you were immersed,

I went up to the living chamber, prepared the snack and brought it down here. Before you say anything, hold the tray in your hands."

The tray was warm. No food heating devices in the room and the tray wasn't here before. Yorlik would have needed to walk up to the next deck with the living chamber, unfreeze the treats, prep the tray, heat them, then carry the tray back down to this deck. That definitely would have taken more time than the few moments I was in the simulated environment.

"As you would say, that's a brain twister," I said, picking up a treat and biting into it. The inside was warm and since it was the first thing that I'd eaten since coming out of hibernation, my brain tingled as the substance entered my system. I popped the rest of the treat into my mouth and grabbed another and bit into it.

"So you see this is a game changer when it comes to research and my loneliness and depression," Yorlik said, "I can work on the Rejuv Serum inside the virtual world while you're in hibernation and time will pass in the normal world at a faster pace than in the simulated world. I set up alarms for chores and emergencies. I can focus on my research without downtime and mood swings getting in the way. The work to get the entire lab and all the components of the Serum research into the machine's data system was a real chore."

"I understand the psychological advantages," I said, popping the rest of the treat into my mouth. "But won't the real experiments need to happen in real life to make sure the results are correct?"

"I only intend on using it when you're hibernating and the real tests will happen in real life," Yorlik said, "I don't know how you eat those things. They smell like rancid body odor."

I picked up another one and popped an entire treat into my mouth at once. "Delicious," I said, chewing with my mouthful, "The perfect nutrients after hibernating."

Yorlik's face scrunched in disgust. "I'm convinced this device will help me to figure out the new Serum in more ways than research. It's a great escape. This is where the unthinking happens. I didn't show you the simulation for my estate. I've done a whole lot of sailing. When you were hibernating, I was relaxing, letting go of those research brain twisters in one of my favorite places. Kind of ironic, sailing the When All Else Fails while I'm sailing through space on the WAEF. Meditative," Yorlik said, "The other day, after a session in this beauty, it dawned upon me to examine the soil from a different angle, and I may have made a step in the right direction. I've found a substance in the soil that may have been the main factor in the age reversal and stoppage. I'm just not sure if it's the culprit or if it's bonding with other elements. So whether the discovery happened due to the unthinking or the machine was stimulating a portion of my brain, I have no idea, but I'm certain it's going to help in finding a solution."

When Yorlik worked out the kinks in the machine and built a double interface, we could sail together on the WAEF. I still cherish those moments. The joy that Yorlik derived from that scenario was an incredible sight. The simulated manifestation of Yorlik grinning ear-to-ear at the rudder as the wind caught the sails and blew back his hair and the boat cut through the glassy lake with fish jumping in our wake was something to perceive. Once I had to leave the simulation early to run an errand and I peered over at Yorlik wearing his helmet grinning in reality.

That simulation made me homesick, too. On Prevor, water is sacred. We worship its presence on our planet as the giver of life, the place where we sprang forth. Water is part of every religious ceremony. We marry on a platform over the deepest part of the oceans and we mate there for the first time and our females give birth there and the eldest expire there and we're sent back into the deep when life leaves us. I'd already grown fond of Yorlik. There was a mutual respect between us. Yet experiencing Yorlik on the simulated boat on the simulated lake related directly to my Prevorian spiritual roots, cementing a bond between us until the end of Yorlik's days.

Maybe the VPR simulator didn't lead directly to the discovery of the new Serum, but I believe Yorlik's communing with the water enhanced his consciousness to bring about the solutions and save his sanity. My people would say, in a rough translation, 'The ocean provided.' Religious sects on my planet are devoted to staring into bodies of water for days upon days or swimming in the depths to achieve peace and enlightenment. In a way, Yorlik was Prevorian at the core and adopted ways of

Prevorian space travel. Since there was the differential between the concept of time in the simulations and the normal duration of time, Yorlik placed himself in the simulator for extended periods as he automated functions around the WAEF, producing a virtual hibernation for himself.

Seems disrespectful to boil down years of painstaking research to a brief summary about how Yorlik extracted the substance in the lava-planet soil and delivered it into his system elongating his lifespan to accomplish his mission, but no reason to go into a long dissertation here.

In short, the water, heat, and fans applied to the lava-planet soil in hydroponics generated the soil residue which flowed into the vents and got caught in the oxygen generators' filters. Then the residue was converted into an anti-aging element by being bombarded by high-concentrations of oxygen over time. The element in the residue finally made its way through the filters in finer form, then was breathed by Yorlik.

Yorlik spoke many times about how miraculous it was that the age reversal occurred through sheer happenstance although it took years to unravel it into applied science. He contemplated just allowing the soil to affect him through its journey from the hydroponics bay, but thought it best to have control over the soil's influence on him. He put buffers in the vents of hydroponics to stop the residue from leaking out, which restarted his aging for a few years, because he wanted to research if the soil was having any detrimental effects along with its benefits.

I don't know if you've found it in your research, but Yorlik invested his own money to insure that the WAEF possessed a functioning lab, not just to analyze soil samples, but for synthesizing chemicals and examining substances down to a molecular level. Just as he paid for an Industrial Parts Replication Device (IPRD) in case a major part of the ship broke or a spare part malfunctioned so it wouldn't be necessary to turnaround the ship and return home. The investment in the lab and the device was one of the reasons why Yorlik discovered the new treatment, manufactured it and delivered it into his system so the mission could move forward. The IPRD was handy when we needed to build components for the new engines and the energy-field generator units, and put the finishing touches on the VPR. Once Yorlik concluded that the VPR was perfected, he used the IPRD to mold and streamline the VPR simulator's sunglasses and helmet of brick-like circuitry into a one-piece which produced a comfortable fit and eliminated the sensation of weight on the head during a simulation, further enhancing the experience.

Using the IPRD, Yorlik manufactured an apparatus of his own design which covered both his mouth and nose allowing him to breathe a mixture of the residue element and oxygen for a determined dose over a specific length of time. The word 'serum' did not truly fit the delivery process anymore. Yorlik began calling it, Rejuv Treatment. His research revealed that through consistent application of this treatment he could halt the aging of his cells. He hypothesized larger doses could reverse aging, but in

Howard Libes

further research, he found that damaged cells.

One day, Yorlik woke me from hibernation, waving around a half-full bottle of Malrap and a long sheet of paper full of test results from his half year of Rejuv Treatments. His face possessed the same smile from the sailing simulation.

"I did it. There is nobody here to say it…so I'm going to say it, I'm a genius. Took me close to 10 years, but a lesser man would have taken longer or given up. The treatment works." He lurched as if the ship had hit an object, but the Malrap was affecting his balance. He took another swig from the bottle.

I was still laying prone with Yorlik standing over me. "Why don't you sit down in the living chamber and I'll join you?" I said.

"I'll take you up on that," Yorlik said, turning and heading towards the door that led to the living chamber, then veered off course to the right and back to the left, smacking into the wall to the left of the door. The door slid open and he fell through, then the door slid closed. I heard him say from the other side of the door say, "I think there's something wrong with the artificial gravity."

Later, I found Yorlik leaning back with his eyes closed in a pilot's chair spinning in circles. "I have a theory," Yorlik said with his eyes closed as I approached, "If I spin the opposite way the room is spinning, then I can make the spinning stop."

"I don't perceive the room or ship spinning."

Yorlik snorted, releasing a laugh, and stopped spinning in the chair. He said, "No. No. No. When my people drink too much Malrap, the drink affects our motor skills and balance. Probably some other stuff too…like explaining things intelligently."

"I remember from my initial experience with the drink, but I don't understand," I said, "If you're celebrating, why make yourself feel bad?"

"I probably overdid the celebrating. You were asleep…"

"Yes, I was hibernating."

"…and I overdid it…I woke you up, because I wanted somebody to celebrate with." Yorlik picked up the empty Malrap bottle from where it stood beside the chair. Drank from it. Realized it was empty and sighed.

"I understand. Congratulations on your achievement."

"Thank you," Yorlik said and belched, "Oops."

I escorted Yorlik into the living chamber, assuming less damage might be done there, and sat him down in a recliner. He leaned back and sighed, staring up at the ceiling. "You know," Yorlik said, "You're a great guy. You're a lifesaver and I'm not just talking about that maneuver on the lava planet. That was funny. Well not funny, but weird. Well maybe not weird, but…something else. I mean I fall into a lava tube and here's this for lack of a better word walking alien fish. I guess those would be words, climbing towards me. I had no idea what was going to happen. You could have been coming down to kill me but I was going nowhere. I was pretty messed up…"

"Yes you were." I found a bottle of Malrap in the living-chamber food prep area, and poured a modest amount. Somebody had to celebrate with Yorlik and keep their wits about them.

"Yes I was. I was messed up. Broken. Immobile. And here you come climbing down towards me. This half-fish, half-man, no offense. My species first contact with an intelligent alien being and I'm literally off my feet, and so much for diplomacy, and I'm at your mercy, undignified and I was scared. I'm not too big a man to admit it and not sure what was going to happen.

"I mean I'm a man of science, but my adrenalin was pumping and I'm in considerable pain. I was not rational at that point and you swoop me off that ledge, lift me like I weighed next to nothing, throw me over your shoulder like a sack and carry me up into your ship. I was thinking this could be the end of my mission, the end of my life and what do you do? You listen to me and ferry me to the WAEF and repair me. I have to be the luckiest being in the universe and then I happen to bring dirt onboard the ship that has properties that will keep me alive and relatively youthful for as long as this mission will last. Dirt. Unbelievable. Dirt. Like the universe is watching over me. And on top of all that I have you as a friend for the entirety of this ridiculous journey. I've never met a nicer...Prevorian."

"You've never met another Prevorian."

"That is true. That is true," Yorlik said, "But I just want you to know that I owe you my life. I cherish our friendship and I can't say that I've ever felt closer to anybody else with the exception of my family."

"I'm honored by your words," I said, "I'm honored to be acquainted with you, too."

"You are like my family. Like my brother."

"I feel the same way," I said, lifting the glass of Malrap to my mouth and taking a sip.

"A toast!" Yorlik said, looking down at both his hands, "I don't have a drink. How did that happen?" He attempted to get to his feet, but I put my hand on his shoulder, halting him.

"Do you really think you need more?"

"Need is not the issue here. We have not celebrated my success, my genius, my discovery..."

"Okay," I said, "You stay right there though. That's best." I poured a small glass of Malrap and handed it to him.

"Probably right. Probably right. Always looking out for me." Yorlik said, holding up his glass, "To you, to me, to us, to When All Else Fails, no matter what happens, we have each other and may this sector where we're headed continue the good luck we've encountered on this journey so far." With that, Yorlik gulped down the entire glass of Malrap, leaned back in the recliner, closed his eyes and moments later began snoring.

Yorlik's "good luck" didn't come again for quite some time. On Prevor, this idea that a force operates for good or bad in a person's life doesn't exist. Life comes from the power encompassed in the universe and simply happens. On a trip spanning decades, we experienced a fair amount of Yorlik's so-called bad luck, too. Our troubles

ranged from micro-fractures in the hull to a field generator blowing out which sent the WAEF into a high-velocity
spin, breaking Yorlik's arm, uprooting hydroponics and
shattering valuable equipment that wasn't bolted down.
There was a multitude of tech problems with the circuitry
and computing devices. And as we moved closer to our
destination, one of the planets appeared less viable and
Yorlik's two chances to discover a new planet for his people
became what he called an "all-or-nothing proposition."
That's naming a few in the 18 years, traveling to the sector.

Routine is a cornerstone of long-term space travel, not
only as a necessity, but a way to keep the mind from leading to the darkest corners and probabilities of the journey
ahead. Close to 50 years trapped inside a metal container,
could drive any species crazy, hibernation and the VPR
simulations aside, there is no alternative to vacating your
prison cell and moving around outside of your normal
environment. Space walks were for repairs, but they were
not the same as stretching the legs on firm ground.

Using my star charts as a guide, I examined space on
the hyper-telescope between the WAEF's location and
the viable planets' sector, and plotted a course to a few
moons and planets where the WAEF might land for a few
days, allowing Yorlik and myself to walk around in our
spacesuits. We could not only inspect the hull and make
repairs, but traverse the terrain, enjoy the views, dig up
soil samples, and generally see what we could see.

Yorlik was an explorer at heart and he was enthusiastic
about the idea. He was inspired to build a two-wheeled

vehicle which traveled on tough terrain, powered by the Prevorian tech that was used in my craft's engines. The SEEDER program had provided a ground vehicle, but Yorlik conceived a better design in his spare time and built it, recycling parts from the SEEDER vehicle.

Obviously, the stops delayed reaching the sector, but Yorlik didn't mind. He cared even less when the adventures began and he appreciated how much these outings elevated his mood beyond the capability of the simulations. After lift off from these outings, Yorlik was a happier and more energetic individual, and couldn't wait for the next stop.

Then the stop on B-452 happened. This was a moon orbiting a gas giant planet. The grey landscape was dull, scarred and pitted by meteor showers, but the scene was picturesque with the entire sky dominated by the colorful giant that had captured B-452 as a satellite.

Landing was easy and we setup the WAEF systems to acquire analysis of the atmosphere and seismic activity of the moon, then we stepped into our spacesuits and exited the ship, inspecting the hull and engines for necessary repairs. Once Yorlik scooped a few soil samples and placed them in the science lab, he broke out the vehicle which he called All Else. We rode tandem and the vehicle possessed a vidcam mounted on the front to collect the imagery of our trip.

We traveled for a quarter of the day and as we drove around the rim of a deep crater, Yorlik spotted a spacecraft at the bottom. A quick inspection with binoculars showed a crashed craft of an early space flight design. Yorlik suggested moving the WAEF closer to utilize his ship's equipment to analyze the discovery. My Prevorian paranoia about contact with other species kicked in, but Yorlik reminded me of my current situation. In the end, I acquiesced and we landed the WAEF closer to the edge of the crater.

B-452 was one-half to five-sixth the gravity on Prevor or Koda so we rappelled down the side of the crater with equipment to provide readings on the ship and Yorlik mounted a cam onto his helmet so we could review the vid after we were done with our investigation.

As we planted our feet at the bottom of the crater, I was still weary of this expedition, but Yorlik was enthusiastic about the prospect of viewing alien tech and he wouldn't be deterred by my concern. This was a short-range craft, and I was surprised I hadn't spotted traces of this civilization in my examination of this region via hyper-telescope.

I began to panic when I saw a light flashing above the side entrance to the craft. Yorlik was walking ahead of me so I reached out and poked him in the shoulder. "Yorlik, stop!" I yelled into the comm mounted inside my helmet. Yorlik halted and I pulled up beside him.

"I know you're excited," I said, "I know you want to get inside so badly but don't forget your observation skills. Look above the door."

"You're right. What do you suppose that means?"

"I have no clear idea. It could be an alarm system. We

could be on vid right now on some other world. The ship could be rigged to explode if we attempt entry."

"That would put a crimp in our day," Yorlik said, "Let's just go to the door and knock."

"I suppose that's funny."

"Nothing. Not even a chuckle. Really? Well, at this point we might as well look around the hull and go from there. No touching. I'll be a gentleman. This is a first date."

Reluctantly, I followed Yorlik as we walked around the hull. My early observations were correct. The conduits leading from the craft to the engines mounted to the hull demonstrated a fuel source with limited range. The engines were what my people would call "first generation" space flight. At a point where the hull was torn, the composition of the alloy appeared thin and inadequate for lengthy space flight. Yorlik pointed at a sizable break in the rear hull, turned on his helmet lights, and walked through the break into the craft. I stood in place, not wanting to follow, but if anything happened to Yorlik due to my complacency and fear, then I would have a difficult time forgiving myself.

I must have been standing there pondering for a time, because when I entered the hull through the jagged crack, Yorlik was nowhere to be seen. I stood in a loading bay with a mechanical arm mounted to bring objects onboard while in flight which meant their civilization had attained multiple space shots. I passed through the bay into a room meant to prep for space walks and depressurization, then entered into the cockpit which had taken the brunt of the crash. One side of the hull was caved-in metal and whatever had lined the hull, now littered the floor, crunching under foot.

Yorlik stood over the control console at the front of the ship, flipping inactive switches. At his feet was strewn shattered transparent material from the cockpit window. He spotted me and waved me over.

"I don't think a rescue mission is coming for them," Yorlik said, pointing at a body in a spacesuit of a bulky primitive design, strapped into the pilot's chair. A similar suited body was strapped into the co-pilot's chair. They were both upright four-limbed beings like myself and Yorlik.

"Someone could still be coming to rescue them," I said, "We should leave them here."

"I agree," Yorlik said, "If not, this is the proper burial for them and I doubt it, but somebody might come for them eventually. Do you know this species?"

Yorlik flipped open the reflective visor of the pilot's helmet. The head was hairless, round and gray. Bulbous eyes. No eyelids. Lipless mouth. Even in death, the terror of the crash was preserved in the extra wide eyes and the open mouth which possibly let out a scream of some sort relevant to this species in such a disaster.

"No, my people mapped this sector, but never surveyed the planets. From the look of the tech, they couldn't have traveled far from home although they may have drifted dead for centuries and crashed into this moon."

There was nothing to scavenge and Yorlik captured

everything on his cam so we headed back to the WAEF. From the time we left the alien craft, Yorlik was quiet and all of the excitement leading up to the day's expedition had left him. He said nothing of our findings and when I pointed out a comet shooting across the horizon, he made no comment. A rare event for Yorlik to be without words. We arrived at the WAEF, placing the All Else into the loading bay, sealed the airlocks, removed our space-suits and Yorlik was silent the entire time, walking into the ship without saying a word.

I tracked him down in the control room, flipping switches on the main control console and prepping the WAEF for takeoff.

"Are we leaving?" I said, "I was planning on perform-ing a run up of the engines to make sure they're ready for full power and set a course for the sector before lift off."

"Let's get off this rock. We can do those things from space," Yorlik said. He was upset to the point of almost crying before he finished the sentence.

"You want to tell me what's bothering you?"

"Please strap in for lift off," Yorlik said, seating himself in his pilot's chair and clicking his harness into place. He flipped a few more switches and the engines began to hum up to power for lift off.

I sat down next to him and secured my harness. "Please tell me what's happening before we lift off."

Yorlik was staring out the window into the grey land-scape. "Being out here, I've lost touch with the immediacy of my mission. I know we can't move any faster and we've taken the quickest safest route to where we're going. Now I see this crash site and the death and I can't help thinking those creatures come from somewhere. They probably mate and have families who have lost them. Seeing those creatures out there reminded me that life is happening on Koda. All of a sudden, I missed my family, my people more than I have in a long time. Not that I haven't had these thoughts before, but the reality hit me hard. They probably think I'm dead, and believe I've ended up in a crater somewhere and have mourned my passing. I've been absent from their lives for decades and they've probably moved on as I labor out here to make their lives better. It's just overwhelming sadness at my inability to share my life with them. They are ghosts to me, sheer memories as I am to them," Yorlik said, "Now, let's get out of here." He flipped a switch and the engines roared.

Yorlik turned his sense of loss into a greater concern for what was happening on Koda in his absence. He assisted me in completing my rescue pod, and we both upgraded the range of the hyper-telescope and applied its tech to produce a hyper-listening post. Yorlik decided that once the WAEF turned around and headed for home he wanted to know what type of planet he'd be arriving on.

Yorlik's view of his species was highly skeptical. When he drank too much Malrap or a synthetic Malrap he created when the original crates were depleted, he sometimes murmured that his species did not deserve to survive and maybe he should simply turn around and save his family. In more lucid moments, he looked at the greater achievements of his people and their kindness, and he pushed on to complete his mission.

I know I've gone on long and you probably have many questions, but one point I've failed to discuss in detail here is the fact that Prevorian engines propel a ship at a high rate of sub-light speed. Although the engines we mounted on the WAEF propelled us slower than a Prevorian craft, due to the WAEF's design deficiencies, relativity was put into play since we were approaching close to the speed of light. Taking note of relativity, our journey in transit to the viable planet and back to Koda took 48 years for us, but 73 years in Kodan time. The entire journey including engine conversions and time on the planet took 76 years. Yorlik always wondered if he arrived 24 years later with the WAEF's engines, how that would have impacted our current plan.

When Yorlik was headed home with his discovery in hand and the Hyper-Signal-Capturing Device or HSCD was within range of Koda, the captured news affirmed Yorlik's fears about his people. We were approximately 10 years from Koda and less than half a year from my drop-off. The domes were not built yet, but the overall plans were in place. The wealthy exploited the government for research and development funds, and the politicians in their pockets let the fleecing continue as the environmental crisis was in full effect. Oceans were rising. Sea life was near extinction. Water was rationed and the temperature was climbing planet-wide.

Yorlik spent day after day in the loading bay where we

setup the HSCD, leaning back in a chair with listening hubs in his ears. He was obsessed with knowing every detail of Kodan history since his last communication with the planet. I began taking over his chores, and brought him his meals. The plants in hydroponics began withering. He slept little. Black circles formed under his eyes. His hygiene lapsed, and his stink was unbearable. He grew a beard, and his hair touched his shoulders.

Then one day, I found Yorlik hunched over the HSCD unconscious. I carried him to the med bay and hydrated him intravenously. He slept for a day or two, and I happened to be checking on him when he awoke with a scream. He was disoriented. "What's going on? Is everything all right?" Yorlik said in a panic.

"Everything's fine," I said, "I brought you here a few days ago."

"Thank you, Mado. I don't know what I'd do without you," Yorlik said, "Everything is not fine though." He sat up in bed.

"Yes I'd imagine so," I said, pushing Yorlik to lay down. "Nothing will be better unless you pull yourself together."

Yorlik adjusted the bed so he could sit up and talk. "I won't get up. How did I get here? Did you carry me?"

"Yes and you're heavier than I remember."

"I haven't been taking very good care of myself ."

"I was kidding about the weight, but you haven't been taking care of yourself. According to the med equipment, there are no maladies except for dehydration and exhaustion. I'm remedying that now."

"More my state of mind," Yorlik said, "The machine won't detect it."

"Then how would you like me to proceed with treatment?"

Yor laughed. "I'm not sure if you meant that as a joke, but that's funnier than the other one about my weight," Yorlik said, "When my electrolyte levels are normalized, I'll tell you what I'm thinking."

A few days passed and I was in the control room checking the trajectory of the WAEF for the optimal and safest flight path to my drop-off point when Yorlik entered the room. His hair remained long but trimmed and he retained the beard, cutting it back closer to his cheeks. He was wearing a cleaner uniform and seemed in better spirits.

"You look better," Mado said, "How do you feel?"

"I'm better," Yorlik said, seating himself in a pilot's chair, peering off into space, "Thanks to you, once again."

"You would have done the same for me and you have done the same for me in the past," I said, seating myself next to Yorlik, "I'm glad to see you back on your feet."

We both stared out the window in silence. In a relatively short time, we planned on taking leave of one another. Probably never to see one another again. These moments, sitting next to one another in the control room looking out into the universe was another communal ritual of ours.

We sat in that fashion for awhile until Yorlik said, "So I have a rather large favor to ask of you" There was an earnestness in his voice I had not heard in years. "If I'm not being too presumptuous, you and I have developed a relationship over these years that I would define as more than friends. We've become family, have we not?"

"I believe we've discussed this before and I hold that sentiment as well."

"That's good to hear," Yorlik said, his tone now turning emotional, "Because I'm about to ask something of you that is…that is…I'm not sure how to say it. On the surface it's absurd, but the stakes being what they are, I'm compelled to ask you to return to Koda with me. I've run tests on my cellular degeneration after the Rejuv Treatment and it's a fast ride downhill. I can stave it off for a short time. but I can't bring the soil back with me. That means there is no way in my lifetime to make things right for the Kodan people. I need you by my side to devise a plan and make Kodans see this new planet is the answer, and nobody knows space travel better than you. I don't think I'll be around long enough to see whatever plan we hatch come to fruition. I need somebody who I trust to make sure it all works out."

Like when Yorlik asked me to journey with him to the viable planet, I told him that I'd think about it. In this case, on the way to Koda, our current course would pass the border of the Prevorian Protectorate for my drop-off in the pod. It was a simple maneuver and I dreamed of going home. If we landed on Koda, I might never return considering the government aversion to space flight. I spent days pondering how I felt about Yorlik's plea. I understood his desire to save his species, but there was my own existence on Prevor awaiting me. I told Yorlik about my reservations, but of course, he had already thought of what I'd say. That's when he told me about forming Prevor Industries and if we couldn't put together a workable plan, then I could always build a ship of my own with the proceeds from my corporation and return home.

YOR

After Mado's detailed story about traveling with his great-grandfather, Yor went to work on the WAEF's engines. He was installing the parts on the sixth engine, which were tooled by the Prevor Industries manufacturing division, to make it complete. To keep the inspectors from suspecting anything, the plan had always been to prep the engines for museum viewing and wait until a day before it was necessary to inject the core with the Volidian power source. The material to create the power was rare, but Mado found a supplier on the black market. Once the engines were powered, Mado was confident that he could ready them for launch on short notice. Mado had talked to the Global Assembly earlier in the day and they were excited about the WAEF unveiling being pushed to the upcoming Breeze Celebration.

Yor thought about the story he was told as a child about how his father ended up being acquainted with Mado through the Great man. Yorlik had befriended Mado, introducing him to all the right people to start his corporate empire and Mado helped Yorlik retrieve the WAEF. Based on what Mado had told him, it all made sense: Prevor Industries and the HGD provided the seed money for the WAEF restoration and the overall plan. And if Mado's story was true, then this was mapped out decades ago in outer space. It was all hard to believe.

Yor was sore, tired, and bleary eyed when he finished work on the engine. He found Mado in his lab welding a circuit board. He was deep in concentration over his work. Yor stood there watching him from a distance, still wondering if he had dreamed the entire unveiling of Mado as an alien creature and Mado's tale of traveling with his great-grandfather. Maybe he had Trianin poisoning. That would certainly make more sense than these revelations.

"You going to stand there like a lump? There's more work to do," Mado said, continuing to work on the circuit board, "If you're hungry, I can order some food although it's almost curfew and not much will be open."

Yor walked further into the room stopping beside Mado. The work on the circuit board was standard refurbishment for old tech. "No, I'm thinking more about sleep. I was going to head over to Insol's, but I was thinking about sleeping in my own bed. I promised my mother that I'd talk to her tomorrow, but I have a million questions for you before I leave," Yor said.

Mado didn't answer. He was focused on the welding.

"Why don't you have one of your assistants do that?" Yor said.

"This is a specific component for the WAEF and I don't trust anybody else to do it except maybe you, and you were working on the engines," Mado said, "Was that the first of your million questions?"

"Not funny, Mado," Yor said, "I'm tired and I'd like to get some clear answers."

"You seem irritable. You sure you don't need to eat something," Mado said, "Didn't my story answer some questions?"

"Yes, but as usual, you left out a few of the more relevant details," Yor said, "Like why did we...?"

"Hold on," Mado said. He shut down his welder, then walked over to a lab console and began pressing buttons. Doors around the lab began locking. "Just want to make sure we've got complete privacy and we're not interrupted. Proceed."

"I know you said you were attempting to parse information for when the time was right, but if you were onboard my great-grandfather's expedition and were aware of the discovery, then why the entire scheme with the journal? It seems overly dangerous and unnecessary when you were with my great-grandfather all along."

"It was both dangerous and necessary."

"See this is what I'm talking about. Maybe it's all those years of you dancing around the truth without lying. Maybe I should ask more specific questions." Mado was correct. He was cranky. "So this morning you thought the time was right to reveal to me that you're an alien being who was in space with my great-grandfather, because of what happened at the library?"

"Not because of what happened. You and I both knew that detention would happen considering the size of the journal and the time necessary to scan it," Mado said, "After the library, we had always assumed the time would come to tell you about my true origins since that was going to be the last step before the Breeze Celebration. You prematurely went to the library and it triggered pushing up the timeline on the plan and telling you."

"Wait. You said, 'We.'" Yor could hear his irritation leaking out in the tone of his voice. "Who is 'we'?"

"'We' was me and your great-grandfather."

"How? How can that be? The man has been gone for 16 years now."

"That is true, but…" Mado said, "I can see that you're not happy right now. Please let me explain the bulk of what you want to know and then you can ask further questions. I promise it won't take that long."

Yor sat down in Mado's work-table chair. "Okay, I don't believe that it won't take long," Yor said, throwing his arms in the air, "But I'm all yours. Regale me."

"The journal is Yorlik's actual writing, containing valuable thoughts and insights into his travels," Mado said, "One of Yorlik's only requests to the Global Assembly in the WAEF deal was housing the journal in the Royal Library. Yorlik hinted to them if they changed their mind about space travel, then they might want to preserve the journal for future use instead of destroying it like all the data, since there was information in the journal about the location of the discovery.

"He told them it might be easier to hide his discovery in the library and suggested they up security there. The government approved the request, and established the library's high-security SEEDER journal section to control the information inside. Yorlik wanted them to want the journal and keep it safe."

"That's what I always thought, but I don't recall anything specific about the discovery?"

"In the last handful of pages, Yorlik writes about the prospect of finding a planet and mentions the general area of space where the planet resides, an area spanning hundreds of light years. It would take them forever to find it without coordinates."

"I recall that passage although it seemed vague," Yor said, "So why convince them that they needed it?"

"There was a practical reason for wanting them to want the journal. He, or we, decided the journal was the best place to hide the star charts to the viable planet since the government made Yorlik destroy all evidence and data surrounding the discovery. We initially had the charts on a holo-device memory-core, but those cores become unreliable in retaining data over the long term."

Mado strolled over to the work table where the scanner from the library laid. "This is not an ordinary scanner. Inside this scanner is a device that uploaded the contents of the data storage devices in the Detention Facility where the government houses the codes to control and in our case deactivate the defenses on the ground and in their cruisers and satellites.

"So getting arrested was not just the extra time it took to scan the journal, but was a ruse to break into the GSS. When the government was reluctant to let you read the journal, which we expected would happen, I agreed with them that it probably wouldn't be a great idea for you to see Yorlik's more scathing opinions about them at the end of his journal, which we put near the end specifically for this part of the plan. I suggested a good compromise was a time limit. Of course, this would mean you'd get arrested. We thought that it would be best not to tell you about the star charts or the GSS infiltration, so depending on what interrogation method they used, you still knew nothing."

That's kind of brilliant, Yor thought. His father always talked about the genius of the Great man, and Yor assumed his great-grandfather's maneuvering had ended with his death. He had obviously been wrong. He felt proud of his father and great-grandfather...and Mado, but Yor was irritated at being kept in the dark, and still harbored some doubt. "So I'm expected to believe this is all part of a plan that my great-grandfather put into play over 20 years ago, like Prevor Industries?"

"Yes, more like 30 years ago," Mado said, pressing a few more buttons on the lab console. The windows to the lab turned opaque. Active Glass was another invention of Mado's and a big earner for Prevor Industries. Active Glass was not real solid glass, but a field of energy that acted like glass and could be altered to different shades. Every new house in a dome had it.

"May I sit there?" Mado said, pointing at his work-table chair where Yor was seated. Yor relinquished the chair, then Mado sat down and began typing rapidly into the keyboard below the main lab viewing screen, which was much larger than the normal screen in the average citizen's home, about three meters wide and two meters tall, and was mounted on the wall of the lab. An image of the first page of Yorlik the Great's journal appeared on the screen.

"Here we have the journal," Mado said and began typing again, then the page was magnified over and over until Yor was looking at stars, at the universe, in a way that he'd never seen before. "Here we have star charts."

In Yor's early education, teaching about space travel and the universe was considered frivolous and unnecessary, and astronomy became a specialized field with security clearance. Yor only saw artist's renditions of outer space in his studies. During the environmental crisis, seeing stars in the sky at night became difficult and more so living in the domes where the city light's reflected off the solid dome glass.

"That's incredible. Mind boggling," Yor said, walking closer to the screen. He felt like he couldn't get close enough.

"If one knew how to read them and knew the coordinates of the viable planet," Mado said, "One could find their way back there."

"That's genius!" Yor said, louder than he expected.

"Thank you," Mado said, "That is Prevorian tech, but Yorlik's idea."

"The man was a genius," Yor said.

"He was more intelligent than most of your species," Mado said, "I'm glad you believe it all now. I was beginning to think your skepticism would stop you from seeing the truth."

"I always knew he was special. I mean, I spent my life studying to learn more about him, but this…and the plan that he set in motion so long ago, duping the government."

"He did have a knack for planning, assessing, and setting complex scenarios in motion."

"How did he know I'd follow the path I did?" Yor said, "He only knew me as a child."

"Well, you literally told him that you were going to figure out what he wasn't telling you. And he fed you enough to stoke your excitement in the subject. Your father affirmed Yorlik's insight about you and we all knew you were a gifted child," Mado said, "And there was a Plan B if you decided to take another path in life."

"So my father knew all about this?"

"Yes, he fully supported the idea."

"He was part of the plan, too?"

"He was part of the plan, but only in a sense that he continued being himself and building his cause. We didn't want the government to have any idea he was part of a greater plan. Your father was a true warrior in the Prevorian sense. He never stopped believing in his ideals and he wouldn't stop in the face of mortal danger. I respected him greatly."

"What about my mother? What does she know about you?"

"She has no idea I'm from another planet, and we want to keep it that way. Your father was the only one who knew, and I told him just before Yorlik passed. Your mother was told about the discovery, because Yorlik wanted her to perform the erasure procedure otherwise she knew nothing of the plan. He was afraid she'd figure it out. She always seemed to be on the verge of adding it all up, but Yorlik kept her out of the loop. We all wanted her focus on you, nurturing you and educating you. The less she knew the better, in case anyone decided to interrogate her."

"My mother performed the procedure?"

"Yes, she was a skilled med we all trusted. The consensus was not telling you. We all came to the conclusion you'd be angry at her. Look at your outburst when you found out about your father's treatment at the hands of the government."

"I would've liked the benefit of the doubt, but I guess that's logical," Yor said, still looking up at the stars on the screen. "On one hand, I'm honored that my great-grandfather trusted me as part of his plan. You know, I always had the highest admiration for him. On the other hand, I always thought my accomplishments and my relationship with you, working as an intern, learning about the WAEF and my chair at the University was based on merit and now it seems my misgivings have been confirmed. This has all been given to me based on this plot that my great-grandfather laid out years ago."

"That's ridiculous," Mado said and began typing into the keyboard again and the screen went blank. "How many times do I need to say it? You earned everything yourself. There are few people on this planet who could have grasped what I've taught you about the WAEF and her systems or any of the other projects you've worked on here. Everything in your academic career was entirely your own doing. I just endowed the chair at the University, and you were unanimously given that position by your peers. Let's put it this way. If you were a moron, I would be working this plan in a whole different way."

"Okay I guess I'm overly sensitive about it," Yor said, grabbing his satchel from where he left it earlier. "I should probably get going, but what do I, or we, tell my mother? She's going to want answers tomorrow."

"Why don't you stay in my penthouse's spare bedroom tonight? I'll prepare some food and we'll figure out what we're going to say to your mother tomorrow, then go see her together."

RAJER

Rajer opened the door to the bedroom and discovered Mar asleep on the couch. Her viewer sat on the table next to it. She had come home from her late shift at the med clinic and fallen asleep there. That was two night's in a row she'd slept on the couch. In the nine years they'd been living together, that had never happened.

He sat down in the armchair beside the couch and watched her sleep. He thought he knew her well and they'd always been honest with one another, but the events that transpired two days ago had left him feeling deceived. *The other night was more than I expected, but we'll get over it.* Since they both had the day off, he hoped they'd clear the air between them and find a way forward together like always. *I knew from the moment we met that her past was complicated.*

They'd been introduced by a University mate and colleague of Tetrick's friend, Ador. Rajer was well aware of her late husband. Tetrick was infamous around the globe for his speeches against the DOME project. True believers and others ripe for conversion, who wanted to see and hear the grandson of the legendary Yorlik the Great, flocked to his gatherings.

Rajer never told Mar, but he attended one of Tetrick's speeches. *I guess that I have secrets of my own,* he thought.

That was years before Rajer met Mar. He graduated from University and sought government employment like thousands of others, because it guaranteed housing in Capitol City with an exclusion from the DOME Residence Selection Process when the dome was built. Achieving government security clearance was grueling even for a financial examiner. One of the tests was attending a Tetrick Vanderlord lecture, then being asked a series of questions about Tetrick's ideas. Rajer thought the exam was strange, but he assumed it was another loyalty test. He wanted the job, so he bought his ticket to *Doom of the Domes*.

When Rajer arrived at the venue, he was surprised at the line stretching city blocks and the wide demographic of people waiting— men and women, all class groups, age groups, and cultural groups from around the globe. The venue was packed with close to 10,000 citizens and Rajer sat up in the rafters. Tetrick was projected on massive viewing screens on either side of him.

Tetrick was an imposing persona. He was the spitting image of his grandfather, except Tetrick appeared more animal than intellectual. A flow of jet black hair with streaks of grey, regal nose, strong chin, and broad shoulders. He wore a button-down shirt with a few top buttons undone, a tuft of chest hair coming out from under the shirt. He was constantly catching his breath, overwhelmed by his physical performance. He was not standing in front of the lectern, but energetically striding back and forth on the stage with a wireless microphone.

Sweat poured down from his forehead into his eyes and he held a handkerchief in hand wiping away the perspiration as he ranted how the DOME project was a thievery of finances better spent on a renewed SEEDER program. He stated his case against breaking ground on the domes, on how the Global Assembly spent 72 percent of their annual budget over the past 80 years on research and development for the domes with no construction, on how the DOME project developers were getting richer while the domes would never save the entire planet's population. If the domes were ever completed, what happened when Koda's finite resources were depleted.

Rajer was impressed by the enthusiasm of the crowd. During parts of the speech people were speaking Tetrick's words verbatim along with him, as if they'd been to one of these gatherings before or watched illegal vids of this speech on their viewers. When Tetrick mentioned his grandfather, the crowd stood and gave a deafening cheer. Yorlik the Great had just finished moving the WAEF to his estate. He had appeared on viewing-channels shows for almost a year, becoming a lauded public figure.

Rajer remembered the end of Tetrick's lecture. The phrases and sentences were unforgettable. Tetrick stood at the front of the stage. "Our planet is dying. There is no denying it now," he said, holding out his arms imploring the crowd, "Our best scientists have concluded we've gone far beyond the environment ever healing…I see the highest price ever paid for mass mausoleums…Inevitably we'll reach a stage where a countdown to our demise, to our final breath as a species on Koda will be reached and there is no hope, and then it won't matter anymore how many units line the pockets of the wealthy...Our species won't die fighting for life, but we will die with a whimper under glass." At the end, Tetrick went silent and stood still with his head bowed and the entire crowd went silent with him, waiting for Tetrick to say more, then he turned on his heels, walked off stage and the lights turned on. The crowd filed out as if they were leaving a holy place after a funeral. Rajer recalled walking home, thinking about how he was about to swear his allegiance to the government Tetrick had condemned.

For the test, Rajer sat alone in a chair in the middle of an empty white room, white walls and no other furniture. The entire ceiling was white and smooth with a bank of lights mounted inside. No vidcams were mounted in the corners of the ceiling. Rajer was convinced the cams were inside the ceiling along with devices measuring his heart rate and analyzing his body language for truthfulness with administrators sitting in another room monitoring the readings.

A welcoming female voice, emanating from a hidden speaker said, "Good day, Rajer Jeps."

"Good day to you," Rajer said, breathing in a measured way to relax himself and keep the readings normal.

"What did you think of Tetrick Vanderlord's speech?"

"A spectacle," Rajer said, "Tetrick Vanderlord said many things. My overall impression was the speech was intriguing, but I have not studied the facts so I can't say whether his conclusions on the DOME project's fallibility are correct or not."

Silence ensued. In the white room containing no clocks, no blinking light, and no sound except for his breathing and the rattling of the chair when he made small movements, Rajer had no idea how long he sat there. The lack of measured time felt almost painful until the prompter spoke and Rajer practically leapt out of his seat.

"Rajer Jeps. That concludes today's test. You will be notified regarding your employment status in no less than twelve days. Thank you for your interest in working for the Global Assembly and please leave your ID with the receptionist on the way off the floor. Powers-that-be bless our global union."

Although Rajer was awarded the job, he wondered what that test ultimately measured and how his words caused him to pass. Years later, he met Mar.

Now, he lounged in an armchair watching Mar sleep while he sipped on a warm morning protein beverage. She wriggled a bit, opened her eyes, and smiled as she noticed him and stretched.

"You have one of those for me," Mar said.

"Ready in the kitchen when you are," Rajer said, walking over to the couch and kissing her on the lips. "I'll get it right now." When Rajer returned with Mar's beverage, she sat up and stretched again.

Rajer handed her the beverage. "Careful it's hot," Rajer said, sitting down next to Mar and planting a kiss on her cheek.

"I'm glad this is our day off. I could use a break," Mar said, sipping at the beverage. "Any sign of my son?"

"No, not a glimpse of the Professor. I can comm him and see when he's coming home."

Mar patted Rajer on the hand. "Let him be," she said, "I have a feeling he'll be back soon enough. In the meantime, I'm going to take a shower and we can talk before he gets home."

"Would you like me to join you? Always good to conserve water," Rajer said.

Mar smiled. "I like the idea, but I'm looking forward to thinking about the day ahead. In the meantime, you must see this reformatted vid," Mar said and opened her viewer to the image of Yorlik.

"Wow," Rajer said, "That's him. I've never seen him that way."

"Yes. He looks even more haggard than when he landed. This wasn't a public appearance. The government was highly conscious of keeping up the Yorlik the Great myth even if they disagreed with each other," Mar said, "Ready."

Rajer nodded and Mar pressed the start key, picked up her beverage and left the room.

When the vid ended, Rajer was dumbfounded. He took a loyalty oath that included death for acting out against the government, but the contents of the vid didn't fit the truth he was sworn to uphold. Over the years, he had his misgivings about the government policy of spying on citizens, the violent means the DOME riots were handled, and the supposed rigging of the Residence Selection Process, but his loyalty to the Global Assembly was entangled in his livelihood so he kept silent.

When Mar returned to the living room, Rajer beckoned her to sit down and said, "I'm not sure how to react. This is counter to history." He reached over, removed the wafer from Mar's viewer and examined it. "This is a 20-year-old wafer in its tech and the date on the wafer, but…" Rajer said, shaking his head. He was speechless "Imagine if this got out…oh my…Tetrick…" He turned to Mar and their eyes met.

"Yes," Mar said, "Tetrick risked himself to get the word out in his own way. Labeled a subversive, and his body and will beaten down until neither could live anymore." Tears welled in her eyes.

"Oh my dear," Rajer said, embracing her, "What do we do?"

"We wait for Yor to come home."

Rajer spent the day reading through the contents of the secret compartment. Tetrick's DOME research was revealing and backed his speech. Rajer read stolen high-level Global Assembly briefings which confirmed all of Tetrick's accusations about government policy. He didn't know how Tetrick obtained these documents, but being in the government for years, Rajer recognized the names on the memos—Global Assembly reps, department heads, advisors to the Leader—and the official letterhead with distinctive printing and watermarks for security purposes was impossible to fake. Yorlik's vid sent a shock through Rajer's existence, but this evidence entirely altered his worldview.

There was also a pile of paper communications between Tetrick, Mado, and Joro Camtur. There was discussion of future plans to resurrect the WAEF, which was happening now, but this was a few years before the WAEF was moved to the estate.

Mar told Rajer that Tetrick didn't trust comm transmissions. That's why he communicated by paper. He'd print up one to send by private messenger to the intended receiver and another for himself, then back it up on a wafer and delete the file from his viewer's data system. Paranoia in his case was well-founded.

The stack of communications with Yorlik was cryptic. There was a great deal of talk about the type of clouds in the sky that day, and a weather forecast for the upcoming days. There were references to a plan for building a platform, too. Mar said that neither of them were much for carpentry.

"You know me," Mar said, "My instincts are usually correct. I believe that the Great man created a long-term plan, which over the course of time ended up involving my son. Time was a different aspect of reality to him. He was in space for more than half his life. He also said I was the constant in this plan…and here I am, and I'm not going to sit around as some unused pawn anymore."

"I'm behind you one-hundred percent," Rajer said,

"You know that, right?"

Mar kissed Rajer on the lips. "I know."

Later that day, Yor walked through the front door with Mado. Mar rushed from the bedroom to greet her son. She had displayed a calm disposition the entire day, but now hugged Yor like she had not seen him in years. *She is a soldier. She has been through this type of chaos in her life before.*

During the embrace, Mado stood behind Mar and Yor, smiling in that awkward way he did. When Mar released Yor, she stepped to Mado and said, "Good to see you, Mado. I believe it's time we talk about this plan." Mado's eyes widened. His body language stiffened. Mar had hit the nail on the head.

ORN

O rn said to Harmin, "We'll talk again soon" and he walked across the hall and knocked on the office door.

Twenty-seven days ago, the Leader had diverted Orn from the Vanderlord investigation to find a scapegoat for the Msituan dome collapse. The arrests took longer than he'd anticipated, and after days of interrogations, he obtained a confession for the terrorist act. The viewing channels broke the news and the Leader was pleased, but now Orn was back on this case.

Mellick Zonor answered the door. Orn was aware from his investigation that Mellick Zonor was born into a merchant family from Nor. Being a Norian himself, Orn was familiar with the young man's ancestry. The curly red hair, the distinct long straight nose and the blue eyes indicated a direct descendant of the Nor ruling class who had been vanquished by the Global Assembly in the separatist upheavals.

"Can I help you?" Mel said.

Orn could read from Mel's shaky voice and body language he was wary of Orn from the outset. In the well-scrubbed halls of the Royal University, Orn came off as an aberrant visitor. He also assumed Vanderlord had told Zonor to be on the lookout for him.

"I believe you can," Orn said, placing his shoe against the door jam.

"I don't believe I can," Mel said and closed the door, putting a mark in Orn's well-polished shoe. Orn grabbed the frame of the door, pushing it against Mel's resistance until it was open halfway.

"Now, look what you've done to my shoe. You can help me here, or you can help me at the Detention Facility. Either way works for me," Orn said, noticing Mel observing his scarred hand holding the door. "I can have two Global Guards drag you out of this fine upstanding place of study and talk to your Dean about your status here, or you can invite me into your office for a chat."

"I guess the choice is clear then," Mel said, letting up his resistance on the door and stepping back into the office.

"Wise decision, Professor," Orn said and stepped into the office. Mel retreated into the small one window office and sat down at his desk. Orn switched off the light by the door. Over his shoulder, he saw Harmin smiling in pleasure at the scene he'd just witnessed. Orn shut the door with a slam and sat in the seat opposite Mel, then scraped the legs of the chair against the floor as he pulled it as close to the desk as possible. Mel cringed at the grating sound.

"Comfortable," Mel said.

"That's not the point here," Orn said, "But I'm situated well enough."

"I'm..."

"I know who you are Mellick Zonor. I know every detail of your life up to this moment, including how you achieved this position with the help of Yor Vanderlord."

"Who are you? I mean your name. I know who you represent."

"Not relevant, although I'm glad you know who I represent."

"So what can I do for you? I have a busy day ahead of me."

"Oh yes, the back breaking work of filling young minds with your version of the truth. So many of your colleagues have lost their positions due to treasonous acts. Hard to believe that SEEDER studies was allowed to have their own department, but the Leader has a soft spot for that particular moment in history. He thinks it reveals the pioneering and innovative nature of the Kodan people, and the program is a favorite of Mado Prevor, a personal friend of the Leader."

"The Leader is correct about the SEEDER program's impact…"

"I don't care!" Orn said, slamming his palms down on the desk. "That's not why I'm here. I'm here to discuss your friend, Yor Vanderlord and his anti-Global Assembly activities."

"I don't know what you're talking about."

"If I had a unit for every time somebody in your position has said that to me, I'd be a rich man. Let's just cut to the chase shall we. One Norian to another."

"You're from Nor?"

"Yes. Not from the sweet-smelling seaside like your people although your family's future was on the downturn when you came into this world. Your poor father couldn't keep fishing when there was no fish to be netted. Quite the dilemma. And he couldn't exactly sell off his boats for a profit. How many people needed them? But you found your place in a nice cushy job in academia and got out of Nor before the crisis hit full bore," Orn said, "I digress, and you said you're busy, so tell me about Yor Vanderlord's plans?"

"Again, I have no idea what your referring to."

"You know I witnessed first-hand the Norian impulse to rebel. It was before you were born, but I grew up in the midst of the separatist movement that literally destroyed the city I lived in. I watched the separatists doing their work, day after day, with the majority of the public supporting their contemptible lies, for whatever good that did."

"I take it from where you're sitting now, you weren't one of the majority."

"I was young and concerned with putting food in my belly," Orn said, "But the point is, I know that treasonous impulse still exists in many Norians. I've seen the records. Members of your family were listed as seditious during those times. Some of their lives were extinguished by the Global Assembly, so you grew up with anti-government sentiment and that influenced your current actions. You're just a product of your environment. May I use your viewer?"

Mel opened his viewer and turned it in Orn's direction. Orn entered a secure GSS address and code to access a specific vidcam feed, then turned the viewer so he and Mel could watch at the same time and pressed the vid to play. Mel's father, mother and teenage sister appeared. They were dirty and their clothes were filthy rags that hung off their bodies. Two Global Guards stood behind them with their weapons drawn, pointed at Mel's parents heads.

"Please," Mel's father said, "Please son. Help us. We've been told that if you give them what they want, they'll fly us to Capitol City and let us have a life there with you." Mel's mother and sister began crying. Tears flowed down Mel's fathers face tracking in the dirt on his cheeks. "You have no idea what we've been through the past few years. Living in refugee camps, sleeping in the mud, avoiding outbreaks of disease in the camps by fleeing into gang-controlled territories. Your sister…what your sister has endured…" Mel's sister fell to her knees sobbing hysterically.

Orn pressed the pause button.

"What is this?" Mel said, his torso shaking as he grabbed onto the desk for leverage. "What is this?" Mel hollered, spit flying from his mouth.

"Now, no need to yell. Let's be civil, Professor Zonor," Orn said, "This can all be settled rather simply. You can murder them or save them. It's in your hands. Just tell me what I want to know."

"I don't know anything," Mel said, standing and knocking over his chair. He turned his back to Orn and looked out the window, suppressing the sound of his sobbing.

Orn walked to Mel's side, standing close to him and spoke softly with his lips close to Mel's ear, "You and Vanderlord are close friends. You might be his closest peer beside the girl that he sleeps with. I know he's planning something and I have a hard time believing with your history of organizing rallies for dissent you'd be standing on the side as your best friend organizes a major plot against the big bad Global Assembly."

Mel took a few steps away from Orn and wiped at his eyes. "You'd ask me to betray Yor or you'll take the life of my family?"

"I know you've been searching for them for quite some time. They don't have much of a life right now. I'd probably be doing them a favor if I put them out of their misery."

"So say I can tell you something, how can I trust you'll do what you promise and send them here?"

"You can't. But if you don't tell me anything, you can be sure that I'll comm the superior officer of those Global Guards, and I'll wait here so you can watch all three of them executed. Although I could tell from the way that one of those Guards was looking at your sister, that he wouldn't mind quality time with her before we kill her."

Mel let out a breath that almost sounded like a growl and walked around the desk so it was between them. *He wants to hit me*, Orn thought, *He knows better so that's a good sign.*

Mel shoved his hands into his pants pockets. "Yor compartmentalizes each of our activities. I have no idea what everyone else does and I don't even know what exactly he wants me to do until less than a day prior to the action. That's the protocol he's set up. Nothing has happened yet. All I know is whatever is supposed to happen, will happen around Breeze Celebration." Mel took his hands out of his pockets and began pulling on his hair.

"I believe you," Orn said, walking past Mel and opening the door.

"Wait. What about my family?"

"I'll think about it. In the meantime try and find out something more meaningful and come down to the GSS building."

"But I don't know your name."

"If you come down to the GSS, I'll show up eventually," Orn said, leaving the office with Mel sobbing.

As Orn walked down the hall and passed Yor's office, Yor stepped out. "Good day, Professor Vanderlord," Orn said, continuing down the hall. He relished in the fearful look on Yor's face and could hear him running down the hall behind him toward Mellick Zonor's office.

While Orn was in Msitua his subordinates had laid the groundwork for the Vanderlord investigation, but now he needed to build on it. He had his work cut out for him. Breeze Celebration occurred over three days, starting tomorrow evening, culminating in the parade on the final day. He was looking forward to the challenge.

YOR

Yor felt exhaustion behind his eyes and in his limbs as he sat behind his office desk. He and Mado had been working non-stop on the WAEF for the past 27 days, putting the finishing touches on the systems, assuring that the ship would be ready for the upcoming Breeze Celebration. His door was halfway open and he heard what he thought was screaming coming from down the hall.

He exited his office and the man from the interrogation room smirked as he passed him in the hallway and said, "Good day, Professor Vanderlord." He heard Mel sobbing and his heart raced and he ran down the hall. When he entered the office, Mel stood in front of his desk weeping and wailing. He yelled at Yor, "Get out of my office! Get out of here now!"

"What happened?" Yor said, "Are you all right? Did that man do something?"

"Get out!" Mel yelled louder, walking towards Yor and pointing towards the door.

Yor backed up and when he cleared the threshold, Mel slammed the door in his face. Yor stood there for a moment, shaken. Mel had begun weeping again. There was nothing Yor could do about it. He would attempt to talk to Mel when he calmed down, but he couldn't help but feel responsible for Mel's misery. It wasn't hard to reach the deduction this had something to do with the plan.

Yor turned around and Harmin was standing in his office doorway.

"Wonder what happened?" Harmin said, "He seems distraught."

"You didn't hear anything? You didn't see that man?"

"No, nothing," Harmin said, "I've got papers to grade." He took a step back and closed his door.

Yor walked further down the hall. Insol's door was shut. She was teaching a class right now. Ador's door was ajar and Yor knocked. "You in there, Ador?"

There was no answer and if nobody was here, then it was strange for Ador's door to be open. With that man in the building, he was further concerned. Yor knocked and call out again. There was still no answer.

"I'm coming in," Yor said, pushing the door open.

Ador was slumped over his desk, face down and it didn't look like he was breathing.

"Ador," Yor called out as he ran to him. He stopped beside Ador and lifted his wrist, taking his pulse. He was alive.

Ador mumbled.

"What was that?" Yor said.

Ador turned his head to the left towards Yor and said, "I said if you want to hold my hand, then you need to take me out to dinner first."

"I thought you were dead," Yor said.

"I'm feeling that way." His arms shook as he attempted

to lift himself up from the desk. Yor took hold of him and assisted him to sitting up in his desk chair.

"You don't look so good."

"Always good to hear. I don't feel so good," Ador said, running his hand over his head and a clump of hair fell to the floor. "Can you hand me that waste basket?"

Yor spotted the basket and picked it up. A rancid smell emanated from it. "You sure you want this?"

"Yes, quick."

Yor handed him the basket, and Ador vomited into it.

"You should go home," Yor said.

"You haven't been around lately. I know you've been over at Prevor's," Ador said, coughing. "I've been under the weather for awhile, and I've already taken days off. I'm trying to play catch up on work here."

"Have you seen a doctor?"

"I'll be fine. Just a clinging to a cold."

"What's with your hair falling out? And you look like you've lost weight."

"Old age probably," Ador said and laughed.

"That's crazy talk and not funny. You should go to a med."

"You sound like my partner. I hate meds. No offense to your mother."

"Shika is correct and I can find someone to take your classes. Promise me that you'll go see someone."

"I'll let you know," Ador said, vomiting into the basket again and wiping his mouth with the back of his hand. "What brings you down here?"

"I was in my office and I heard Mel crying. That GSS man was here. He obviously said something to Mel or did something to him. Mel chased me out of his office."

"I told you that man was bad news."

"He hasn't shown himself in awhile. I thought he just backed off."

"He wants to know what you're doing, and he's not going to stop until he gets some answers."

"By not going to stop, you mean?"

"He's going to hurt the people you care about. Mentally. Physically," Ador said, "I see that look, Yor. You didn't think you were going to get away with this scheme without blowback. That jammer can only stop so much."

Ador grabbed the arms of his chair and threw his head back, closing his eyes. "Wow that was a doozy."

"What?"

"The room just spun around a few times."

"Ador, please. Go home and see a med. Call my mother and setup an appointment. Do you need me to walk you to the rail car station?"

"You're probably right. I should go home. I can make it to the station."

"And let me know if you need me to take over your classes."

"Will do, kiddo. Oh sorry. I mean, boss."

Yor laughed. "You're the one person on the staff who has known me long enough to address me that way...in private," Yor said. He bent down and gave Ador a hug. As he was walking out of the office, Yor said, "Please let me know if you need anything from me or my mother."

Yor walked down the hall and knocked on Mel's door. There was no answer. He knocked again. Silence. "Mel, are you in there? If you are, then you don't have to answer," Yor said, "I understand that man upset you. I feel guilty about bringing this kind of suffering onto someone who I love as much as you. We should have known we were bringing this onto ourselves. Look at the world around us. I've come to the realization that I was aware all along, but I preferred not to think about the consequences. We live in an academic environment that appears to encourage free expression, but we both know that's not true. I want to make a difference in the future and I hope that you still do, but I understand if you change your mind."

There was still no sound from inside the office. Maybe Mel had left the building so Yor started back to his office.

"We're in this together," Mel said, "We've always said it and I still feel the same way."

Yor smiled and continued down the hall.

MADO

"Are we done here?" a warehouse worker on the ground floor yelled up to Mado who was standing on his lab's second-floor balcony. The worker held a large remote control pad which required two hands to hold.

"Yes. Close it up," Mado yelled back.

The worker pressed a button on the remote and took a few steps outside of the building as the massive door lowered and closed, leaving Mado alone with the WAEF.

Mado had spent the morning supervising the removal of the automated repair devices and excess equipment around the WAEF. He could have asked one of his employees to manage the task, but he didn't trust anybody at this sensitive point in the plan. He hired top-notch recruits and his security checks on his employees were rigorous, but if the government turned one of them to spy on him, he never would know until it was too late.

The floor had been cluttered with pieces of equipment for years, and now that the ground floor was clear of everything except for a heavy-duty equipment mover and a few crates, the WAEF dominated the space. *Ready to come alive again*, Mado thought as he looked down at the ship. Prevorian craft possessed organic components so they were regarded as alive when functional. Mado was looking forward to flying the ship and opening up the throttle.

Mado descended on the lift and walked up into the WAEF, ending up in the control room. He told Yor he had a place of honor for his great-grandfather's foto that would meet his approval. He mounted it on the panel above and beside the main control console so his friend would always have a view out the window.

Mado removed a large cylinder from his jacket pocket, a holo-device memory-core, and inserted it into a round slot below the holo-device's operating screen and keypad. Manufacturing these outdated memory-cores was an expensive part of the WAEF restoration. Mado could have installed a newer mapping system, but the inspectors saw this device as an all-ages interactive crowd-pleaser when the WAEF became part of their museum. Mado felt nostalgic about it, too.

The core was accepted into the device and the star charts converted from Yorlik's journal were made accessible on the operating screen. Mado had downloaded the pages of Yorlik's journal into his heavily firewalled personal database in the corporate system, then converted them for the holo-device and uploaded them onto the core. His next step would be deleting the charts from the Prevor Industries corporate system so no trace of the charts existence could be found there, but he needed to confirm they worked here first.

He punched in the galactic coordinates to the Prevorian homeworld and charted a course from there to a small planet orbiting a Dwarf star near Koda's planetary system. The holo-device interacted with the ship's systems and the lights in the room dimmed to make the presentation more distinct while the device stitched together the necessary charts to manifest the most economical and safest path to the destination planet, Terminus A-1, which was named by Yorlik. When the operating screen showed routing was complete, Mado pressed the Display button on the keyboard. The table glowed, then projected points of light representing star and planetary systems above it. The Prevorian homeworld and Terminus A-1 appeared as blue and red dots with a line from one to the other wending its way through the stars and planets.

Satisfied with the interface, Mado switched off the map, and ejected the core which he put back in his pocket and the lights in the room brightened. He was anxious to perform a final run-through of the entire ship's systems including firing up the engines, but he was waiting for Yor. Mado wanted him in attendance for any hiccups that might arise in the WAEF's systems so Yor could correct them himself. Mado had schooled Yor on the systems and he was confident Yor could analyze any situation, postulate a solution, and make the necessary repairs to resolve the problem. That was no easy task on a ship as complex as the WAEF. But new glitches were sure to arise and if the time arrived where Mado wasn't around, he wanted Yor to handle the unexpected.

Yor should have returned by now from the University, but Mado was not worried yet. He calculated a time for a mating session as a factor in Yor arriving later than his estimated time of arrival. To pass the time, Mado inventoried the supplies in the science lab and the med bay to confirm they were complete, then he did the same for the food replicator in the living chamber. He requisitioned all of these supplies off the black market so the government wouldn't be alerted to their intended use on the WAEF. Mado descended to the hallway of storage compartments, examining each compartment to make sure the crates filled with spare parts and surplus supplies were secure, then verifying that each compartment door was locked for when the WAEF moved.

Inside the final compartment, he felt for a hidden latch where a wall met another wall. The latch appeared as part of the wall, but fingertips could detect where the wall was springy. Mado found the spot and pressed. The wall slid away and Mado entered moving sideways. He and Yorlik fabricated this space by manufacturing a fake wall and using a small part of the storage compartment, This was how Mado was smuggled onto Koda. The walls were shielded here so any scans of the ship would appear normal while Mado hibernated with food and water until Yorlik found an excuse to return to the ship and sneak him off. Mado had rediscovered this hiding place when the ship was brought back to the complex. He wanted to make sure it was secure before the Celebration. He and Yorlik were particularly pleased with this bit of subterfuge.

Then Mado headed to the engine room. He was proudest of his work here. His last experience with the

WAEF's original engines happened on the final portion of Yorlik's journey home. He and Yorlik spent days together dismantling the propulsion system they'd assembled from Mado's craft and restoring the WAEF's engines from the parts they'd set aside 51 years earlier in case they were needed again.

When Yorlik returned, the government removed the essential engine parts and power source from the ship. Mado rebuilt the engines from the original blueprints and schematics, uncovered by Yor's research. He reconstructed the first engine piece-by-piece, puzzling it together with Yor by his side in order to guarantee that Yor understood exactly how the propulsion system operated, then Yor assembled the final few engines by himself.

The inspectors were in awe of the restoration job on the engines, but they had no understanding of the tech. They were satisfied as long as the parts were shiny for display at their museum.

Every once and awhile an inspector would point and comment on how fantastic a specific part appeared.

Mado would ask, "Do you know what that does?"

The inspector would respond, "Oh no, I've seen it in historical documents though and it looks tremendous."

In order to keep up the charade, Mado hadn't installed the engine's power source until a few days ago. He had thought about installing the Prevorian engines into the WAEF after the inspections were done, but with the schedule bumped up to the approaching Breeze Celebration, he had limited time and a backup plan for upgrading the engines was set in place years ago. He had performed a few cosmetic tech upgrades and considered converting the ship's internal systems to more advanced tech, but again, time had run out.

Mado exited the ship and took the lift up to his lab. On his way up, he drank in the image of the WAEF ready for her unveiling and when he reached the balcony, he stood there like he was love-struck, admiring the vision of his affection.

That's when Yor appeared by his side. "That is some sight. I never thought I'd see the day. The hull is incredible. Gleaming. I've seen fotos of the ship before its first launch when it was brand-new. Your workers have done it justice."

"Yes, it is quite the picture as your great-grandfather would say." Mado entered his lab, and the proximity sensors activated his equipment. The main viewing screen brightened to a viewing-channel program displaying images of the WAEF on its first launch as two viewing-screen personalities discussed its scheduled appearance at the upcoming Breeze Celebration.

"Those are the exact fotos I was talking about," Yor said.

"I was watching this earlier. We're all over the news." Mado turned up the volume on the viewing screen.

A female viewing-channel personality wearing a dress of grey with purple dots, the same colors as the Global flag, and a lapel pin of the Global symbol said, "Breeze Celebration attendance is estimated at a record high this year with travel bookings to Capitol City up four-fold from the previous year."

"Very very exciting," the male personality said, dressed in a suit of purple with grey pinstripes and wearing the same pin.

"Yes it is, but that shouldn't stop any of you from coming out for the festivities. The recent renovation of the Global Arena doubled its capacity and there's always the parade floats. When All Else Fails is expected to roll down the entire route through Capitol City and into the Arena." Graphics displayed the route of the parade from start to its finish at the Arena. "It's a little different this year considering the size of the spaceship," the female personality said and giggled.

"It is big. Very big. And you can view it all here. We'll provide complete coverage of the parade and all the speeches including the commemoration of the When All Else Fails restoration by the great-grandson of Yorlik the Great, Yor Vanderlord the author of the best-selling *Power Over the Future*, which covered the failure of the SEEDER program and the launch of the When All Else Fails."

The female personality said, "You don't want to miss it and of course, our Global Leader will deliver the introductory speech…"

"The failure. What a load of crap," Yor said

Mado turned down the volume. "So I'm assuming the speech is ready?"

"I sent you a copy for your feedback."

Mado punched a few buttons in the keyboard below

the viewing screen. The speech replaced the viewing channel on the screen, and Mado flipped through the pages,
then he switched back to the muted viewing-channel
news, showing footage of Yorlik's return to the planet. "I
like it. Especially the part where you mention your father.
He needs to be remembered as a fallen hero on Koda."

"You read it. It was only up there for a second."

"Yes. My brain perceives at a faster rate. I've consciously never displayed this ability in front of you before.
Now that pretense doesn't matter," Mado said, "How did
your mating go?"

"Mating? Do you mean meeting? I didn't have a meeting," Yor said, laughing.

"No, I meant mating. I can smell it on you. I presume
with Insol. She is beautiful in your species standards."

Yor blushed. "The mating went fine. Is this part of
the no pretense Mado, too?"

"Yes," Mado said, "I presume better than fine, since
you two mate quite often. No need to be embarrassed.
My senses are much more perceptive."

"I'm not sure I'm comfortable with this conversation,
but I get it Mado. I'll just need to get used to it," Yor said,
"We had a visit from that GSS man today."

"The same man?"

"Yes, he visited Mel who was distraught to say the
least."

"Did Mel tell you anything?'

"No."

"That's troublesome."

"Troublesome? We're getting close to Breeze Celebration and he appears again. I'd say it's more than troublesome. Makes me think that we should take a step back. Maybe ride out this hearing and try another time."

"I think that's unwise. If he's on the scent, it means he's not going to stop and this might be our only shot."

"Can you say something to the Leader to make him stop?"

"I don't want to call the Leader for that reason. That would be suspicious. I may talk to him in the next couple of days in regard to a project in progress. If I do, then I'll try to slip it into the conversation."

"I have a bad feeling about this man."

"As well you should," Mado said.

The viewing screen displayed an image of Yorlik the Great near the end of his life on the tour supporting the WAEF's move to the estate. Mado turned off the screen. "I don't like those images of your great-grandfather. I care to remember him how I met him. The vibrant, eloquent, strong, genius of a man." Mado saw so much of Yorlik in his great-grandson. He might never possess the scientific genius of his great-grandfather, but he was smart and quick to understand whatever subject he needed to grasp.

"Let's get to work," Yor said. "That'll take my mind off this problem."

Mado worked with Yor from mid-day into late-night running systems checks, firing up the WAEF's engines, and fine tuning them. Nobody at the complex heard the engines at full throttle. Mado instituted a Prevor

Industries mandatory half day of work with pay which he enacted a few times a year. With no workers around, it also guaranteed the restaurants and cafés near the complex were closed. Only the complex's security guards working the main gate heard the engine tests and Mado paid them extra to hear nothing.

Mado hadn't experienced the roar of the engines in decades and he was thrilled when the WAEF came alive. On one test, he created a fault in the engine relays that overloaded the circuits and shut them down. He tasked Yor to debug the problem. Yor solved it in no time and activated the engines. When they finished the tests, they stood tired outside the WAEF admiring it.

"I wish we could just fire it up and fly it out of here," Yor said.

"You and me both. I was thinking the exact same thing earlier before you showed up," Mado said, putting his arm around Yor, "But we don't want to give ourselves away just yet. Nobody knows it's flight worthy except for us."

"I know. Although I'm weary about this GSS man, I'm both anxious and excited to make it all happen."

"Understandable, but maybe you should spend time with your mother."

"Damn! How late is it? She's probably asleep by now. I was going to sleep over there tonight."

"I know that's why I said it."

Yor patted Mado on the back and ran up the stairs instead of waiting for the lift to come down, disappearing through Mado's office door.

Left alone with the WAEF, Mado stood staring up at her again, then closed his eyes, conjuring the sense of the ship's gravity in his bones compared to Koda's gravity which had enslaved him for the past 24 years. He was the only person on this planet who could tell the difference. He was a Prevorian Space Traveler at heart and he never wanted to forget it.

ORN

The day after his visit to Mellick Zonor, Orn sat on a bench along a path running through the Royal University campus. The buildings were some of the oldest on Koda. Built from stone quarries depleted over 400 hundreds years ago. Capitol City had been the seat of Kodan power for nearly a thousand years. Before then, Koda consisted of a handful of countries until Leen the Magnificent conquered one country after another in his bloody battles for planetary unification. He took this city in one of the final battles and claimed it as the capitol for the Global Monarchy. Since then, no major warfare had touched Capitol City so this campus had survived the test of time.

Orn watched as young Kodans walked to one lecture or the other on the crisscross of campus paths. When the Leader had taken rightful control after the riots, Orn attempted to convince him that this place was a breeding ground for treason and should be permanently shuttered. That certainly would have made Orn's job easier. Thinkers were troublesome in maintaining rule. Orn had seen the troublemakers from these institutions in the separatist movements, but the Leader told him that Koda would need these thinkers to move their agenda forward and they'd simply limit them from wandering outside Global

Assembly policies through surveillance and loyalty. The Leader said those who strayed would be made examples through reprogramming or elimination, but Orn understood that was never the end of it. Tetrick Vanderlord was an example of an academic who Orn eliminated, but his thoughts were like a virus passed onto the next generation and now Yor had organized his own cadre here.

For today's assignment, Orn selected a less traveled path to avoid any students questioning his actions, but just in case, he stationed two undercover GSS officers, dressed as students, at either end of the path to reroute anyone down here other than his intended target. Eventually, he spotted Insol Renta heading in his direction. He could see how the Vanderlord boy would be attracted to her Shamban charms. She walked like a Shamban as she glided instead of moving in a gait. Orn blocked her way.

"Excuse me," Insol said and took a step to the right to maneuver around Orn who moved in front of her. "Excuse me." She stepped to the left and Orn blocked her again. "Do we have a problem?" Insol said, "What is the meaning of this?"

"The meaning?" Orn said, "That's what an academic would ask."

"I'm late to my lecture and this isn't funny."

"I agree. There's no humor intended," Orn said, "I'd like to have a word with you about your boyfriend, Yor Vanderlord. Join me on this bench."

Orn immediately saw recognition in Insol's eyes.

She looked down at Orn's hands and his identity was confirmed.

Orn said, "Yor told you about me? I'm touched. Now, sit down."

"I don't think so," Insol said, making a quick move to her left to pass around Orn who lost patience and grabbed her by the arm. She fought to pull away and yelled, "Stop!" Orn increased his grip on her, and she cried out in pain, but continued to resist him.

"I asked you politely and look what you made me do," Orn said, "You can run off, but that won't bode well for your future or your boyfriend's. Now, sit down on this bench or we can go to the Detention Facility." Gripping her arm, he could feel her body surrender so he released his hold on her.

Insol sat down and Orn positioned himself next to her so she'd feel uncomfortable. He expected her to shift away, but she stayed put. She wasn't afraid of him. Shambans were tougher to crack than other Kodans. *They'd been fighting what they deemed their oppression for so long they seemed to come out of the womb fearless,* Orn thought.

"What is it you want? You horrible little man," Insol said, turning and facing Orn down.

"Now that we're settled so cozy on this bench, I'm glad that you understand who I am. Always makes for an easier interrogation."

"Go on," Insol said, "I get the game: Frighten me, then attempt to get information out of me. I suspect you know I've been questioned by GSS officers before."

"Yes, I know, but let me make it perfectly clear, I'm not one of those officers. I can do whatever I please to get the information that I want."

"You are full of yourself, aren't you?"

"I'm surprised you waste your time with a sissy like Vanderlord. Do you pity him?"

"I don't think you'd have any clue what it's like to have a genuine relationship."

"You certainly live up to your file," Orn said, "But this chit-chat is wasting my time."

"Did I hit too close to home?"

"Tell me what Vanderlord is planning, and don't insult my intelligence. Don't tell me that you don't know what I'm talking about. I already know something is happening on Breeze Celebration."

"If you already know so much why do you want me to tell you?"

"There's more to tell and I'm sure you're in on it."

"Are you going to show me a vid of my closest relatives and threaten to eliminate them? If you know me so well, then you know my relatives are well-armed and ready to shoot on sight."

"I know you're at the University on a protected Shamban visa, and I can't drag you into the GSS for more than a day, but I could do lots of damage in a day to get the truth out of you."

"My, oh my, you are a scary man," Insol said, "If you talked to Mel and got him to tell you about Breeze Celebration, then you're aware Yor compartmentalizes our activities. I have no idea what's being planned, but I have faith in Yor."

"Your disloyalty to the Global Assembly disgusts me," Orn said.

"I bet that turns you on, doesn't it?"

Orn peered into the eyes of this defiant woman. Her attempt to get under his skin was working and that was mostly due to Orn's overall frustration with his orders. If the Leader had given him free reign over this investigation, then Vanderlord would be at the Detention Facility with Orn using pliers to pull the truth out of him and having a fine time trying. He felt like he was operating with one hand tied behind his back, but Orn's job was taking orders and carrying them out to the best of his abilities.

"You're a lucky young woman," Orn said.

"What makes me so lucky? Because I've had the honor of being in your presence."

"No, because I'm going to let you go. I believe you know more than you're telling me, but we'll have to pause this interrogation until later and that will be my pleasure."

"I am the lucky girl."

"You have no idea."

"No, I have a clear idea of what you and your people are capable of. I've seen first-hand the trail of devastation that you've wrought on Shamban Freedom Fighters," Insol said, standing up from the bench. "You're despicable and your presence makes me want to wretch."

"One moment before you leave." Orn jumped up and grabbed Insol's arm behind her back, restraining her.

He looked directly over her shoulder at Yor Vanderlord's office window, auto-dialed a number on his comm and said into the receiver, "Look out your window." When Yor appeared at the window, Orn bent and twisted Insol's arm to the point where he could break it with just a little more pressure. Insol screamed in pain. Yor reacted in horror as he watched the agony on her face.

"Now you see," Orn said, whispering into Insol's ear. "I can break you whenever I want." He eased off a bit, then asserted more pressure to the arm and she screamed louder. Yor looked terrified, then he disappeared from view.

"You know," Insol said, struggling to speak through the pain. "You have really bad breath."

Orn wanted to snap her arm in two. He thought about doing it for fun, but he had other plans for her. He eased up and let go. Insol grabbed her arm and gasped in pain. Yor Vanderlord was running down the path towards them.

"You should probably go easy on that arm for awhile, but keep the pain in mind," Orn said, turning about-face and heading towards the campus exit.

RAJER

Rajer sat in an Old Quarter café waiting for his friend to join him. He usually brought a lunch or purchased one at the cafeteria where he worked, because eating out was cost prohibitive on his salary. Since the domes and the perpetual increases in cost of living due to tighter resources, only wealthy citizens ate out and many of them lived in Capitol City, close to the seat of power. The people sitting at the tables around him were far above his pay grade. They were Global Assembly reps, regional lobbyists, or the wealthy working a political angle for their advantage. They wore spendy suits. Rajer wore his government worker attire of button-down shirt and slacks. His security badge was in his pocket. He noticed more than one glance of curiosity from the other patrons and Rajer felt out of place, but as he sipped on a glass of water, he saw this expense as worthwhile.

A waiter came up to the table and asked if Rajer wanted an appetizer or a hot beverage while he waited, and Rajer declined. He'd already waited half his allotted lunchtime and his dining companion hadn't shown up yet. He was afraid that he might end up paying a gratuity for just sitting here, but that would still be cheaper than ordering anything. He pulled out his digi-tablet from his satchel and read the latest news. There was a big spread on the upcoming Breeze Celebration with fotos of Yor and Yorlik the Great set next to one another. The family resemblance was obvious. He was proud of Yor and he was at this café, because of him.

Rajer looked up and his old friend Lek Valsted was pulling out the chair on the other side of the table. They were roommates at the University, and he was Rajer's best man at his commitment ceremony. Rajer saw him a year ago at his daughter's birthday party, but they hadn't seen each other as much over the past ten years since Lek began a family and was promoted to GSS head analyst, where the hours ran past curfew all the time. Lek was a tall thin man who never seemed to age except for the grey hair spreading across the black mop of hair on his head. He was dressed like Rajer, just another government worker.

"Sorry I'm so late."

"No problem. You look tired," Rajer said, "GSS keeping you busy."

"Always gets crazy around Breeze Celebration time, but especially this one," Lek said, seating himself and pushing himself closer to the table. "Policing against incidents before they happen. Every government building and installation is considered a prime target. The Leader is paying close attention to this one. He wants security tight as a drum."

"You can probably blame it on my boy."

"Yes, this WAEF unveiling is an extravaganza. Lots of security headaches. People coming to Capitol City from far and wide using their special travel permits. Extreme vetting of all individuals from children to the elderly. The Global Assembly isn't sparing any expense on the event," Lek said, "Doesn't look like you're sparing any expense here either. What's the occasion, Raj?"

"Yes, nothing is too good for you, my friend," Rajer said, "And I figured this sort of place is less likely to be bugged and no vidcam outside the door."

The waiter came by the table with a pitcher of water and a menu under his arm. He filled Lek's glass and placed a menu in front of him.

"Don't be so sure," Lek said, nudging his head towards the waiter.

"Can I tell you about the specials?" the waiter said.

Lek shrugged his shoulders. Rajer smiled at him.

Lek said, "Why don't you come back in a few minutes?" The waiter bowed slightly and departed.

"Thanks. Those specials would set me back, and Mar doesn't know I'm meeting with you."

"Since when do you keep secrets from one another."

"That's a long story, but it seems like we've been doing it for some time."

"Trouble in paradise?"

"More like complications in paradise, but it'll pass. How are things in your world?"

"You mean my home life? I'm never there and Linara reluctantly puts up with it. I told her to blame you and your family," Lek said, sipping at his water. "We should probably talk faster and get to the subject at hand before we're asked to order."

"Did you look into the concerns I mentioned over the comm? Do you know of any plans for my family?"

"Raj, I told you when you were going to propose to Mar that she was a fantastic woman, but you were committing to the Vanderlords and it wasn't going to be easy especially since she had that boy."

"I do remember the conversation through a Malrap haze at my bachelor party, and you've been a great friend over the years in helping me sort out problems when they've come up. Yor has been trouble every now and then, but I care for him like he was my own son. I'm not sure if he feels the same way. He's not that demonstrative with his feelings, but that doesn't matter because I love his mother."

"I know you do."

"So what do you know? I don't mean to rush you. I have to get back to the office."

"You don't need to apologize. I'm the one who was late," Lek said, "I did some digging, but I came up with nothing, and from what you've told me about recent events, with my clearance, that's unusual. I didn't want to dig any further, because I don't want to alert anybody I'm snooping around. Let's just say, if this man was at the WAEF's homecoming, then he goes way back in the system and he must be close to the Leader. Sounds like he is taking a personal interest in this case, and that can't be healthy for you, Mar, or Yor."

"That's disconcerting."

"I was reminded of a GSS legend about a man who

lurks around the interrogation rooms and appears on the tougher cases around the planet. Your description fits him, but nothing is known about him. I don't know what Yor has gotten himself into, but if it's produced this sort of interest, it must be something big. This could easily blowback on you and Mar. How much do you know about his activities? I have a feeling that you know more than you're letting on."

"Now, you sound like a GSS man."

"I can't help it. That's who I am."

"Yor is good at keeping details to himself," Rajer said. Although he didn't like lying to Lek, he was sworn to secrecy on that night at the bungalow when Yor came home with Mado, and he and Mar were told of their plan.

"I know that you've been supportive of the young man over the years, but as your friend, I'd advise stepping back."

"You know I can't do that. That would be like abandoning Mar."

"I knew that's what you were going to say. You've always been loyal to a fault."

"I've put up with you all these years, haven't I?" Rajer said and they both laughed. "Here comes the waiter. Anything else?"

"No. Just be careful and don't do anything stupid. I know how you tend to let your emotions rule you. That's one of your most endearing qualities, but it could get you in trouble."

The waiter approached the table. "Have you looked at the menus?"

"We've got to get back to our offices. I'll just pay the gratuity," Rajer said, placing his units on the table and pushing back his chair. Lek followed suit and they walked out of the café together.

In the streets of the Old Quarter, workers on ladders installed streamers of colorful banners depicting each of the nine dome-city logos, the Global symbol, and an image of the Leader between the surveillance-cam poles. Hammers rung out as workers built Malrap vending stands and memorabilia kiosks. Trucks pulled up, dropping off Malrap-stand components like chairs and tables and cases of glasses. The Old Quarter streets would be officially closed at the end of the work day and curfew would be extended for the beginning of Breeze Celebration.

"The three nights of Breeze Celebration start tonight," Rajer said, "Let the Malrap drinking begin."

"Those days have passed us, my friend, but we did have some fun in the old days."

"You know it," Rajer said, slapping Lek on the back. "Why don't you return to the Plaza by yourself? If you're right, then we don't want to be seen together. I appreciate what you found out."

"Of course, Raj. Please be careful," Lek said, "See you on the other side." He walked off, winding his way through the construction site.

YOR

The time display on Yor's viewer told him that his colleagues were late for their meeting. He wondered if they were having second thoughts like him. Everyone close to him seemed in danger. The man terrorized Rajer and Mel, then abused Insol. Yor wondered whether Mado was correct about staying the course. He had gone against Mado when it came to the library and that didn't turn out well. Would the man end his reign of terror even if they put a stop to their plans? The Breeze Celebration parade was tomorrow and Yor had been working for years toward the outcome of their plan. *I should be feeling excitement instead of dread.*

Yor had already activated the jammer. He opened the drawer to his desk and looked at the collection of memory wafers. Distributing these to his colleagues today was the key to the Breeze Celebration having its maximum global impact.

His comm buzzed, displaying Ador was calling. When he picked up, Ador's partner Shika spoke to him. She said Ador was unconscious in the intensive-care unit at a clinic and they were saying he might not live out the night. As she spoke, her voice cracked and she began crying.

"What's wrong with him?" Yor said.

Shika composed herself and said, "They say it's some

sort of radiation poisoning. One of the last things he said before he lost consciousness was for me to call you and tell you his condition. How could this have happened?"

"I have no idea," Yor said, "But I will make it down there as soon as possible. Take care of yourself."

Shika hung up.

Yor understood all too well how this happened. During the DOME riots, the opposition leaders and anti-DOME academics withered away and died mysteriously until their autopsy revealed radiation poisoning Yor always thought this was a symptom of his father's death, and Ador's dose must've been substantial to take him from his condition days ago to intensive care today. Radiation poisoning was rare, and the only organization with access to radioactive materials—the hulls of decommissioned SEEDER ships and military weapons—was the Global Assembly.

Bottom line: The man was sending Yor a message. Yor got it loud and clear. He put his head in his hands. He didn't recall the last time he was this uncertain.

"You don't look great," Mel said, standing in the office doorway. "Were you out at Breeze Celebration last night?"

"I wish. Shika just called. Ador is in a clinic dying of radiation poisoning."

Mel sat down in an armchair and Yor joined him.

"I feel horrible," Mel said, "I did this by telling that man about Breeze Celebration. He's doing whatever he can to scare us and tear us apart."

"He shocked you into telling him," Yor said, "You were thinking about your family."

"I don't know what I was thinking. I was weak. You can't trust somebody like him," Mel said, "I'm not backing out on what we've started now. I'm in it for the long haul."

"That's good to hear. Now, where's Harmin?"

"He's in his office. He said he doesn't have time for the meeting and wants me to relay whatever we discuss."

"He is so maddening."

"You know I hate dealing with him as much as you, but we both know he's involved with us for a different reason which is why we included him in the first place," Mel said.

"True," Yor said, "I'm a little concerned that Insol isn't here." Yor walked over to his desk where he'd left his comm and called her. She didn't pick up. He decided not to leave a message, because someone might be listening.

"No answer," Yor said, opening his desk drawer and removing the wafers.

"That's alarming, considering our circumstances," Mel said, "What have you got there?"

"Tomorrow is the day and here are the wafers. I've got lots to do and not much time so I need to get a move on. I haven't seen my mother in awhile and who knows how tomorrow will turnout."

"We've laid the groundwork and we're coordinating everything so others need to hold up their end of the bargain," Mel said, "You'll be fine and you've got Mado to back you up."

"Check on Harmin and make sure he uploads the contents of his wafer before sundown. All the details of your respective assignments are on the memory wafers. Also, please make sure you've given each of us, except for Harmin, access to your respective viewer so one of us can open your wafer files in case you get arrested or incapacitated. Can you handle Ador's assignments?" Yor said, handing Mel the wafers for Harmin, Ador, and himself.

"I've got it handled."

Yor placed Insol's wafer in his satchel, then he had second thoughts and handed it to Mel.

"What's this?"

"Insol's wafer. I've got a backup, but you take this one just in case. I don't want to leave anything to chance and I'm spooked by Ador's situation and Insol not answering her comm. I'll contact you if you need to deal with her assignment too although that's spreading you a bit thin."

"I'll await your call," Mel said, popping up from the chair. "I'll be fine. Go see your mother. Let me know if you get ahold of Insol and send me the details of where Ador is staying. I'll try and get down to the clinic."

Yor held out his arms to Mel and forced back tears.

Mel walked over and embraced Yor. "Good luck, my brother," Mel said, letting go of Yor and stepping back, "Since you were the kid asking questions about the SEEDER program, I've had faith in you. I know you won't disappoint tomorrow."

"Thanks, Mel. I hope that I'm up to it, because right now I'm having some serious doubts."

"Chin up. Great people have your back, even your

great-grandfather must be watching you from the beyond."

"That's closer to the truth than you can imagine."

RAJER

Rajer ended his shift and exited the Budgetary Standards building, stopping at the top of the steps leading down to the street that was teeming with Kodans. Breeze Celebration was in full swing. Many were looking up at the buildings in amazement, as if they were seeing them for the first time. These were probably the travelers who received special permits to attend Capitol City's Breeze Celebration. Of course, the other domes had their Breeze Celebration parades, but Capitol City's was the main celebration on the planet and this one was being hyped as a once-in-a-lifetime experience by the viewing channels and the government.

In a time when the Breeze Celebration seemed more obligatory than celebratory, the Global Assembly saw the WAEF unveiling as an opportunity to return the event to its origins, a festival upholding the ingenuity of its citizens in overcoming an environmental disaster that would otherwise have decimated them. They perceived the Capitol City parade with the WAEF passing through a mobbed Plaza and the frenzy of a sold-out, 200,000-capacity Arena as their way of gaining greater approval of their rule so the government was more than willing to open the floodgates to attendees from around the planet.

That was the gossip around Rajer's office anyway. As

other government employees streamed past him and down the stairs to the street, Rajer thought about Mar's vid of Yorlik's confession and how easily these citizens could be manipulated by the government. *Yor and Mado have the government's eagerness for control playing into their hands.*

The Global Guard would close the Plaza streets to traffic at curfew and set up barriers for tomorrow's parade. Rajer had worked in this district the majority of his adult life and had never seen it so decked out for Breeze Celebration. Streamers and banners flew over every block. Gigantic viewing screens were being mounted on the side of the Plaza buildings. The Malrap vendors had sprung up at least two to a city block and next to them were kiosks selling pennants and placards with the images from the banners and an image of the WAEF with the words 'When All Else Fails' printed on it. *Glorious*, Rajer thought, *If only the Great man were alive to see what transpires tomorrow.*

"You headed home there, Jeps or you going to camp out here?" Rajer turned to see his office mate Zebron standing next to him. Rajer didn't like him, but he put up with him since they were crammed together in the same work space. Zebron was boorish and a suck-up who was constantly campaigning for a promotion and never noticed that his superiors had a similar view of him as Rajer.

"Just taking it all in. Quite the spectacle."

"For the good of the globe," Zebron said.

"For the good of the globe," Rajer replied.

"Although I can't wait for this trash to leave the city and the streets to stop stinking," Zebron said, "Tomorrow is a big day for you and your family. Maybe see you then…if you're lucky." Zebron bounded down the stairs and pushed his way into the flow of people on the sidewalk and disappeared.

If Rajer was going to catch an express rail car home, he needed to get moving so he descended the stairs into the river of pedestrians below. He passed through the Plaza into the Old Quarter where the streets had been closed to traffic since yesterday evening. Food and craft booths lined the streets ready to open for tomorrow's parade festivities. They would be selling food from all over Koda and crafts from the city's artisans. The memorabilia kiosks would do most of their business on the day of the parade, but a few were already busy with out-of-dome visitors who were eager to get into the spirit of the event or city dwellers who wanted to make their purchase ahead of the expected throngs. A child crossed Rajer's path holding a parent's hand, waving a WAEF pennant in the other and smiling and giggling. The sight lifted Rajer's spirits and put him in the mood to celebrate. He told himself that he could always catch the next rail car home, and began scoping out the Malrap vendors.

On the face of it, the Malrap vendors were the biggest financial winners in the Breeze Celebration. They were the only vendor open for the entire three days, and the government subsidized the retail price to a lower cost, increasing sales overall across the planet for the event. This wasn't purely to aid the Malrap industry and intoxicate the masses on Breeze Celebration. The government taxed each barrel and bottle of Malrap throughout the year, and the Breeze Celebration subsidy was a 10% reduction in the tax. This maneuver increased the sales of barrels and bottles by millions, producing trillions more units than usual in tax income for a normal three-day period. As a person working in the Budgetary Standards office, Rajer was privy to the collection of Breeze Celebration Malrap tax income and how the accumulated trillions of units, disappeared into a secret blacked-out account that he couldn't see without higher clearance.

Rajer found a vendor that wasn't too crowded. Each vendor sold bottles for consumption at home or on the streets the day of the parade, and each installed a mini-bar with stools and a table or two for leisurely Malrap drinking by the glass. When Rajer reached the vendor's mini-bar, he heard Zebron's voice booming from one of the tables. "There are so many of them. Why come here and stink up the streets? They can see the damn parade from home."

Rajer continued to the rail car station courtyard where he spotted a Malrap vendor in the morning on his way to work. Business was booming there. He sat at the bar and ordered a small one. From his seat, he viewed the entire Royal skyline—the cathedral, the library, the palace—the stunning ornate and intricate architecture against the monolithic streamlined Global buildings. He recalled the soaring beauty when the sky was behind it instead of the framed transparent panes of the dome.

"So why is this happening this year?" said a loud voice emanating from one of the tables. Over his shoulder, Rajer saw two rail car maintenance workers. They both wore the bright-orange coveralls of the men who worked on the tracks. "Is this some sort of anniversary?" From the slurring of his words, it was clear that he'd drank more than a small one.

Rajer drank down his glass and asked for another. The bartender suggested a larger one to save money. Rajer checked the clock mounted over the rail car station. He and Mar were supposed to meet Yor, but if he caught the rail car after the next one, he'd still make it home in enough time so he ordered a larger one.

The bartender filled a large glass to the top, "That's a lot," Rajer said, "I'll never make it home."

"Some don't," the bartender said, "Rough day?" He was a burly man with a shaved head and scars on his face. Maybe a victim of a few Malrap brawls.

"Today wasn't bad. The past thirty days have been rough."

"Do tell," the bartender said, wiping the bar with a rag and giving a sincere look of interest.

Malrap bartenders were rumored to be government agents who were paid by the quality of their intel. Rajer knew the entire downtown had vidcam coverage so one was spying on the location.

Rajer took a healthy swig. "Oh you know, family stuff."

"Been there. You have a child?"

A crowd of government employees still wearing their security badges surrounded the bar clamoring for Malrap. They were mostly Yor's age. Chances were they didn't have a family waiting for them at home. Breeze Celebration with its Malrap consumption was a great way to meet and become acquainted with your future commitment-partner. The term 'Breeze Celebration baby' was connected to the sexual promiscuity attributed to the overconsumption of Malrap during the Celebration days.

While the bartender's attention shifted to his new patrons, Rajer took the opportunity to grab his glass and sit at a vacant table. The intoxicated rail car maintenance workers pushed back their chairs, teetered to a standing position, then meandered towards the station. Three of the more youthful government workers from the bar took the rail car workers table. One of the three, a young woman, noticed that Rajer was staring at her, smiled and raised a glass in his direction. Rajer smiled back, embarrassed. He didn't realize what he was doing. This woman reminded him of a younger Mar that Rajer had seen in fotos. She was late twenties with long dark hair flowing over her shoulders, wearing a shirt buttoned down enough to reveal her cleavage which was about the same as Mar's.

"Happy Breeze Celebration," the woman said, "Would you care to join us?"

"No, thank you," Rajer said, taking out his comm as if he were checking for a call. The woman turned her attention back to her friends. He kept his comm on the table next to his drink, continuing to look down at it and sipping his drink, then he couldn't help himself and stared back over at the table. The woman was sitting with two men about the same age who were clearly button-down government workers with security badges. On the man closest to him, Rajer spotted 'Dept of Education and Well-Being' on his badge. Those less enamored with the Global Assembly like Yor, called this government branch the Department of Indoctrination and Brain-Washing.

"So is everyone excited about Breeze Celebration tomorrow?" one of the men said.

"What's to be excited about?" the other man said, "Crowds and more crowds on the streets and in the rail cars. And this speech by the great-grandson of Yorlik the Great. Has anybody seen a transcript of the speech?"

"Hasn't come down to us," the first man said, "It's all being kept at the highest levels."

"How safe is that?" the second man said.

"It's not our place to question," the woman said. "For the good of the globe."

"For the good of the globe," the two men said in unison.

"Anyway, I took a class from Professor Vanderlord at the University when I went back to finish my higher degree," the woman said, "A brilliant man. Kind of cute, too. Have either of you read his book?"

"This shop talk is making me thirsty," the first man said and held up his half-empty glass. "Happy Breeze Celebration."

All three of them held up small drinks and swallowed down their remaining Malrap in one gulp.

"Another round?" the first man said and they all nodded, and he took all three glasses in hand. The woman whispered in his ear and the man chuckled, then he headed for the bar.

"I don't suppose you've read Vanderlord's book," the woman said to the remaining man.

"I haven't read it, but I've read about it."

"The book is a detailed look into the history of the SEEDER program leading up to the fall of the Monarchy and the controversy between the advocates of the DOME project and SEEDER program. You'd expect some bias in the book considering there's a personal connection between the central figure who is arguably the most famous Kodan in modern history and the author, but it's basically balanced in its insight. Depending on your loyalties, I can see leaning one way or the other in the DOME versus SEEDER argument. The SEEDER point of view is laid out in a clear concise manner which hasn't been done in recent years. That's why the book has been so popular in my opinion."

"His father Tetrick Vanderlord was the agitator, correct? It was before my time, but my parents had a friend who was a follower. He was a secondary school teacher who was fired for teaching Tetrick Vanderlord's point of view on history instead of the government-sanctioned textbook curriculum."

"Yes, that was years ago. Tetrick Vanderlord is in the

past. As a people we've put that behind us. The domes are here to stay and he was obviously wrong in his views."

"I'll drink to that," the man said, picking up his empty glass and flipping it open-end down with a loud thump on the table. "Where's our drinks?" The man peered over his shoulder at the bar where his friend was standing in line.

Rajer stared back at his comm, then removed his digi-tablet from his satchel. He read the news. It was dominated by the upcoming Breeze Celebration. Yor had refused interviews with every viewing channel and digi-media outlet which initially displeased the government. Yet this action caused an anticipation regarding his speech and was the most talked about topic in the news, living rooms, and work places across the globe. And this coverage caused the government to back off on their insistence that Yor participate in interviews. Rajer was impressed by the impact of Yor's strategy, although Mado was due credit, too.

Rajer perused a story on the unprecedented turnout expected in Capitol City. Another story covered how the demographic of travelers between domes was typically the wealthy, but regular citizens were spending their hard-earned income, traveling to Capitol City for the unveiling of the restored WAEF. *The hype is working*, Rajer thought.

"It's about time," the man at the table said as the other returned from the bar.

"Did you see the line? You can get the next round," the other man said.

"Excuse me, sir?" the woman said, louder than her companions. "Sir? You over there staring at your digi-tab?"

The woman was holding out a large glass of Malrap towards Rajer. He was only halfway through the one that he ordered earlier. "We've got an extra one," the woman said.

"I haven't even finished this one," Rajer said, holding up his glass.

"We've got one too many," the woman said, smiling, "We wouldn't want it to go to waste. It's Breeze Celebration, right? Join with your citizens to celebrate the survival of the Kodan people. Come on over."

Rajer looked down into his half-empty glass. He was not usually a Malrap drinker, and he already felt his mind sliding into intoxication. He heard the sound of a chair being pushed back. The woman was headed his way with a full large glass in hand. It was uncanny how she had a similar appearance to Mar at that age. Even in her bland government outfit, Rajer found her ravishing. Along with the government-approved light-blue button-down shirt, she wore darker tight pants which accentuated her hips and posterior. She was his type of woman, too—assertive and smart. He was feeling a stirring he'd only felt for Mar since they'd been together. He was sure the Malrap was taking over. *I have to admit. I kind of like it,* Rajer thought.

Now, the woman stood across the table from him. "You sure you don't want to join us," the woman said, lifting her glass towards Rajer. "A toast. For the good of the globe."

Rajer did not want to be discourteous and not

responding to the Global Assembly's salute was blasphemous in most government-worker circles. He held up his
glass, looked up at the woman and said, "For the good of
the globe," then drank down the rest of the Malrap in his
glass and the woman drank half of her glass.

"You're positive you won't join us? We still have that
extra glass. Looks like you're empty."

The two men were smiling at Rajer. One of them
pointed to the full glass. The other was waving him over.
The rail car station clock showed more time needed to
elapse before the next express rail car home. Rajer sensed
he was losing control. He was imbibing Malrap on an
empty stomach which was never a good strategy for a
casual Malrap drinker. "I probably shouldn't," Rajer said.
He hadn't meant to say that out loud.

"You looked over at the station clock. Do you have
a car to catch? Somebody waiting for you?" the woman
said, moving closer. Rajer could smell her perfume. Her
scent reminded him of an old girlfriend, one of his first,
who taught him the finer points of sexual interaction.

"Yes…and yes," Rajer said. He wanted to say a sentence that was a bit more eloquent, but his mind couldn't
find the words

"Well that sounds like a yes to me. I'll make it easy
for you." She walked back to her table, saying something
in a low volume to the two men that Rajer couldn't hear,
and brought the full glass back to him, placing it on the
table in front of him. Before Rajer could say anything she
sat across from him.

Her scent overwhelmed him and he couldn't control his eyes which gravitated to the buttons undone on her shirt and the sight of her cleavage and bosom. His heart was racing. "I'm sorry," Rajer said, grasping onto the full glass as if it would keep him from falling out of his seat or losing more control. "I don't mean to be impolite. Thanks for the Malrap. I generally don't drink this much."

"You don't say," the woman said, pushing her chair in further. "It's Breeze Celebration so might as well cut loose. That's what this celebration is all about. I assume you work for a government agency."

"Yes. Nothing as engaging as the department of in... education."

"Oh yes," the woman said, reaching down to her security badge. "Forgot I was still wearing this. We were so excited about getting out of the office and engaging in the festivities that I forgot to take it off." She removed the badge and placed it on the table between them, brushing Rajer's hand still holding the glass.

"Sorry," Rajer said, sliding the glass closer to himself. Rajer saw on the badge that her first name was Roneh.

"Sorry for what? You're a skittish one, so shy. No need to be concerned. That one sitting over there is my partner." She pointed to the man who had gone to the bar. "I've heard all his stories though and he's heard mine. I thought it might be nice to chat with another person, and you seem pleasant. I'm from the department of ineducation though."

"I didn't mean anything..."

"Sure you did. That's all right. I've heard it all before: Department of Indoctrination, Department of Ignorance, Department of Intolerance and Disbelieving, Department of Disinformation. I could go on. Everybody has a job to do and it's not always easy. Isn't that what the government posters say? The ones they hang in our offices to ease our days along. I get it. What did you say that you do?"

"I didn't. I'm a financial examiner in Budgetary Standards."

"I never would have guessed it," the woman said, then called over to her companions. "He does work for Budgetary Standards." Immediately, one of the men looked annoyed, reached into his pocket, and began counting currency in the direction of the other man.

"What's that about?"

"They had a bet where you worked."

"Is that why you're sitting here?"

"Not at all. I was serious about what I said. I enjoy meeting people and Breeze Celebration is the best day for it. Malrap makes everyone friendlier."

Rajer lifted the glass to his mouth and took a healthy sip. *What am I doing*, Rajer thought, *Must be the Malrap and now I've got more.* "I guess that's the truth. You remind me of my partner."

"I'm flattered. She must be quite a woman. A beautiful woman," the woman said and chuckled.

"I think she is, but she also speaks her mind and damn the implications which sometimes creates friction. At the end of the day, I completely appreciate it. One of the reasons I love her."

"I like friction," the woman said and chuckled.

An awkward silence ensued. Rajer sipped at his Malrap.

"You have children?" the woman said.

"No. We never had a child, but my partner has a child from another marriage."

"That can be difficult sometimes."

"There were rough patches. Some rougher than rough patches. Tough stepping in for another parent, but my partner was always there to make everything better and the boy finally came around."

"Boys can be tough especially when it comes to their mother re-marrying. Is the father still prominent in the boy's life?"

"No. He passed before I met his mother."

"Powers-that-be keep him. So you married a widow with a young boy. Lots of men wouldn't take that on. You're a good man. You must really love her. How old is the boy now?"

"He's 24 years old. Still lives at home. No family yet."

"What does the young man do for employment? Did he follow you into public service?"

"He followed his father."

"So what's his profession?" the woman said, drinking her Malrap.

"He's a professor at the University," Rajer said, taking a long swig from his Malrap and realizing that he somehow finished his glass. "Wow! How did I do that?"

The woman laughed. "Malrap works that way sometimes. So what does he teach at the University?"

The man who the woman pointed out as her partner brought over another large glass of Malrap and placed it in front of Rajer removing the empty glass. The woman kissed her partner on the lips and he walked off.

"Thank you!" Rajer said, calling after the man as he walked back to his table. "I think...what was your question?" Rajer's mind and body were now sodden with Malrap. He consciously wanted to push this glass away, knowing he had lost control, but that being the case, he gulped down half the new glass' contents.

"What does your stepson teach at the University?"

"Actually, I have to admit I was eavesdropping on your conversation earlier. You were talking about him. Yor Vanderlord. He is an incredible young man and we're proud of him."

"Eavesdropping. You naughty man," the woman said, brushing Rajer's hand holding the glass. Rajer did not move away this time. "He says, Yor Vanderlord is his stepson," the woman called over to her companions. Other people in the bar looked over.

Rajer waved at the people in the bar looking his way.

"I'm in the company of the stepfather of a famous person. The man who is going to give the Breeze Celebration keynote speech tomorrow in front of the entire planet. That's really something. You have any idea what he is going to say?"

"If I did, the speech wouldn't be much of a surprise."

"A surprise? Don't be so coy," the woman said.

"Am I being coy?" Rajer said, patting her hand on the table. He was flirting with her. Consciously, he comprehended what he was doing. He probably shouldn't be doing it, but it felt great in the moment.

"Yes, you are being coy. You naughty boy. I see now you were just acting shy. Will you be in attendance tomorrow when your stepson gives his speech? You and his mother?"

"Yes I will. We will."

"I'm sure his mother will be beaming with pride over her baby boy. What is her name?"

"Mar," Rajer said, sipping at the new glass of Malrap.

"Mar. A pretty name. She must be proud of her son achieving so much at such a young age, but then his great-grandfather was a prodigy himself so kind of runs in the family. If she chose you after her brilliant husband, then you must be quite remarkable."

"I'll take that as a compliment," Rajer said, taking a bigger drink.

"You should, because I meant it that way," the woman said, sipping from her glass.

Rajer felt her shoeless foot working its way up his thigh and he became aroused. He didn't stop her, although he knew that he should.

"I appreciate it. Sometimes it's difficult," Rajer said, wondering what he was doing. "Almost like I'm a second-class citizen in the household. The boy looms large."

"I bet. I bet. His book was a best-seller and now the restoring of Yorlik the Great's spaceship and giving this speech in front of the planet that everyone is excited about. You must give me a preview."

"I don't think I should."

"Please," the woman said, working her foot around. "Please. I won't tell another person. I promise, not even my partner and his friend over there."

"I don't know."

"You know you want to tell me. You don't want our friendship to end on a sour note, do you?"

Rajer was positive he didn't want what she was doing with her foot to stop. He peered over at the clock above the station and couldn't believe that he missed the second rail car he'd been waiting on. He had the time to tell her now and a half glass of Malrap in front of him and what she was doing with her foot felt sublime.

"Please," the woman said, leaning towards him displaying her breasts and the scent of her perfume engulfed him. "Please."

Yor would be furious, but what could this woman say or do that might alter their plan. *How could it hurt?* he thought, *I won't giveaway the entire speech, just the gist of it.* Yor read an early draft in front of him and Mar.

"I probably shouldn't," Rajer said, taking another healthy swig of Malrap. "But since you asked so nicely I can probably give you a taste. A little preview. I can only paraphrase, of course."

"Of course. That would be incredible," the woman

said, working her foot around some more.

Rajer was aware that he shouldn't. All logic inside him was screaming for him to stop before it was too late, but he couldn't help himself. "He is going to start the speech talking about the restoration of the WAEF and the great achievements of his great-grandfather and the sacrifice he made for his love of the planet and its people, that the WAEF was a symbol of all the incredible achievements of the planet's citizenry..." *I need to stop there*, Rajer thought, *I need to stop now*. He might put Yor in danger if he went any further, but the pleasure was too great and the Malrap overcame his ability to give up the pleasure and stop himself. He began to hate himself, but that didn't stop him.

"...and then he will launch into the grand farce of the DOME project, forestalling the inevitable. If we as a people don't restart our mission for a new home somewhere in the universe, then our resources will eventually run out and we we'll be facing the same dilemma as before the domes. There will be lotteries and our families and friends will be banished to the hellish world outside the domes until only the wealthy and their cronies survive..."

The woman removed her foot and stood up. "You got that," the woman said into the bracelet on her wrist and walked out of the bar with her companions. Rajer was flabbergasted. He was numb. He was not sure what had happened, but he was certain that it was not good. He gazed down at the unfinished Malrap in his glass, then gulped it all down.

Rajer left the Malrap vendor and decided to walk around the station courtyard a few times to sober up before the next rail car arrived. His legs were rubbery and he veered around the courtyard, almost losing his balance a few times, then he noticed a food kiosk, selling fried kelsaw. The delicacy was known for neutralizing the effect of Malrap in the metabolism and he was intoxicated enough that he purchased two servings. He sat down on a bench, devouring them, and staring up at the station clock.

Rajer was ashamed at himself and concerned he had destroyed what Yor worked so hard to achieve. He worried he might lose Mar's respect and love. He worried he might lose his job and the government-sanctioned bungalow that was home to his family who he betrayed through his stupidity. He took a few deep breaths and wiped the grease from the kelsaw on his pants. *What have I done?*

Before he entered the station, he bought a bottle of Malrap. He thought he might need it.

MAR

Mar experienced a rough couple of days at work. Not only was the med clinic busy with their usual patient load, but it was overrun by the victims of the Breeze Celebration's Malrap binge which was a three-day health hazard. Med facilities were packed with broken bones and head injuries, attempted suicides, wounds from fights with sharp objects, shootings from ex-soldiers' government-issued weapons, domestic abuse, and Malrap overdose which brought on temporary-to-permanent blindness.

Mar arrived home exhausted and found the front door open. Since Yor was detained and Rajer was accosted by that man, her concern for her family's security was heightened. She took a few deep breaths while meditating on the global peace symbol, the open hands of peace, painted on the door. *Maybe Rajer forgot to lock up on the way to work. Sometimes he did that.*

Mar entered with caution, slowly opening the door with one hand and in the other was her comm which was set to auto-dial the authorities at a touch of her finger. The house was quiet and she took a few steps in, but left the door open behind her.

"Hello mother," Yor said, lifting himself up from where he'd been laying on the couch.

Mar was stunned. "Yor! For the powers-that-be sake, you scared the life out of me."

"I thought you were made out of tougher stuff," Yor said, walking around the couch and hugging her. "Shall I close the door?"

"Been a long day," Mar said, tightening her hug on her son. "Considering what's coming, you're correct, I need to put on a tougher skin."

"Sorry about frightening you, but I do still live here," Yor said, closing the door.

"Yes, you do, but you've been working late and sleeping over at Mado's and Insol's so I never know when to expect you," Mar said, "Just been a crazy few days at work. Malrap madness is upon us."

"Sit down. Can I get you anything?"

"No, I just want to get off my feet and visit with you," Mar said, sinking into the couch with Yor beside her. He removed the jamming device from his satchel, placed it on the table and activated it.

"I hate that thing," Mar said, flicking it with a finger. "Signifies everything I hate about this entire business. Heading toward danger just like your father and you see how that turned out for him...for all of us. Maybe I made a mistake naming you after your great-grandfather. You've got too much of the Vanderlord in you already." She clutched at his arm.

"Isn't that part of what you loved about father?"

"Part of it. That's true. I just don't see why you have to lead everything. Not like you inherited the position from your father."

"I guess there might be some truth in that inheritance. If I wasn't his son, would I feel compelled to defend what he gave his life for?"

"He gave his life for you."

"Yes, but he gave his life for something greater, the survival of the people who live on this planet, who are living a lie created by greed that will eventually collapse around them. What happens then? You know Insol received documents from a compatriot who broke into the government data system and found clandestine plans to build a handful of spaceships for the Global Assembly and their families to escape when the domes fail. They know the end is coming in a few generations, that these domes will not last under the conditions of the deteriorating environment…"

"Please Yor, I don't need the speech right now. You are so your father's son."

"…and they've amassed these fortunes to build spaceships for themselves."

"And where will they go?"

"The plans are for long-distance ships to travel for decades, maybe centuries, using new cryotech on the passengers. They'll have no destination, but will end up searching like great-grandfather. They made great-grandfather delete everything and he never gave them precise coordinates."

"Seems criminal to condemn these people to wander in space for decades."

"At least they'll survive. Anyway, once the truth gets out, these plans will be void."

"I don't want to argue. I believe in what you're doing, but I'm your mother so I'm concerned about you. That's all."

"It'll work out fine."

"I believe in you, Yor. I believed in your father. I just don't know if I can stand the same thing happening to you that happened to your father. You're so young and have such a bright future…and I know what you're going to say, what future?"

A comm buzzed. Yor took his comm out of his satchel and answered it. "Hello…Yes…What?…I'm so sorry… You know I loved him…I'll tell her…Let us know if you need anything. Take care of yourself."

Mar saw sadness creep into Yor's face. "What's wrong?"

"That was Shika Wint. Ador is dead."

"How? I didn't know that he was sick."

"Radiation poisoning."

"Those bastards!" Mar yelled, then she saw the tears welling in Yor's eyes.

"This is all my fault. I tried to convince Mado that we should back off. That man has been harassing my staff, my friends. I saw Ador a few days back and he didn't look well, but I had no idea how bad. Shika just called me this morning and told me that Ador was in intensive care. It happened so fast. I didn't get to say goodbye. This is my fault," Yor said and began to cry.

Mar took him into her arms and held him as he wept,

and she began to cry, too.

The front door opened to the sound of crowds on the street, air horns and fireworks going off. Rajer entered carrying his work satchel in one hand and a bottle of Malrap in the other. He shut the door and stopped in front of the couch. Mar looked over at him, still holding Yor. "What's going on?" Rajer said, "You two look like somebody died."

Yor began crying again.

"Actually somebody did," Mar said, "Ador Wint died. Shika just called. Radiation poisoning." Mar saw the look of recognition in Rajer's face. He knew what that meant, too.

"Wow," Rajer said, "I don't know what to say." He looked down at the bottle of Malrap in his hand. "I've got an idea."

Rajer headed into the kitchen, returning with three glasses, and sat down in the chair by the couch and began pouring generous portions of Malrap.

Mar released her embrace on Yor and he wiped at his eyes.

When Rajer was filling the last one, Mar said, "Not too much for me."

Rajer and Yor exchanged a glance and Rajer filled the glass to the top, then handed it to Mar. She laughed. Rajer knew what she needed better than herself sometimes.

"Would you care to make a toast?" Rajer said to Mar.

"All right," Mar said, raising her glass. "To Ador Wint. A gentle and kind soul who was supportive of this family through tough times. And if it wasn't for Ador, I wouldn't have met Rajer."

"And I couldn't have had a better friend and mentor. He could always make me laugh," Yor said as his voice cracked under the emotion. Mar put her arm around him.

Rajer lifted his glass. "I'll drink to all of that."

They all took a drink. Mar sipped at hers. She hated the drink. The smell reminded her of a Malrap-sodden Tetrick in the days before his death. Tetrick refused to ingest the government-issued pain meds so he dulled the pain with Malrap.

Rajer drank about half his glass. Yor drank down the entire thing.

"I don't know how you do it," Rajer said.

Yor poured himself another glass. "I'm not fond of Malrap, but Vanderlords are partial and impervious to this elixir," Yor said, "Mado told me the Great man had a taste for Malrap, too."

"Partial, yes. Impervious, no," Mar said.

"So we all have a pretty clear idea what happened to Ador. Is that a correct assumption?" Rajer said.

"It's my fault," Yor said.

"That's ridiculous," Mar said, "You didn't poison him. More than anybody else, Ador had a clear idea of what could happen if he became the focus of the GSS."

A hard knock at the front door made Mar jump in her seat.

"I'll get it," Rajer said. "Must be some Malrap drunk at the wrong address."

When Rajer opened the door, Mar heard a voice from her past say, "May I come in?" and her body went cold. Rajer's face was paralyzed with fear.

"I don't know," Rajer said, sounding a little intoxicated. "Is this an official visit?"

"I'm here, aren't I?" the voice said, "No need to be rude. We're all acquainted here." Then the man stepped around Rajer into the house.

Mar recognized him right away. He had gained weight. He had aged. He wasn't evil enough to stop time. Mar saw him the last time about twelve years ago. After her confrontation with him at the GSS, the man began escorting Tetrick home from the Detention Facility himself. He always had his arm hooked around Tetrick's arm, holding him up, then handed him off to Mar, smirking the entire time. He was the face of her misery all those years ago.

Mar stood and pointed at him. "I don't want you in my home."

The man grabbed the frame of the open door, the scars on his hands appeared deeper than she remembered, then he shut the door behind him. "You can either listen to me here or we can all take a ride to the Detention Facility. I have a vehicle and men outside. I don't think any of you want that."

"Then don't come in any further. Stand right there and tell us what you need to say," Mar said.

Yor stood next to Mar and held her hand. Rajer stepped back a few steps as if the man was a rabid dog. Mar noticed that Yor was attempting to block the jamming device from the man's view.

"When did we first meet, Mar? About 24, 25 years ago? You were pregnant with this one. A joyous day when Yorlik the Great returned to Koda. Do you recall that?"

Mar stood silent. She was not going to be drawn in by his banter and make this scene seem normal. She wanted to yell at him, but she controlled herself. She didn't want to give him the satisfaction.

The man continued, "Of course you do. I met your boy and your new husband awhile back. I'm sure you heard about it. Looks like you're not in the mood for small talk, but the reason I'm here..." The man noticed Rajer was standing near him. "Rajer Jeps, no need to stand so close. Please sit down so I can fully address the entire family at once."

Rajer hesitated as if he wanted to say something and make a stand against this man, instead he sheepishly walked back to the chair and sat down.

Mar didn't think any less of him. More than anybody in this room, she understood what this man represented and what he could do to them. He could destroy their lives with a wave of his hand. She squeezed Yor's hand tight until he flinched and looked at her. She glanced at him thinking *Don't say anything stupid,* hoping he could read her thoughts via the expression on her face. The man strolled into the living room, observed a foto featuring a young Tetrick and examined it. Yor seized the opportunity. He let go of Mar's hand, palmed the jamming device, sticking it in-between the couch cushions, then seated himself. He tugged on

Mar's shirt and she sat down, too.

"Let's get to the issue at hand, shall we?" the man said, turning away from the foto. "Thirty days ago, I met Rajer and Yor and I believe I made myself clear regarding the consequences of activities that might run counter to the Global Assembly's political agenda. Tomorrow is Breeze Celebration. Yor is presenting his great-grandfather's restored spaceship to the planet and giving the keynote speech. The excitement on the viewing channels is exactly what the Global Assembly wants. To be honest, I told the relevant powers in the government that I didn't like this Breeze Celebration publicity stunt. I heard about it and I hated it. This family has been a pain in my side for over 24 years, starting with your husband and father, then your great-grandfather. My predecessor lost his job over Naivim Vanderlord's antics…" His voice trailed off. He'd gone off on a tangent, and he was lost in thought attempting to get back to his point. He seemed flustered.

Mar wanted him out of her home. "We've been model citizens for years. Why are you back in our lives all of a sudden?"

The man snorted through his nostrils, then performed a military about face, marched away from them, peering down at the floor. The cabinet had never been moved back properly and there was a distinct mark in the carpet where the cabinet had resided for years. She assumed the man was trained to heed such details. When he turned back around, his anger was palpable, clenching his fists. He marched towards the couch and stopped almost exactly where he previously stood. He was breathing heavier and his body was taut like an animal about to pounce.

"I'm attempting to give you fair warning. I could drag your son into detention for the jammer he hid in the couch or tear this place apart to see what I can find. I could take away your life in this cozy bungalow, placing each of you in a detention cell for the rest of your lives. Don't take me for the fool. I'm well aware that something is brewing here, but I'm being held back by my superiors who believe their hold on power is based on publicity and pandering while I firmly land in the camp where the only way to hold on to power is asserting it by force. So let's cut the model citizen crap, shall we? I know that Prevor is somehow involved too, but I can't touch him."

Then the man pointed at Yor. The scars on the back of his hand were hideous as if they were done by a jagged piece of metal. "I've been watching you and your colleagues. I know you think that you've got the world sorted out and you'll make it what you want, but I will dismantle your existence piece by piece starting with your mother," the man said, taking a few more steps forward and pointing at Mar. "So watch your step at Breeze Celebration. I'll literally be right behind you. Am I making myself clear?"

Silence ensued while the man waited for an answer. The Breeze Celebration noises outside could be heard along with the low hum of the bungalow's power source. Yor reached over and held Mar's hand. He was smiling. She was terrified.

Yor said, "I hear you and you're making yourself clear."

He let go of Mar's hand, stood up, and took a few steps so he was face-to-face with the man. "You level threats and terrorize me, my family and my friends, but I don't fear you. Mado Prevor had a conversation with the Global Leader a few days ago and although Mado doesn't know your name and the Leader wouldn't tell him, Mado told the Leader we might not be able to deliver what we promised at Breeze Celebration with your dark cloud hanging over us. Obviously, you need to talk to the Leader, because he implicitly guaranteed that moments like the one you've orchestrated here wouldn't happen. We can call the Leader and tell him about your belligerence or you can apologize to my mother and leave her house now." Yor sat back down, glaring the entire time at the man and took Mar's hand once again.

The man exhaled and closed his eyes. He was composing himself to make his next move. Mar was afraid what that might be, then the man walked into the kitchen. She couldn't hear what the man was saying, but he was obviously using his comm and was talking to somebody. She heard him say, "Unbelievable!" then cooking pans crashed to the floor.

A few moments later, he returned to the room and stood in front of them. He was clearly angry, but composed. "I sincerely apologize for any inconvenience, Mar Jeps. My intrusion into your home and my tone of voice were uncalled for. If I caused you any distress, I was out of line and I hope you can forgive me and not take my actions as any sort of provocation by the Global Assembly.

Rajer Jeps, I apologize to you as well. Yor Vanderlord, I wish you the best of luck at Breeze Celebration and please understand that my words were of a unilateral nature and not the language of the Global Assembly. I bid you all a good day." The man marched toward the door, opened it halfway, then called over Yor.

When Yor arrived at the doorway, the man said something in his ear, then stepped out of the bungalow. Yor yelled out the door, "Damn you!" then slammed the door shut and stormed back into the room. He refilled his glass with Malrap, drank it down in one gulp, and plopped down onto the couch, visibly shaken.

"What did he say?" Rajer said.

"He told me that Insol is in the southeast med clinic. She was attacked on the streets by a mob of men, brutalized and sexually assaulted. He said, 'I'm not really sure how that could have happened. Such a pity.' Then he winked at me and left."

"I don't know what to say," Rajer said.

"I know what to say," Mar said, "We both know that bastard arranged the attack. He knows no bounds. First, Ador and now Insol."

"I know what I have to do," Yor said, "I need to comm Mado and tell him that we need to call off tomorrow or temper what we've planned. Nobody else can get hurt because of me. Who's next? You or Rajer?"

"You will not," Mar said, "You will not. You will do what you planned to do. This family will not be intimidated by the likes of that monster."

"Mother…"

"Don't 'mother' me. I know I've been worried about your safety and this is a trying time for you, but you've gotten this far with your intellect and Mado's help. The plan you told us about is brilliant. You're about to address the entire planet with the truth. Now is no time to back down and let them win, let that monster win. You can't let them believe what they've done to Insol, Ador, and your father is okay, and that we're timid sheep who will just back down. You have to set the record straight for every Kodan and let them decide their future."

Rajer and Yor were smiling at her.

"What?" Mar said. "That's how I feel."

"I'm constantly reminded why I love you," Rajer said.

"You never fail to amaze me," Yor said, hugging her.

Yor poured another glass for himself, then topped off the others. He stood and lifted his glass. Mar stood and Rajer followed.

"I'm not sure what the future holds," Yor said, "But let's hope this is the beginning of a brighter one."

"I'll drink to that," Mar said and drank down her entire glass of Malrap. Yor and Rajer followed suit. Mar's body shook in revulsion at the quantity she'd consumed. "I don't know why anybody drinks this poison."

"I should head over to the med clinic and see Insol before curfew," Yor said, "I need to wake up at Mado's in the morning."

"I have something to tell you first," Rajer said.

YOR

As Rajer told Yor about meeting the woman at the Malrap vendor earlier in the day, his face contorted, attempting to hold back tears, but he wept by the end of the story.

Yor felt bad for Rajer, but he couldn't help himself and smiled.

His mother went over and embraced Rajer. "Yor Vanderlord! Look at Rajer. Why are you smiling? I didn't raise you to be so insensitive."

"I know it looks that way," Yor said, "But this uncontrollable weeping is a product of the large quantity of Malrap that Rajer ingested. I'm sure you feel bad about what happened, Rajer, but this is textbook Malrap withdrawal. Mother, you should know that."

Yor carried the Malrap bottle into the kitchen and threw it in the trash. When he returned to the living room, Rajer was wiping away his tears and his mother was still comforting him.

"I'm truly sorry, Yor," Rajer said, weeping again.

"No damage done. The speech I read to you and mother was an early draft and now it's more multi-media."

"How? What are you going to do?" his mother said.

"I want to tell you, but at this juncture, Mado and I have decided that we should keep all of tomorrow's details to ourselves," Yor said, "The ambush on Rajer will actually work to our advantage. The man now thinks he knows how everything will go down tomorrow. We've manufactured expectations for him, and we already have a contingency plan in place and a few safeguards. You'd be amazed at Mado's foresight. He calculated somebody would spill the text of the speech since a handful of family and friends have read it or heard it, and he already had an alternative plan ready."

Rajer grabbed his forehead with both hands and screamed in pain. His mother stared into his pupils and took his pulse.

"And again, Mado thought this would happen too," Yor said, opening his satchel and removing a small vial containing a clear liquid and handed it to his mother.

"What's this?" his mother said.

"Mado was sure that somebody we knew would be drugged with a truth serum that the GSS uses. Wasn't just Malrap that made you spill the speech, Rajer. They wanted to be positive you'd tell them what they wanted to know. I'm surprised they didn't do something to increase your heart rate, too. That serum will usually provide a bad headache, but add in the Malrap and the headache will pack a wallop. Mado concocted this to relieve the pain of whoever was drugged. I've been carrying this in my satchel since shortly after the library incident."

Yor saw the look of disbelief on his mother's face. Yor knew that look. Mado's sheer brilliance in working out solutions to problems before they ever happened was mind-bending. Of course, he wasn't from Koda and he was an advanced species which explained a great deal.

"I'd like to know what's in this? Medical curiosity, of course," his mother said, scrutinizing the fluid in the vial.

"Yes I know," Yor said, kissing his mother on the cheek. "Mado said that you'd ask."

Yor went to his bedroom and shut the door, leaning with his back against it and taking a deep breath. He was shaken by the appearance of the man and the news about Ador and Insol. Maybe the Malrap was causing the panic attack. Yor wasn't a regular Malrap drinker even when he was a lower classman and Malrap binging was his University classmates way of having fun. As a child, he watched his father intoxicated, ranting and raving, throwing and shattering objects against the walls of their home, and it turned him off to the drink as an enjoyable pastime. Now, he took a few more deep breaths.

"Are you all right in there?" his mother called to him.

Yor forgot about the thin walls. He sat down on the edge of his bed holding his knees, feeling sick. He thought about the encounter in the living room with the man. Confrontation wasn't anything new to him: Being the head of a department at the University, he handled colleagues' egos clashing and students feeling they'd been graded improperly and treated poorly by himself or the staff under his supervision. Dealing with this man was a different level entirely.

Mado had foreseen the recent ambush on Rajer, but he hadn't predicted the man showing up at the bungalow and threatening Yor and his family especially after talking to the Leader. He hadn't predicted what happened to Insol. The man's movements seemed to be blocked from Mado's incredible ability to predict and plan into the future. Maybe it was because Mado didn't know how to think like a sadist.

On an intellectual level, Yor always understood the magnitude of their plan and its impact on his life, his mother's and Rajer's, but the reality was beginning to dawn on him. He ran into the bathroom and vomited in the sink.

There was a knock on the bedroom door. "You sure you're all right in there," his mother said.

"I'm fine. Just a little sick. Not much of a Malrap drinker. I'll be out soon. I just need to get a few things together," Yor said as he cleaned up the mess.

Everything is set in motion. There's no turning back now, Yor thought. He had implicated dozens of people in his own outlandish dream and they'd all agreed. Now it was almost time to pull off his most significant part of the plan and maybe what happened in the living room between him and the man proved he was up to the task.

Still, the man had made it perfectly clear that Yor shouldn't take his threats lightly. Mado recalled hearing about the man's first appearance at the landing site from Yor's great-grandfather, and Mado postulated that this man showing up now, meant he had never gone away, but had been lurking on the edges of their lives, keeping tabs on them. The only reason Mado was never visited by the man was his importance to the Global Assembly.

Mado was tenacious when he was on the trail of a mystery in need of a solution. So in the days since Yor's arrest when Mado was not dealing with Prevor Industries business or working on the WAEF or dealing with the government's incessant Breeze Celebration requests for viewing-channel or digi-media outlet interviews, he was on a mission to discover this man's history.

To start, Mado ordered a sketch of the man from Yor's memory of him, rendered by a Prevor Industries graphic artist, then Mado searched the government employee ID system and the results were negative. That was no surprise. The citizen ID system served up nothing. Not surprising either. Breaking into the military and GSS records turned up no information. Mado could not locate fotos of the man in historical digi-media from the day of Yorlik's landing. Finally, Mado broke into the GSS vidcam database, scanning for the man over ten years and still uncovered nothing. The man was a ghost. Mado said frustration wasn't a Prevorian state of mind, but lack of success in this case produced signs of exasperation.

When Mado told Yor about his entire investigation, he said, "I was concerned about this man when he was erased from that rail car station footage, but my recent research makes me even more wary. Men who exist for decades within any bureaucratic organization with no documentation have leeway to act in immoral ways. Usually they work for men who don't want to dirty themselves with the ramifications of their decisions. I've encountered men like this in corporate and government scenarios on your planet, but none like this one who is so entrenched in the shadows with literally no traces."

Yor had challenged the man in a moment of fear and he was concerned that he made a grave mistake, but Mado's influence came over him. "There's always a plan," Mado would say, "Always a solution to the next problem in order to move forward and make progress."

Yor would discuss the latest events with Mado and they'd work out how to proceed. At the moment, Yor needed to pack, stop to see Insol at the med clinic, then travel back to the complex before curfew, which was extended the day before the Breeze Celebration parade. He was less panicked and more single-minded on what lie ahead with the Malrap ejected from his stomach.

Yor folded his clothes beside his travel bag. He pondered his choices and realized these were precisely the same items he packed for his *Power Over the Future* publicity junket. On the tour, Yor was aware that many of the enthusiastic fans at his readings were attending to see the great-grandson of Yorlik the Great or were interested in what Tetrick Vanderlord's son was saying. There were always a handful of his father's followers at the end of every reading in every dome who asked if Yor foresaw a mass movement against the tyranny of the Global Assembly in the future and the renewing of the SEEDER program. Mado predicted these people would approach Yor, so they mapped out two days in each dome: One day was for the reading, and viewing-channel and digi-media interviews; the other for connecting individuals with a 'fan club coordinator' who would vet them to insure they weren't government spies, then install them as part of the movement. Those were constructive trips.

Yor placed his clothes into his bag and wondered if there was anything he was missing, but he had no context for the journey ahead of him. He had asked Mado, "Is there anything specific I should bring with me?"

Mado paused, taking longer than usual to answer a question, then said, "Something that reminds you why you're taking the risk."

Yor walked over to the wall where a digi-foto hung of himself at five years old sitting on his father's shoulders, his mother next to him and his great-grandfather between them. Everyone was smiling. In the background, the brown lawn stretched to the Vanderlord estate. Yor possessed a vague memory of the foto being taken by Joro Camtur. His great-grandfather was still healthy although he held tightly to his cane. They'd all picnicked on the lawn and celebrated what would have been the day of his grandfather's birth. Yor remembered his father saying, "Now all the generations of Vanderlords are represented in flesh if not spirit. Let's take a foto." Yor's mother thought she shouldn't be in the foto so they'd have a picture of the three living Vanderlords together, but his great-grandfather wrapped his arm around his mother and said, "You're as much a Vanderlord as any of us." The memory was distant, like a dream he had the night before. He was left with a stream of feelings—happiness, security, warmth, love. All of these individuals shaped his personality and his existence. He felt blessed by the Powers-that-be to have these people as his guides in life. He detached the foto from the wall and placed it on top of his neatly folded items and sealed up his bag. *Time to go*, he thought.

When Yor exited the bedroom, his mother and Rajer were talking in the middle of the living room. He could tell that his mother was about to cry. Rajer put his arm around her.

"Mado's potion worked like a charm," Rajer said.

"I'm glad," Yor said, hugging his mother, "I should get going."

"My baby boy," his mother said, releasing him from her hold. "You Vanderlords. You know how to make life exciting. I'll give you that. You can't stay a little while longer?"

"I can stay if you can change the curfew schedule. Insol's clinic is on the other side of the city and then I head over to Mado's. Curfew is later because Breeze Celebration is tomorrow, but it'll take me longer to get around with all the rail cars stuffed with intoxicated citizens. They say this is the most crowded Breeze Celebration in Capitol City history."

"That's all because of you, my boy," Rajer said, stepping forward and embracing Yor.

"Thanks, Rajer. You're a good man. I know I don't say it much, but my mother is lucky to have you, and I do love you. I know I never say it, but now seems like a good time to verbalize things since we don't know what tomorrow will bring. I realize now I should have said it sooner and more often."

Rajer released the hug and gave Yor a playful shove. "It's been fine. As your mother said, 'You know how to make life exciting.'"

"And what's all this talk about 'we don't know what tomorrow will bring.' You'll be superb tomorrow," his mother said, "As Rajer said, the reason the city is so crowded is because of you."

"Mado had something to do with it," Yor said, "Sorry. I appreciate the words of support. That man shook my confidence."

"Yes, he did. That's true," his mother said, "But don't give him power over you. These people from around the globe are here to see When All Else Fails in all its glory and the great-grandson of Yorlik the Great."

"And the Great man had something to do with it too," Yor said.

"Yes, 'the old man', as your father used to call him was an indomitable figure," his mother said, "Even in death, he reaches out and influences the future, influences our lives."

"I was saying something like that the other day."

"He loved you dearly. He would be proud of you, but he certainly complicated our lives when he reappeared."

"I should go," Yor said, "I'll see you both tomorrow." He removed his overcoat from the living-room closet. The coat was his father's. Brown leather from a Rexok which was now extinct. Then he lifted his satchel and his travel bag and kissed his mother on the cheek as he headed out the door.

"Tell Insol we'll come and visit her soon and our thoughts are with her," his mother said.

"Will do," Yor said.

Outside, the streets and sidewalks of the residential enclave and its shopping district were crowded with intoxicated revelers and the Malrap vendors were packed with patrons. Yor was pleased to see the Celebration had even invigorated the city's residential areas. No children were on the streets. This was adult time. Global Guards were patrolling in full force.

As he approached the station, somebody yelled out, "Hey, hey Professor Vanderlord."

Yor ignored the person who was obviously an old student, then he felt a hand on his shoulder. He halted, put his bag down and the person stepped in front of him. She was wearing government-worker attire with a 'Dept of Education and Well-Being' security badge.

"Big day for you tomorrow, Professor?" she said.

"Yes, big day. I'm in a rush though. Nice seeing you."

"You don't remember me, do you?"

Yor just wanted to catch the rail car and make his way to Insol, but at the same time, he didn't want to be rude. He paused for a moment to collect himself and gave her a long look until her identity dawned on him. Since Yor had last seen her, she had lost weight and wore her hair differently, putting more thought into her looks. Roneh was her name. She was a student who reported him to the head of the Planetary History department and the Dean of the University for teaching traitorous material about the Global Assembly in one of his first years as an instructor. University policy dictated that the instructor was not given the name of the student leveling charges to hinder any classroom bias, but she had gone out of her way to inform him that she was the person who brought the charges. She was proud of herself and wanted him to know she was the student who got him fired for spreading malicious facts about her beloved Global Assembly and Leader. Of course, Yor kept his job.

"I'm Roneh Rayush," she said.

"Yes, I know who you are. I'm in a hurry."

"I would imagine. Tomorrow is a momentous day for you."

Yor smelled the Malrap on her breath. "Yes, I need to…"

"Looks like you're headed somewhere," Roneh said. She used that I'm-smarter-than-you-are I've-got-one-over-on-you voice that Yor hated about her.

"I don't think that's any of your business."

"No. You're right. You're right," Roneh said, patting Yor on the arm. "So I bet you're excited about tomorrow. You get to spew your blasphemous words in front of the entire planet. One thing that baffles me and I'd be remiss in not asking such an informed academic as yourself this question…" She wobbled on her legs. The Malrap was playing on her equilibrium. She put both her arms out straight to regain her balance.

"Maybe you should sit down. There's a bench over there," Yor said. He took hold of her arm to escort her.

She tore her arm out of his grasp. "Don't you touch me. Don't touch me. I'm fine. You traitor. Answer my question."

"You never asked and I need to..."

"How did you dupe the government into allowing you to speak in front of the entire planet? I went out of my way to report you to the proper agencies. I even met with some creepy man who was highly interested in what I had to say about your teachings. When I heard you were scheduled to be the Breeze Celebration keynote speaker, I reached out to that man again and now I work for him."

"That's great for you. I need to catch the next rail car."

"I'm sure you do. Still that bag is interesting," Roneh said and reached down, lifting it off the ground. "Heavy."

Yor grabbed the bag away from her. "Goodbye," Yor said, picking up his bag and moving towards the station, then he felt the bag get caught. Roneh was clutching onto it.

"I know you. I know you. You believe you'll open your mouth and the entire planet will swoon to your ideas. But you know what," Roneh said, pulling the bag in her direction with Yor tugging back. "I believe, I truly believe that life will continue in bliss for the next 100 years, according to the plan set forth by our Leader."

"I'd appreciate if you let go."

She continued pulling at the bag and Yor resisted her.

"Nobody cared what your great-grandfather thought or your father thought and nobody will give a damn what you think."

Yor had enough. He yanked the bag out of her grip and she lost her balance, falling to the sidewalk. "I guess we'll see about that," he said, then ran for the station, looking back at her.

"I knew it!" Roneh yelled at him from where she sat on the ground. Global Guards were heading for her. "I knew it! I know what you're doing. You've got them all duped. Somehow you've got them all duped. I will not let you get away with it. I will be there at the Arena. I will not let you get away with it!"

When Yor reached the rail car platform, he was out of breath from his sprint and stood there in the crowd, panting and sweating. He placed the hood of his coat over his head even though the station was warm. He had no desire to be recognized any further.

After tomorrow, everyone on Koda will know me, Yor thought *Power over the future indeed.* He laughed as he heard the rail car coming down the tracks.

MADO

From his current vantage point, looking down on the military park below, Mado spied the WAEF sitting on the mobile carrier where all the Breeze Celebration parade floats were gathered. The WAEF was roped off and guarded by Global Guards. Parade participants, government officials, viewing-channel pundits, and digi-media celebrities surrounded the ship for a foto opportunity with the WAEF behind them. The hull glistened in the sunlight, streaming through the dome glass. *Look at my girl,* Mado thought.

In his career as a Space Traveler, he traversed the universe for hundreds of years in typical Prevorian spacecraft and he felt no connection to them except for their functionality. The only person who could have perceived the metallic hull and its aerodynamic curves with similar affection was Yorlik himself.

Mado was overwhelmed by his fondness for the spaceship when he opened the retractable roof in his lab building and the cables were attached to the WAEF's hull. Three hovering air-battle cruisers lifted the WAEF off the floor, up through the roof and into the domed sky. His spirit soared, seeing the WAEF fly again even if it wasn't on its own power, because that's what it was meant to do.

When the WAEF had been airlifted from the estate to

his complex, Mado was anxious the government's shoddy metal cables would fail and damage the ship. This time, he had no such fear. He designed the cables himself from Prevorian tech, and the cruisers easily lifted the WAEF's enormous weight without strain.

Since the government heard about his testing the cable for use in moving the WAEF, they had been petitioning him to purchase the tech for their military. Mado told them that he'd consider it. He used their desire for this product as another thing to hold over the Global Assembly to gain concessions on how the WAEF and Yor's participation in the Breeze Celebration would occur—the interviews, the placement of the WAEF in the Arena, Yor's entrance to the keynote podium—and to prevent them from prying into his affairs in general.

Mado was picked up by a Prevor Industries corporate cruiser at the complex's landing zone and dropped off at the military park which was situated near an edge of the dome. It was a short flight. Usually, this vast empty field was used for parking military aircraft, gathering troops or military training exercises. It was chosen today for two main reasons: the size accommodated all the floats and the WAEF as a staging area; the park was positioned so the parade route could both traverse roads wide enough for the WAEF and its carrier and impact the largest number of the city's population before entering the city center.

When Mado disembarked the cruiser, he was mobbed by viewing-channel reporters. He told them how much it elated him that this scientific achievement by his friend and mentor Yorlik the Great was being recognized and celebrated by the entire planet, and he thanked the Global Assembly for their support. Then reporters shouted questions, asking how he felt about the parade, whether the restoration of the WAEF did justice to his friend's memory after all these years, and where was the great-grandson of the Great man and what would he say in his much anticipated speech at the Arena. Mado worked out his best version of a smile.

His façade as a quirky, eccentric, shut-in tech developer was easy to maintain. Say little and smile a lot. Unveil new gadgets to the awe of the populous and gain more and more of their admiration as he made their lives more convenient and enjoyable in this cataclysmic time in their planetary history. He was beloved for his works and for simply being the reclusive inventor. The probability of being viewed the same way by the Kodan citizenry after he and Yor executed their plan was less than 50% at best. *I hope they'll understand my actions on this day, like most of my gadgets, are in their best interests.* Mado realized this was a condescending thought, but after years of living amongst the Kodans, he could not help but see their flaws and care about them at the same time.

Mado put up his hand to end the question-and-answer session and he was surrounded by Global Guards who escorted him away from the reporters to the VIP tent where only parade organizers and government officials were allowed. The tent sat on a man-made rise, created for military exercises, and that was the vantage point from where he was currently admiring the WAEF.

Mado's old friend, Joro Camtur, approached and told him the floats and the WAEF would lineup soon to begin the parade. Joro was the lead Breeze Celebration organizer. The government was always looking over Joro's shoulder to insure the parade went off without a hitch, but Joro was smart and well-organized and he had become invaluable member of their team. Mado couldn't have wished for a better inside man.

When Yorlik returned to the planet, his old friend and business partner had been dead for years, but his son, who was an old man, and his grandson Joro were invited to the estate for family dinners. Joro was a bright young man who had his misgivings about his grandfather's contributions to the DOME project. Tetrick and Joro hit it off and became best of friends, and somewhere along the line, they hatched a scheme with Yorlik to station Joro within the workings of the Global Assembly using his most abundant resource, his wealth.

The two staged a falling out at a party following one of Tetrick's rallies, which included a bloody brawl between them. This made the headlines in all the global media outlets, and Joro followed up by touring the most prominent viewing-channels shows, bad-mouthing Tetrick and his anti-DOME movement. Everyone on the planet bought his animosity. Even a few powerful figures in the Global Assembly befriended Joro and introduced him to the Leader himself. Joro became part of their inner circle. Upon the passing of his father, Joro inherited a vast fortune, and over the years, he spent a great deal of his time greasing the Leader and key figures in the Global Assembly with his financial bounty, making his ruse stick.

Now, Mado strolled through the crowd of government officials with Joro by his side. Joro introduced the officials to Mado and told them the time had arrived to board their flight to the Arena. They were all dressed in their Breeze Celebration finest, representing the colors of their regions and districts. Mado was acquainted with many of them and complimented them on their regalia and how good it was to see them. The Global Assembly rep from the region where the ore for the cables was excavated, raved about the cables performance in conveying the WAEF and how he looked forward to creating a facility to mass produce them. Mado nodded his head and worked out a smile. Another excellent feature of his peculiar persona was those gestures functioned as a plausible reply, but carried no meaning.

When the majority of the crowd filed out and Mado and Joro were the only individuals left under the tent besides the Global Guards, Joro asked him, "I'd like to have a word in private with you, Mado Prevor of Prevor Industries."

Mado followed Joro to a vacant corner of the tent. "Mado Prevor of Prevor Industries?" Mado said, "That might have been laying it on a bit thick. People know we're friends."

"I know. I'm nervous," Joro said, wiping what Mado

assumed was sweaty palms on his brand-new suit which
was the colors of the Global symbol and probably purchased for the event. "Everything is all set. I made sure
there's a large perimeter around the ship when it's parked
at the Arena and the ramp was built for Yor's entrance.
Lots of questions were asked and that man who you
were warning me about appeared at my office. You were
right about him. Scary. Like others, he was wondering
why such an expansive perimeter around the WAEF was
necessary. I told him that you said there was a danger of
lingering cosmic radiation from the WAEF's hull having
a harmful effect on anyone close to the ship. He was
doubtful of the radiation excuse. He said, 'If so, how is it
being placed in a museum?' and I told him you said that
the museum was a contained environment and it could
be dealt with easier there. The man didn't buy it and
actually snorted in derision and asked about the ramp. I
told him you also said that the benefit of the ramp, other
than bridging the gap between the ship and stage, was that
Yor's walk to the stage would lend theatrics to the event.
He didn't buy that either. Then I told him that's what
you had said and the plans were approved by the Global
Assembly Committee on the Breeze Celebration and to
take it up with them. He wasn't pleased by my response
and made a vague threat about hindering my future inclu-
sion in government events. I told him I'd take one event
at a time and right now the upcoming Breeze Celebration
was my..." Joro stopped when a high-ranking Global
Guard approached and stopped at attention before them.

"What can I do for you, Captain?"

"Sorry to interrupt, sir," the Captain said, "As per your order, we've alerted all the float drivers and participants, and commed the WAEF carrier driver that we'll soon begin lining up the parade in the prepared sequence. All the digi-media and viewing-channel corps have been instructed to leave the park and if they so desire, station themselves at the exit for broadcasting. We're ready to line up the vehicles on your order, sir."

"Please commence lining them up, Captain, and thank you for your exemplary service."

"Thank you, sir. This is a valued assignment. I'll oversee the activity myself and make sure it works out exactly as we were briefed." The Captain performed an about-face and exited the tent in disciplined measured strides.

"Where were we?" Joro said to Mado.

"You were telling me about your conversation with that man. You didn't get his name?"

"No, he steered around telling me. I don't think he believed anything I said, and he left angry and frustrated with our conversation."

"Yes, I've had those kinds of conversations with you as well," Mado said, working out his best smile. "I wouldn't be too concerned. When everything happens, you may be questioned, but in the end, fingers will be firmly pointed at Yor and myself. All you know is what I've told you."

"True. My overall concern is success. I'm less worried about myself. All I want is the best future for my children and their children. I understood what I was signing up for back in the old days with Tetrick. I'd like to see him vindicated instead of vilified," Joro said, "By the way, how is Yor? Where is he? I'm assuming inside the ship?"

"Yes, inside the ship and he's probably wondering where I am. Looks like they're starting to move the carrier into position."

"The ship looks wonderful, Mado. You've performed an exemplary job."

"Thanks. Yes, she does. I'm pleased by her," Mado said, "Don't miss the grand finale."

"I'm looking forward to it. Been a long time coming."

"I couldn't agree more."

Joro escorted Mado back to the tent's entrance, and wished him luck. Mado continued downhill to where the carrier had taken position in the parade line up. A few Global Guards lingered around the carrier and when they saw Mado coming, they set up stairs ascending to the carrier deck.

Mado climbed the stairs to the deck and removed a comm from his pocket. "Ready when you are," Mado said into his comm and the docking bay door opened and Mado took a step up into the ship.

Yor waited at the docking bay console. When Mado was inside the ship, he pressed a button on the console to shut the door.

Mado saw immediately that Yor was in a state of heightened stress and agitation. He was grasping his chin with his thumb and forefinger over and over again. "One of the only things that can ruin what we've set in motion is panic. So you need to relax, do whatever helps you stay calm," Mado said, "Let's go look at the parade from the control room."

When they arrived in the control room, Mado told Yor to sit down in the pilot's chair. The WAEF was the Breeze Celebration parade's main attraction so the ship traveled at the rear of the procession, and the floats were lined up in front of them in a semi-circle before heading out of the park. From the control-room window, they had a clear view of each float ahead of them. They could even observe them close-up because Mado installed Prevorian magni-tech in the control room window, unbeknownst to the inspectors who saw no difference in this window versus the old one. Mado placed his hand on Yor's shoulder and examined him. Yor was still distressed.

"How was the flight over here? Cozy, buckled into the pilot's chair? I assume the flight was smooth. The cables' design minimizes any sort of jerking around."

"It was fine," Yor said, "Everything go all right with Joro?"

"Exactly as planned. Joro's got his part covered," Mado said. He could have mentioned the man visiting Joro, but better that Yor didn't know. He pointed out the window. "Now enjoy the parade. We've got time before we get to the official parade route."

Directly in front of the WAEF was the float representing Capitol City. A model of the city center was built in the middle of the float, the architecture of the Old Quarter and its stone streets, the Royal Quarter, Global Plaza and the Arena were replicated with delicate precision. The WAEF practically looked down into the model as if they were about to fly over it. The Capitol City float also carried the Mayor and the descendants of the Royal family, wearing their crowns. Traditionally, each float transported a handful of representatives from their dome wearing the garb of their region who waved to the crowd or musical and dance groups from the regions who performed.

Yor used the magni-tech, surveying the other floats ahead of them. In front of the Capitol City float was the float for the Mauan region. Once known for a landscape stretching hundreds of thousands of square meters carpeted with blossoms, not seen anywhere else on Koda, it was a desolate landscape today. Some blossoms still existed in limited numbers in the hot houses of the region's dome. The float attempted to depict the region's former beauty. Artificial multi-color blossoms stretched across undulating rolling hills. Robotic flower birds hovered and zipped over the float in a simulation of drawing pollen from the blossoms. The float was the most colorful and lifelike in the parade, and was almost as large as the carrier beneath the WAEF.

Ahead of the Mauan float was the Shamban float, which represented the global area with the most fertile crop output before the environmental crisis. This was the region where the WAEF landed on its return. These days, the region was known for its severe dust storms, growing nothing of nutritional value, and its terrorist faction, but the float represented what it had been in the past. Synthetic reproductions of crops were spread out beside models of farm machinery and a storage silo. A few Shamban citizens dressed in old-time farming garb rode the front of the float.

Yor increased the window's magnification, scanning over floats in the far distance. He stopped on the float of the Msituan region depicting the once glorious rainforests and rare animal species who roamed there. Most of the animals were extinct, but some existed in the dome's zoo. There was the Mlimoan region with volcanic mountains featuring actual climbers pretending to ascend a model of a high-altitude peak. Further ahead, Yor zoomed in on the float with holographic aquatic creatures jumping in arcs out of the blue waves on the surface. "That's Nor," Yor said, "I imagine that's what your world must look like."

"The blue part is right," Mado said. He had read about this region. Nor was a once proud country which had been conquered by the Global Monarchy. Their separatist movement had been a constant problem for the government before it was crushed. When the crisis hit the region, millions died as the ocean rose, flooding the cities along the coastline. As marine life disappeared, their fishing industry vanished. Disease and starvation followed. The Global Assembly's response was limited and like with other regions, they used the excuse that the financial constraints of the DOME project hindered them from helping with relief assistance.

Mado was astounded by the enormous loss of invaluable life and perceived the entire parade as a planetary funeral procession. *So much life wiped out due to so much ignorance,* Mado thought. The Global Assembly in their misguided way wanted to parlay a parade, glorifying global cultures which had been wiped out by the crisis into a pageant of unification and survival. *This is a travesty.*

"The floats are beautiful," Mado said, "But on the other hand, they're truly sad."

Yor looked up at Mado. "I was just thinking the same thing."

The parade exited the military park into an unpopulated warehouse district, then slowed to a stop. Global Guards marched past the carrier on each side of them heading toward the front of the procession.

"What's going on?" Yor said.

Mado could see the panic again in Yor's eyes. "Probably nothing," Mado said, "Or nothing to do with us."

Mado's comm buzzed and he walked to the other side of the control room before answering. Joro was on the other end and told Mado that the government received a credible threat to the proceedings so they dispatched Global Guards at the front and rear of the parade and beside every float. The order was sent directly from the Leader. The GSS believed this threat was a precursor to a larger attack. Joro had no other details. Mado thanked Joro and asked him to keep them updated on any further developments. With the Global Guards presence and caution in play, the parade would move slower than planned. Mado told Yor to meet him in the living chamber.

This could put a serious crimp in our plans, Mado

thought. The files on the memory wafers, which Yor gave to Mel, Insol and Ador, were programmed to open at dozens of specific times providing instructions throughout the day on how to communicate with their operatives and statements to send viewing channels and digi-media at their discretion. The files on Harmin's wafer were automated to transmit at one specific time and this was a key element in the plan. Harmin's files would implicate him in a cyberattack which would cause the government to focus their first arrest efforts on him. Mado never told Yor the true depth of Harmin's duplicity against Tetrick. Yor's level of disdain for Harmin was high and Mado didn't think infuriating him further was necessary. Yor and Harmin worked together, and Yor tended to not cloak his feelings well.

When he and Yor were in the living chamber together, he directed Yor to have a seat across from him.

"What's going on? Who was that on the comm?" Yor said.

"Joro," Mado said, "But before we speak, I need you to center yourself. You seem out of sorts and I need you to be fully with me and not distracted. Is there something you haven't told me?"

Yor told him about Ador, the man coming to the bungalow and the ex-student who worked for the man confronting him. "Kind of been an avalanche, and I'm convinced it was coordinated by that man. Insol was viciously attacked. I visited her at the southeast med clinic before I went to the lab last night. She was in an induced coma. Hooked up to monitors. Broken ribs, arm, shoulder and leg. Severe concussion and brain swelling. Face beaten black-and-blue and unrecognizable. The brutality was shocking. I sat with her for as long as I could, but considering the rigidity of this morning's schedule, I had to reach the lab before curfew ended," Yor said, "What did Joro say?"

Sadness fell over Mado for the loss of Ador and the harm done to Insol. He took responsibility for his part in bringing pain to them and those who loved them. His mind raced with probabilities for the future based on this news. "That's awful. All of it. Seems like the wrath of the government has come down around us. Why didn't you comm me last night?"

"You couldn't have done anything about it. Everything happened so fast and I didn't want to distract you. I arrived at the lab and you were discussing post-Breeze Celebration Prevor Industries business with your assistant Gols and security issues with Commander Warver so I went to sleep. Since early this morning, you've been focused on making sure the WAEF made it to the military park in one piece and we've been separated since the ship was moved," Yor said, "We haven't been able to talk, and what good would it have done to tell you now? What did Joro say?"

"I don't know. The level of violence is an indicator of the man's determination to figure out our intentions and possibly his frustration with not being able to touch you or me."

"That's reasonable, but what's done is done and how can we be truly apply reason when there's nothing of the sort around us? What's waiting for us down the road? We're stopped and there's no telling if that man comes knocking and it's literally over for us. Who knows what they'll do to you once they find out who you really are? Maybe dissection."

"I'd prefer that not happen. It'd be rather unpleasant," Mado said. Yor did not look amused, but more panicked than before. "First of all, I'm not concerned about that man right now. I know it seems trivial to see it this way considering what's transpired with Ador and Insol, but the man is poking around. He's rattling you to see if he can shake loose what's going to happen, but he has no idea and the Leader has him in his place otherwise he would've arrested you already."

"Ador said a similar thing."

"I'm saddened by his death, but he knew what we were doing, that people would get hurt, including himself. He probably had a clear idea on the source of his illness."

"Maybe that's true. He wouldn't see my mother about it."

"I would wager he knew there was no cure," Mado said, "I need you to put all of this tragedy and drama out of your mind. I understand that's difficult, but as long as we move forward with our plan, meeting any changes in the timeline with our own alterations, there's a high probability that we'll succeed. You can't lose your head."

"Easier than it sounds," Yor said, crossing his arms and

clutching at himself.

"I can change how you feel. Do you trust me?"

"Of course, but how?"

"Close your eyes and take a few deep breaths," Mado said. Once Yor's eyes were shut, Mado leaned forward, placing both his hands on Yor's shoulders, and closed his eyes. He imagined himself with Yorlik in the VPR simulation, sailing on the WAEF, on the lake behind the Vanderlord estate, the wind blowing in their faces, the spring air full of the fragrance of flowers blooming on the shore, the sound of the boat cutting through the water and Yorlik grinning with joy. Mado opened his eyes and released his hold on Yor and leaned back in his recliner. Yor now sat there smiling with his arms by his side, breathing in a relaxed manner.

A few moments later, Yor opened his eyes and said, "What just happened?"

"How do you feel?"

"Completely different. What did you do?"

"A Prevorian bonding ritual that shares emotions. I've used it sparingly since I've been on Koda. Your anxiety was stopping you from thinking straight so I filled your mind with emotions that will help you think more freely. I thought this was the best way to get your mind back on track. I apologize. Some find it intrusive, but I need you to be available."

"No. I can see how people would think it's an invasion of privacy, but that put me in a much better mind space. I know what I was feeling before, but the darker emotions have been pushed out of my head. A sort of mood enhancer."

"Of sorts," Mado said, "I don't want to rush you, but we need to get down to business here. I assume we're still going forward with the plan and these complications haven't made you change your mind."

"Without a doubt. I'm sorry," Yor said, "I kind of lost control."

"It's understandable," Mado said, "We need to proceed with confidence though. A wise man once told me when you proceed into a battle, you enter it without mercy, remorse, or concern for the other side. That's the only way to operate as a soldier. In this case, it's not a true battle, but it might as well be. If we don't win, the outcome is dire for us, the people backing us and the entire planet."

"Who said that?"

"Who else?"

"Let me guess," Yor said, "My great-grandfather. He certainly had it figured out."

"He was wise in many ways, but he wasn't without his misgivings. Your father was a lot like him. Sometimes it's those lingering doubts, questioning yourself that make you great. You'd be foolish not to have them," Mado said, "If I might be so bold, they were a few of the bravest men I've ever met, but there's a thin line between confidence and doubt. They stayed the course with their confidence in their cause, and in your father's case it didn't end well. We should keep him in mind on this day. His memory will keep us steadfast. You with me here?"

Yor stood up and Mado did the same. Yor placed both his hands on Mado's shoulders. Mado placed his hands on Yor's shoulders.

"Yes. We're in it together," Yor said.

Mado tightened his grip on Yor's shoulders and Yor did the same. "In it together," Mado said, "Before I tell you what Joro said, you need to focus on what's truly happening instead of what could happen. You ready?"

Yor nodded and Mado told him what Joro said, then Yor walked over to the kitchen dispenser and filled a glass of water. He drank down the entire glass, then he opened his comm and calmly spoke to someone on the other end. When the conversation ended, he walked back over to Mado and sat down.

"So I just talked to Mel," Yor said, "First off, he is already taking care of Ador and Insol's assignments. I also asked him yesterday to make sure that Harmin uploaded his wafer's files when we told him to do it. Mel never got the chance. Right after he gave Harmin the wafer and told him not to upload until sundown, Harmin knocked on Mel's office door and wanted to know how to open the files. Mel said it was priceless as Harmin tried to play dumb like he didn't understand the instructions. I suspected he would upload it right away after Mel gave it to him because he'd want to open the files and see exactly what they contained. I knew I couldn't trust the bastard. He'd go out of his way to comm the government if he found anything he believed was treasonous."

"So we know the files are on his viewer?"

"Yes, Mel went back to Harmin's office with him, saw they were already uploaded, then reminded Harmin the files were time-locked so he'd have to wait for them to open. He might attempt to remove them when he realizes he can't open them himself, but once they're uploaded, they're embedded in his viewer's system so we're set there," Yor said, "So do you think it was Harmin who called in this threat? I wouldn't put it past him."

"The order came from the Leader so it had to be someone at the GSS who has his ear. If I were to venture a guess, I'd say that man convinced the Leader to at least take precautions. The Leader is so wrapped up in what this Celebration will do for his popularity that he wouldn't go any further without solid evidence, and there is none," Mado said, "Any thoughts on how to proceed?"

"Improvise."

"That's risky."

"What other choice do we have? Harmin's files will release the virus triggering the shutdown of all government systems at the programmed time. Our window of operation is based on their backup systems kicking in and they start when the normal systems are down for a specific time period. Do you have an idea on how to change the time settings on Harmin's virus from here?"

"I don't have access to that sort of equipment here."

"Then the only other choice is abandoning the plan altogether which also means contacting all the operatives in the field from acting before we get to the Arena. I don't see that happening. We should just work on the assumption that the window will close on us and improvise."

"I actually have a few contingency plans already in place, but you may not like them."

"Then don't tell me."

"Are you sure? The course of events will change your existence radically."

"More than what's happening already. I trust you, Mado. We've come this far and there is no turning back now," Yor said, "I definitely don't want to know. I just don't want something else on my mind when I'm giving my performance. Before we arrive at the Arena, I'll edit down my speech to give us more time. Let's pray to the Powers-that-be this parade gets moving soon."

"Let's do that then. You work on the speech. I'll get the contingency in place."

MAR

The packed rail car emptied onto the crowded platform of the Plaza station and the masses inched towards the exit doors, which were not designed wide enough to accommodate this deluge of people. Rajer grabbed Mar's hand. She had never attended a Breeze Celebration, but she had watched them on the viewing channels since the DOME project was completed 8 years ago. Mar enjoyed the spectacle of the Breeze Celebration, but loathed what the government was trying to achieve by producing it: blind loyalty to poorly conceived policies. She turned on the viewer before they left the bungalow and the channel was already reporting record-setting attendance. That was more than evident while waiting all morning to get into their neighborhood station and catch a rail car. That was the longest Mar ever waited for a rail car in the nine years she'd been living in her current bungalow, but she had planned for the congestion so they'd arrive at the Arena on time.

In the courtyard around the station, a band was playing traditional songs from around Koda. Families of diverse global ethnicity wheeled tots in strollers and fathers carried children on their shoulders, waving pennants with the image of When All Else Fails or the Global symbol. It seemed like pennants the color of the Global

Howard Libes

symbol dominated the airspace over the crowd, giving some idea of the thousands upon thousands headed towards the parade and the Arena. Parents with children steered clear of the Malrap vendors who were working through their patrons at a brisk pace. At the entrance to the vendors, Global Guards stood at attention. *The government is earning a big payout and don't want any bad publicity,* Mar thought.

The crowd inched forward ahead of them as they moved up the Old Quarter street, which was closed off to anything but foot traffic. Mar was fascinated how people who looked like they were visiting from other domes kept their heads down, afraid to make eye contact with strangers. Since the Global Assembly took charge, they created a public-service campaign to warn citizens to beware of strangers especially when traveling faraway from home. In the campaign's viewing-channel ad, a person talks to a stranger who tells them something seditious and the person transforms into an anti-government protestor. They're arrested, then a prison door slams shut, locking the person in a cell. The ad states "You never know who that stranger might be. Mind your own business."

Rajer was still holding Mar's hand, and Mar kissed him on the cheek. They kept moving forward, but at this point they didn't have much choice. The street was so crowded that going against the flow, attempting to veer off in any direction other than forward, would have taken considerable effort.

In front of Mar was a family, a tan-skinned man and

woman with their female child of possibly five years old. Mar could tell right away that they weren't from Capitol City. They peered around at the buildings and pointed with awe at their surroundings. The little girl waved a WAEF pennant in one hand and held her mother's hand in the other. The father held the mother's other hand.

Suddenly, the crowd's forward movement halted. Standing on her toes, Mar saw a Malrap drunk who pushed through the crowd heading towards the Arena, knocking people over in his wake, swinging a Global Leader pennant overhead. The crowd yelled at him. Global Guards were in pursuit.

The mother pulled her child towards her.

"What's happening, Mommy?" the girl screamed to her mother in a similar accent as Insol's.

Mar bent over to the girl and said, "It'll be fine. Nothing to worry about."

The mother turned and shot a dirty look at Mar. "Please mind your own business."

"Are you from the southern climes?"

"What business of that is yours? Mind your business," the woman said, holding her daughter up against her. The girl appeared frightened as she looked at Mar.

"Just curious, and I believe you're scaring your daughter. I have a friend from there and I noticed your accent," Mar said.

The woman looked down at her daughter who was visibly shaking. The man picked up the girl and hugged her.

"I apologize," the woman said, "We're visiting and we

were told at the aircraft drop-off to not trust any strangers."

"I understand," Mar said, "I have a son and I was defensive of him when he was young, too. Instinct, really. Are you visiting here specifically for Breeze Celebration?"

"Yes it's a special one," the woman said as the crowd began flowing forward again and she walked beside Mar. "This crowd is craziness. We came to see the WAEF. My partner here had an expiring travel permit and there wasn't a better time to use it. Such a historical event, but this crowd is making me afraid for my daughter's safety."

Her partner was walking ahead of them, carrying his daughter who was peering at Mar over his shoulder. She still clutched the stick of the pennant in one hand, holding tight with both arms to her father.

"Do you live here?" the woman asked.

"Yes, my partner and I live here," Mar said, lifting her hand that Rajer was holding.

"Hello," Rajer said.

"This must be an exciting place to live," the woman said. "All the beautiful architecture."

"It has its moments," Mar said, "Like this one."

"Yes, although this happens once in a lifetime. My little one wouldn't sleep last night. She couldn't wait to get down here to see the parade. I don't know how much we'll be able to see with this crowd."

"Oh, they'll have viewing screens up and down the parade route."

"That's good. All she can talk about is the WAEF. Isn't that right, my sweetheart?" the woman said and ran her finger down her daughter's nose.

The girl giggled and sang, "When All Else Fails, we'll find our way across the universe to a brand-new home, what a wondrous day, Yay! When All Else Fails, where the birds will fly in the sky so blue, what a wondrous day, Yay! When All Else Fails, where the fish will swim in the bountiful sea, what a wondrous day…" Then she threw up her arms with her father holding her and hollered, "Yay! When All Else Fails, where the flowers will bloom where the air is clean and there are no worries but to dance and sing, what a wondrous day, Yay! When All Else Fails will lead us there, where joy and happiness will reign supreme, what a wondrous day, Yay!"

"I haven't heard that nursery rhyme since I was a little girl. How did she learn it?" Mar said.

"All the children learn that song where we come from."

"Not here in Capitol City."

A woman walking ahead of Mar turned around and said, "My children learned it, too. I'm from the Mauan region."

"Mine too," a woman walking behind Mar said, "We're from another dome though."

As the crowd's pace quickened, Mar still holding Rajer's hand, walked up closer behind the man holding the girl. "Can you sing that for us again, dear?" Mar said, squeezing Rajer's hand.

"Can I Mommy?" the girl said, smiling.

"By all means," her mother said.

"Please go slow so I can learn it again, okay?" Mar said.

"When All Else Fails, we'll find our way…" the girl sang, "Now you."

"Join me, Rajer," Mar said, "When All Else Fails, we'll find our way…" Rajer sang with her.

"…across the universe to a brand-new home…"

"…across the universe to a brand-new home…" The mother sang-a-long with Mar and Rajer.

"…what a wondrous day, Yay!" the girl sang and threw up her hands, waving the pennant.

"…what a wondrous day, Yay!" The woman walking ahead of them sang-a-long with the four of them.

By the time they reached the end of the rhyme, it seemed like the entire crowd around Mar was marching and singing, "…where joy and happiness will reign supreme, what a wondrous day, Yay!"

Rajer yelled, "One more time!" and the crowd around them sang the rhyme from the beginning again. Mar looked around at the smiling, singing faces, and the crowd seemed to get louder and more confident as the rhyme continued and it ended on an ear-splitting, "Yay!" *Thousands must have been singing,* Mar thought as the crowd cheered and strangers began talking to one another.

At the Plaza, the crowd was so dense that it was impossible to get up close to the parade route. The people nearest the route had probably arrived as nightly curfew ended to obtain a curbside view. The government had installed billboard-size viewing screens on the side of the buildings on every block of the Plaza leading to the Arena and around the outside of the Arena so all in attendance could see the parade. The Plaza screens would broadcast the ceremony happening inside the Arena as well. At the moment, the screens were blank, and the Arena gates were shut until the WAEF entered the stadium so every citizen would have a fair shot at getting inside to see the ceremony.

Mado acquired special Arena passes for Mar and Rajer, but Mar refused to use them. She had no desire to view Yor's speech high above the field in a stuffy executive box populated by wealthy strangers. She wanted to be among the Kodan people watching Yor's speech. Mar had worked out a strategy for her and Rajer to move through the crowd and stand as near the Arena as possible before the gates opened. She wanted to make sure they entered the Arena early enough to position themselves on the field in front of the stage to see her son give his speech up close.

The mother from the southern climes took her daughter in her arms and they both waved goodbye as they disappeared into the crowd. Rajer still held Mar's hand. Mar let go and linked arms with Rajer.

"Shall we," Mar said and they wound their way through the crowd towards the Arena.

YOR

Yor completed the new edit of his speech, then returned to the control room and sat back down in the pilot's chair. A short time later, the carrier driver called up on a special comm rigged for the event that fed through the ship's intercom system, saying the procession would be moving shortly.

Yor realized since the last government inspection, Mado upgraded the entire main control console to brand-new tech. The old switches and buttons were there, but the 100-year-old tech with a read-out monitor for each system was now replaced by an up-to-date tech viewing screen with continuous readout, monitoring the entire ship's systems at once. Although he'd been looking at it all day, he was so overwhelmed by his panic he never saw it. The carrier lurched, and began rolling forward, traveling down the avenue between warehouses. In the distance, Yor could see the downtown skyline.

The door slid open behind him and Mado appeared by his side. "I've got a timer going so we know when Harmin's virus is sent and when the effects will be overcome. It's going to be close. How did editing the speech come out?"

"I've got it down as much as I can. I couldn't cut it down any further."

"I've been working on the contingency in the engine room."

"In the engine room? I don't want to know," Yor said, throwing his hands in the air at Mado, shooing away any explanation of what he was doing, "I see you've done some refurbishing here." He pointed at the control console.

"I was wondering when you'd notice."

"There's something I've been curious about."

"Please ask," Mado said, "I'm an open panel of circuits."

"That's just it. You're always making jokes and sometimes they make more sense than others. It's charming and I find it amusing, but I was curious if that's part of your planet's culture."

"Not at all," Mado said, "Not at all. That's your great-grandfather. He taught me joking and tried to teach me how to smile although I never got the hang of it. Prevorians don't have the cheekbones for it."

Yor laughed. "That might be the funniest thing you've ever said to me."

"And I wasn't even trying."

Yor continued laughing and Mado attempted to smile. "Yeah that really doesn't work for you, but don't stop trying."

"I'm glad you're feeling better. I've got some work to finish. Comm me when we start the parade route," Mado said and exited the control room.

The parade was progressing forward at a slow pace. With the Global Guards marching on the procession's flanks, it would be some time before they reached the active part of the parade route. Yor noticed Mado had mounted his great-grandfather's foto on the panel beside the control console.

The foto sat by his bedside growing up so its current placement only seemed fitting. The joy on his great-grandfather's face and in his body language always made Yor smile. He realized he now had the resource to discover the story behind the foto, and he'd already garnered more history on Yorlik the Great than anyone on Koda, although he couldn't tell anyone else because of the source. *Funny how that worked out.*

The carrier rolled along leaving the warehouse district for the old industrial district with similarly wide roads. When the Capitol City dome was built, the air-circulation pumps, the real-glass panels, and the metallic beams were manufactured here. Now, dome replacement parts were built here, but a majority of the buildings were vacant. The buildings hadn't decayed much without weather erosion, and the government was planning on converting the structures into housing when the population numbers reached the necessary tipping point. This was also where the SEEDER ships were manufactured including the WAEF. When Yor was a child, his father took him on an outing to one of the buildings in this district where a commemorative plaque marked where the SEEDER program headquarters was housed.

Up the street, Yor saw maybe 50 people milling around on the sidewalk in the middle of a block disinterested in the passing parade. They were men and women who wore blue coveralls with work gloves jutting out of their back pockets, and others in button-down shirts and slacks. He assumed they worked down here. When one of them spotted the WAEF heading towards them, she alerted the crowd, jumping up and down waving her arms. She reached down to something leaning against the wall behind her and held up a homemade sign that read, 'Manufacturers of Capitol City Love the WAEF' and a bunch of them held up 'When All Else Fails' pennants. Yor reached for the outside-intercom switch, which was in the same place on the new control console, and flipped it on. He faintly heard the crowd at first, but as the carrier edged closer, they grew louder.

Yor pressed the talk button on the PA and said, "Hello from the When All Else Fails." The crowd ran in unison to the end of the block to greet him. Yor heard them clearly now. "That's Yor Vanderlord…how would you know… who else would it be?"

"Yes, it's Yor Vanderlord from the WAEF control room," Yor said. The crowd hooted and hollered and waved their pennants and homemade signs as they walked on the sidewalk beside the carrier.

"It's wonderful to see you out here on Breeze Celebration. Thank you for the incredibly gracious greeting," Yor said. One woman held up a sign reading, 'We Love You, Yor. Take Us to a New Planet.' Yor was thrilled. "Thanks so much. My great-grandfather would thank you too, if he were here. I don't know what else to say. I love you guys, too."

A bunch of them yelled "We love you, Yor," then they all began chanting, "When All Else Fails, When All Else Fails, When All Else Fails…" One overenthusiastic man ran into the street towards the carrier, waving a WAEF pennant and a Global Guard stiff-armed him, knocking the man to the ground and stepping on his throat.

Then the carrier made a right turn away from an industrial rail car underpass that neither the floats or the WAEF could make it under, and the crowd was gone. A few blocks later, the parade turned left towards the city center again, the skyline moving closer.

The crowd's chanting caught in Yor's mind like a familiar song you've heard that won't leave your brain. *When All Else Fails, When All Else Fails, When All Else Fails.* Yor looked at his great-grandfather grinning in the foto. *When All Else Fails, When All Else Fails, When All Else Fails.* Yor broke out in a grin of his own. He felt much better than he did earlier. More confident in what lie ahead. Mado said that his great-grandfather taught him how to joke, and the Great man's sense of humor seemed to be on full display today. Yor thought, *After a century wandering the galaxy, looking for a needle in a haystack, he'd either be wiser or crazier or both, and he'd need to laugh at the universe and himself to survive.*

Again, Yor read through the edit of his speech on his digi-tablet. He told himself this was the final time. The speech read better after cutting the fat which consisted of off-topic bile directed at the Global Assembly's oppression, and the subject matter was more poignant now. He wanted the speech to say what it needed to say about the government's deception without harping on it. His mind wandered again to his concern over how his actions would affect his family and friends even though they were supportive of him. Although his mother could handle herself, he worried about her and the part she and Rajer agreed to play after the day's events. *Worry won't change anything now though.*

Feeling happy with the speech, he turned off his tablet. He'd given speeches before and once he started speaking, he'd be fine, but he began to develop jitters when he thought about delivering his speech in front of a packed Arena and the entire planet. He looked back at his great-grandfather in the foto grinning and couldn't help but grin again himself. *I'll be all right.*

Up ahead, the Global symbol banners hung from the unused lines between the old power and communication poles which meant they were approaching the active parade route. Yor called over the intercom for Mado who appeared in the control room surprisingly fast.

"Were you down in the engine room?" Yor said as Mado stood beside him again.

"For a short while, then I was working through some files in the science lab."

"Files? Which files?"

"I was studying the converted star charts. I haven't really examined them in their entirety in decades," Mado said. He removed a holo-device memory-core from his shirt pocket, walked over to the holo-device and inserted it. The century-old SEEDER tech whirred to an increasing pitch while powering up. When the whirring leveled off in pitch, Mado pressed a few buttons, and the control room lights dimmed and stars were projected.

"Does this map mean anything to you?" Yor said, joining Mado by the holo-device.

"Hold on."

Mado peered at the operating screen, pressing a few more buttons and the image rotated as he pressed them. "This is Koda right here. This is your sun," Mado said pointing to a few small specks of light at the far end of the projection. "Over here is the Prevorian Protectorate." He pointed to a cluster of stars at the opposite side of the projection. He pressed a few more buttons and spun the axis of the image so Yor was now looking down on the chart and the vast distance between Prevor's system and Koda.

"How long would it take to reach the system containing Prevor?"

"By the WAEF's engines, maybe 20 years. Prevorian engines would take less than half that time."

"Never being out there, it's difficult to fathom the distance," Yor said, walking around the image. "So while we're talking about star charts, can you show me where the viable planet resides?"

"That's exactly why I was pouring over the charts. With the latest twist in our plan and the extra time in the ship, I thought this might be a good time to show you," Mado said and began typing into the holo-device keyboard, staring at the operating screen. Yor walked over to him. The screen revealed as many files as pages in the journal.

Mado pointed at the screen to show Yor what he was doing. "I'm linking a string of charts together to create a comprehensive map so you can see the breadth of the journey. Might take a few moments. This device processes slowly. I couldn't replace it until the inspections were over, then I was focused on the new control console and I didn't have the days to get both done. And to be completely honest, I feel sentimental about the old tech and didn't want to tinker with it. A little slow, but we all get that way when we get older," Mado said, walking over to the control room window. "Might as well enjoy the incredible crowd while we're waiting."

Out the control-room window, Yor was astounded at the mass of citizens crammed on the sidewalks on both sides of the procession. Yor was always cautiously optimistic about the prospective turnout, and he was heartened by what he saw.

"So tell me about this planet you discovered with my great-grandfather?" Yor said, sitting back in the pilot's chair, viewing what seemed like a never-ending crowd, screaming, waving their pennants, and chanting "When All Else Fails, When All Else Fails, When All Else Fails…"

Mado said, "Over the years in space, Yorlik had to choose between what data to save and what to erase, because the ship's data-core capacity wasn't designed for a century of space travel. When Yorlik installed the WAEF's systems, the common way of sharing files was data-core to data-core via cables. No memory wafers existed. So we had no method to remove the enormous amount of fotos, vids and scientific data files that existed on the ship's data-core in regard to the planet and save them.

"Before we returned to Koda, in light of the political situation, we had to make a choice about what to salvage so we took the charts which could be stored on a single holo-device memory-core and could easily be hidden, then smuggled off the ship. I encrypted the data-core so the government couldn't just steal the evidence when they commandeered the ship. There was no way they could crack a Prevorian encryption, and Yorlik erased the files on the entire data-core in front of Global Assembly officials as part of the WAEF deal so they couldn't possess them. After the deletion session, Yorlik arrived at my residence and drank quite a bit of Malrap, but it made his resolve for the long game stronger.

"So how can I do justice to those erased vids? You've seen the ancient vids and fotos of Koda, but to witness unsullied unbridled virgin nature in person is something else. Thousand-year-old trees. Waterfalls cascading from icy peaks, dropping hundreds of meters, landing in a thunderous roar that never stops. Hundreds of thousands of species from microscopic to the size of this ship in the ocean, on the land, and in the air. Flowers blooming within a span of a few weeks encompassing colors the range of the light spectrum. The seasons changing

Howard Libes

from frozen landscape to vibrant existence. Every species giving birth with the hope of life everlasting. The richness. The scent of flowers and even the excrement of animals smelled exquisite. There's no way to relate the sensory experience.

"We spent 484 days drinking it all in. Cataloging it all. Sadly all lost in the deletion. Yorlik wanted to be certain that he'd found a new home for his people after traveling all that way. There was a humanoid life form evolving there and we attempted to keep clear of them for the most part and observe them. It was difficult to ascertain whether they'd evolve beyond their primitive ways. Their existence was one of Yorlik's greatest dilemmas. There was no doubt the planet was rich in life and water and the climate was perfect in the majority of land masses, but Yorlik was concerned about the impact of your people upon what might be the planetary legacy and birthright of these humanoid creatures. Yorlik argued with himself whether bringing your people there would be robbing these creatures of what was rightfully theirs. He asked himself whether there was enough habitable land masses to go around. This was a debate we had together and he had with himself many times on the way back to Koda. That debate ended the day we heard the first transmissions from Koda and learned things were environmentally worse than expected, then we decided to prep for a new plan, a new future that involved returning to that blessed orb we'd discovered."

Mado walked back to the holo-device, and typed into

the keyboard, then pressed the Display button. An image appeared which seemed to incorporate the holo-device's entire projection capability creating the illusion that the points of light and nebulas were spilling over the edges of the table. Mado hit a few more buttons, spinning the image on its axis so they were peering down on the projection. "This is a composite of over two dozen star charts. I put them together to show you a direct path or as direct a path as possible from Koda to the planet. I could have gone bigger with the charts in our possession, but the holo-device wouldn't show it all at once and this will do the trick for now," Mado said, "For perspective, Koda and Prevor are in this sector." Mado pointed to a small area about the size of Yor's palm in the lower quadrant of the projection.

"Wow. It's endless out there. How did you deal with it?"

"You have to let that reality go when you're traveling through it. You just focus on your destination."

"Do you miss it?"

"Space travel was my career, my profession and part of my essence for as long as I can recall. Even as a child, I wanted to be out there, then I discovered I was suited for it. I was talented in that way. Up until I landed here with your great-grandfather, space was my home for the majority of my adult life. As you would say, it was my calling."

"So you miss it?"

"Yes and no. Not as much as you'd think. I've been engrossed over the past 24 years implementing your great-grandfather's plan, building a corporation to pay for the plan, rebuilding this ship, working with you and getting to know your family, and just tinkering with tech. I've enjoyed doing all those things on Koda, and I've become a different being here," Mado said, "Although, there are times where I yearn to get back out into space. So I guess I'm torn."

"So what are we looking at here other than a large slice of the universe?"

Mado said, "Here is Koda..." He pressed a few more buttons and a brown dot appeared in the area where he pointed a few moments before.

"And where is the planet?"

"Your great-grandfather was concerned if the government ever became smart enough to figure out the journal was in reality a trove of star charts that they'd destroy the journal or at the very least bury it somewhere for future use. So we needed a backup plan, somewhere to hide the planet's coordinates. If they destroyed the charts, then at least we'd have the coordinates. Making it there alive would decrease exponentially without the charts, but at least we'd know where to point."

"Smart, but nothing would surprise me at this point."

"One moment," Mado said and detached the foto of Yor's great-grandfather from the panel, then removed a magnifier from his back pocket that he used for repairing the micro-circuitry on the WAEF "We captured this moment on the day that we were leaving the planet to come back here and deliver the news. Yorlik wanted something he could put on his mantle and remember the joy of the discovery. We had no clue what it would mean in the future. The planet is a speck in the background, but the most important part of the image is the control console which was fortuitous," Mado handed the magnifier and foto to Yor. "Look below your great-grandfather's right elbow and read the numbers on the spatial coordinate positioner to me."

"I knew it," Yor said, jumping up and down and pointing at Mado. "I knew it. I always knew those were coordinates to somewhere special. That's the reason why I kept asking you about it. When you evaded my questions for the umpteenth time, I asked a Professor of Astronomy who was a friend of my father's about those coordinates."

"Yes, I was aware you had some idea about the foto's relevance, but I didn't think the time was right to reveal the truth…until now," Mado said, "Remember when you asked me about the foto right after the library incident, I told you that your great-grandfather gave it to you so you'd keep it safe. He knew you'd cherish it and keep it close. When you found it, he might have been as happy as the day the foto was taken. Your great-grandfather saw you were endowed with an aptitude for gathering knowledge, an open-mindedness and a rabid curiosity. He knew you'd be the perfect keeper of the truth. He was a man of science and not a mystical man, but he saw your discovery of the foto and your interest in it as a sign that everything would go as planned and that gave him peace at the end of his life."

"I don't know what to say," Yor said, feeling emotion come over him, "That means so much since I admired him my entire life, and he died when I was so young."

"Yes, our lifetimes don't always line up with other souls the way that we'd wish," Mado said, "Was Professor Camoti the astronomy professor? He was always asking your great-grandfather questions."

"Matter of fact, yes. But when we investigated the coordinates, they didn't match with a planetary body and there weren't any planets within light years."

"Yes, I imagine that would've been the results. When I initially gave your great-grandfather the Prevorian charts to analyze sectors for a viable planet, we adapted them for the holo-device which is in synch with the ship's spatial coordinate positioner and the navigation system. That meant converting the WAEF from the Kodan coordinate system to a Prevorian coordinate system which is much different than the Kodan system, because you're starting with a different planet of origin," Mado said, "The numbers in the ship's spatial coordinate positioner are Prevorian. There's no way Professor Camoti, you, or anyone on Koda could have known that fact other than myself and your great-grandfather."

On the foto, Yor centered the magnifier under his great-grandfather's right elbow and a spot on the control console, then increased the magnification until red marks appeared. He continued magnifying until the red unblurred to numbers on the spatial coordinate positioner. He remembered when he did this for the first time as a child. His great-grandfather didn't know anything about the coordinates because his memory was erased, and his father knew nothing about the ship. Yor researched on his own for over a decade and found no answers to why his great-grandfather was so happy in that place in outer space. "There they are," Yor said when the numbers were clear.

"Please read them to me."

"153648028947," Yor said and as he spoke the numbers, Mado typed into the holo-device.

"For perspective, here is Koda," Mado said, pointing to the brown dot again. "Are you ready?" Mado held his finger over a button on the device.

Yor was excited. His jitters were gone. He knew what Mado was doing. He'd bring his finger down on the Display button and one of the stars would change color, revealing the planet. "I can't even relate to you how ready."

Mado pressed the button.

RAJER

The parade was running late and the crowd was jam-packed in the Plaza and around the Arena. People were becoming edgy, hollering at each other as they competed for position to get closer to the street where the parade would pass. A few skirmishes broke out. Global Guards quickly stepped in and removed the offending parties to the cheers of onlookers.

When the lead float turned out of the Royal Quarter into the Plaza, the viewing screens began to broadcast the parade. People cheered as much in relief as jubilation. As the float for each region passed on the viewing screen, a loud cheer went up from those region's citizens in the crowd which made it seem like the entire planet was represented in the Plaza. Rajer had his arm linked with Mar's, taking in the spectacle, then Mar grabbed Rajer around the waist and kissed him passionately on the lips. They separated staring at each other. As always, Rajer couldn't believe how lucky he was to have this woman in his life. Then Mar's eyes shifted upwards and she yelled, "Look!"

Up on the screen, the WAEF was approaching. Yor stood on top of the WAEF in Yorlik the Great's space-suit without the helmet waving to the crowd which was going wild. People cheered, applauded, and screamed Yor's name. Two young adults jumped the barriers and ran beside the carrier waving their pennants before being tackled by Global Guards in riot gear and the crowd in the Plaza released a collective groan. Then the two were restrained by the Global Guards and evacuated out of the viewing-screen frame.

Yor was smiling, strutting back and forth along the roof of the WAEF and waving down at the crowd, appearing as happy as Rajer ever saw him. Somebody in the crowd began chanting "When All Else Fails, When All Else Fails, When All Else Fails…" then a few more people joined him and a few more and in moments, there were thousands of people chanting at an incredible volume.

Rajer leaned over and said in Mar's ear, "That's your boy."

Mar pointed at her ear and mouthed the words, "I… can't…hear…you."

Rajer repeated himself, yelling in her ear over the din of the crowd.

Mar leaned in close to Rajer, kissed him on the cheek and yelled into his ear, "Yes, he is and yours, too."

Rajer pointed at himself and smiled.

"Yes," Mar yelled. "I know you two had your differences, but you were there when he needed a father, when he needed a man in his life as an example."

"I know. I love the little snot-nosed know-it-all."

"Too bad we can't get closer to the street."

The crowd reached a fevered pitch with tens of thousands still chanting "When All Else Fails, When All Else Fails, When All Else Fails…" and the cam kept focused on the WAEF riding the carrier with Yor on top smiling and waving, then each parade float veered off to the left and the WAEF headed straight into the Arena's vehicular entrance and disappeared. The chanting petered out. The viewing screens went blank, then the metallic clank of the Arena entrance-door bolts unlocking rang out one-by-one around the Arena and the dozen automatic Arena doors slid open on their skids and slammed metal-on-metal to a stop.

Rajer grabbed onto Mar's hand and they were swept by the crowd through an Arena entrance into the rotunda where Global symbol and regional banners hung from the rafters. Mar led the way to the field-level entrance and they ran down the stairs to the real green grass of the field. Synthetic grass was the usual sight around the city, but for Breeze Celebration, real grass was grown at the cost of invaluable water rations and cut before the ceremony so everyone could relish in the smell. At any cost, the Global Assembly wanted to dispel thoughts the planet would not renew itself to its former riches.

As they dashed across the field towards the stage, still holding hands, the happiness on Mar's face delighted Rajer. The WAEF was finishing its parking maneuver and came to a stop, a distance from the stage, parallel to it. Workers moved a ramp in place which extended from the stage to the WAEF's docking bay. Rajer wondered why the ship was parked so far from the stage, but Mado told them explicitly he was leaving them in the dark about the day's specific plans so he and Mar wouldn't be implicated in their actions.

Rajer reached a security barrier with Mar, keeping them a fair distance from the actual stage which was just above the height of an average person so nobody could see the goings on backstage, but they had a view all the way to the WAEF. Mar turned and hugged Rajer as they both panted to catch their breath. He held her tightly as he looked up at the Arena around them.

When the construction schedule for the entire DOME project was announced, the Global Arena was sold to the public as the last immense municipal construction project and the cornerstone of the Global Plaza where the government would gather citizens for important announcements and rallies. As a government employee, before the dome was sealed, Rajer attended a few events here to support Global Assembly policy. The stands were filled by requiring attendance for government employees and giving out extra ration coupons although the viewing-channel audiences across Koda were told the capacity crowds were due to the enthusiasm of the citizenry. On those days, above the oval of stands was a blue cloudless sky and the heat was unbearable.

Now, the sky could be seen behind thousands of ultraviolet-blocking transparent panes in metal frames which the government spent half a year and millions in units to spotlessly clean for Breeze Celebration. The stands were filling with citizens and the field behind Rajer was an impenetrable wall of people carrying pennants and homemade placards reading, 'When All Else Fails...We're Ready to Go,' 'Take Us Away, Yor,' 'When All Else Has

Failed…Isn't It Time That We Admit It?' Under normal circumstances, such statements would be considered sedition and their creator detained, but if the Global Guards started arresting citizens and tore apart these signs today, then they might start a riot in front of viewing-channel cams and the entire planet.

"An amazing turnout," Rajer said, releasing his hold on Mar.

"This certainly is the biggest Breeze Celebration ever," Mar said, squeezing Rajer's hand.

Rajer felt a tap on his shoulder and turned to face the woman from the Malrap vendor. She was wearing her government ID which meant she was working the event.

"Nothing to say to me, Rajer," she said, "I thought that you'd be happy to see an old friend. I've read in your files you're a polite man. I'll have to revise that impression."

"Who is this woman, Rajer?" Mar said, "Is this the woman from the other day?"

"Yes and he was a complete gentleman except getting aroused by my footsy with him and gawking at my breasts, but I have to admit that I was putting it out there for a reason," she said, "You must be Mar Vanderlord."

"No, I'm Mar Jeps," Mar said, "You have nerve, young lady."

"You are as fiery as I've read in your file. I can see your son in you. You must be a treasonous bitch just like him."

Mar slapped the woman across the face with an audible smack. A welt immediately appeared on her face. The crowd around them took notice.

The woman didn't budge, staring at Mar. "Impressive," she said, the tone of her voice just as steady and condescending as before the slap. "I *am* impressed."

"I can do it again if you like."

Rajer thought about stepping into the skirmish as more people around them were paying attention to the standoff.

"Although I do like a little rough play, I think I'm fine with your initial assault," the woman said, deepening the condescension in her tone and taking a step closer to Mar so they were practically touching noses. "I'm glad you're here with Rajer."

"I wouldn't have missed it for the world," Mar said, not budging from her stand.

"Well, it's good to hear all your maternal instincts are in full play, because by the end of the day your son will need your full support."

"What does that mean?"

"Oh you'll see," she said and walked off into the crowd.

"What does she mean?" Mar said to Rajer, concern creeping into her voice.

"Stay here, I'll be right back," Rajer said and took off in the direction of the woman, but hands grabbed his shoulders and stopped him. Rajer looked over his shoulder at Mar. She was furious and her hold on his shoulders was painful. Rajer reached over and placed his hand on one of hers and held it there until she let go of him.

"I'm sorry," she said, grabbing Rajer by his shirt and looking directly in his eyes, "But are you crazy? What are you thinking?"

"I don't know. I was obviously going after her."

"Obviously, but what were you going to do when you caught up with her?" Mar said, patting Rajer gently on his face with her other hand. "Powers-that-be knows, I appreciate you being so considerate, but what are you going to solve? Don't you think she's baiting you?"

"I know, but I'm not going to let her ruin everything."

The people around them were still watching so Rajer said to the crowd, "Everything is fine here. Just a family squabble. Please go back to enjoying your Breeze Celebration."

Then he pried Mar's hand off his shirt, turned her toward the stage, and draped his arm around her. "We don't want any attention drawn to us, do we?" Rajer said and kissed her on the cheek.

Right then, a cheer went up from the Arena crowd as Chal Mikahl, the most-seen viewing-channel announcer on the planet, walked with a hop in his step to the podium. Two gigantic viewing screens installed on either side of the stage became operational so the entire Arena crowd could watch each speaker up-close. Chal was a short bald man wearing a lime green suit with a multi-colored tie—purple, red, orange—and a bright blue shirt. He was known for garish dress, that was his calling card along with his short stature. He was much beloved by the planet. An attendant about Chal's size, wearing white shirt and pants, followed Chal with a box which he placed before the podium. Chal jumped up on the box and appeared above the podium. The Arena went wild.

"Hello citizens," Chal said, wearing a wireless microphone. "Welcome to Breeze Celebration." The crowd let out a resounding simultaneous cheer. "We are here to celebrate the grand achievements of our people, and there are few things on this planet that signify the triumph of our people more than the spaceship created and flown by our beloved Yorlik the Great in his valiant quest to discover a new Kodan home…"

"When All Else Fails, When All Else Fails, When All Else Fails…" Two-hundred-thousand people chanted in unison. Rajer looked over at Mar who joined the crowd, smiling, punching the air with her fist at the end of every word.

"Yes, yes…" Chal said, holding up his stumpy arms with open palmed hands attempting to get the crowd to quiet down. "And now the moment you've all been waiting for, the opening of the dome."

The Arena was built specifically in this place for this event. Directly above, a pane visibly bigger than the others in the dome structure, slowly slid back opening the dome to the outside. Everyone in the Arena was looking up, waiting for the moment when the pane was completely open, including Mar. *She is radiant,* Rajer thought.

When the pane was open all the way, a cheer went up from the Arena. The dome's air-circulation facilities were powered down to half capacity, but not turned off and a few moments later, Rajer and the rest of the citizens in the dome felt the heat from the outside which was moderated by the air circulators. Anti-DOME advocates predicted, not too far in the future, the dome wouldn't be opened for Breeze Celebration, because the heat outside would be searing and the air circulators would be ineffective at controlling the temperature even at full capacity. The Global Assembly denied this would ever happen.

"What a wonderful sensation, isn't it?" Chal called to the crowd. "And now a few words from our Global Leader."

Mar turned to Rajer and smiled. He smiled back, then Mar turned back to the stage.

Rajer snuck off.

MADO

In the silence of the control room, Mado sat in the pilot's chair, watching the enthusiastic crowd as the WAEF passed through the Royal Quarter and moved onto the Global Plaza, and he thought of his friend Yorlik and how much this would mean to him.

If he turned on the outside intercom, he could have heard the crowd loud and clear and basked in their adulation, but Prevorians felt joy in a much different way than humanoids with their thrills, chills, smiles and bumps on the flesh. Prevorian joy was far more transcendent, and the imagery outside the window with no sonic stimuli only served to intensify it: There were the homemade signs expressing an understanding and affection for the WAEF's mission—'Find Our Next Home, We Trust You,' 'We Need to Live, Not Survive, When All Else Fails is the Future'—and the sheer fervor of the crowd with children on their parent's shoulders beaming with happiness at the sight of the WAEF. Mado was injected with an overwhelming vitality, making him feel like he could levitate above his seat through sheer force of will. He recalled moments in his existence when this sensation overcame him—his first love, his first launch into outer space, sailing in the simulation with Yorlik, discovering the viable planet, the WAEF arriving at the Prevor

Industries Complex. There were more moments in his hundreds of years of existence, but those were the first to his memory here and now.

Then the crowd began working themselves into a frenzy, streaming toward the ship and pushing up against the barriers on both sides of the roadway. Mado flipped on the outside intercom. The crowd was cheering and applauding, hooting and hollering, and chanting, "When All Else Fails, When All Else Fails, When All Else Fails..." Mado noted the entire throng was gazing toward the roof of the WAEF and he heard one person say, "We love you, Yor." Mado punched a few buttons on the main control console and the viewing screen with continuous readouts of the ship's systems changed into a display of the outer-hull vidcam feeds. He flipped through the feeds—front, rear, docking bay, port, starboard, loading bay, bottom of hull—and saw nothing, but when he switched to the roof cam, his heart raced faster.

For an instant, Mado thought he saw his friend Yorlik alive and well, but of course, it was Yor wearing his name-sake's spacesuit, calling out to the crowd, encouraging louder chants with his arm movements, waving to the crowd, and smiling. A surge like he'd never felt before shot through his body. At first, he thought he might have the capacity to experience joy like humanoids after living among them for decades, but he chalked it up to surprise and being caught off guard.

Mado had wondered where Yor had gone after their discussion about the viable planet. He assumed Yor was preparing for his speech. It wasn't planned or expected for Yor to climb out of the overhead hatch to the roof. This was effective off-the-cuff inventiveness, further energizing the crowd. *Improvisation. Maybe Yor had the right idea after all.*

On the roof-cam feed, Yor gave his final waves to the crowd before descending through the hatch as the WAEF approached the Arena. A few moments later, the control room door slid open and Yor stood there in the spacesuit, smiling.

"You catch any of that," Yor said, pointing to the screen turned onto the roof cam.

"I did...and it was fantastic," Mado said and an impulse with no forethought caused him to rush toward Yor and embrace him, holding him tight. He felt Yor hug him back.

"Wow, I don't believe you've ever hugged me before, Mado," Yor said, "And you're much stronger than I thought."

Mado let go and stepped back. "Sorry. Did I hurt you? Prevorians are many times stronger than humanoids. Different muscle structure. Sorry. Something came over me."

"No. Don't be sorry. I don't see that weird smile of yours, but I hear something different in your voice. I like it. You seem a little out of control which I don't think I've ever seen. Like you're overjoyed."

"Overjoyed. A Prevorian being overjoyed? Maybe that's it."

"I mean it might be strange if you were like this all the

time. We'd never accomplish anything, but right now it seems right. This is almost a century in the making," Yor said, "All of that hard work, building to this moment."

"Yes, that must be it." Mado said, attempting to gather himself. "And you resemble your great-grandfather in that spacesuit."

"I was looking at the foto earlier, thinking there was a noticeable family resemblance."

"I was truly taken aback."

"I was putting on the suit and preparing for my speech, then I just couldn't help but get out there."

"Possessed by your namesake's spirit, perhaps," Mado said, "Please feel free to take initiative. Now get ready for the speech. I have a few things to do like set up the sonic cannon, then I'll meet you by the docking bay door."

"How are we doing on time?"

"I don't think we're going to make it, but I made a secured comm to a few operatives inside the government who told me that systems and communications are down right now. We'll be in control of the PA and vid, and the viewing-channel broadcasts won't be taken down. Our problems will be afterward."

"We probably should have discussed the contingency, but again right now I don't want to think about it."

"If that's your instinct, then go with it."

Yor exited the control room and Mado picked up the foto of Yorlik from on top of the operating screen of the holo-device and placed it back on the panel beside the main control console.

Mado recalled earlier when he punched the Display button on the holo-device and the viable planet was marked blue, the look on Yor's face was far from what Mado expected. He thought Yor would display awe or glee, but Yor stared blankly at the projection.

Mado waited patiently for Yor to react, then finally broke the silence by saying, "Here it is."

"Yes. There it is," Yor said, "It's so far from Koda, so far away. How far is it?"

"The journey back to Koda took us about 30 years with the converted engines on the WAEF, and that was going a little out of our way to drop me off at the edge of the Prevorian Protectorate. Maybe a year less on a more direct route. Four or five years less with proper Prevorian craft and engines. Hard to say exactly in a journey of that distance. I've been working on new tech which may allow us to arrive sooner."

"How do we get all the citizens there?"

"I believe that's a quandary for another time," Mado said, "But here it is, right in front of you. Your great-grandfather's discovery. Isn't this something you've been wanting to see forever?"

"Yes. You're right. You're right. What am I saying? I'm looking at the single greatest achievement in planetary history and I'm seeing evidence that it actually happened... and its actual location," Yor said, "You're right. I lost my mind for a moment. This is...I'm not sure what to say."

"That's closer to the response I predicted," Mado said, "There are daunting tasks ahead. No doubt."

But we still have to get through today, Mado thought.

Now, the WAEF's carrier was positioning itself behind the stage, and Mado needed to get moving. He ejected the holo-device memory-core and inserted a blank core into the device so if anyone accessed it they'd find nothing, then he locked the core containing the charts into a hidden drawer under the operating screen and keyboard. These charts could not fall into the wrong hands, and even if the wrong party somehow found the drawer, nobody on this planet could decode his DNA to open it, and if they tried more than a few times, then they'd destroy the contents.

At the main control console, Mado made certain all the vids were uploaded for broadcast during Yor's speech including the one vid that was sure to shock the planet.

MAR

"So we move forward and pray to the Powers-that-be that we will persevere, we will survive as a people living within these domes, within the glorious achievements of our civilization, and we will walk in the breeze once again," Vidor Plemso the Global Leader said. He closed his eyes, holding up his arms, palms up towards the open dome pane as if to feel a breeze and the 200,000 citizens in the Arena cheered and stood imitating their Leader. Mar examined the Leader's image on the giant viewing screens: This was the same man Mar met with Tetrick at Yorlik's landing, and it appeared he might be wearing the identical suit from that day, but his hair was gray and his face had a few more lines. He'd led the planet for 26 years now, 14 years as President and 12 years as Leader.

Mar was troubled over Rajer's disappearance. She was afraid he'd do something reckless. He felt castrated by yesterday's confrontation with the woman, and Mar could tell today's encounter had put him over the edge. She didn't know where to start searching for him. The Arena was too large and packed with people.

"This day we celebrate the When All Else Fails and the accomplishments of Yorlik Vanderlord or Yorlik the Great who not only gave us longer life and happiness with our families, but gave us a glimmer of optimism when we were mired in uneasiness over the environmental crisis. Our citizens could gaze up at the night sky and pray for his return with news of a discovery that would improve our future. When I was a boy, my father would take me to a meadow at night, away from the city lights, and we'd gaze up and marvel at the stars above. And I'd ask my father if he could point to where Yorlik the Great was traveling and he'd say, 'Son, I'm not sure where he is, but he is searching to make our lives better.'"

Two-hundred-thousand Kodans in the Arena began chanting "When All Else Fails, When All Else Fails, When All Else Fails…"

The Leader continued over the chants, "While waiting for his return, as a people we steered a different path and discovered a different solution that was far more practical than the SEEDER program. Yorlik the Great returned in the WAEF, failing in his mission, but regardless, he earned every Kodans adoration and respect for his ingenuity in striving over a century in space to achieve a better future for the Kodan people. In the days and years that followed since his return, we've learned from his example and our gratitude has endured and grown…" As chants of the ship's name grew louder, the Leader paused and waited, then spoke louder into the podium microphone. "Yes, yes and today we return that adoration and respect yet again, embracing him in perpetuity with the restoration of the When All Else Fails. We owe many thanks to the SEEDER program and Yorlik the Great for showing us the way towards our salvation. This ship is a lesson in imagination and determination, which ushered in the creation of the domes and rescued the Kodan people from extinction."

The crowd produced a sustained cheer and again the Leader waited for them to quiet down, looking pleased. "And now without any further delay, I'd like to introduce a shining example of Kodan youth. He is Professor of Planetary History and Director of SEEDER-program studies at the Royal University, the author of the best-selling book *Power Over the Future*, and restoration consultant on the When All Else Fails..." The crowd began chanting the ship's name again, clapping their hands in unison. The Leader raised his voice again to make sure he was heard, "Yes, yes, I'm proud to introduce Yor Vanderlord." The crowd erupted—screaming, shouting, hooting, applauding—and chanting "When All Else Fails, When All Else Fails, When All Else Fails..."

The Leader turned and held an arm out toward the WAEF, smiling. The viewing screens cut from the Leader to the docking-bay door at the end of the ramp which slid open and Yor stepped out wearing his great-grandfather's spacesuit including the helmet with the sun visor down so his face was hidden as the cam zoomed in on him. The crowd continued their din.

Then there was a burst of static and fuzz on the viewing screens, the crowd noise lowered, and Yorlik the Great appeared on the screen from the day he landed back on Koda. At first, the picture was frozen on the Great man's image, the wildman from space, like the startup image on Mar's viewer. The Leader appeared confused and frantically searched the edges of the stage behind the podium, then the image came alive with the viewing-channel vid from the day when Yorlik confronted the Global President in front of the entire planet. Since the riots, this vid was banned from being shown on media outlets.

The crowd went silent as Yorlik spoke, "I'm thrilled to return home, President Plemso. For years upon years, I've dreamed of my loved ones, of my family and friends, and this wondrous planet full of life that is seemingly unique in all the universe, but I was aghast as I approached the globe and took readings on the environment and noted the degradation that has taken place in such a short planetary period of time. I can only imagine the greedy forces at work to maintain the status quo in the face of such a disastrous tide…"

Then the viewing screen showed Yor at the end of the ramp. The crowd erupted once again. Yor removed the helmet, placed it inside the ship and the docking-bay door slid closed. Mar was awestruck by the enthusiasm of the crowd as if her son were the Great man himself. She could not believe this was happening, it was like a dream. She thought about how Tetrick would be filled with pride and she looked around the crowd, growing more concerned for Rajer's well-being.

Yor waved to the crowd as he walked down the ramp toward the stage. The Leader was all smiles again, meeting Yor where the ramp met the stage and putting his arm around Yor's shoulder as they walked together to the podium. The Leader leaned close to Yor and said something in his ear, then Yor said something into the Leader's ear. The Leader stopped smiling and looked appalled, then collected himself as they arrived at the podium. The intensity of the crowd never waned.

"My fellow citizens," the Leader said, "The great-grandson of Yorlik the Great, Yor Vanderlord."

Yor stood in front of the podium, holding up both his hands to the raucous crowd and said into the microphone, "Thank you, thank you for the wonderful welcome." The crowd noise abated. "Before I begin, I'd like to thank the Global Leader for the fine introduction." Yor turned and shook the hand of the Leader who proceeded to walk offstage. Mar noted the look of consternation on the Leader's face as he strode out of sight. "I'd like to thank my great-grandfather. None of this would be possible without him." The crowd cheered and Yor held up his hand to get their attention before speaking again. "I'd also like to sincerely thank my mother..." Mar was shocked to see her face on the viewing screens. She was embarrassed by her looks. She hadn't suspected that she'd be spotlighted in front of the entire planet. If so, she might have dressed in better Breeze Celebration garb and made sure her hair wasn't disheveled from running. She waved to Yor and blew him a kiss. "...and my stepfather..." The cam panned to the right and left of Mar, then stayed on her. "...for their constant support in all the years restoring the WAEF, and I'd also like to thank my father, Tetrick

Vanderlord who…" A chorus of boos filled the Arena. "….was my guide through the history of the SEEDER program when I was a young man and always gave me the straight and honest truth…" Someone in the crowd yelled out, "Traitor!" The person was close enough to the stage that the entire Arena heard the remark through the podium microphone.

"Yes, some may call him a traitor, but on this Breeze Celebration, the truth is the best way to pay our respects to Yorlik the Great, and those who flew off into space before him, and the scientists, electricians, welders, and machinists who built these brilliant spaceships. Some of those people might have been your forefathers. They vested their hopes and dreams into these ships which wandered the universe searching for a new planet, a healthy planet where the Kodan population might relocate as the planetary environment deteriorated toward the point of no return. When All Else Fails was Yorlik the Great's home for over a century, ferrying him from one corner of the universe to the other, and he could simply look at the welds on the hull to remind him of the planet that he'd left behind full of resourceful people who shared in his vision for the future." A cheer went up and the crowd began chanting, "When All Else Fails, When All Else Fails, When All Else Fails…" Yor took a few steps back and let them revel. He smiled down at Mar, then stepped up to the podium.

"Here on Breeze Celebration while honoring this stupendous history, we have a duty to be truthful." Yor stopped briefly and looked over his shoulder at the back-stage area, then turned back to the crowd.

"Some truths are evident, my dear Kodans. We launched ships to the stars hoping to find another planet as bountiful as our own against all the odds that such a place existed. We gave up on that mission and decided to place all our hope in the domes. We spent a century researching and building these spectacular structures with clean air to breathe, clean water, regulated temperatures, and filtered sunlight. We gave up our liberties and our voice in governing to make it through the tough transition from planet dwellers to dome dwellers in the hope that some day the environment would heal itself and return to its former glory, and release us from tyranny. What other choice did we have, but to hope? We survived because of the eternal hope that we've displayed in the face of adversity. In my humble opinion my dear Kodans, that is the message of Breeze Celebration. That is what brings us here to celebrate." The crowd erupted into cheers again.

"And while we hoped, while we scrambled for survival, lies altered the course of Kodan history to the detriment of the majority of people and the enrichment of others. Why would we let such a thing happen and not rebel against it? Citizens, we did, but the Global Assembly became adept at silencing those Kodans who spoke against the lies, who spoke the truth like my father." Booing and hisses broke out in the crowd. "Yes. The truth is hard to swallow, especially when its been denied for years. My great-grandfather once told me 'Lies can be just as powerful as the truth,' but I believe the truth is more powerful than any lie. So on this Breeze Celebration when we honor Yorlik the Great, I impart you with the truth about his journey: My great-grandfather left Koda with all of your hope and he held onto that hope for 122 years and in that time, he fulfilled your hope by discovering a habitable planet." Two-hundred-thousand people gasped, and the Arena buzzed with chatter.

"You heard me correctly. He found a planet that fulfilled his mission, that justified our hope in him and when he returned, he was told in no uncertain terms by the Global Assembly, by the Leader that you should remain ignorant of what he discovered."

The crowd noise built louder. People were yelling, "Get off the stage…Traitor…" Groups of people were chanting "Lies, lies, lies" and booing. Mar was surprised the Global Guards hadn't stormed the stage.

Yor leaned toward the microphone and said, "I know it seems unbelievable, but you should hear the truth from the primary source."

The viewing screens behind Yor turned to static and fuzz for a moment, then Yorlik the Great appeared on the screen, "Hello citizens of my beloved Koda," Yorlik said. This was Yorlik about the time that the WAEF was delivered to the estate hangar. He was beardless with short hair, standing in the estate's library.

"I'm not sure when this will be seen, but my end is coming soon. This could be 20 years in the future and I will be gone from this life for at least that long. I made

a pact with the Global Assembly and I promised that I wouldn't tell anyone their secret in my lifetime, so here we are. I will get directly to the point. When I landed on Koda, after so many years in space, I was excited to tell the Global Assembly I'd discovered a planet that fit all the parameters of my mission, a beautiful planet, teeming with life, and I possessed documentation and data on this new world to prove its viability. Instead of sharing in my exuberance, the Global President himself censored me. I wasn't to utter a word or there would be dire consequences for myself and my family. I pleaded with the President to let the citizens decide their fate, but if you're watching this vid, then nothing has changed and that saddens me. You have maybe a century before the domes built on avarice rather than enduring quality will fail and the materials to repair them will be exhausted and Koda's vital resources will completely run out and it will be a race against time to figure out how to survive. Here, I've given you a solution to this dilemma and Powers-that-be bless you all."
The vid froze on Yorlik's serious demeanor.

The crowd was hushed.

Yor was moving down the ramp toward the ship.

The viewing-screen vid cut from the frozen image of Yorlik to a vidcam moving through an environment in half light with strange noises. It took Mar a moment to comprehend this was a jungle. The cam panned from rays of sun piercing a dense canopy of trees overhead to a lush green flora below. Birds chirped and squawked. There was screeching and the movement of animals running by the lens. Then the cam cleared the jungle into an open space, where a lake was being fed by a thunderous waterfall under a clear blue sky, and the cam panned around to Yorlik who was holding the vidcam with the lake and waterfall behind him. Mar could guarantee that no Kodan in this Arena or watching at home had ever experienced such an eco-system.

When the vid ended to fuzz and static, Yor was more than halfway back to the ship, and the woman who confronted Mar and Rajer, climbed onto the stage. She aimed a stun weapon at Yor and yelled "Stop!" which was picked up on the podium microphone and echoed throughout the Arena.

Yor halted and turned to face her, then walked backwards as the docking-bay door slid open behind him.

The woman marched down the ramp toward Yor. "Stop!" she screamed, "Or I will shoot you in the name of the Global Assembly."

Yor felt for the open doorway behind him and began to step backwards into the ship.

"This is your last warning," she screamed, aiming at Yor who held up his hands.

Then Rajer appeared onstage and dashed down the ramp at the woman who heard him coming and was turning toward him as he tackled her. The gun fired twice as they fell off the ramp out of sight.

Mar went cold.

YOR

Y or watched in disbelief and grabbed onto the sides of the WAEF's docking-bay doorway when Rajer tackled Roneh Rayush and they both plummeted into the pit behind the stage with the gun firing. They fell among the unconscious bodies of Arena security, government officials, the Global Leader and his staff, Global Guards and the Breeze Celebration organizers and stage crew. Yor even caught a glimpse of Chal Mikahl laying sprawled out on the ground in his gaudy clothes. They were all rendered that way by Mado's sonic cannon which he had mounted behind a panel that slid open in the rear hull.

Yor stepped further into the ship and the docking-bay door closed. Mado stood at the docking-bay console, observing the scene outside on a viewing screen.

"What happened?" Yor said, walking to Mado's side and closely examining the image on the screen. "Can you see Rajer? Is he all right?" He plucked out the earplugs that made him immune to the cannon.

"He's out of the docking-bay cam's range. This cam doesn't have the ability to magnify. That might be him here," Mado said, pointing to the bottom right-hand corner of the screen.

"How're we doing on time?"

"The engines are ready and I've released the clamps on

the carrier. We need to go," Mado said, pointing at the screen where backstage personnel were standing up and holding their heads.

"Let's go then," Yor said.

"See you in the control room."

Yor was removing the spacesuit when he heard the engines powering up. By the time, he arrived in the control room, the engines were thundering. Mado sat in the pilot's chair. Through the control-room window, Yor saw Global Guards and Breeze Celebration staff, scattering away from the ship with their hands over their ears, shocked at the sound and heat of the WAEF's engines. In the midst of those people, Yor spotted the man with the scarred hands. He stood unmoving with his arms crossed and Yor could have sworn that the man was glaring directly at him.

"The effects of the sonic cannon are wearing off and the government will overcome the virus shortly," Mado said, "Reinforcements will be on the way soon and all the government defensive systems will be coming back online. We've got to go."

"How was that woman not knocked out by the cannon? And how did Rajer get there?"

"I don't have answers to those questions," Mado said, punching buttons on the control console. "I haven't flown this beauty in decades. Hold on."

The ship lifted off and Yor grabbed the back of the pilot's chair with both hands as the WAEF shot straight upwards. The stands full of spectators blurred by, then the ship was hovering over the top of the Arena.

"Hold tight," Mado said, and the WAEF sped forward and upwards at what appeared to be a 45-degree angle, then leveled off and executed a 180-degree turn. They flew over the University campus, the Royal Quarter, the Plaza and the Arena where the ship slowed and hovered. "Still handles like a dream," Mado said, "Now let's see what she can do."

The WAEF soared upward at a steeper angle, heading for the open Breeze Celebration pane. Mado pointed at the roof-cam display on the control console. The pane was closing. Harmin's virus had been neutralized. "Time for Plan B. Luckily nothing inside the dome can catch us and closing the pane is their only move."

"What's Plan B?"

"You told me not to tell you. We need to work on communicating better," Mado said, "Hold on."

Mado lowered the ship's nose, then rocketed forward in a steep descent. Mado punched a complex code into the remote transmission box to the right of the control console. The Prevor Industries Complex was coming up fast and the ship wasn't slowing down.

"Aren't we going too fast and getting a little close to the ground?"

"We're okay. I'm pretty sure," Mado said, clutching the steering mechanism. The WAEF creaked and rattled as it leveled off and passed directly over the outer gates of the complex.

"Pretty sure?"

"Oh I'm sorry. Definitely sure."

"You're right. We do need to communicate better," Yor

said, grasping tighter to the back of the pilot's chair. Outside the control-room window, it seemed like the WAEF was close to scraping the rooftops of the buildings, speeding towards the dome's glass pane behind the complex.

"Mado…stop!"

"Now would not be an opportune time."

Yor firmly believed they were about to crash and he thought about how his life had led to this bizarre ending, then he noticed the pane was gone.

The ship barely fit through the space in the empty frame, then rapidly gained altitude outside of the dome. Still gripping the chair with both hands, Yor positioned himself so he was standing beside Mado. "When did you put Active Glass in that pane?"

"I was still building the facility when they were constructing the dome and I told them it would be less hectic if my workers installed the panes. Over the years, I've paid those workers and the DOME inspector a hefty sum for their silence. They're still on my payroll."

"Those must've been large emitters."

"Colossal. Active Glass was invented and designed for that pane, then I marketed it."

"You are full of surprises, Mado, though I'm not sure I like it all the time," Yor said, "I knew we were using the vid of great-grandfather talking about his discovery, but you failed to mention the vid of the planet."

"Oh that vid? That was a snippet your great-grandfather and I saved on an old vidcam drive. I kept it with me in my hiding place when we landed on Koda," Mado said, looking up at Yor with an awkward smile. "It was effective. Don't you think?"

The proximity alarm rang out.

"Looks like we're not going to make our rendezvous in Shamba. Air-battle cruisers are approaching," Mado said, "They're armed and we're not, and after what happened at the Arena, they're not going to have much patience for us."

"Is there a Plan C?"

"Yes, but you should go back and buckle yourself in."

"I'll be fine here," Yor said and positioned himself behind the pilot's chair again holding on with both hands.

"No. You'll need to buckle yourself in."

Two Global Assembly air-battle cruisers positioned themselves directly in front of the WAEF, and the rear-cam showed two more behind them. They were each one-third the size of the WAEF, but were armed with missiles and pulse weapons.

Yor dashed back to the chair by the holo-device and fastened the straps.

"You ready?" Mado said, punching buttons and throwing a few switches on the control console.

"Yes, but I don't know what's going to happen."

"Then we're in the same boat."

The WAEF maneuvered directly above the cruisers and rocketed past them, ascending at a sharp angle, then straight up. The engines roared, and Yor was pinned to his seat. He felt like he might lose consciousness, then the view of the sky out the control-room window dissolved to more stars than Yor had ever seen before.

HOWARD LIBES has been a writer for more than 30 years and is a graduate of the University of Oregon Creative Writing Program. He edited the 2,300-page manuscript of *If They Move ... Kill'em: The Life and Times of Sam Peckinpah* by David Weddle (Atlantic/Grove Press) and worked as a collaborator—writer and interviewer—on *Among the Mansions of Eden: Tales of Love, Lust, and Land in Beverly Hills* by David Weddle (William Morrow/HarperCollins). He has been a freelance writer for many publications, including *Los Angeles Times Magazine*.

Currently, he is tapping into his lifelong obsession with science fiction and writing the SEEDER series.

Made in the USA
Lexington, KY
27 April 2018